KNIGHT OF THE BROKEN HEART

The Eglinton Knight series
Book 2

Margaux Thorne

ARE YOU SIGNED UP FOR DRAGONBLADE'S BLOG?

You'll get the latest news and information on exclusive giveaways, exclusive excerpts, coming releases, sales, free books, cover reveals and more.

Check out our complete list of authors, too!

No spam, no junk. That's a promise!

Sign Up Here

www.dragonbladepublishing.com

Dearest Reader;

Thank you for your support of a small press. At Dragonblade Publishing, we strive to bring you the highest quality Historical Romance from some of the best authors in the business. Without your support, there is no 'us', so we sincerely hope you adore these stories and find some new favorite authors along the way.

Happy Reading!

CEO, Dragonblade Publishing

**Additional Dragonblade books by
Author Margaux Thorne**

The Eglinton Knight Series
Knight of the Jaded Heart (Book 1)
Knight of the Broken Heart (Book 2)

CHAPTER ONE

Eglinton Castle, Scotland, August 28, 1839

A MELIA SCANNED THE crowds, her lower belly knotting in anticipation. She always had that uncomfortable, ticklish squeeze before a good swindle. And this swindle was looking to be the very best.

It would be so easy. The crowd was like one giant herd of cattle, all jumbled together, grazing in a fat heap while it waited for the show to begin. There was electricity in the Scottish air, a buzz of excitement—and not a little bit of righteous pride. Because these fat cows had done it. These were the chosen people who'd managed—by hook or by crook—to get a ticket to the Eglington Tournament, which was no small feat.

The crowd was content. But, most importantly, it was ... happy. And happy meant distracted.

Amelia blinked away all the coins dancing before her. She shifted to the young lady standing at her side whose face was as green as the turf the throng was joyfully smashing with its expectant feet.

"Pull yourself together!" Amelia hissed through her pleasant expression. "Smile, for goodness' sake. No one will let you near them if they think you're going to retch all over their clean clothes."

The girl's forehead creased apologetically, and she heaved an enormous breath. "I'm sorry, Amelia—"

"Shhh! Don't say my name!" Amelia whispered, her congenial expression faltering. "What is wrong with you? I taught you better than that."

The girl's coloring morphed from green to crimson, and a line of perspiration dotted her smooth forehead. The sun might have dipped behind a heavy dollop of thick clouds hours ago, but the air was sticky with moisture. Even Amelia was sweating, although that had more to do with the multitude of layers she wore underneath her brilliant ensemble.

"Just take another deep breath and focus," Amelia said, softening her voice. Tough love was obviously not the way with her newest student. "This is no different from London. Come, let's walk a bit. We look silly standing here; we should mingle. The last thing we want to do is gather attention."

To get her moving, Amelia nudged the girl with her hip, though the nervous thing tripped twice before settling into a calm amble.

Amelia had to get the girl under control quickly or this day wouldn't be as successful as she needed it to be. She'd planned to go to the tournament alone, but Molly had declared that Amelia couldn't go without a partner. A bulk-and-file trick *was* the most successful in these types of tight situations. And Molly was usually right about these things. One didn't become the leader of the most infamous women's gang in London otherwise.

Still … Amelia's doubts clung to her like sticky burdock burs. She'd only been mentoring Jenny for two months, and although the girl was getting more confident, she still had a way to go before she would make a decent knuckler.

Taking a few minutes, they waded amongst the anticipation-crazed mass.

The women had traveled from London the day before and left their hotel early that morning to reach Lord Eglinton's castle grounds a full two hours before the medieval tournament was set to start. Amelia had had a hunch that visitors would congregate early in an effort to claim a prime spot to view the knights as they barreled down the lists for the joust. Only a limited number of tickets had been made available for seats in the grandstand. Everyone else had to make do with standing on the hills overlooking the structure the earl had built especially for the day.

In the months leading to the event, the newspapers had estimated that twenty thousand people might show up to watch the first medieval tournament the country had held in three hundred years. The staggering numbers had made it undeniable for Amelia—she simply had to take part in the historical occasion ... in her own way. But as she ambled past all the spectators, nodding politely, smiling serenely, she concluded the newspapers had misjudged. For once they hadn't overstated the situation, because twenty thousand was egregiously low. Amelia couldn't be certain, but she guessed there were no less than one hundred thousand people milling around her. All ripe for the picking.

Jenny stumbled again, and Amelia rolled her eyes. *This girl ...*

"Why don't we start easy?" Amelia said. She suspended their progress just outside the perimeter of the crowd where the earl's grounds started a gradual incline toward the rolling, tall-grassed hills and bucolic, munching sheep. From the elevation, Amelia had a spectacular view of the potential marks. "Look about. Who would you choose first?"

Put on the spot, Jenny cracked her knuckles one by one, causing Amelia to shudder. Not only did the popping sound make her insides crawl, but Amelia also knew Jenny well enough to recognize it as her tell. And, in their line of business, tells were as useful as two-legged dogs.

"Um ..." Jenny stalled uneasily, skimming the hordes of people. Amelia gnawed at her bottom lip, keeping her annoyance in check. Honestly, the girl looked like she was perusing the meat counter at the local butcher's. It was not *that* difficult. Though there was something to be said about taking one's time and not falling in headfirst without planning and thought. Those were the girls that ended up being shipped to the colonies—or worse, hanging from the wrong end of the noose.

"What about that one?" Jenny said, flicking her pointy chin to a portly man just at the edge of the crowd. "He's perfect … don't you think?" she added tentatively.

Amelia eyed the mark closely. He *would* have been perfect … if his clothes fit a little bit better. "I don't think so," she answered sagely. "You're right to consider him. His size makes him perfect for leather working, but there's a problem. Do you see how tight his coat is?" She continued without waiting for a response. "It makes for a hard dive. Nothing clean or quick about it. Too much rummaging and squeezing about."

Jenny rolled her eyes and muttered, "I could do it."

Amelia pretended not to hear her partner. Getting into an argument was the last thing they needed. In the short time they'd known each other, Jenny had shown herself to be prickly and sensitive to criticism. A war of words never ended readily or quickly with the arrogant girl. "Try again," Amelia urged. "Look for someone with loose clothes, a lot of layers, someone who won't feel your hand. That's the key. It shouldn't be too hard. The fools made it easy for us with all their costumes."

The apparel had been an unexpected blessing. Not all, but most, of the people who attended the tournament had gotten into the spirit of the day by donning medieval garb. Princesses and ladies littered the audience with their Tudor-inspired skirts and ruff-lined necks. The men were not immune to the festivities. Flouncing tunics and hose-clad legs were, unfortunately, running rife as well.

Amelia's mouth watered. All that heavy fabric could only help their cause.

Jenny made a humming noise and went back to her search. Amelia had already chosen ten people she was going to buzz, but she needed to give the girl a chance. Success would only bolster Jenny's belief in herself. The sooner the girl became a brilliant pickpocket and helped Amelia pay off her debt, the sooner Amelia could go to sleep at night with both eyes closed. Maybe not *every* night, but a few nights a week would be much appreciated.

"There," Jenny said, excitement tinging her voice, much in the same way a bloodhound's bark altered when he caught a scent. "Definitely that one."

Amelia followed her sights to a man, most likely in his early thirties. Ordinarily, Amelia would have never considered him. He was tall and lean, in good shape, most likely still fast. But he was also surrounded by two young children and was holding a third on his shoulders, his arms hooked over a skinny boy's knobby knees. Children made it awfully hard to run after a pickpocket.

Amelia's face split into an approving grin. "Yes, good. Let's go. Stick to the plan."

"I always do," Jenny said with irritation before echoing the same easygoing expression as Amelia. Lengthening her spine, she adjusted her bonnet, patting the fake blonde curls framing her face. Amelia could tell Jenny yearned to scratch at her scalp. Wigs were always uncomfortable, which was why Amelia never wore them over her straight black hair, opting to pin it back severely under her bonnet instead. However, Jenny's wig was a special gift from Molly that served to hide her blazing carrot-red tresses. When the plan was to be as inconspicuous as possible, that particular shade—though beautiful—was a liability.

Idly, Jenny and Amelia made their way over to the man and his brood. To anyone watching, the duo must have looked like everyone else in the crowd. Two sisters, perhaps, enjoying a stimulating day away from home. Nobody could have divined the calculations going on behind the women's placid eyes, the strong leg muscles underneath their fine skirts, the nimble fingers covered in their lace gloves. They would never have likened them to sharks as they slowly, effortlessly, languidly swam in for their first kill of the day.

Amelia struck first. It made the most sense. Pregnant women were so awfully clumsy, after all.

"Oh, I'm so sorry, sir," she said, tripping and losing her feet.

She would have landed face-first in the grass if not for the two steady hands that snatched her from the precipitous fall. Thank the Lord he was fast. Sometimes, the marks weren't so agile, and Amelia had to pick dirt out of her teeth for hours afterward.

"Are you all right?" the man asked, pulling her back to standing. Amelia made a meal of it, floundering a bit, huffing and heaving at her billowing skirts as she straightened in front of him. The effort wasn't long, maybe a little dramatic, but nothing out of the ordinary. It was just perfect, actually, if she said so herself. Not for the first time, Amelia mused that she could have been an actress in another life. If things had been different. Actors lie for money as well, though they're considered acceptable in polite society.

"I'm fine, I'm fine," Amelia said breathily, batting her eyelashes at the man—her savior. Men loved it when she did that. Her big brown eyes had been hailed enough. Molly had always told her they were her best asset. They made Amelia appear honest and angelic—two things she was decidedly not. What man didn't like to do a bit of rescuing—especially at a medieval tournament? If Amelia knew anything about men, it was that they were simply creatures … animals, really. Their egos liked to be stroked, among other things.

"I cannot believe I did that. How clumsy of me. Thank you, again," she said, simpering.

"Not at all," the man said, puffing out his chest and re-hooking his arms around the boy's legs on his shoulders. The gentleman had no idea his billfold had just been lifted. No idea at all.

Before Amelia could shuffle off, he stopped her. "You have to be careful," he said self-importantly, nodding to the belly bulging out from her middle. "You look to be due any day now. Your husband must be a generous man. I wouldn't have allowed my wife out of the house in your condition." He chuckled, bobbing his son up and down. "Sometimes I wonder why the Lord entrusted women to hold such important cargo. Being the weaker sex and all."

Always the professional, Amelia kept up her even-tempered countenance. Every once in a while, when her conscience asserted itself, she felt a smidgen of pity for the people she stole from. But not now. Not when this dolt reminded her so much of Molly's old beau, Walter, a vile man who got a sick perversion out of making every woman he encountered feel like she was lower than the dirt under his stolen boots. Amelia desperately hoped this simpleton had stuffed his billfold with his life savings.

"You have such a beautiful family," she remarked. "Three children. What a blessing."

His eyes gleamed. "Ten. My wife is watching the others at home."

"Ten! Good Lord." *Good Lord, indeed.*

The man nodded, his pride undeniable. "Yes, the Lord is good."

Amelia wasn't so sure the man's wife would agree so readily. With one last nod, she wished the family a happy day and dove into the crowd, getting lost in the bustle.

A few minutes later, Jenny sidled up to her side, saying nothing, just giving her a glance that told Amelia everything she needed to know. Still ... Amelia had to ask.

"Please tell me it was heavy?"

"Above average," Jennie replied with a smirk. "You kept him talking so long I was able to nick a handkerchief as well."

"What did I tell you?" Amelia said, smiling down at her bump. "Men love helping women in delicate situations."

"I can't believe you thought of that. It's absolute genius." The awe in Jenny's voice made Amelia's smile grow even bigger. It wasn't every day that Jenny offered praise to her mentor. Usually, Amelia only heard resentment in the woman's voice.

Though she didn't have one maternal bone, Amelia had the overwhelming urge to stroke the feather-filled pouch attached to her stomach underneath her dress, but alas, her costume didn't allow it. The brilliance of the design was that her real arms were actually hidden *inside* her clothes, close to her body. The arms everyone saw—the gloved hands lovingly draped around her stomach—were fake. She'd had them constructed especially for the trick.

And it *was* genius—though she wasn't the kind of person who would call herself a genius. However, if Jenny wanted to, then Amelia wouldn't be so rude as to contradict her.

She'd gotten the idea for the costume one afternoon while she was walking along the always-busy Piccadilly, scouting out potential jobs. She'd noticed a pregnant woman fall to her knees. It seemed like the entire block stopped to help her. Not one, but five men had dropped what they were doing to bring the woman back to her ungainly feet, clucking over her like mother hens. At first, Amelia couldn't believe it. She even followed the woman for six blocks afterward, thinking the pregnancy was a scam. When the woman eventually entered a proper row house on a very proper street, Amelia had to deal with the fact that nothing nefarious had happened. The pregnant lady had fallen, and everyone rushed to help her. That was it. For a person who looked upon general good deeds with a sense of incredulous disbelief, it had been a revelation.

Pregnant women were a gold mine. *Married* pregnant women, that was. They were never rebuked or chastised, and the world considered them absent of malice. As vessels of the future, they were all that was good and right in the world and were never treated with anything as boorish as suspicion.

Amelia had only been annoyed she hadn't thought of the ruse sooner. It was perfect for a diver like her who preferred to work alone. With her hands hidden inside her dress, she could pretend to fall near an unsuspecting man and lift his pocket watch while he helped her. Anyone watching could attest that her "hands" had never veered away from cradling her virtuous belly.

The only downfall was her speed. Amelia was a great runner, fast as lightning; however, she was nervous about sprinting in the cumbersome contraption. Even fake pregnant women were easily winded, it seemed.

"So, who's next?" Jenny asked.

Just as Amelia had expected, Jenny's apprehension considerably abated after their first dive. Now, with her accomplice's head on straight, it was time to get to work and then vanish before anyone realized they'd been fleeced.

After only a few days in Scotland, London was calling. Amelia had never been so far north—she'd never actually left the city before in her twenty years.

It was surreal witnessing firsthand that people existed outside the city, and that they even preferred being there. Amelia wasn't sold on country life. The air was too fresh, the people too apple-cheeked and healthy, the smiles too welcoming. It left her constantly on alert, as if all these good intentions were merely an act. Fronts for duplicity.

Being away from the only home Amelia had ever known unmoored her more than she thought it would. She couldn't allow it to throw her off her game.

Everything was riding on this day. Everything.

But if Amelia was suffering from any kind of inner dilemma, she couldn't afford to let Jenny witness it. The girl's luminescent skin was flushed with anticipation now. Showing any weakness would only hurt them both.

Amelia pulled her shoulders back and lifted her chin, making sure to punch out the belly. She was Amelia Driver, the best pickpocket in London. The Eglinton Tournament was made for her. She was no gallant knight, but she would be the true winner today. Molly's favorite pupil might not be able to knock a man off his horse, but she could make his head spin. When she was through with him, he'd be seeing stars.

But he wouldn't be seeing her. No, they never did. Because Amelia Driver was that good. No one ever saw her coming.

CHAPTER TWO

"I DON'T KNOW why you didn't let the girls come," Michael whined, glaring up at his father. "They're going to make me pay for this when I get back. You have no idea."

Eli offered his nine-year-old son an apologetic frown. "You shouldn't be afraid of your sisters, Michael. They're only two years older than you."

Michael wasn't the least offended by the rebuke; he merely gave his father an incensed look. "But there's two of them, isn't there?" he pointed out with the exasperation of someone who was explaining something for the tenth time. "And they bite."

Eli sighed, nudging his glasses up his nose. He stretched his head above the crowd, using his height to his advantage. Gazing over the mob, he could just make out Eglinton's castle across the far side of the field. Unfortunately, there was no procession lining up outside it.

Taking out his pocket watch, he checked the time. One in the afternoon. The tournament was a full hour late, and it didn't appear to be starting anytime soon. That alone was reason enough for not allowing the girls to accompany them. They hated waiting. Who knew what mischief they had gotten into? Eli shuddered to think of the possibilities.

"That is precisely why they couldn't come," he told his son firmly. "If they cannot behave like ladies then they do not get to enjoy the benefits. Ladies don't bite."

Although their mother had, but Eli would be keeping that unsavory information to himself.

His son granted Eli a fresh scowl. For a moment, he was taken aback at the uncanny resemblance of the boy to his mother—especially when he was pouting. The same jet-black hair and olive skin. The same deep-set eyes that retreated into his face, making him look perpetually exhausted. The same red splotches that covered his entire cheeks when he was angry (as he was now) that made it seem like he'd been splashed with crimson paint. Eli dearly hoped his son never took to the vice of playing cards as his mother had. Michael was a sweet boy, though he could lose the reins on his emotions; his tells would be a boon for the unscrupulous individual.

"Some benefit," his son groused.

"What's that supposed to mean?" Eli bit back, hotter than he'd intended. If Michael had qualms about standing up to his sisters, he obviously didn't with his father. Eli didn't hit as hard, apparently. In fact, he didn't hit his children at all.

"It means," Michael huffed, pointing to the grandstand, "that we should be sitting over there with everyone else."

Everyone else? *Oh.* His son meant everyone like them. Real lords and ladies, not those just dressed up, pretending to be.

Yes, Eli had to take that one on the chin. It *was* his fault that he hadn't acquired a ticket for the grandstand. But Lord Eli, Viscount Barrington, so rarely was around other aristocrats that he'd begun to forget he was one—much to his son's displeasure. He had no great love for the noxious gossip and backbiting of London and preferred the solitude of his country house where he could get lost in his plants—which was precisely why he and his son were bumping elbows with the other plebians, jockeying to get a decent view of the field.

To Eli's credit, he had *tried* to get tickets; he'd just been unlucky. Having said that, he probably wouldn't have been so unlucky had he tried to purchase the tickets earlier in the year.

Remembering to do it the week before the tournament most likely hadn't been the smartest decision. How was Eli supposed to know there was going to be such a staggering demand for the silly show? What was so bloody interesting about a jousting contest? It wasn't even real. It was all make-believe and incredibly anachronistic. Half the people around him were dressed in a hodgepodge of combating centuries. The man to his right was sporting a Roman toga, though the dagger he wore in his belt was clearly Edwardian. It made no damn sense!

Eli cast a furtive look at his son's disappointed form. Now probably wasn't the time to point out the chronological irresponsibility to Michael. The young boy couldn't be reasoned with. All summer long he'd read every article he could find on the tournament, studying and memorizing the knights and their standards. If only Michael showed as much interest in the real history of these kinds of events—the social and political machinations of the medieval era. His son had a substantial mind. Like a Venus flytrap, the boy held on to information with an unrelenting grasp. It was too bad his interests lay with this superfluous nonsense, Eli lamented. Cheering on the same gilded people who were so quick to turn their noses up at others.

Arguing would do no good. Eli had tried it enough anyway. For today, at least, he would allow his son to enjoy the frivolity. Wasn't a knight's creed to live another day to fight? Eli would do just that. He wouldn't say a word. Tomorrow would come soon enough to espouse the virtues of land management and stewardship for their estate. Michael would be the future viscount, after all. It was never too early to learn about soil fertility.

Eli was giddy just thinking about it.

"I *am* sorry," he said, placing his hand on Michael's shoulder. It looked so odd to Eli, sitting there, dwarfing his son's small frame. He could feel the tiny bones underneath, the sharp edge of Michael's clavicle reaching across to fit in the socket. For all his bluster, Michael was still such a little thing. A child. Every fiber in Eli's being tightened in preparation to protect him.

He went on, "But standing never hurt anybody, and when the procession begins, we can push our way to the front."

Michael twisted his lips as if unwilling to believe his father. "You'll really push?" he asked.

"Well, I'm not going to throw a nun to the ground and traipse over her neck, but I think a modicum of pushing might be acceptable."

A smile broke forth, showcasing Michael's missing front tooth. "How about a vicar?"

Eli squinted at the overcast sky. "Is the vicar very tall?"

Michael nodded.

"Like 'Jack and the Beanstalk' giant tall?" It was the only fairytale that Eli could stomach. Any story involving beanstalks healthy enough to reach the sky was all right with him.

Michael nodded again.

"Then yes, of course. If there's a freakishly tall vicar standing in our way, he's definitely hitting the dirt."

Michael fell into a fit of laughter, and Eli sighed in relief. There ... that was better. It wasn't every day that he could get his son to laugh; it certainly wasn't every day they could enjoy each other's company. He told himself to enjoy it while he could.

Life was rushing by too fast for Eli. It felt like it was only last year that his wife had left him with three small children. But Marianne had been gone for eight years now, so long that the children had no memories of her. Eli was the only moderator of his children's past ... for now.

Michael released a bored, exasperated sigh. He ran his fingers through his short hair, highlighting the hasty cut he'd needed last week after the twins "played barber" one night while he was fast asleep.

Michael, ever worried about being called a snitch by Cecily and Kitty, hadn't even told Eli. The governess had informed him. Right before she quit.

The twins hadn't been too put out by her abrupt departure. One could even say they were glad to see her go, since they were the reason behind her haste. They were always the reason behind it.

Over the past nine months, the household had gone through nine governesses. Sometimes Eli wanted to throttle the girls. Nine governesses! Nine! Did they have any idea how difficult it was to find one acceptable governess, let alone nine?

Who knew little girls could be so difficult? Eli surely hadn't. Lord knew their mother hadn't been—at first. She'd at least waited until they were married to display her particular brand of difficulty. In hindsight, he wondered if everything would have been different if she'd shown her true self from the very beginning. Their families had pushed the match, so Eli thought it unlikely. Marianne had grown up on a nearby estate in Essex. When Eli first met her, she'd been quiet and docile, sweet and forgiving—everything a man like him had been conditioned to appreciate and want. At twenty, he'd been enthralled. Young and naïve, Eli thought Marianne was as well. He'd been wrong.

Eli felt his son tug on his fitted navy-blue jacket. Michael had pleaded with him to wear striped hose and bushy pantaloons, but Eli had adamantly declined, informing his son that, once lost, a man's dignity was gone forever.

"Is it starting yet?" Michael asked.

Eli glanced toward the castle. Some people (bagpipers?) appeared to be gathering, though certainly not enough. There were no banners raised or music playing. The knights were still a far cry off. "No," he answered. No use sugarcoating it.

"Can I look?" Michael asked.

Eli returned an ignorant stare. "How?"

"On your shoulders?" Michael pressed his palms together in a holy plea. "Please!"

Edward tucked his hands under Michael's armpits, but a booming baritone stopped him short.

"My lord! I thought it was you," a familiar voice called out. A bunch of people split at the sound, making a path that Moses would have been enviable of.

The figure came into focus. "My God, Gerald. What on earth are you doing here?" Eli asked, stretching out his hand to forestall the man's bow. Gerald shook it with gusto, his cheeks and his eyes bright and merry. For a botanist, Gerald was merrier than most, though Eli suspected it was because of the man's affinity for breeding apples that he, in turn, transformed into the best cider in the country.

"Me?" Gerald responded with a jovial cackle. "What are *you* doing here? I don't think I've ever seen you outside your estate."

"I'm here with my son," Eli answered, directing Michael to stand in front of him. The botanist shook the boy's hand before tilting his head at the father curiously.

"That's right." Gerald chortled as if this news was the funniest thing. "I forgot you had a child."

"He has three," Michael cut in.

Gerald blinked at Eli like he'd never seen him before. "My, you stay busy."

Eli's expression grew sheepish. "I had two at one time."

Gerald laughed. "Well, you've always been efficient." He bent to Michael. "So, my boy, you dragged your father out here to see the knights, huh? Good on you. I, for one, know how difficult it can be to get your father anywhere. Who are you most excited to see today?"

"Lord Charles, the Knight of the Sun!" Michael replied so quickly it came out as one long word. "The newspapers say he's the best!"

"The Earl of Somerset, eh?" Gerald said, rubbing his substantial jaw. The man had studied apples for so long, he was beginning to look like one, though it could have been all the drinking that made his skin so pink and round. "Yes, I hear he's fearsome to be sure. Good man, that Lord Charles. Very good man. An honorable knight if I ever saw one." Placing his hands on his knees, Gerald leaned closer to Michael. "I know him," he said, sotto voce.

Michael's eyes lit up like it was cloudless night sky. "You do?"

"Of course I do. So does … uh …" Gerald paused, his expression clouded over with strain, as if he were suddenly remembering something. "So does your father."

Michael directed his disbelief to Eli, who felt like he'd been scorched by the child's joy. "*You* know Lord Charles?"

Eli shrugged. "I've met him a few times. I think we were at Oxford together, though I'm a few years older and Lord Charles wasn't exactly known for studying."

"I'll say." Gerald chuckled. "His idea of the social sciences differed from your father's."

Father and son wore matching frowns, though for very different reasons.

"So … you weren't friends?" Michael asked, unable to hide his chagrin. The maroon spots were back on his cheeks, though Eli suspected it was from secondhand embarrassment for him.

Eli gave his friend a weighted look. Gerald never did know when to keep his mouth shut. "Well … as I said … I'm older," Eli said slowly, searching for the most diplomatic way to explain that he and Charles were as different as water and oil. And they shared a history Eli would prefer never to explain to his nine-year-old son. "And we were interested in different things."

"You mean he was interesting," Michael said sullenly.

"That's enough," Eli shot back, immediately ashamed he got so rattled. He maneuvered his lips into a semblance of a smile and shook his head at Gerald as if to say, "Kids!"

Gerald had the grace not to act scandalized by their interaction and placed his hand on Michael's shoulder like the two were co-conspirators. "Now, my boy, I understand this tournament is all shiny and exciting, but you mustn't forget all the amazing things your father has done."

"Like what?" Michael asked.

"He's absolutely brilliant. A genius!"

Eli should have put a stop to it; it sounded too much like pity. Besides, he wasn't the kind of person to go around telling people he was a genius. Although it would be rude to contradict his friend while he was addressing Michael.

Gerald went on, "The breakthroughs your father is making with strawberries are truly astonishing."

Michael's shoulders fell. "Strawberries?"

His desultory tone was unmistakable. Eli didn't agree with his son, but he couldn't blame him, either. To a young boy, there was nothing heroic about strawberries.

Gerald was not put off. "Did you know by cutting off the stalks of one and—"

"It's all right, Gerald," Eli broke in, fiddling with his glasses. "He doesn't need to hear it."

Gerald jutted his jaw into his chest, creating three chins. His face was comically confused. "No, trust me. He'll like this. By snipping off the head of one plant and taping it to a different root system—"

Michael's eyes glazed over.

Eli put out his hand to squash the conversation. "Really, Gerald. The boy already knows. Let's just enjoy the day, shall we?"

The boy didn't know, actually. Eli was quite certain that Michael knew nothing about what he did or the importance of it. He probably just viewed him as another eccentric aristocrat obsessed with plants—which, to be honest, wasn't that far off.

Gerald cleared his throat. "Of course, of course, my apologies," he said, coming back to his full height.

Eli stood there for a few awkward seconds, waiting for his friend to make his goodbyes. Even this felt unnatural for him. All of his friends were attached to his work. Encountering them in the outside world made him feel like a completely different person. One he wasn't sure he liked.

And if anything was clear from this day, it was that Eli wasn't sure his son liked him either.

CHAPTER THREE

"WHAT DO YOU think?" Jenny asked with a mischievous quirk to her lips. "Should we call it? There's still plenty more out there," she added quickly.

Amelia regarded her accomplice. Jenny's blonde wig bounced merrily against her cheeks as they meandered through the crowd. She looked like an angel fallen from heaven for the day, certainly not a pickpocket who had ten pounds of loot stashed underneath her plain brown dress.

Amelia's first instinct was to say no. The partners had only been working the crowds for an hour, but already she could feel the strain of the stolen trinkets secreted away in the hidden pockets of her clothes. This day had been her wildest dreams come to life. They'd easily taken enough money for Amelia to pay back Harry's Boys, and then some.

It was just as she had expected. The spectators had been too preoccupied to notice sticky hands diving into their pockets. However, any pickpocket worth her salt had to appreciate the signs, and the wind had shifted—both literally and figuratively. The crowd's tenor had changed.

The procession near the castle was still showing little signs of starting, and restlessness was as palpable as the coming storm. The air had thickened with warning and an ominous wind had kicked up, blowing top hats and parasols across the fields. Rain was imminent—as well as annoyance. Pickpocketing from a mass of disgruntled people was infinitely more difficult than joyful ones. Their frustrated bodies warped in on themselves; their limbs were less free, their tolerance for jostling even less so.

"I'm not sure," Amelia hedged. "You've gotten quite talkative with the last few."

Jenny's eyes went wide, indignant. "I don't talk too much!"

"You do," Amelia replied, lowering her voice. The girl had done well today, and she needed to know that, but there was always room for improvement. "We are supposed to be ghosts. In and out, not saying or doing anything that will make anyone remember us. It's why our clothes and hair are so boring. We're meant to fade into the crowd. The more you talk, the more you'll stick in someone's mind."

Jenny chewed on the inside of her lip.

Amelia sighed. "Spit it out."

"It's just ..." Jennie *tsked*. "I like speaking to some of them. It makes me feel normal. Sometimes it gets so boring only discussing work."

"What are you going on about? We talk."

Jenny arched a thin golden eyebrow. "About the jobs. Don't mistake me. I know how lucky I am to be trained by you. But sometimes ... I don't know." She bobbed her narrow shoulders. "You've become quite drab. At least when you had the flowers, you could talk about other things. Sometimes I wish she hadn't ordered us to stay away ... maybe you wouldn't have failed."

Failed. That insidious word. It was all Amelia heard. Again and again in her brain. *Failed.* Everything else faded away as it stabbed her like a pickaxe to the chest. If it wasn't for the enormous belly holding her forward, Amelia was certain she would have fallen back on her behind. *At least when you had the flowers ...*

Well, Amelia didn't have the flowers, and there was little use bringing them up because they were gone. Why cry over spilled milk? Or dead petals?

Still … despite her reputation in the gang, Amelia wasn't made of stone. If Jenny only knew how often she ruminated over her flowers. Every thought of every day centered around what she'd lost, the flower shop that she'd opened, the life she'd dreamed of creating outside of thieving. But she'd failed. *Miserably.* She'd lost everything and now she was up to her neck in debt, paying back the cold-blooded blokes she'd borrowed from to make her dream a reality. Why had Amelia borrowed from ruthless sorts like Harry's Boys? Oh, that's right, because she only knew ruthless sorts.

Did Jenny think Amelia had just forgotten? That flower shop had been her future, and now it was gone. Talking about it wouldn't bring it back. Talking about it felt like scratching at an open wound—it only made everything worse.

"I'm sorry," Jenny said blandly, an afterthought. She studied her nails through her demure lace gloves. "I shouldn't have said anything."

In an instant, Amelia cleared her expression. She didn't know how much hurt Jenny had spied, but it was too much. "Let's just leave it," she said, the ground wobbling beneath her. For once, she couldn't blame the pregnancy suit. Her equilibrium was always challenged when she thought of the moment that had slipped through her fingers.

She had been so certain the shop was going to be a success. She'd poured her blood, sweat, and savings into it. When it had gone under, she couldn't help but take it personally, and she'd had to crawl back to the gang with her tail between her legs. It had been a harsh awakening, and that was saying a lot for a girl raised on the gritty London streets.

"You know what?" Amelia said, demonstrably upbeat. "Maybe we have time for one more. Why not? As you said, it's been so easy today." She was tired of failing. She felt like winning a little bit longer. If only to wipe away Jenny's pity.

Jenny clapped her hands. "You're exactly right … except …"

"What?" Amelia snapped, irritated at the girl's constant second-guessing. That's what a big bag of gold hidden underneath your skirts did for you … it gave you an obscene amount of conceit.

Jenny hesitated. "Don't you always say the most important rule is *get out while the gettin's good*?"

Amelia glared, forcing Jenny to shift her gaze away. "Do you want to make some money or not? That was the plan. If you're not woman enough for the job then maybe you should have stayed in London. I told Molly I could do this by myself."

"She said you were being reckless."

"She was wrong!"

Jenny slapped her mouth shut with a grimace. Amelia wasn't going to apologize. She hadn't said anything that wasn't true. Besides, if the girl couldn't take a little confrontation, then how was she going to deal with the greater disappointments in life? At seventeen, Jenny was only three years younger than Amelia, and yet it could have been a lifetime. She was new to the streets, having just run away from home, where a drunk father and neglectful mother still lived.

At least she had chosen to leave instead of being the one who was left, Amelia thought bitterly.

Taking a moment, Jenny regrouped, composing herself quickly without one tear falling. Begrudgingly, Amelia gave her credit for that.

"What about him?" Jenny said, staring off over Amelia's shoulder, mercifully redirecting the conversation.

Amelia knew better than to turn. "Tell me about him," she said.

"Well … he's carrying his pocket watch right in his front pocket …" Jenny continued to study the victim. "And it looks like he has a small child with him. It will be so quick. In and out. And then we can go back. We haven't lifted one pocket watch all day."

That was true. And Amelia loved a good pocket watch. It was effortless to steal them and easy to hawk them on the streets. Men loved showing them off and always kept them in the pockets of their vests with the chain hooked around a button for safekeeping. As if that chain could stop her.

But something inside her resisted. Amelia had allowed her ego to get in the way. Molly had always taught her to leave her emotions at the door of any job, and here they were running rampant, all because Jenny had injured her pride and mentioned the flower shop. They should go. There was no reason to stay. They'd been so lucky. Why risk it?

Amelia twirled around and followed Jenny's gaze to their target.

From the corner of her eye, she watched him in the middle of some sort of uncomfortable conversation with a thick-boned man and what she assumed was his son. Unlike the others around him, the gentleman was dressed somberly in crisp navies and brown trousers. No dandy there. Most likely a fussy, dour teacher, or maybe even a cleric. Under his top hat he had dark brown hair that somehow resisted being mussed by the wind, as if he'd ordered it to do so. He seemed like the kind of man who could do that. His face was pinched, his chin lifted like he was above everyone around him, and indeed, whenever he was bumped by someone walking past, his expression tensed with greater irritation.

When the gentleman barked at his son, causing the boy to recoil, Amelia knew she wouldn't be passing up this opportunity. She would enjoy it too much. She always cherished stealing from a haughty man's pockets. It was like she was balancing the scales of the universe. What did that man have to be so upset about? By the looks of his dress and comportment, he had money. He had a family and, no doubt, self-esteem, and yet he was still unsatisfied and miserable in life. Others, like Amelia, were born with nothing—less than nothing—and had to fight and claw and scream for any kind of place in this world. And even though it was still never enough, she could at least find the time to smile, even smell a rose or two.

When someone was as pathetic as this man, nicking his pocket watch really made little difference. His day would be ruined regardless because he had woken up choosing to believe it anyway. So, despite Amelia's better judgment, her years of making a living off the streets, of always looking out for herself with the utmost caution and care because there was no one else who was going to do it for her, she went against her gut.

Amelia waited for the right moment, when the portly acquaintance offered his farewells, before she started through the crowd. "I get to handle this one."

"You don't want my help?" Jenny asked.

Amelia shook her head. "No, just watch and learn."

Jenny fell into step next to her. "You don't even want me to create a diversion? Trip into him? Step on his foot?"

"Nothing like that. All I'm going to do is talk."

"Talk?" Jenny squawked. "You just told me not to talk. He might remember you."

Amelia rolled her eyes, fastening her trademark serenity on her face. "Men like that never remember a woman in a crowd," she said, her jaw tight. "They see women as below them, and therefore, beneath their notice. Trust me."

"All ... right," Jenny stammered. "But then we're done?"

"Then we're done."

Amelia didn't waste any time. She aimed right for him. The dour man was taller than she'd thought. Her head barely reached his whiskered chin. That would make things easier for her, she thought. Tall men were usually slower—both physically and mentally. The blood seemed to have a difficult time traveling all the way up to their brains. Another point in her favor was his glasses. If he ran after her, she'd have to find a way to knock them off his face. He couldn't find her if he couldn't see her.

On closer inspection, Amelia deduced the little boy was indeed the man's son, though the likeness wasn't immediately apparent. The boy's coloring was darker, with tanned skin and midnight-black hair. But their scowls ... those matched perfectly.

A rush of sadness filled Amelia for the boy. It appeared that dissatisfaction could be taught, passed down from father to son along with the proper way to bow and sneer down at a lady.

Well, not this lady. Never this lady.

"I'm sorry, sir. I hate to bother you. But have you seen my small dog?"

Slowly, as if dragging himself through mud, the man drooped his neck toward Amelia. She wasn't ready for what she saw. She'd been waiting for contempt, supercilious uppity-ness, but what she received was far worse: ambeivalence.

"No," came his terse response. His light blue eyes, made even more startling behind the cage of his glasses, rested on her for a fleeting second before dashing away. Apparently, the vacant fields were far more interesting than her.

Amelia furrowed her brow, pooling water on her lower lids. It had taken her years to master tears, and now she could command them at will. It was yet another reason why she was the best—dedication to her craft.

"Oh dear, oh dear," she whimpered, quivering her lips. "I don't know what I'll do if I can't find him. My son will never forgive me."

His bored gaze still on the field, the man replied casually, "Then perhaps you shouldn't have brought a dog to an event such as this one."

The nerve! Amelia didn't spend her life with the most compassionate people, but this man's lack of concern was staggering.

For his part, the boy showed signs of being human. "What kind of a dog is it?" he asked, his face wrinkled in distress. Amelia recognized more of his father in him. They both shared the same square jaw and high cheekbones, although the boy's didn't cut as deeply, since he had the delicious cheeks of youth still in abundance.

She gifted the child with a sparkling smile, noticing that it also got the father's attention. "She's a pug—Coco. The sweetest little thing you've ever seen."

"A pug?" the man said, leaving no room for ambiguity on

what he thought of the breed. "The fat, little things with the pushed-in faces?"

"Exactly," Amelia replied, winking at the boy.

The man scoffed. "Interesting choice," he muttered. "They can't even use their noses properly."

"They're lap dogs," Amelia said, not understanding why she was indignant for a dog that didn't exist. For extra measure, she pushed out her stomach. "And they're delightful with children."

The father zeroed in on her stomach. He stared at it for a moment, his jaw flexing, before he returned his impassive expression to her. "We cannot help you."

"Cannot or will not?"

"Does it matter?"

Amelia's smile stalled over her teeth. "I suppose not." She nodded to the boy. "Thank you for your time, gentlemen. I should be on my way. I'm afraid I'll just have to miss the joust; I won't be able to rest until I find him."

"It's going to rain," the man remarked before she could pretend to leave.

Amelia arched her brow. "Does it matter?"

He smiled then, or at least moved his lips infinitesimally in an upward motion that resembled a smile. Amelia hadn't been expecting it, and an uncomfortable tickling feeling came to her stomach, confusing her. A scar above his lip turned white, becoming more noticeable. Long and deep, it carved deep in his skin from the bottom of his nose just off center to his top lip. Bewildered, Amelia wondered how she'd missed it before. She blamed his eyes.

"I suppose not," he answered.

"What?" Amelia asked, genuinely lost on what they were talking about.

His scowl resurfaced. Apparently, not following his conversation was a cardinal sin. "I said," he answered sharply, "I suppose not. When you asked if it mattered that it was going to rain."

He shifted uncomfortably as if nervous to admit that he'd

been following their conversation closer than she had. She was just as surprised by that fact.

It almost made her not want to do what she did next. Almost.

Issuing a high-pitched scream, Amelia lunged forward toward his chest, craning her neck over his shoulder. "There. Right there. Oh, there's my sweet boy!"

She wished she could have pointed. That could have added to the scene, but the costume wouldn't allow for it. Her fake hands were still busy cradling her belly.

While her *real* hands were busy lifting the pocket watch from the man's inside front pocket.

So easy. Like stealing candy from a baby.

Only … something went horribly wrong. Amelia was so used to her targets following her lead that she didn't notice when the man failed to look behind his shoulder. His gaze hadn't left her at all.

And for the first time in her life, Amelia Driver couldn't get her fingers away quick enough.

She tried to pull back, but the man's hands clamped on her waist.

"If you'd please, madam," he said, his warm breath scorching her alarmed cheeks, "your dog isn't inside my coat."

CHAPTER FOUR

THE WOMAN FLINCHED, her indignant heat palpable between their clothes as her chest flattened against his. "What are you talking about, sir?" she asked, voice heavy with recrimination.

"Your hand," he said, his tone icy. "Remove it."

"My hand?" she echoed, tilting her head up slowly, her words reaching him in a summer breeze of a whisper, the kind that made one tremble from the unexpected coolness.

That was precisely what this woman was—unexpected. From the big brown eyes that looked like they could swallow him whole to her petite frame that he had no doubt could carry him if she put her mind to it.

Grit. The woman had grit. And absolutely no shame. Because she refused to extract her hand.

In fact, she started to move it … in the wrong direction.

Her eyelashes fluttered as her lips parted just inches from the skin of his neck. "What's wrong with my hand?" she asked.

Eli gritted his teeth. No shame.

The thief was a blatant professional, using her body and heavy shirts to shield her actions from everyone around them. Eli would have to be a simpleton to mistake where her adventurous hand was heading. Just as she was at the cusp of cupping his balls (which, unfortunately, were not as apathetic as he wanted them to be), Eli grabbed her wrist, flinging her away from him.

"Father!" Michael cried with wild eyes. The innocent had no idea what the dastardly woman had been up to, only that his father was treating her unkindly. "How could you do that?" He grimaced apologetically to the woman. "I don't know why my father is behaving so rudely. I will help you find your dog." He reached for her hand—the same one that had only seconds ago been rooting near Eli's crotch.

"Michael, stay away from her," Eli barked, swatting his son's hand back.

The woman interrupted them with a rude noise in her throat. "You didn't have to smack his hand. He was only being sweet. I'm not made of poison, you know. He won't get hurt by touching me."

How in the world could she be angry at him? She was the thief!

"I have a feeling he might," Eli replied. Michael gasped, and Eli threw him a weighted look, telling him to stay out of it. The child was too young. He'd only lived within the friendly confines of his home where everything was always the same, from the people who worked there to the furniture that had been in their family for generations.

Michael had no experience with women of loose morals ... not like Eli. One had to be stern, or they'd walk all over you, taking all their arms could carry.

Though, Eli had to admit, she'd almost had him.

Between her lovely brown eyes and her sweet oval face with skin as smooth and creamy as any indulged duchess, the woman's nefarious intentions were almost too wild to be believed. And that was saying nothing about her age. Eli had read that these pickpockets started young, but she couldn't be older than eighteen, and she was already an old hand. Eli recognized that right now.

A man such as he could always tell dedication in others. Just because this woman's commitment was on the criminal side, it didn't mean she didn't take her choice of business seriously.

However, that also meant she would have to face the consequences.

Snaking his hand around her upper arm, Eli couldn't help but notice how malnourished she was. Her limb was as light as down. He could wrap his whole hand around it. He almost felt sorry for the babe in her belly. To grow up with a mother like this … The poor child had no chance.

"What are you doing?" she screeched, wiggling out of her grasp. "Get your hands off me!"

Eli stretched his neck, searching through the crowd, ignoring her outrage. "It isn't fun, is it?" he asked.

"What?"

"Having someone touch you when you don't want them to."

That seemed to bleed through the woman's reasoning. Suddenly, her face collapsed, and tears (real or not, Eli did not know) streamed down her face. "Let me go," she pleaded, hanging her head, giving him an ample view of her long, slender neck. Such a pity it could end up in a noose. Her tears trailed down that neck, picking up speed. "You have no idea what's it like. My husband … He said he'd kill me if I didn't come back with anything. He makes me do this. I have no choice."

"Father?" Michael asked.

Eli blinked. He'd almost forgotten the boy was watching the whole thing. He tried to take the woman's arm, but she evaded him again. Such a slippery, wily thing she was. Her senses always seemed to be on. Even while sobbing, she still had complete control of her faculties and her relation to everyone around her.

"Don't worry, son," he said, offering Michael a confident nod. "We're just going to take this poor woman to the nearest constable. He'll be able to help her find her little … lost dog."

The woman's eyes blazed a black inferno, and if she had something sharp, Eli was certain he would be bleeding at this moment. "Have you no compassion, sir? My life is already such a sorry existence, and you're only making it worse."

Eli frowned, finding the people around taking interest in the altercation. He hated being the center of attention, which was probably why he'd gravitated to plants at such a young age. The idea of strangers staring at him, thinking things about him that he couldn't control, made him want to pull his hat down and cover his eyes like a child.

"Stop making a scene," he seethed in the woman's ear. She surprised him. She smelled clean, like citrus and lavender. It was … pleasant. "You did this to yourself."

The tears had mercifully ebbed, leaving trails of pink stripes down her face. Did she cry so easily because she did it often? Early in life Eli had learned things the hard way and, as a rule, wasn't swayed by emotion anymore. Even so, he stared at those rivers of ruddy skin, wondering if her husband ever offered her a decent handkerchief to console herself.

The woman sniffed, licking her lips, and Eli felt her protuberant belly brush against him. "If you have no compassion for me," she said sadly, "please think of my children. My husband is watching the other two. He hurts them when I don't bring him what he wants. Please, sir. I beseech you. Have mercy."

If her hands were the things that had gotten her into this mess, they were ultimately the things that saved her. Because they rested on her stomach, and it was the most maternal, beautiful thing Eli had ever seen. His wife, Marianne, had never enjoyed being pregnant; she hated how it changed her body, and bemoaned each of her pregnancies. Like a devilish Madonna and Child, the picture before him spoke to Eli in ways he hadn't anticipated. He would never consider himself a religious man— men of science rarely were—and yet her behavior woke something he assumed he'd lost years before.

Eventually, the woman slinked away, head bowed in beatific contrition. "I am at your mercy, sir." Her voice trembled, her wobbles wretchedly effective. "But I swear to you. If you let me go, I will leave my husband and do everything in my power to live a virtuous life. This is my chance. You and your beautiful boy have opened my eyes."

Michael positively beamed. Just like the knight he hoped to be one day, he'd had a role in saving the beautiful damsel in distress.

Beautiful? When had Eli decided that? The little pickpocket was acceptable at best, even with her fathomless eyes. However, there was something about her ... not that he was really contemplating it. But ... if he was forced to explain it ... her attractiveness was all about motion. A painting would never work for a woman like her. It was too staid, would never be able to capture her energy. She was a woman that needed to be experienced in movement. Only then would someone truly understand her appeal.

Not Eli, of course, but someone. Her husband, most likely, even though he seemed like a right bastard. How did those brutish kinds of men always get these women to marry them? Must be the initial excitement. Eli, for all the merits Gerald attached to him, could never be mistaken for a passionate being. Marianne had certainly not considered him thus. And, according to his son, he was not knight material either.

But Eli could be merciful. Despite what Michael believed, even regular men could have chivalric characteristics on occasion.

He cleared his throat. "I'll hold you to it, then," he said, causing the woman's head to snap up.

She regarded him warily. "You're letting me go?"

Michael let out a squeal, and Eli felt like he was ten feet tall. "If you promise to renounce this life of sin."

The tears began to flow again. "Yes, oh yes! What a wonderful man you are." The pickpocket kissed Michael's cheek. "Oh, dear boy. I hope you know what a lovely father you have. He's a prince among men. A true knight!"

Michael laughed, no doubt at Eli squirming under all the adulation.

"I should go," the woman said. She turned away, but whipped back instantly, her bonnet falling askew across her head, showcasing shiny ebony hair. Eli's fingers tickled. He had a harsh desire to right the bonnet upon her head, though he held strong in his position. This whole encounter had been unseemly. Best not to make it any worse.

The woman gulped as if working up the courage to speak. Shyly, a smile fluttered across her face, and she glanced down at her belly. "My child will have a chance now. Thank you, sir. What is your name so I may name it after you if it's a boy?"

Eli was stunned. No one had ever wanted to name a child after him—not even his own wife. He coughed gruffly. "Um … Eli."

She nodded, as if he'd confirmed her suspicion. "Eli," she said. "My knight Eli. Thank you, sir."

"My name is Michael," the boy said, not wanting to be left out.

The woman nodded at him with affected sincerity. "Sir Michael, my hero."

And then she was gone, vanishing as quickly as a dandelion puff in the wind, no trace of it ever having tickled your face.

Eli and Michael stared at one another helplessly. Father and son looked wrung out, like they'd just survived a tornado. And the damned tournament hadn't even started yet!

The tournament. Eli had almost forgotten that was why they were stuck in their interminable wait. If anything, the woman had provided a nice distraction. He usually didn't approve of distractions, but in this instance, he could allow it. It had all worked out in the end. No harm, no foul.

Michael started to wiggle, reaching up on his tiptoes to search around. "When is it going to start? I'm so bored!" he mewled.

Eli sighed. They were back to that. Squinting toward the castle, he reached into his vest pocket, but his hands only felt the familiar fabric. *Not* the familiar pocket watch. He fluttered the jacket against him, checking every nook and cranny, realization slow but inevitable.

Her hands. It couldn't be. They hadn't moved. Not once.

CHAPTER FIVE

J ENNY BOUNCED ON the bed, making the trinkets clink as prettily
as Sunday church bells. "It's like we robbed a pirate ship," she
exclaimed, flopping back on the mattress to wave her arms
through their booty as if she was taking a swim. In her flurry, she
knocked a few wallets onto the floor.

Amelia snatched them up. "Get a hold of yourself," she admonished the girl, though even she had a hard time keeping a
stern countenance. A bed full of treasure could have that effect on
anybody. *And* there was the fact that she'd escaped by the skin of
her teeth. That kind of rush was hard to relinquish. Amelia was
positive she'd be feeling her sense of triumph—and the man's
chary blue eyes tattooed on her for the next month. "We don't
have time to revel in our conquest. They'll be plenty of time for
that later. Let's pack up so we can get out of here. I'm nervous we
waited too long as is it. That storm doesn't look good."

Amelia prowled to the window of the room and brushed the
thread-worn curtain aside. They'd left the fields just in time. Rain
had started falling in sheets, saturating their clothes and weighing
them down more than their booty, by the time they'd reached
the inn. The change had been apocalyptic; the fair blue sky had
turned black so quickly it was like God himself had placed his
entire hand over the sun. Amelia didn't know how the rest of the
tournament would play out—or if it would be canceled. And if

there was one thing Amelia didn't like, it was not knowing the outcome.

She returned to the bed, blowing out an exasperated breath as Jenny continued to bathe among the rings and bracelets, paper money, and coin purses they'd pilfered. Colorful and glistening, the spoils looked as delicious as petits fours lined up on the other side of a confectionary window. "I'm serious," Amelia barked, the anxiety finally winning over when Jenny didn't budge. "We have to go. If people return anytime soon and realize they've had something stolen, they'll take one look at us and put two and two together." She threw an empty sack at Jenny, who caught it before it hit her in the face. "Start stuffing."

"Oh, fine," Jenny grumbled, popping up to sit. Amelia ignored the face the girl pulled. "It wouldn't kill us to enjoy ourselves for a little bit," Jenny muttered. "After all, this is probably the biggest job we'll ever pull in our lives!"

The more handfuls Amelia tossed into her bag, the more she couldn't argue with that. This was a monumental win. She'd known they'd done well by the number of people they'd targeted, but even she couldn't have guessed *how* well. Now, gazing at everything in front of them, it was almost terrifying. She could understand why her accomplice was so giddy. It was the kind of job that made a name for oneself; however, it also got one noticed by every policeman in the country.

"I'll enjoy all this once we get back to London and sell it," Amelia replied tersely. Her gut clenched. Something didn't feel right. She chided herself to calm down. They'd done a fine job, damn near perfect. They'd followed the code and gotten out while the gettin' was good.

Only now she couldn't shake the fact that she'd left something behind, which made no sense. The moment they returned to the inn, they'd done an inventory check, making sure they hadn't dropped anything that would tip anybody off. They'd accounted for every glove and scarf, earbob and handkerchief. But something still rankled, and Amelia concluded it had everything to do with the man and his son.

"We don't have to sell everything, do we?" Jenny asked. "Surely there are some things we don't have to tell Molly about? Things we can keep for ourselves?"

Amelia lifted her head to see Jenny wiggling her hand out in front of her like a young lady showing off her engagement ring to her jealous friends. Only, Amelia didn't know many young men who could afford the green bauble on Jenny's finger. The size of a small nut, the emerald could rival anything in the queen's coronation crown. It was wondrous, but also wondrously dangerous. The ring wasn't exactly a piece of jewelry one could wear without eliciting loads of attention—a pickpocket's worst nightmare.

"Don't even think about it."

"What?" Jenny squawked defensively, hiding the ring with her other hand against her chest. "No one has to know."

"That's not how we do things," Amelia said. "And it's reckless."

Jennie floundered back on the bed, causing more wallets to hit the floor. "*Not how we do things. Not how we do things.* You're always telling me how we do things. I'm sick of it."

"I'm sorry you don't like it," Amelia said patiently, "but it's for your own good. Everything we do is for our own good."

Jenny reached to the ceiling, catching the lamplight on the stone. "I know. I know," she complained. "Sometimes I just wish I could decide what is for *my* greater good."

"That's not how gangs work," Amelia explained. "You join a gang for the safety, for the family. Everyone takes care of each other."

Jenny answered with another groan. The young woman had heard this countless times before. Molly wasn't one to shy away from reminding the girls of the virtue of her wide umbrella, but it was why her unit was so prosperous. With close to forty girls working in concert, it could be a logistical nightmare massaging all those egos and personalities. However, Molly Diamond wasn't one to shrug at challenges. When she'd started up the Diamond Girls thirty years before, she'd been resolute in her demands. You couldn't become a member if you weren't unanimously voted in, and that heavily depended on your ability to be a team player. They all looked out for one another. Everything they stole—from a single piece of linen in a shop to a diamond bracelet—came back to the headquarters to be sold. The earnings were split equally among the crew—no ifs, ands, or buts. If you didn't like it, there was the door.

The egalitarianism was a revelation to women who'd always grown up getting the short end of the stick. With Molly, they always knew where they stood and how much they were worth—just as much as the person standing next to them. But there were sacrifices for this type of society. Dues had to be paid, and a percentage of each of the scores went to a communal pot that was saved to pay legal fees if a girl found herself in trouble. And if a barrister couldn't get a girl free, then the money went to help take care of her family while she did her time. It was the only right thing to do.

Amelia could understand her partner's reluctance. That extraordinary ring would be something Jenny loved like her own child. It would be a constant reminder that this life—not always as heroic as Robin Hood made it appear—had a bright side. It wasn't always perfidy and looking over one's shoulder. It was glamorous and exciting. However, in Molly's gang, that ring would also feed many innocent children when their not-so-innocent mothers didn't make it back home at the end of the night.

"You just won't let me keep it because you're mad at me," Jenny lashed out, tearing Amelia from her thoughts.

"What?" Amelia shook her head. "What are you talking about?"

Jenny's neck drooped while she absent-mindedly fiddled with a pearl necklace that Amelia desperately hoped was real. "You're angry that I left you there, after that man caught you. I can't believe the amazing Amelia Driver got caught," she added callously.

Amelia paused, choosing her words with care. She *had* been angry at first. The second the man had wrapped his hand around her hip, Jenny had cut and run. But that was the way it was. You followed the code even if it showed a lack of loyalty to your partner. Because the real loyalty was to your gang. Regardless of what happened to the person you were working with, the object was always to get back to your crew without getting caught.

And Amelia—for that slim slice of time—had been caught. Jenny had had no choice but to flee. Even if Amelia might have done something different, even if Amelia might have tried to create a diversion to help a friend out of a jam, it wasn't the sensible thing to do. And Amelia was teaching Jenny to be sensible. There was no place for rogues in their line of work. Amelia knew that better than anyone.

She went back to stuffing her bag. "No, I'm not mad at you," she said, cramming in the stolen goods with a little more gusto. "You did the right thing. I'm mad at myself."

"Why?" Jenny asked, her expression relaxing now that her mentor had left her off the hook. "You were brilliant. The way you conned your way out of that was first-class!"

Despite her self-recriminations, Amelia's lips curled up. "I suppose."

Jenny kneeled on the bed, tossing her fake blonde curls off her forehead. In her elation, she'd forgotten all about the itchy wig. "There's no supposin' about it. I've never heard of a person trying so many tricks at one time. First you tried the dog bit, and then the seducing bit, and then, when that wouldn't work, you still got him to pity you and let you go." Jenny's jaw fell open in guileless wonder, as if she'd just seen the Almighty perform one of his miracles. "I still can't believe it."

Neither could Amelia, for that matter. She never suffered under false pretensions; she knew she was good at her job, the very best. However, the man had been difficult, unyielding, a stone wall of moral certainty. If it hadn't been for the boy … With his help, a light had slid through the smallest of cracks, giving Amelia just the leverage she needed. Everybody had a weakness, a tell, and in the last moment, she'd found it in the man. He might have had a giant stick up his ass, but he also hadn't wanted to disappoint his son. Unfortunately, it cost him. Chivalry usually did. People bemoaned the fact that chivalry was dead. Amelia knew it was dead for a reason.

"Speaking of which, where *is* that pocket watch?" Amelia asked, perusing the stash. She'd lost track of it when she dashed into the room and dumped her treasures unceremoniously on the bed.

Jenny grazed the loot with both hands, yelling, "Ah-ha," as she lifted the timepiece above her head like she was King Arthur pulling Excalibur from the stone. She tossed it to Amelia, who caught it deftly in her palm.

"Well, look at that," she said wistfully, shifting the pocket watch to catch the light.

"What?" Jenny asked, walking on her knees across the bed to get a closer look.

Amelia couldn't take her eyes off the piece, as if the expensive thing would vanish in thin air. "It's a Breguet."

"A what?"

Amelia rolled her eyes. "Honestly, you call yourself a thief."

Jenny replied with an irritated *tsk*. "Just tell me what it is," she said, sitting back on her haunches, the air ripped from her sails.

"Only one of the most expensive watches in the world. Breguet custom-made pieces for Napoleon, Empress Josephine …" Amelia grinned. "I even heard our new miserly queen purchased one last year—a modest one, of course."

"Of course." Jenny giggled, furor building in her tone. "So, what of this one? How much do you think we'll get for it?"

Amelia peered at the piece closely. Its gold plate was near pristine, with virtually no scratches despite its age. By no means a watch connoisseur, she guessed it was made late in the last century. It had Breguet's signature white enamel dial and blue steel hands that were common in the period. What made it truly spectacular was that it was self-winding. Breguet wasn't the first to create watches of that kind; however, his were considered the absolute best and most reliable.

Amelia weighed the timepiece in her hand. The man would miss it. Oh well, his loss was her gain.

"Let me put it to you this way," Amelia said carefully, tucking the watch into the hidden pocket near her breast. "I would have gone all the way to the Eglinton Tournament and been happy to only come back with this."

Jenny gasped.

Amelia smiled. "No, I'm serious; this is special—"

A deep voice interrupted. "I'm well aware of that, which his precisely why I want it back."

CHAPTER SIX

ELI WOULD HAVE compared them to two deer staring down the length of a shotgun, but these women weren't quite as innocent looking. They didn't move a muscle, and their eyes were as wide as the space between dreams and reality.

Taking advantage of their paralysis, he entered the room, closing the door softly behind him. "Did I startle you?" he asked pleasantly. "In your excitement, you forgot to lock the door. I thought about knocking but assumed that wouldn't be necessary for old friends. That is what we are now, isn't it? Old friends?"

"Who *are* you?" the pregnant one asked. No, not pregnant. Eli focused on the tiny woman who only hours ago had tricked him into thinking she could change. Well … she'd changed, all right, only not as he'd anticipated. Her dark brown eyes still swallowed her face, and her black hair still lay plaited tight against her head, but her hands … her hands made him stop. No longer cradling a lovely bump, they clasped together in front of her lithe, *flat* figure—gloveless and red-knuckled, the tendons long and pale green against her ivory skin.

Eli rebuked himself. He should have figured it out sooner. The gloved hands she'd shown earlier were not real. They were too petite, too delicate for someone like her; they lacked strength.

When her fingers began to fidget, he blinked, remembering himself. "Lord Eli, Viscount Barrington," he announced with a stiff bow. "Pleasure."

His thief found this to be anything but pleasurable. "What do you want?"

His gaze climbed back up to her eyes, and they shared a long, drawn-out stare, neither backing down. "I'm going to do what I should have done before," Eli answered. "I'm going to take you to the constable."

The younger blonde woman gasped again, covering her mouth with her hand.

"*Both* of you," he added. "Because that's how it works, doesn't it? You work in pairs?" For the first time, his focus fell on the mattress, where he saw the myriad trophies they'd accumulated throughout the day. Taken from trusting fools just like him. He walked to the bed, and the blonde woman climbed off. With her back stuck to the wall, she sidled her way around the room, giving him a wide berth.

"No, that isn't how it works at all," the pregnant (or *non-pregnant*) woman stated. "I'm the one who stole from you. She had nothing to do with it."

"Amelia!"

Eli's ears perked up. Finally, a name! And by the harsh glare Amelia gave her accomplice, it wasn't a fake.

"Amelia, eh?" he said, crossing his arms. Keeping one eye on her, he scanned the riches some more. "Why don't you tell me where my watch is, Amelia?"

"I will if you let us go after. You'll have your watch; there's no reason to turn us in."

Exasperation flared. "You're hardly in any position to negotiate. Come now"—Eli held out his palm—"give me the watch. If you behave, I'll tell the constable that I know nothing about the rest of this." He waved his arm hastily at the loot. "You will only have to answer for what you stole from me. Just give me what I want."

He couldn't believe the girl. She actually hesitated, as if she still had a choice in the matter. Didn't she know she was done for? There was no other angle, no other way she could get out of this situation. She'd lost. And still, she made him wait. It could almost have been commendable if it wasn't so stupid.

Eli stretched his hand out more. "You're making me angry."

Amelia sucked in a large breath, her shoulders widening like a bird ready to take flight. "I'm not entirely delighted at the moment, either."

"Just give it up!"

"Stop yelling!" she yelled. "I'm trying to think."

"There's nothing to think about," Eli yelled back, his cool completely vanishing. "You've lost. Just accept it."

Her thick eyebrows bunched together. "Accept it? Only losers accept it when someone tells them they've lost."

Eli's arm was stinging, but he continued to hold it out. He resolved not to pull back until his father's pocket watch was safe in his hands. The limb would have to break off before he yielded to this elfish chit.

And she really did look like an elf. With her bonnet off, Eli could make out two pointy little ears with tips that peeked out from the braids at her sides. Her eyes didn't help anything. Not only were they unusually large, but they twinkled—and not in a good way. It was the kind of twinkle that alerted one to scheming, but not joy. Eli didn't spend a lot of time around people; reading them wasn't one of his strong suits. But he would hazard the girl hadn't experienced real joy in years. As youthfully charming as her features were—from the upturned nose to the full cheeks—there was a hardness in the clench of her jaw, a pull in the muscles around her eyes that revealed a depth that most ladies of her age hadn't achieved yet. It was the kind of hardness that only a difficult life could provide.

Curious by nature, for a second, Eli wanted to ask what had caused her so much hurt, why her knuckles were red and scarred, her eyes laden with sadness.

But the damned woman stole the opportunity from him. Before he could register what was happening, pandemonium erupted.

Amelia flung the bag she was holding at Eli's head, obscuring his vision long enough for her to reach down and grab a handful of coins and handkerchiefs from the bed. She pitched them at his face, showering him with so much silk and gold he felt like he was in the middle of a Moroccan bazaar.

Eli heard footsteps and spun around just in time to spot the blonde woman whip open the door and flee. Amelia was right on her tail. She bobbed past him, sidestepping his grasp. She was almost at the threshold when Eli clutched hold of her skirt, yanking her back against his chest.

Like an eel, she slipped and slithered in his arms, using every part of her body to fight. Nothing on Eli's body was safe. Amelia stamped on his feet, threw her head back, attempting to crack his nose, and bared her teeth to bite any skin within limits. She was a cornered animal desperate and willing to do anything—and he meant *anything*—to gain her freedom.

"Goddammit, stop it!" Eli roared when she'd just missed crushing his nose for the second time. It was bad enough that he thought she'd broken two of his toes. He'd be hobbling for a week. "Just calm down."

"I will never calm down!" she rasped, bending her knees into a crouch, trying to escape his grasp. "You'll have to drag me to the constable by my hair. I won't help you turn me in."

He ground out a filthy word from his clenched mouth. If the girl had proven anything today, it was that she would be a pain in the ass. He searched around the room for a rope or something to bind her with, but he came up short. Even that tiny lapse of concentration was too much. The moment he turned all his attention from restraining her, Amelia ducked her head forward and sank her teeth into his forearm with such a wicked bite that he could hear his skin opening.

"For fuck's sake!" he cried, launching them both back to the bed. The mattress sank like a stone beneath them, caving in the middle under their weight. With monumental effort, Eli rolled over Amelia, pinning her hands over her head. She made ragged noises, groaning and growling like a rabid animal. Later he would ponder all the things she reminded him of in that room—an elf, a fox, a wolf; she was nature personified. Dangerous and feral.

Draping his torso over hers, Eli finally succeeded in forcing her to rest. Her chest pumped wildly underneath him, strong and frantic enough to raise his upper body along with her breaths.

"You're hurting me," she whimpered.

"No, I'm not."

Her eyes narrowed to slits. "All your weight is on my wrists. You'll snap them."

He glanced at the wrists, so tiny he could wrap his hands around them, and balanced more of his weight into his hips. "Then you won't be able to dive anymore."

Amelia laughed caustically. "What do you know about diving?"

"More than I did yesterday."

They waited. He could see the levers spinning and shifting behind her eyes as she tried to get out of this latest quagmire. Eli believed her. She'd never stop. But she should believe him, because neither would he.

However, this current predicament they found themselves in wouldn't be beneficial for long. Eli had to find a way to control the woman without lying on her. Even if it didn't feel altogether unpalatable.

As if sensing his dilemma, Amelia rammed her pelvis into his, doing absolutely nothing to move him off her and absolutely everything to *move him.* "Get off me," she seethed.

Eli's neck hung over her shoulder, and he resisted the pull to rest his forehead on the bed. He clamped his eyes closed, sucking in air, trying to think of ways to calm his attentive lower half. *The crowds at Piccadilly Circus ... cricket matches ... the plague ...* but his methods didn't work. His body refused to accept reason.

"Just wait." He blew the words out of his teeth like a man expelling his soul.

Naturally, Amelia didn't listen. She pumped into his pelvis again, and, for an agonizing moment, Eli saw stars. Agony and ecstasy.

"Goddammit, I'm trying to think!" Or *not* think, for that matter.

She cackled, her hot breath scalding the skin on his neck. "Hard, isn't it?"

His head shot up. "What?"

"It's hard … trying to think when someone's pestering you."

"Oh." Yes, pestering.

Clearly, he hadn't been with a woman in a long time. That was the only explanation for his body's blatant lack of objectivity. Because this woman was foul, a blight on society. On the other hand, she was also very, very soft. For being such a small thing, she was exceedingly strong … and supple. It was amazing what a real woman's body felt like when it wasn't hiding a ridiculous amount of stolen wallets and an army of handkerchiefs.

Handkerchiefs …

Eli scouted the bed and got an idea.

"Don't move," he warned, burning her with his harshest glare, the one that always made the twins listen for a few precious seconds before they went back to causing trouble.

"Not a chance," she shot right back.

With a put-upon sigh, Eli slid up her body, jerking back and forth whenever she tried to knee him in the groin. Dismissing all thoughts of gentlemanly behavior, he pinned a knee in the center of her chest while he amassed the handkerchiefs.

Not to be outdone, Amelia also cast ladylike behavior aside and regaled him with her colorful vocabulary. He even learned a few new words, which made for a productive day. Eli fought her for her arms, tying (and double-knotting) each one to a bedpost with the handy silks.

Amelia's face was as red as a strawberry in July when he was done. Eli suspected his was as well.

With her limbs spread wide across the mattress, Amelia surprised him with a wicked chortle that tickled him straight to his rod. The damn thing would still not go down. "Now what are you going to do?" she said, admiring his handiwork. "Carry the bed to the constable's office?"

Eli hadn't gotten that far in his planning, though he wasn't about to tell her that. Wiping his sweaty hands on his pants, he trudged off the bed to the window. With all their ruckus, he had failed to register the rain that continued to pound against the windows and roofs. It was a biblical downpour if ever he'd seen one.

"Where's your son, by the way? Did you leave him at the castle?" Amelia asked, her tone oddly conversational.

Eli continued to survey the outside, where he saw people hurrying to find cover in all directions. This was the only inn in the village; it would be inundated soon. "What? Of course not. He's sharing a room with my valet."

"Wait. You mean to tell me you made him *leave* the tournament? A little boy who'd probably been waiting all year to see the knights in action? What kind of a father are you?"

Eli pretended not to care about her rampant disapproval. He shrugged. "A responsible one. Finding you was more important. Michael will understand that … in time." Try as he might, his voice wobbled on that last bit. "Besides, it was raining."

"A little rain never hurt anyone."

"Neither did a little common sense," he flung back. Filling his lungs, Eli resettled his composure. The woman did have a knack for throwing him off center. "Besides, I doubt Eglinton even went through with the tournament. I'm sure he decided to reschedule."

Amelia shook her head, annoying him further with a *tsking* noise. "Not likely. Did you see all those people? They were there for a show, and they weren't going to leave before they got one."

"People will act in a sensible manner. They'll see reason."

She squinted comically at him as if he was an animal at a zoo she'd never encountered before. "You don't know people very well, do you?"

"I knew you well enough to find you."

"Yes … how did you manage that?" Amelia replied as if she was asking him for directions to the park. Eli couldn't quite get his head around their exchange; it was damn near cordial and unbelievably discombobulating.

"I followed you," he said, coming back to stand over the bed. "You really should learn to look over your shoulder. One would imagine that's the first thing they teach you in pickpocket school."

Her confident veneer cracked. She lolled her head to the side to stare at the wall instead of him. In a day of embarrassing skirmishes, Eli took it as a small victory.

"There's no such thing as pickpocket school."

He eyed the treasures surrounding her. There must be hundreds, maybe even thousands, of pounds worth of stolen goods. "Then how did you get to be so good at it?" he heard himself ask, his interest winning out.

He waited for an answer. Amelia scrunched her lips, opening her mouth and closing it as if waging an inner battle. Her self-preservation won out in the end. "Shouldn't you be with your son right now? He might be afraid of the storm. You really don't intend to keep me here all night, do you?"

Eli hadn't planned on it, though now that she pointed it out, he realized that was exactly what he would have to do. There was no way he would be able to locate the constable in this weather. They'd have to wait it out.

"I appreciate your concern, but you mustn't worry about my son," he said, flashing a winning smile. "We're staying at this inn as well. It is the only one in town, after all."

Amelia groaned, closing her eyes.

"Oh, don't be so hard on yourself," he went on, enjoying her torment. "You weren't counting on the storm to maroon you here, and you definitely weren't counting on me."

"You can say that again," she murmured irritably.

Eli laughed.

"If you're going to keep me here all night, will you at least take all this loot off the bed?" Digging her heels into the mattress, she arched like a kitten, forcing Eli to look away. "It's killing my back. I'll never be able to get to sleep."

He contemplated her for a serious minute. It would be the polite thing to do, but he didn't trust that she wouldn't try to make him a eunuch again if he got too close. Not to mention his cockstand had just abated, and he was loath to get it started again.

Gentlemanly attributes died hard, and with a withering stare, he made his decision, scattering the bits and bobs at the edge of the bed. "Don't try anything."

Eli kept his focus on his work, but he could almost hear her smile as she replied, "What would I try?"

He scoffed, sliding an astonishing number of wallets to the floor. Even with a partner, how had she accomplished all this in only a matter of hours? "Women like you always think you can get what you want."

Laughter came deep and heavy from Amelia's chest. "Women like me, huh?"

Eli didn't respond, only nudged her on her side to remove any items beneath her.

When she returned to her back, she pinned him with an icy glare. "Hateful harlot, right? An abomination to the world? Ruining good men with temptation and sin? Yes, that's me." Her words had a bitter tinge, as if she'd just bitten into the pith of an orange. "A veritable Jezebel."

The bed seemed to sink even more under her tirade. Eli rounded to the other side, clearing off the mattress. When he rolled her again to reach underneath her other half, he pretended not to notice the lonely tear that trailed down her nose.

He failed. "Attractive," he said, returning to standing. Slowly, her eyes—equal parts limpid and sorrowful—blinked up at him. Eli wiped his hands on his pants, suddenly noticing how small this room seemed for the two of them. "I meant attractive women … like you. Now if you're done feeling sorry for yourself, let me get some rest. You might be attractive, but you're also annoying as hell."

CHAPTER SEVEN

HOW ELI THOUGHT Amelia was going to get some sleep was beyond her.

Attractive? He thought she was attractive? Well, that was something. Amelia could definitely work with that. She ignored the fluttering in her chest while she ruminated on that fortuitous information. She hated the man, for goodness' sakes! Why should she care if he thought she was pretty? It wasn't like she hadn't noticed the effect she'd had on him. The poor man had desperately tried to hide his stimulated lower half for most of their altercation. It had been wicked of her to keep thwacking her pelvis into his, though it served him right. He shouldn't have tied her up like a common criminal.

Amelia might be a criminal, but there was nothing common about her.

Which was why she waited to untie herself. In a quandary like this, novices would have worked on getting loose the moment the gentleman's breathing had fallen into a steady, sleep-induced rhythm; however, Amelia knew better. She waited for the eyelashes. One had to resist the temptation to flee until the eyelashes began flickering intermittently in repose. That meant the gentleman had truly gone to Nod and her chance at escape was at its best.

Amelia wiggled her wrists just shy of making the bedpost

creak. The bastard had knotted her up tight—though not tight enough. Using her teeth, she loosened the knot on one hand. She was free and working on the other in two minutes flat. She'd have to thank Molly when she got back to London. Molly had had the brilliant idea to start tying Amelia up in bed when she was a child. Every night, Amelia would have to break out before she could go to sleep. The first night it had taken her until dawn—the second night, a few hours earlier. By the time she turned nine, she was free in minutes. And Molly didn't stop there—she started using handcuffs. Amelia would never be able to shake the disappointment in herself. It had taken her two years to master escaping those.

Stuffing the handkerchiefs down her dress (waste not, want not), Amelia slid off the bed. Asking the viscount to clear everything from the mattress had been a stroke of genius. There was nothing to rustle or cause any noise as she came to her feet. Gently, without straining one plank of wood, Amelia tiptoed across the floor past all the loot she was leaving behind. She consoled herself by pressing her chest, the spot where she carried the pocket watch snug against her heart. That was all she needed anyway. Everything else would have been pure greed.

Her hand hesitated on the doorknob. This would be the tricky part. Her body tightened in anticipation. If (or when) Eli heard her, he'd start a chase. But he had no idea how fast she was—another of Molly Diamond's drills. Thanks to her brilliant leader, Amelia could run and run and run and run. One could even say she could run like her life depended on it—because it usually did. There was no way he'd be able to keep up. And if he did for a time, she'd lose him in the storm. It was her only chance. The rain had yet to yield. The gale banged on the hotel like snooker balls against the rails. And when all else failed, hopefully, the viscount would think of his son and see reason. A pocket watch wasn't worth deserting his son for a wild goose chase in the Scottish hills—even a Breguet.

Amelia twisted her neck, absorbing the man's sleeping form

as he lay on his side on the floor next to the bed. To use Eli's word, he was certainly attractive—if one liked men with giant sticks up their asses. As a rule, Amelia did not. They were bad for business. This one, though … this one gave her pause, regardless of his buttoned-up demeanor. His dark brown hair was short and cut close to the head, and at this late hour, his whiskers were thick, threatening to cover half his face. Amelia wondered what he would look like with a full beard. If it would come in brown like his hair or have a reddish tint to it. She imagined it would be as deep as the oriental poppies she'd just viewed at Kew Gardens. It would hide his strong, square chin, but Amelia didn't think that was necessarily a bad thing. He seemed to be a man who approved of distinguished airs, and it would provide him that.

Even with his eyes closed, Amelia could see the color in her mind. Not so much bluebell blue but gentian blue, as rich as cobalt. Too rich for a man like this. Too deep for a priggish man who lacked fire.

Though he hadn't been completely bereft of a flame. Amelia was not startled often, but even she was taken aback when Eli had wrapped her in his solid arms. Tall men so rarely had that kind of strength. It made them such fun to steal from. But this man … When Eli trapped her, she could feel the energy coursing through him, the masculinity pumped and primed through overindulged muscle. It felt … shocking … and comforting in an odd sort of way. If Amelia hadn't been so busy trying to smash his feet, she might have tried letting him hold her while she rested her head on his forearms. It might have been nice … for a brief stretch of time.

She wrestled her gaze away and returned to the doorknob, the cold brass uninviting against her palm. Those fanciful thoughts were never helpful. Amelia had allowed them at one time, but they'd done more harm than good, ultimately leading her here. A woman in her line of business couldn't dream about a future. Her life was all about the now. The moment one started letting oneself think about tomorrow was the exact moment one lost sight of today—

A hand looped around her ankle, branding her with its squeeze. *Dammit! Not again!*

Amelia kicked like a maniac, yet the hand wouldn't budge. She looked down to see the viscount awake, furious, and very, very determined.

Balancing herself against the door, Amelia picked up her free foot and aimed for Eli's groin, but he must have read her mind. He blocked her heel with his hand and didn't let go. Instead, he twisted her foot, sending an excruciating pain all the way up her leg. She cried out helplessly, falling to the floor, back in the steel-trap arms of her son-of-a-bitch captor.

Amelia lay there for a long time, raggedly panting, tears falling freely, the wood of the floor cutting against her cheek.

Eli scrambled up behind her in a spooning fashion, throwing his arms and legs over her own until she was entirely encased within his long body. His words grated against her ear. "You are such a piece of work, you know that?"

Amelia couldn't stop the tears. That was something she *hadn't* been able to manage in all her years of training. Once Amelia opened the waterworks, she had a difficult time putting the lid back on at will. It was as if her body was a geyser and, once released, had to unload all the pressure it could in the time it was allowed. As annoying as it was, she had to admit she always felt better afterward.

Though she doubted she would feel that in this instance. Embarrassment scorched her insides. Embarrassment and failure.

More bloody failure.

How had her life become such a disappointing mess? And now she was finally caught. Served her right for dreaming. Dreams were for other kinds of girls. Girls who could afford futures.

Amelia might as well just let him take her to the constable. Who knew? It might even be the safer option. At least if she was transported off to Australia, she'd be far away from Harry's Boys.

When they found out she didn't come up with the money to pay them back, she was as good as dead in London anyway.

Eli grunted, his chest vibrating against her back. Though he was thoroughly disgruntled, his voice was still heavy with sleep. "That was stupid."

"I had to try," Amelia whispered plaintively.

"Now, do you see that you have no other choice?"

She paused, pressing her lips together so a sob wouldn't escape. She wasn't afraid of his pity; she didn't give a damn about that. It was her pride that waited until her voice could be trusted—that was all she had left.

"You always have a choice," she said softly. Even girls who had no futures had choices. The only problem was that most of them were never good.

⟫⟪

AMELIA'S FOREHEAD TICKLED. She moved it back and forth, scratching it against a prickly, warm surface. It was delicious and foreign, like running her hands against a furry, exotic flower stem.

She tried to pull away, but her motions were quickly squelched when an iron hold locked at the base of her back, keeping her in place.

Amelia opened her eyes to darkness, the room still shrouded by night, and the memories rushed to the forefront of her drowsy mind. She had no idea what time it was, though guessed it was close to dawn. She was astonished that she'd allowed herself to sleep at all, especially in this intimate position.

Her head was situated against Eli's, tucked just underneath his chin, while her arms were bent and cuddled in between them, providing the only barrier keeping their fronts from touching. Unfortunately, there was nothing to block their legs, which were thoroughly tangled.

Amelia should have been mortified. She never allowed this

kind of intimacy—especially with men determined to pitch her to the authorities. The anguish of the day was clearly to blame; however, she suspected it was more than that.

With Amelia's nose dipping into the cavernous hollow between Eli's neck and chin, she inflated her lungs and came away with a delicious scent. He smelled bitter, though not in the way one would expect. The bitterness was crisp and fresh, like unripe fruit, like seedlings starting out on their journey to the sun. Amelia had the sneaking suspicion that if she peeked at his hands, she might find dirt under his fingernails. The tangy, earthy aroma clung to him like sap to a tree. If she licked his skin, would he taste sweet?

Eli shifted, and he maneuvered her closer, jamming her nose against his neck. Closing her eyes against the coming morning, she allowed herself to rest her head there, taking breaths that revived her with a small semblance of peace. Those inhales brought her back to her shop, cutting stems and arranging flowers, planning bouquets with the unending hope that they would be bought for someone special.

Rose. Lilium. Phalaenopsis. Dianthus.

A tiny spark of hope bloomed deep within Amelia. Australia had plants—some of the most exotic and beautiful in the world. Maybe a new life in a penal colony wouldn't be the worst thing. *If she was lucky enough to escape the noose.* It was rare that female pickpockets were hanged—but not unheard of.

Eli muttered something, and his hands increased their pressure on her back. She cuddled into him more, sinking her legs in the space between his thighs. She should startle him, wake him up, pull his hair, scream in his ears until his eardrums broke.

But she didn't.

Instead, Amelia stayed right where she was, letting this incorrigible, hateful man hold her. Because, in the end, how bad could a person be when they smelled like a greenhouse? That's what it was. He must have a greenhouse at his home; that was the only thing she could attribute the fecund aroma to. And he spent a lot of time in it, so much that even his elegant clothes trapped the lovely scent.

It smelled like home. Not the one she came from. Amelia had no memory of what that had smelled of, though she could guess there was nothing fresh about it. No … he reminded her of the home she had wanted. The home that would never be.

If Amelia hadn't been so lost in her maudlin thoughts, she might have picked up on his hand sooner. As it was, she didn't register it climbing up her back until it was resting delicately in the valley between her shoulder blades.

She froze. What was he doing?

The hand continued its lazy journey, sliding up to stop once more at the back of her neck, immediately making her tense. Whenever a man had her by the neck, he was usually trying to strangle her (habit of her trade), but this was an altogether different sensation. Slowly, rhythmically, Eli began to massage her skin, gently at first before adding the kind of exquisite pressure that made her toes curl.

Amelia's breathing quickened, turning the skin around his neck hot and damp; she arched against him like a lion taking its first stretch of the morning while his other hand—still on her lower back—pressed so that she stretched over him, into him.

Eli muttered again, but Amelia couldn't make out his words. His head had begun to wander, his chin scratching the tops and sides of her face. It was all so horribly decadent, her senses being bombarded on all sides by his sleep-drunk movements.

When Eli dropped his head toward her, Amelia noticed his eyes were closed—he was no doubt still asleep. She didn't know why that failed to alarm her; she'd been warned that men were not to be trusted in any sort of amorous situation. However, a man had never touched her like this before, so delicately, as if everything he was doing was all for *her* pleasure. And only hers.

Amelia could use this. She could use him. She wasn't above employing her feminine wiles to get out of a tough situation; however, she'd never used them to excess or in a situation like this. So tight. So close. So out of her control.

Could Amelia mix business *with* pleasure?

It might be the last time that anyone touched her with any kind of tenderness ever again. Why not relish it? She'd been taught not to put any stake in the future. Life was all about the here and now.

Well, Amelia's here and now was coaxing her into a kiss. Just. One. Kiss.

One kiss never hurt anybody.

CHAPTER EIGHT

AMELIA HAD BEEN kissed before, more than she'd care to admit. However, if she were to count the kisses she'd actually agreed to, the number would fall precipitously. But even those few kisses she'd initiated and welcomed, naïvely and in the flush of youth, couldn't compare to what she shared with Eli.

Because sharing was, indeed, the proper word for it. Amelia had never known the act to be shared between two people. She'd always been the one giving, the one being taken from, to fill the need and void in the other person. This was anything but that.

Eli's lips skated across her, back and forth, back and forth, as if he were building the courage to cross that invisible barrier of no return. There was no yanking or prodding. His hand continued its lackadaisical massage like it had all the time in the world. Like the beginning of the act was just as important as the rest. His breath was soft and calm against her responsive skin, but he didn't rush, instead allowing their bodies to open up to one another like morning glories experiencing the first rays of light at dawn.

It was Amelia who eventually trespassed over the threshold, who initiated the true contact, igniting a spark as their lips finally met. Again, assumptions were a funny thing … Amelia immediately went rigid, thinking Eli would grab her then, tug on her body, deepen the kiss with animalistic yearning.

But he confounded her. The kissing didn't deepen; their bodies didn't crash together in rough lust. Eli continued to kiss her fleetingly, excruciatingly soft, as if she was a crystal bowl that might break, something Amelia had never been compared to in her life.

After a few more heady seconds, her muscles relaxed, her shoulders climbed down from her ears, and she let herself experience—really experience—what she was taking part in. She let herself be in the game instead of watching the play from the outside.

Eli's mouth tasted like rosemary and thyme and other herbs her tangled web of a mind couldn't place. His lips were full, and he had the confidence of a man who never had to force his demands on anyone. He lured her with dizzying kisses, licking her lips with the sort of temptation that a saint would have had a difficult time denying. Their bodies continued to rock into one another, no one initiating anything other than the desire to touch. Amelia was more than cognizant of the swollen member between his legs, but it didn't seem to concern him. *She* was his concern. He drank from her as if he was experiencing chocolate for the first time.

When Eli's tongue stole inside, Amelia opened readily for him. He swept in her mouth with torpid curiosity, exploring at his leisure … sampling. The act was hypnotizing with its lack of hurry, which wasn't to say there wasn't passion. With Amelia's arms still locked against his chest, she could sense the frisson hiding beneath his surface. She snuck her hands inside his coat and ran her fingers over his thin shirt, reveling in the ridges and bumps, the muscle and hairs. An uncharted land. A man she could scout and tour, a man she could relish.

As if gaining permission from her own breach, Eli's hand crept along her side until it reached her front. It stayed there for a long time, not moving, until Amelia pressed her chest against it, giving it encouragement to continue.

Amelia had a thing about hands. After all, they were her number one asset. One could tell so much from a handshake, a dive, a wave, the way a man touched his hat in greeting. The calluses on the palms, the lumps on the knuckles, the length and cleanliness of the nails. All of these were insights into the person.

Eli's hands were large and commanding, long-fingered and rough-tipped, as if he'd spent his childhood learning an instrument. They were the hands of a person who did things, not watched things get done.

And Eli was doing things to her. Amelia surprised herself when a low purr escaped her lips. His hand began at the front of her throat, tracing the fragile line of her tendons like a waterfall cascading toward the top of her dress. He didn't try to burrow his hands underneath, tugging the stiff fabric for purchase. Rather, he coasted over the material, reading the surface of her body like a blind man reading braille. Amelia shivered from his light touch, shaming herself with the incessant need pooling low in her stomach. How could she want a man she hated so much? How could life be so unfair?

When Eli reached her breast, there was no more hesitating. He held her like a peach he didn't wish to bruise, caressing her with his fingers, inciting her nipple to a point before skimming over it with the breezy glide of his palm. The faint touch ignited something in her, and for once in her life, Amelia didn't dive into a man's pocket but into his mouth.

She tasted him with a fervor she'd never experienced before, wrapping his tongue in hers, licking his teeth so she would always remember his flavor. Something had been unleashed, and she was unable to stop it. With the first flush of true passion, Amelia was gluttonous at once.

Eli chuckled as she wrestled her hands from in between them, grabbing hold of his shoulder, his hair, anything that would bring him closer. Finally, he reacted to her need. His hands grew bolder. His tongue scalded hotter. His body pressed harder. It was unmitigated bliss.

Eli's lips never ventured far, kissing the sides of her neck for a few breaths before going back to her as if there was an invisible string anchoring them that they were afraid to break.

However, Amelia knew more than anyone—everything breaks in the end, no matter how careful you think you're being.

Eli's hand was on her breast, gripping and stroking it with delicious force, when suddenly he stopped.

His palm shifted upon a hard surface, and Amelia froze.

Those deep blue eyes popped open, shattering Amelia's illusion of what they'd just shared. All hint of fire was gone, and they turned into bloodless crystals. Eli's mouth retreated just enough for their lips to no longer be touching, though their breaths mixed freely and wantonly. His hand moved higher, and his fingers began to probe around her heart.

Eli scooted away, his legs painstakingly untangling from hers. All Amelia could do was wait, embarrassed, ashamed, proverbially doused with cold water, as he continued to mine her for the familiar shape just underneath her clothes.

Unleashing an annoyed growl, Eli started at her buttons, undoing close to ten before he could open her dress wide enough.

Amelia lay there dumbly—a frozen fool—not offering any help while he rooted in her hidden pockets, taking special care not to graze any more of her than he needed. Like he'd made the mistake of thinking she was Queen Anne's lace but realized she was hogweed and was loath to touch her for fear of a blistering rash.

At last, he landed on his watch and yanked it from her pocket, scooting his body away as soon as he'd gotten what he wanted. As dawn crept into the window, Amelia brought herself up to sitting, slowly rebuttoning her dress, hoping her pride could be pasted together as easily.

Eli shuffled to the wall, sitting against it with his knees bent out in front of him. Taking his glasses from inside his coat, he placed them over his nose. Amelia could see him clearly now, especially the cruel twist of disgust written all over his face as he perused the precious piece.

"I didn't harm it," Amelia said, her voice choked with disuse.

Eli brought it closer to his face, making it abundantly clear that her word meant nothing to him. As he searched it, there was something in his eyes she couldn't quite place. Disappointment? Regret?

Disgust? Of her?

It would explain why he refused to look at her even as she picked herself up and went to the bed, straightening the covers if for no other reason than she was feeling increasingly foolish and needed something to do.

"The maids are just going to come in and take them off again to clean them," she heard him say gruffly.

Amelia kept working. "I don't like to leave a mess."

His bitterness was unmistakable. "You mean you don't like to leave a trace. Trick of the trade, I'd gather."

Amelia's spine straightened, and she planted her hands on her hips, rounding to him. Eli could sulk all he wanted because he'd kissed her, but she was finished with him insulting her.

"I'm sorry I kissed you," she said, fighting the blush that was erupting all over her cheeks. "But what's done is done. I would appreciate it if you would take me to the constable and get it over with. I don't want to listen to your barbed tongue all morning."

Mentioning his tongue made her flush even more. Bad choice of words. Now all she could think about was the way the tongue had felt as it licked a path across her teeth.

She was almost certain Eli was thinking the same thing. Two large red blotches formed over his cheeks. He looked like a child who had found her mother's rouge for the first time.

"You kissed *me*?" Finally, Eli lifted his head to regard her fully, frowning in consternation. "*I* kissed you. And I'm not angry at you; I'm angry at myself. I can't believe I did that ... I'm the one who acted inappropriately; you ..." His mouth pinched as if it was reluctant to release the words. "You played along to take advantage of me again."

It was like someone had stabbed her in the stomach with a lightning bolt. No one—especially not a man—had ever admitted to taking advantage of her before. Taking advantage of someone was what the whole game was about. If you were dumb enough to get taken advantage of, the last thing you needed was an apology for it.

Amelia wasn't sure what to do, what to say. The idea of a man explaining himself to her, let alone apologizing, was foreign to the extreme. "Played along?" she sputtered. "I didn't whore myself to you, if that's what you are implying."

He cringed at the foul world. Amelia rolled her eyes. Gentlemen and their gentle natures.

"As you say," Eli grumbled to his feet, raking his hands through his hair with such frustration that the brown locks stood at all ends. He didn't seem like the stick-up-his-ass viscount now, though a full morning beard tended to do that to a person. It was brown, just brown, Amelia surmised. No hint of red or gray.

"I don't want to keep arguing about this," he said, stomping to the side table, which held a small hand mirror and basin and ewer. He poured out some water and splashed it on his face, using the rest to comb his hair back with his fingers. He stayed at his ablutions for a long time, much too long to be considered normal. As if he was mulling something over, Eli kept splashing the water on his face and scrubbing his skin until Amelia was worried he'd scratch it off.

Eventually, with a sigh, he straightened away from the water, replacing his glasses. Like a surly bear, he scratched at his beard before turning to her, piercing her with a glare. "I was fully awake and entirely at fault and, apparently, completely out of my mind. That's the only explanation for it."

Amelia snorted. *Naturally.* That was the only reason a man like him would touch a girl like her. He really knew how to build a person up in the morning.

She was about to offer that hot retort when his next words cut her off. "And now I will atone for my mistake."

"A-atone," Amelia stammered. *Mistake?* Her stomach did a flip. "You mean you're going to let me go?"

Eli's confused scowl made it feel like he'd stripped her naked and thrown her into the ocean. And *not* in a good way. "Let you go? No. I already told you I wasn't going to stop until you've paid for what you've done. I apologize if I misled you to hope your *attentions* would buy your freedom."

Amelia palmed her face, scouring aggressively at her eyes. This man was going to be the death of her, whether he sent her to Australia or not. Her arms flopped down to her sides. "What, then? Are you going to tell the constable to go easy on me? Please, save your breath. That only makes them treat the inmates worse."

Eli went back to the mirror, dusting the dirt off his shoulders. He was avoiding her again, and Amelia swore she saw uncertainty in his reflection, something he tried to hide with the arrogant tone of his voice. "I've decided not to take you to the constable."

"Then ... what?"

He flashed a grim, apologetic smile, as if he was already regretting his decision. "I'm taking you to my home."

Amelia's feet began to back away. She held up a hand to ward him off. It was entirely unnecessary, since Eli hadn't taken one step toward her. "No. No. No," she said, shaking her head like a wet dog. "I don't do that. I'm a thief, not a whore."

Eli's face crinkled up in disgust—at her or at him, Amelia wasn't sure. "What kind of man do you take me for? I don't want you like *that!*"

Did he have to sound so repulsed? Amelia bit at her lower lip. "Well, what did you expect me to think? You ... and ... I ..." She trailed off in quiet discomfort, staring at the place on the floor where they'd just kissed. Could he have forgotten so soon?

She heard him huff. "That was nothing. Forget it ever happened. I already have."

Someone seriously had to talk with Eli about his conversational skills. Amelia had a thick skin, but this was ridiculous. Just because one could say something, it didn't mean one should. However, that was for another day. She had to stay on topic, especially when the topic was insane.

"Then why do you want to bring me home with you?" she demanded, willing her feet forward. Eli didn't budge, wouldn't even meet her halfway. He was determined to keep as much space between them as possible.

"I have a job for you," he replied. "If you complete it to my satisfaction, then I will let you go. Free as a bird."

Amelia lifted her chin. "I don't do *jobs*."

Eli matched her stare. "You'll do this one."

She squinted. It had only taken him a few moments with a mirror and water, and he was back to looking like the elegant gentleman. A crusty, imperious one.

"You don't strike me as the type of man who is ever satisfied. It sounds like a losing situation for me. How do I know you won't lock me up in handcuffs in some decrepit ancestral castle dungeon?"

"Because I don't have a dungeon. Or a castle. I do have handcuffs, though ... seventeenth century, I think."

Amelia laughed despite herself. "Forgive me for not being comforted by that information."

Eli folded his arms. "I promise not to lock you up forever. With any luck, you won't have to stay longer than a couple of weeks."

"You promise?" she asked, hope again beginning to grow.

His mouth tightened. She wondered if his son questioned him often; he didn't seem to have much practice with it. "I promise."

"Stick out your hands."

"What? No," he said.

Amelia cocked her head. "Just do it. I won't go with you until you do it."

Eli's arms folded even tighter into his chest. *Such an ass.* "If you don't go, I'll march you straight to the constable right now," he countered.

"Is that how you want to spend your morning?" Amelia asked with a cocky edge to her voice. "I guarantee I won't make that little journey easy for you."

He glowered so hard and so long that she thought his face might freeze that way forever. Eventually—with another huff of irritation—he thrust out his hands. "There! Is that fine, your majesty? I'm not wearing any rings, nothing for you to steal."

Amelia peered over the hands, not touching them, since she had a distinct feeling Eli might rip them away if she tried. "Turn them over," she said with the authority of a surgeon. "Palm up."

Eli did as she asked, and she saw what she was looking for. Dirt under the nails. Either he planted in his spare time, or he buried the bodies of girls like her in the fresh dirt outside his home. Either way, she'd have to take a chance. She motioned for him to put his hands down.

"Good," she said. "But what about the satisfaction part?"

"What about it?"

Amelia arched a brow. "Can you be satisfied?"

He arched his brow right back, so sharp it could cut a dream in half. "You certainly better hope so."

CHAPTER NINE

"HOW DID YOU get those scars?" Michael asked, disturbing the blessed quiet that had sheathed the small group ever since it had loaded into the carriage. Last night's storm had done its worst; however, Eli's driver had assured him they would have no problems starting the journey to Barrington House that morning, though they would have to go slow. Two days was how long it had taken them to get to Ayrshire, and Eli desperately hoped they could still make decent time on the way home.

That way, there would be less time for unfortunate questions like the one his son had just posed to the thief Eli had brought into their midst. Earlier that morning, when he had told Michael that they would be traveling home with Amelia, he'd delicately explained the woman's unsavory history and ordered his son to keep his interactions with the thief to a minimum. Obviously, that little speech hadn't been effective.

Now, all eyes fell on the white, puckered scars on the tops of Amelia's hands that she didn't even try to hide with gloves. "Don't answer that," Eli barked at her.

She shook her head, issuing a small smile. He wished she would stop doing that. The last thing he wanted to do was think about the soft curve of her lips, the way they'd angled to his so insistently the night before. "Oh, it's fine. I don't mind," she said breezily.

ty, plush brocade seat at her side.

Eli ignored her, but when she continued to haunt him with an inquiring expression, he finally relented. "He likes sitting up top … the fresh air is good for the soul."

"Then why don't you sit up top?" she challenged.

Eli would never admit to getting used to the chit, though there were some signs he was beginning to recognize—like the way her right eyebrow rose ever so slightly before she threw out a sarcastic quip, or the way her head tilted a few degrees to the left when she was ready to question him.

For Michael's sake, Eli smiled, though there was no joy to be found anywhere. "How about you go sit up on top?" he countered.

"That sounds lovely!" she exclaimed, raising her fist to the ceiling to give it a knock. Eli pulled it back down before she had the chance to alert the driver to stop.

"Like I would allow that!" he fumed, settling in his seat, looking anywhere but at her smug expression. "You'd make a run for it at the first chance."

"I would not!" She had the temerity to look affronted. "I gave you my word, and I am as reliable as they come."

Caustic laughter bubbled out of his chest, burning him with its acidity. "I doubt that."

There she was, looking all insulted again. What had he said other than the truth? "You don't know the first thing about me," she said, gazing out the window once more. "I am incredibly reliable. My friends always know I'll do what I say I'm going to do. For instance, one time they dared me that I couldn't sit through a mass without moving and still come out with my pockets full of—"

"That's enough of that," Eli interrupted, shooting her with another weighted glance toward the boy. Poor Michael. He was leaning on his knees, head in his hands, hanging on her every salacious word. Utterly beguiled. A fairy creature, Amelia had snared the child with her exotic, magical tale.

"What?" the boy asked. "What were your pockets full of?"

Eli shook his head, and the woman's cheeks blazed pink. "Oh, ah, verses," she said oddly, as if it hurt her to actually tell this lie. "Bible verses to study when I came home."

Michael fell back in his chair, clearly put out by the end of the story. But his curiosity was not appeased just yet. "Where's your tummy?" he asked shyly, shifting farther away from Eli as if readying himself for his father to try to physically put a halt to the conversation.

Fat chance, Eli concluded. He only had one handkerchief in his pocket, and he didn't think it would fit around Amelia's or his son's mouth. Alas, he would have to suffer through the questions and police them the best way he could.

"My tummy?" Amelia repeated, fixing her palm on the flat area in question. Her eyes lit up, and Eli braced himself. There was too much sparkling going on. Something vastly inappropriate was bound to fly out of her mouth.

Her mouth. He didn't want to think about *that,* either. Or the erotic sounds it made when he'd kissed it.

"It seems I'd been mistaken," she explained, eyes wide with wonder. "I thought I was pregnant, but it turned out I'd only eaten too much one day. When I woke up this norming, I was quite back to normal."

"Or as normal as you can get," Eli cut in, not able to help himself. What a load of nonsense she was heaping on the poor child.

Amelia sliced him with a glare.

"Oh, that's good," Michael said, relief evident. He looked at his father. "Some mothers die when they have babies."

He offered the statement so matter-of-factly that it pained Eli's heart. He reached out to put his arm around the boy and hold his tiny shoulders, which had been asked to carry too much in his short life … but the damn woman beat him to it.

Amelia patted the seat next to her, and Michael needed no other invitation. He flew into the seat, burrowing into her side.

Despite her encouragement, Amelia looked bizarrely uncomfortable with the child's affectionate display, not sure what to do with her arms now that he was glued next to her. "Did that happen when you were born, Michael?" she asked.

Eli needed to stop this conversation at once! It was ridiculous and unpleasant and completely inappropriate ... but he didn't. Amelia's voice halted all action. Silky and soft, like sticking your hand in a pile of freshly shorn sheep's wool, it was the epitome of empathy and comfort. He had no idea she'd had it in her.

Without a word, Michael lifted Amelia's arm, placing it around his shoulders, so he could cuddle into her armpit. Eli almost laughed at her bewildered expression. "Yes," the boy answered.

"My mother died when I was young as well."

Michael nodded. "My sisters were still babies too," he added.

"Sisters!" Amelia exclaimed, ducking her head to look at him. "You have sisters? How glorious!" She'd effectively wrangled the conversation onto less somber ground. No doubt for Michael's benefit. It was decent of her, Eli decided.

All solemn contemplation gone, Michael grinned, showcasing his missing front tooth, his cheeks rosy. "Two of them," he said, flashing as many fingers. "Twins!"

Amelia slapped her forehead with her hand, pretending to faint against the cushions. "Heavens above, what a blessing!" She hazarded Eli a quick flicker of her lashes. Was it his imagination, or was she looking at him differently? Yes, twins. His manhood was so competent he could spawn two children at once, ha! Only ... the kind of children he'd spawned was up for debate.

"Twins are quite the catch!" Amelia went on. "I know one person in particular who would love to meet a set!"

"Why?" Michael asked, and there was that sparkle again. Eli wasn't sure what he wanted more, to hear Amelia's absurd story or grab his handkerchief and stuff it down her throat. He decided on the former; Michael was sensitive and becoming rather partial to the ridiculous woman.

"Twins are a boon in my line of work. What they can accomplish is extraordinary! Molly is always on the lookout to bring some into the fold."

"Molly?" Michael asked, brow furrowed.

"My stepmother." She paused. "Or something like that."

Eli had to step in. "Something like that?"

Amelia's tone sharpened. "She is a *kind* of mother."

Eli didn't know who was more confused—him or Michael— but his son, ever the optimist, let it go as if the woman hadn't just offered them a view into her seedy life.

"What could the twins do?" the boy continued, wrestling the story back on course.

With a starry-eyed smile, Amelia laid her head back against the seat. "The better question is what *couldn't* they do! They could run so many tricks it could make a man's head spin. Round and round until he didn't know if they stole his wallet or if he actually gave it to them."

"For Christ's sake," Eli muttered, not even attempting to soften that bit of criminal intercourse.

Amelia ignored him. "But there would have to be complete dedication and practice," she said firmly. "Working like that would have to be precise, and the twins would have to behave with complete control."

Michael giggled, playing with the loose strings of Amelia's dress. Eli hadn't noticed it the day before, but it was much shabbier than he'd thought—old and faded. He wondered if that had been a part of her ruse: old, worn-down mother whom no one would consider capable of fleecing them. Back in London she probably dressed in garish silks with ostentatious feathers and pearls dripping from her creamy neck.

Dammit! Don't think about her neck!

"The twins would never be able to do anything like that," Michael announced with the authority of a know-it-all little brother. "Father is always saying they can't be controlled."

"Oh, I'm sure they aren't that bad," Amelia responded. "Society thinks little girls shouldn't get up to mischief, but they are the same as little boys. Everyone deserves a little fun."

"They are not the same as boys; they are worse!" Michael replied emphatically, his countenance turning serious. He glanced at his father, as if asking if he should explain, and Eli nodded. If the woman thought she could scandalize them with her stories, it was only fair they scandalized her right back.

Eli realized it probably hadn't been fair of him leaving Amelia in the dark about the conditions of the bargain they'd made. After their … intimacy, he'd only wanted to make things right. She hadn't asked for more information, and he'd known better than to give it willingly until they were closer to his home. The fat was in the fire now. Best to just get on with it and make Amelia aware of what was being asked of her.

She was sitting close enough. He could catch her if she tried to throw herself from the carriage.

Michael went on. "They put frogs in my bed when I'm sleeping," he whispered sotto voce. "And they put wine in the dogs' water bowls."

Amelia pinched her lips, stifling a laugh. "I've heard of much worse, believe me."

But he was just getting started. "They cut off Miss Levin's braid when she was sleeping; her hair is as short as mine now."

She tripped over her words. "I-I'm sure Miss Levin was grateful; long hair can weigh so heavy on a woman's neck—"

"They captured a whole jar of red wood ants and hid them in the finished laundry."

Amelia's smile faded. "Yes," she said, shifting in her seat. "That sounds rather uncomfortable—"

"They replaced all the sugar with salt; they melted down all my toy soldiers; they ate all of Father's strawberries!"

"That one doesn't sound so bad!" she said.

Michael's eyes went as round as dinner plates. "We're never to touch Father's strawberries."

Oh, for fuck's sake. Eli would have to explain that one soon.

Amelia was now regarding him with the same ferocity that people saved for axe murderers. He wasn't some crazy strawberry hoarder; it was work!

"You're leaving out the most important part," Eli reminded him.

Michael's little brow furrowed in question.

"The governesses," Eli added.

"Oh!" Michael exclaimed. "They like to burn their clothes."

"Yes," Eli said, enjoying watching the woman's face drain of its color. "Fire seems to be a preferred choice of weapon for my daughters. They've gone through nine governesses because of it."

"Nine," Amelia repeated slowly, like she was trying to pronounce a foreign word for the first time. "That's not *so* bad. How old did you say they were? Eleven?"

"No, not nine in their entire lives," Eli replied. "Nine in the last year. They've gone through close to twenty in their short lives."

"Well ..." she said, grappling to find some nerve in her voice. She jostled Michael's shoulders encouragingly. "You will just have to hire another. Someone will stick; it's all about getting the right fit."

"Oh, we already have," Eli said. He waited for realization to dawn in those dark eyes.

"Who?" she breathed.

He grinned. "I bet Australia is looking good right now."

CHAPTER TEN

"I AM *NOT* a governess!" Amelia fumed.

This had to be the tenth time she'd said it, but it was like the stubborn man had clogged his ears with cloth. Well, she would get through that thick skull of his, because this was not what they'd agreed on. She would hold Eli hostage in the doorway of her inn room all night if it took that long for him to see reason.

But reason and Lord Eli didn't seem to be good friends, not even acquaintances. His expression remained infuriating passive, bored, even, as he waited for her diatribe to end.

"I can't do it. I won't," she said. "I don't know anything about children. I don't even think I was one. What do I possibly know about taking care of them?"

Was there anything hotter than boiling? Amelia had no idea; however, that was where her blood was at as Eli responded in a placid drone, "I'm sure you'll know enough. It's only for a little while, until I can find a replacement for the last governess. And it's like I told you, I just want you to speak with them, tell them about your life on the streets. They need something visible, tactile. I need them to know that if they don't straighten up, they could end up like you."

Amelia's spine straightened so quickly it cracked in a few places. "What the bloody hell is that supposed to mean? *End up like me?"*

He waved an arrogant hand between them. "Don't be a simpleton. You know exactly what I mean. A woman like you … struggling to survive on the streets … lonely and downtrodden."

"I am *not* lonely and downtrodden! I have friends … a family—"

"Like your mother, that's really a stepmother, that's really a mother-like figure?"

Amelia opened her mouth and came up short. What must it be like to wander through life as a man, so sure of everything you said? Must be lovely.

"You know nothing about me!"

"I know you steal from others to get through life," he hit back, the tendons tightening along his neck, the scar above his lip turning white. He paused, straightening his glasses. "All I'm asking is that you share your stories with my daughters, so they realize that I'm offering something better. A real life."

A real life? Filling one's belly and the bellies of others was as real as it got.

"Why didn't you tell me this before?" Amelia asked, the proverbial walls around her caving in.

Eli scratched at his forehead, lifting his dark hair just enough so it stuck up. He seemed to have an issue with his hair; it desperately wanted to run free, and he did everything in his power to stamp it back down again. "It didn't come up before."

Her lashes lowered to half-mast. "You knew I wouldn't agree."

Eli sniffed, leaning across the threshold. Her hand on the door, Amelia pulled it closer, ready to shut it if he came any further. This was the closest they'd been since their night together, and the sharp smell on his clothes immediately brought her back to the way he'd held her, the way he'd wanted to keep holding her—until he didn't anymore.

He had shaved before they started the drive, but his whiskers had already returned, casting thick shadows on his face. She remembered how they felt, how she'd wanted to keep feeling them.

"Are you really scared of two little girls, Amelia Driver? I thought you said you were the best thief in London."

"I *am* the best. I'm just not used to children. That's all. Why did you only bring Michael to the tournament?" she asked, genuinely curious. "Why not the girls too?"

Eli shifted, visibly uncomfortable. "Michael enjoys stories about knights; he begged me to go."

"I'm sure the girls would have enjoyed it," Amelia said. "They seem the kind of adventurous sorts that would like knights as well."

"They're little girls; they should behave as such."

"Says who?"

"Says ... everyone." He shook his head, scratching at his temples again. The color was back in his cheeks. "Life will be difficult—especially for young ladies like them. Their mother—"

His words cut off.

Ah. Now Amelia was beginning to understand. Poor Eli. Actually, poor twins. Since the day they were born, their father had held them up to an impossible standard. Who could live up to a perfect dead mother?

"I'm sorry your wife died."

Eli flushed, glancing down the hall even though Amelia hadn't heard a noise.

"No one tells you how to be a parent," he said, his voice low. "I'm doing the best I can."

Amelia couldn't help but find the ridiculous humor in that. "So, you think bringing a pickpocket into their midst is the best decision?"

Unfortunately, Eli didn't find it to be as funny as her. His lips fell into a grim line as he scanned her from top to bottom. "You're not ideal, I'll give you that. However, desperate men do desperate things."

She blew out an exasperated exhale. Such. An. Ass. "You do

know I have feelings, right? I am a human being, like you?"

He returned a baffled look. "Of course I know that."

She squinted. "And yet you still say the things you say."

"I'm a straightforward person."

"You're an ass."

Eli blew air out of his nostrils like a raging bull. Amelia could feel the restraint pulsing through his body. "Regardless, you are the tool at my disposal, and you will do as you're told. Can I go now? I have to meet Michael downstairs for dinner." As an afterthought, he added, "Your food will be brought up soon."

Amelia still wasn't over the "tool at my disposal" part, but her stomach growled when he mentioned the meal. She'd barely eaten in days, and food *always* came first. "Why am I not eating downstairs with you and Michael?" She didn't want to; however, he should have given her the option. Wasn't he supposed to be a gentleman?

Eli had already begun to walk away.

"Why?" she repeated louder as he reached the stairs.

"Because you're not family."

It was a perfectly fine explanation, but Amelia slammed her door anyway. She slammed it so hard that everyone in the inn felt the vibrations.

THE STEW TASTED like dust in her mouth. Amelia couldn't even appreciate the biscuits—and she had never met a biscuit she didn't like. *Not family!* Not family!

Of course she wasn't family, nor did she want to be!

Despite what he thought, she already had one! Like Molly and Jenny, and Three-eared Theresa and Makeshift Mary, and Evil Eve and Drunkard Daisy.

They might not be the most conventional family, but they were hers. They were all she'd ever had. Probably all she would ever have.

And Amelia would do right by them.

Rooting around the inn room, she found a few pieces of paper and a pencil in the bureau drawer, most likely left by the previous visitor, and then forced herself to take more bites of the stew. It had been an early lesson in life and one that had always stuck with her: never, *ever* leave food on your plate. Who knows when you'll be lucky enough to get more?

Eventually, the well-seasoned meat and fresh vegetables steadied Amelia enough that she could draft her letter.

She had to let everyone know she was still in one piece. Molly must be worried. Amelia had no doubt that Jenny would make it back to London safely. She was young but competent, and would inform everyone of what had happened, and they would all assume the worst. Amelia couldn't allow their minds to go down that road.

She might not be in the best way; however, she was free (sort of) and in a position to still make something happen. *Always look at a problem from a different view, Amelia my girl,* Molly had told her. *Never accept what you see the first time you spot it. There's always another angle.*

The viscount was taking her to his ancestral home. Amelia didn't have experience with the aristocracy, but she was almost certain they all lived in mammoth houses on sprawling estates. By Lord Eli's insufferable behavior, his country home was probably bigger than most. Something she might recognize from a fairytale—if anyone had ever read her any.

Regardless, it was bound to be filled with trinkets and knick-knacks that had come over with William the Conqueror, so much bric-a-brac Lord Eli wouldn't even know it was missing. Silver spoons and Irish lace, pewter candlesticks and Grecian vases …

Country homes were a favorite scam for the Diamond Girls. Tried and tested—crews had been doing it for centuries. The trick started innocently enough. A gang would place a girl in a house working as a housemaid of some sort. She would live there for a month at least, taking inventory of what the great home had to offer. Only when she was ready would she write to the gang, describing what choice loot was located in the house and the best way to find it. If a girl was truly talented, she might include intricate maps of the layout with the kind of detail that would make a master builder jealous.

Then a door would be left unlocked one night—quite accidentally, of course—and some people might creep in. They'd take just enough so as not to incite suspicion. Two months of planning for a half-hour of work. And the spoils would last for a year at least.

It was risky and time-consuming but vastly rewarding. After all, when life hands you eels, you make jellied eels!

Amelia finished the letter informing Molly that she'd send information about the house as quickly as she could. Lord Eli would never know what hit him, which made her a little depressed.

Because Amelia found that she always wanted to hit Eli, and she always wanted him to know that she was the one doing it.

CHAPTER ELEVEN

NATURALLY, THE LITTLE hellions weren't waiting outside to greet him.

After two days of travel and policing an incorrigible woman and everything that came out of her insolent mouth, Eli had finally made it to Barrington. Just a few hours out of London, Barrington could never be considered wilderness, though Eli's father had done his best to make it seem that way. Set within the ancient Epping Forest, the estate always held the distinct feeling that it could get swallowed at any moment and lost forever. As a child, Eli had loved that about his home, and had since done nothing to make it more hospitable to the outside world. Why fix something if it wasn't broken?

Better trained than his daughters, the servants, in their crisp uniforms, lined up outside the palladium structure along the stone steps. Eli wasted no time hopping out of the carriage and calling his chatelaine to attention.

Mrs. Hutchinson's feet hurried over the gravel, causing it to skitter when she stopped to bob her curtsey. He nodded at the mature woman before nodding toward Amelia, who had just exited the carriage. "This is Miss Amelia. She will be staying with us for a few weeks. Please make sure there is a room ready for her immediately," he said.

Even with the way he delivered his flat order, the chatelaine's eyes betrayed her curiosity. She stared at Amelia a moment longer than necessary, and Eli grew restless, just knowing what the staff must be thinking. The only woman he'd ever brought home to Barrington was Marianne, and the servants had known her since she was a baby. This ... was not the same thing, and he didn't want them to get the wrong idea. Eli might be an ass (as Amelia liked to inform him), but he wasn't a lecherous one.

"She'll be working with the girls," he added, annoyed that he felt the need to explain himself. Mrs. Hutchinson's expression relaxed, her interest only slightly abated.

"A governess?" the chatelaine asked.

Eli heard Amelia groan. "Not exactly," he returned. He felt Amelia come up to his side—or rather, he smelled her first. After two days in the carriage, Eli had become accustomed to her scent, and it disturbed him to no end how much he enjoyed it. She had a citrusy smell, like oranges or lemons, but it didn't make any sense to him. The acidic aroma hung on her like she was a fruit tree. It couldn't be a perfume; that would have faded, and it didn't have the oily, manufactured hint to it. His failure at identifying it was driving him crazy, though it could just be *her*.

"Where are you going to stick me?" she asked him sullenly. "The nursery?" He assumed the question was posed to him, since she smiled politely at Mrs. Hutchinson. Amelia tended to be wonderfully pleasant to everyone except him.

He didn't bother acknowledging her. She couldn't be controlled, and he didn't want her to glare at him in front of his faithful servant. He gave the chatelaine a tight smile. "I think the third floor will be appropriate."

"Yes, my lord," Mrs. Hutchinson said with the kind of reverence that began to balance him. He was determined never to let the silly chit know how she rocked him off his center. "Does Miss Amelia have any things I can take?"

"No, Miss Amelia doesn't," Amelia replied before Eli could open his mouth. "He wouldn't let me bring my things—or my belly."

Mrs. Hutchinson's gaze shot right to Amelia's flat midsection. Eli closed his eyes and silently growled. Was she actually upset that he'd refused to let her bring her loot or tricks? The pregnant belly costume was ridiculous! Whether it was genius or not (and he would never tell her it was), Eli would never allow her to keep it. He couldn't imagine the questions the twins would conjure if they found it—or the ideas it would give them.

Words stalled on Mrs. Hutchinson's lips. "So … no, then?" she asked.

"No," Eli agreed, shaking his head as the chatelaine left them to do his bidding in the home, the other servants following closely behind.

"I know this is going to be difficult for you," he said, rounding on Amelia and her insufferable grin, "but I'm going to need you to behave with a little decorum while you're here. Do you think that's possible?"

With a flick of her hand—so quick Eli almost didn't see it—she tugged on his cravat, unraveling it from its perfect tie. Eli muttered a curse, scrambling to right it as she wandered away from him, circling around to get a full view of his home. That was another reason he couldn't wait to get away from her. She was always teasing him, bumping into his side to upset his glasses, tugging at his cravat, or untying his shoes when he wasn't looking. She was a child, a silly, annoying gnat of a child who loved getting under his skin.

Ordering Amelia to stop didn't work. If anything, the more attention he brought to her infantile behavior, the greater joy she got out of it.

Instead, Eli allowed Amelia to take in his home, waiting for all that confidence to drain from her face; the sight of his country estate usually did that to the servants who came to work there. He decided to give her some leeway. She was probably acting up because she was so overwhelmed; it happened to the best of them.

However, Amelia was determined to crush every stereotype

Eli had of women or thieves.

"This it?" she asked, the disappointment in her tone chopping his legs off, making him feel four feet tall. "Where's the moat?" she added. "The turrets and drawbridge?" She crossed her arms, piercing him with a critical eye. "I thought you had a castle."

"I specifically told you I did not have a castle," he shot back. How dare she besmirch his ancestral home!

She shrugged, and he could tell an apology was not forthcoming. "I figured you were being modest. I thought all you fancy lords have castles out here in the country. When we drove through the forest, I was certain I was going to see flags and banners just below the clouds, and a façade as white as snow." She frowned at the façade, which probably had been white at one time but was now decidedly gray and mostly hidden with ivy that climbed up the entire exterior. "It wasn't what I pictured."

"Well, I'm so sorry to disappoint you," Eli snapped. "I had no idea you were so fanciful. If you wanted a castle with a dragon and knights, perhaps you should have stayed at Eglington to enjoy the tournament." He slapped his forehead. "Oh, wait, you left the tournament because you stole from half the crowd. I completely forgot."

Amelia's brown eyes narrowed at him, but they were still entirely too big, too hypnotizing. She came closer to him, and the orange scent returned, tickling his nose. "Don't be upset; it's still rather nice."

Nice? Nice! "It's more than bloody nice," he yelled.

She placed her hands on his shoulder in a comforting pat just as she'd done to Michael in the carriage. Needless to say, it did not have the same relaxing effect. "Just like people, it's the inside that counts. I'm sure the inside is lovely."

Eli shook his head, moving away so her hand dropped back to her side. He didn't have time for her nonsense. She was baiting him, though his recognizing that did little to curb his pique.

"I have to go," he said in a flat voice. "Mrs. Hutchinson will come for you soon and show you to your room. If you need anything, let her know. This lovely"—he gritted the words—"house is incredibly grand, and I doubt we'll be seeing much of each other from here on out. Do your job, and a few weeks from now this whole thing will have been a dream."

She snorted. "Or a nightmare."

"Whatever you make of it."

Amelia's gaze left him again, and she surveyed the grounds, whistling lightly. What kind of a woman whistled? Oh, Eli knew what kind, and when her attention stayed a little too long on the copse of trees in the distance, he was reminded yet again.

"I wouldn't get any ideas if I were you," he said, his warning as sharp as the tips of her eyelashes. "We don't get many visitors out here. If you escape, you could be lost for days before anyone finds you."

The whistle died on Amelia's lips, but she kept her face away, lifting her insolent chin a few more inches.

Eli went on, confident she was listening. "The townspeople are quite the gossips, too, and loyal to me. If you think they won't tell me where they saw you going, you are quite mistaken."

She huffed, cocking her head in his direction. "How many times do I have to tell you, *my lord*, that you know nothing about me? I once hid in a convent for a whole week, and nobody was the wiser."

Good Lord! Who the hell was he dealing with here? How could this elf of a woman do half the things she said she did? She wasn't even that old. She couldn't be more than twenty. Perhaps that was the problem. Young people didn't have the fear that age pounded into you. They thought they were invincible.

"Please don't tell me you stole money from the poor nuns," he replied dryly, not ready—always not damned ready—for her response.

"I would never!" she said, truly aghast. "What kind of a monster do you think I am? I stole wine from the priests' substantial cellar. They were drinking far too much of it and had plenty to spare. Did you know they don't allow the nuns to have any? How is that fair, I ask you?"

He wiped his hand over his face. "Maybe the nuns don't like wine."

She gasped. "Everyone likes wine!"

Eli didn't have a response for that. He was quite certain he would never have a response for that. So he left her there in front of the disappointing—though *probably lovely on the inside*—house, hoping she didn't go snooping and find his substantial wine cellar anytime soon.

ELI SIPPED AT his wine, relishing the easy way the spicy liquid went down his throat. For the first time that day his body was placid, his chest not pumping a beat too quickly, a little too hard. He'd spent the remainder of the afternoon in the greenhouse, checking on his strawberries, recording all the changes that had taken place in the few days he'd been gone. His latest breeding experiment was going better than expected, the two varietals he'd spliced together uniting without a hitch, not one plant dying in the process. Now he just had to wait and see if the offspring proved as hardy as he suspected they would be. Then he'd be ready to write his paper on the new varietal and send it to the Horticultural Society.

Publishing was never the end game for him. Respect from his peers was all well and good, but his main joy came in the work— the questions and answers, the hypotheses and research. That was where his heart was happiest. He had friends who lived in London and filled their days sitting in coffee houses and lecture halls debating the merits of plant breeding, but Eli would be bored spending his hours that way. A true scientist stayed in his lab, not worrying about what might happen, but doing what he could. If Eli's work could create stronger plants that would be more resistant to plagues and drought, then the only reward he needed was fewer starving people and a surviving estate. That was his aim, not if the queen knew his name—though she already did anyway.

A tiny foot kicked the leg of Eli's chair, jumbling him from his thoughts. From his seat at the head of the table, he eyed the little blonde girl sitting at his right. The exact duplicate of the little blonde girl sitting on his left, she was the picture of an angel from heaven—though probably one of the angels that had fallen along with Lucifer.

Sweet, light ringlets hung from her head like corkscrew hazel lying just at her shoulders. That was how he knew it was Cecily. She'd chopped her luscious hair down to her ears last month and had been furious—more furious than Eli!—when he ordered her to grow it back.

In hindsight, he should have thanked her. Now, it was much easier for him to tell the difference between the girls, and much more difficult for them to trick everyone.

"Please don't hit my chair, Cecily," he said evenly, getting an innocent, blue-eyed look in return. All of his children had his blue eyes, but none of them were the exact shade. Cecily's were light blue, as light as her hair, as if she was constantly fading before him. It was in distinct contrast to her personality that tended to smack any room she entered over the head.

"It wasn't me!" she cried before hanging her head and grumbling, "You always think it's me."

Eli didn't believe her put-upon act for a second. If she was staring at the tablecloth, it was only because she was devising something.

When had he become so jaded with his daughters? Oh, he remembered. When they'd ordered Michael to take a bath in beet juice and dyed the poor child's skin red for a whole month.

"*I saw Michael do it,*" the other girl said, sharing a secret smile with Cecily. Kitty. Older by ten minutes, though to her, it could have been ten years. The girls worked in tandem, definitely an egalitarian unit; however, if there had to be a ringleader, it was

Eli clenched his jaw. "*I mind*," he said pointedly, nodding to Michael, who was sitting next to him in the carriage. "For *his* sake."

Amelia's eyes formed murky pools as she released an exasperated noise and turned her head to stare out the window. Good. Crisis averted. There was no need for conversation. After last night—after his unusual behavior—the best thing for them was to proceed with the utmost caution; they were strangers and would never be anything more. Eli did not take lovers ... or he didn't take lovers like her. Being a widower for the past eight years, he'd had experience (admittedly limited) with arranging such ... entanglements. When he did, it was always with the most care and discretion. The woman sitting across from him fit none of those criteria.

And yet Eli had still reached for her in the night.

That morning, he'd done his best to convey that it had been an aberration. A one-off. A loss of mental faculties. His gut had pinched when he saw the hurt his words had caused her. But it was for her sake; surely, Amelia had to know that. There would be no round two, no sleepy, love-drunk smiles shared in the mornings. Nothing would be shared.

Though atonements had to be made for his uncouth behavior. It was the only respectable thing to do, which was why he'd offered her the deal.

After Amelia completed her end of the bargain, she would leave. Eli would go back to his work on the estate, and she would go back to avoiding the noose. They were two distinct people with two distinct futures. Two ships passing in the night, never to see each other again. He was confident he wouldn't even look back to see which direction she headed.

"Why doesn't he sit in here with us?" Amelia asked suddenly. Eli's bewildered expression betrayed him, and she added, "The valet. Why does he sit up top with the driver? There's plenty of space in here."

To illustrate her point, Amelia rubbed her hand on the emp-

usually Kitty.

Eli leaned back in his chair, exasperated. "What do you mean you saw him do it? How could you possibly see something under the table?"

Kitty giggled, her cornflower-blue eyes sparkling, reminding him of someone he was desperately trying not to think about. She wiggled her fingers in front of her face like an illusionist on the stage. "Because of my special powers!"

"What special powers?"

"I can see through things," Kitty said without a hint of shame in the lie. That was what worried Eli the most—not that the girls lied, but that they had no remorse about it whatsoever.

"Prove it," Michael said from across the table where he sat next to Cecily. If Eli were Michael, he would have sat next to Cecily too; it was the safer bet even with her chair-kicking tendencies.

"Fine," Kitty said, thrilled someone had asked her to display her new talents. She set her sights on her brother, who visibly shrank in his seat, no doubt rethinking calling his sister out. Kitty sucked on her lower lip, making a production of the act. Like a true professional, she forced them to wait, creating a heavy atmosphere. Then she clucked her tongue and said, "The top buttons of your trousers are undone."

All heads swiveled to Michael, who slowly, painstakingly, nudged his chair back from the table and looked down. Cecily, naturally, beat him to it. "They are!" She cackled, hunching over his seat. Michael's cheeks bloomed crimson, and he hurried to do up his buttons.

"You shouldn't talk about my trousers. Father, tell Kitty not to look at my trousers!"

"Kitty," Eli drawled, curbing a chuckle. It wasn't funny, so why did he want to laugh? "Don't talk about your brother's trousers. And Michael?" He lifted a brow at his son. "Stop forgetting to button up, son. Anyone could have told you that you forgot to button them. You always do. Your sister certainly doesn't have powers."

"I do too!" Kitty said.

"No, you don't," Eli said.

"Yes, I do!"

Eli strengthened his tone. "Stop this, Kitty. You don't have powers. Now sit like a good girl and wait for your food."

She slumped in her seat even more. "If I don't have powers, then how do I know a lady is just outside the room and is about to enter?"

He lurched forward in his seat, looking around and happily finding no one. "Who? When?"

Kitty's mouth split into a wide smile. "Riiiiiight. Now."

Just as the words left her, a pale pink skirt flew through the doorway. Amelia, exuberant and giddy, didn't appear the least abashed by interrupting their supper. In fact, she made straight for the empty seat next to Kitty.

"Oh, good, I'm not late. I was worried I wouldn't be ready in time," she said, patting her hair for extra effect as she slid into the chair. It took Eli a second to work his tongue off the roof of his mouth; however, he still couldn't get it to utter any sounds—any coherent ones. He might have choked a bit when she put her elbows on the table and cupped her oval face in her hands.

"What … what are you doing?" he finally said. His voice came out guttural and offensive, like he'd torn it from his chest and thrown it at her.

Amelia was innocence personified. The dress helped. Mrs. Hutchinson must have pitied the poor wretch and given her one of Eli's sister's castoffs. The red gown was almost a good fit, though Della was on the taller side, making the gown skate across the floor when Amelia walked. Still … the color was decent on her, highlighting the scarlet of her lips when she became animated. She could almost be mistaken for a lady—if she would keep her damn elbows off the table and her mouth closed, two things she wasn't inclined to do.

"It's suppertime, no?" Amelia asked, driving her insouciance into his chest and twisting it when it hit bone. "I heard a bell and tried to hurry. New hairstyle, do you like it?"

Was Eli supposed to answer that question? The children gaped at the woman and then back at him, probably wondering the same thing. Who asked about their hair at dinner? Worse yet, who nagged for compliments? What did he give a damn about her hair? It was black. And up in some kind of bun in the back. But she'd even muddled that up, because tendrils flowed around her face in a willy-nilly manner, as if she'd had it done up properly and then gone outside in a windstorm before coming into the dining room. Ladies were *never* windswept.

Michael—poor, beguiled Michael—obviously hadn't been told that. "I like it," he said shyly, staring down at his newly buttoned trousers. "It looks nice."

Amelia gifted him a radiant smile. "Thank you, love," she said, and he positively beamed.

Eli sucked on his two front teeth, the sound breaking up the love-struck moment. "Dinner is for family," he said, putting emphasis on each word.

The woman took her napkin and placed it over her lap. He should only be grateful she didn't stick it under her chin. "Oh, I know," she said blithely, resettling her elbows on the table. "But I didn't get a chance to meet the girls today. I looked everywhere, but I couldn't find them." She met his stare and arched an impish brow, causing Eli's breath to catch for a quick second. He wasn't sure how she did it, but when she gave him her full attention, sometimes it was almost too much, like staring at the horizon when the sun was rising. Again, she ruined it by speaking. "By the way, your house is grand and lovely on the inside," she said, her silent laughter making her nose crunch in that mischievous, fairy-like way of hers.

"You must be the twins," she said, dismissing Eli.

It was a foreign feeling to him, one that he didn't feel near enough, but right then and there, he felt nothing but pride for his beautiful girls. Not as easily swayed as their younger brother,

Cecily and Kitty studied Amelia as if she was a slimy, scaly monster who'd just climbed out of the nearby lake.

Unfortunately for Eli, he didn't take into consideration that his daughters were the type of girls that would *love* any kind of monster that would crawl out of a lake—the slimier the better. After a pathetic lack of deliberation, their faces broke out in matching grins.

Cecily struck first, introducing herself and then her sister, even going so far as to point out the length of her hair so that Amelia would remember which one was which. Was it a secret code? Eli wondered. Were they like dogs who could hear high noises that humans couldn't detect? What else could explain the girls' easy acceptance? Could they recognize the wicked nonconformity in each other?

"Pleasure to meet you," Amelia replied. "I wish we could have talked before, but I hope you received my presents I left in your rooms this afternoon."

"Presents? What presents?" Eli asked gruffly.

The twins, completely ignoring him, each pulled out what looked like a copper penny.

His mouth fell open. "You're buying them off? That's how you intend to win them over?" His chuckle was infused with arrogance. It was foolish. The twins would never fall for something so trite. Besides, he'd already tried it, and they never behaved for long after.

Kitty answered with a beleaguered sigh and cast her father a mournful scowl. "She's not buying us off," she explained as if Eli was a troublesome child. "She's testing us."

Amelia smiled, her eyes twinkling. "Testing you? How?"

"You wanted to see if we'd fall for it," Cecily answered. "It's obvious."

"Fall for what?" Michael asked. Thank the Lord, he was just as lost as Eli was.

Cecily held the penny in her palm, tossing it up and catching it. "It's counterfeit."

Amelia's voice came out stiff, challenging. "How do you know?"

"For one, it's too thin," Cecily said with such thoughtful appreciation that she could have been speaking to a professor at Oxford. "And all the Rs are lowercase, as are all the Ns in Britannia. It's not even close. Someone did a very poor job."

"Someone did," Amelia agreed, getting up from her seat. Her gait purposeful, she walked over to Cecily, stopping at the back of her chair. "And that someone is in jail now for his bad effort. It just goes to show that if you do anything in life, you should do it correctly."

"Or perhaps the lesson should be that one shouldn't create counterfeit coins," Eli cut in dryly.

"Yes, that too." Amelia laughed, the musicality of the sound making the children smile.

"You know someone who's in jail?" Kitty asked, with the same excitement as when she'd asked Eli if he'd ever seen a mermaid.

Amelia nodded. "I do, but I don't want to talk about that. I didn't give you the coins to test you, although I'm proud that you did know they were fake. I gave you fake coins so you wouldn't miss them when I show you what I'm going to do."

"What do you mean?" Cecily asked. She twisted in her seat to face Amelia and held the coin out in her hand. "What are you doing to do?"

Quick as a flash (or quick as a London pickpocket), Amelia took the fake penny from Cecily and tossed it in her other hand. Then she brought the hand to her ear, shaking it a few times before bringing it back to the little girl. With a "ta-da!" she opened her palm, and the penny was no longer there. Amelia had made it vanish in thin air!

Cecily was dumbfounded, while Michael squealed joyfully. "What … how …?" she asked. "Was that magic?"

Pleased as punch, Amelia returned to her side of the table, performing the same act on Kitty before taking her seat. "I'm not sure if it's magic, but let's just say Kitty isn't the only one with special powers."

The fact that Eli knew Amelia hadn't been in the room when Kitty made that preposterous statement made him even consider they had a witch in their midst. Which was ridiculous! Amelia wasn't a witch—or magic. She was a first-rate charlatan. A smart one.

Because Amelia had known money wasn't going to sway the twins in her favor. Tricks, on the other hand … She had converts for life.

And Amelia had wanted to do it in front of him. She'd wanted Eli to bear witness to her conquest.

"Now," she said, planting her elbows on the table once more and issuing a stern gaze to the girls. "What's this I hear about you two harassing the laundress with red ants?"

The twins shared a guilty look. "It was only that one time!" Kitty replied. "It was funny, though."

Eli was about to offer a harsh rebuke, but Amelia stopped him. To her credit, she didn't laugh, nor did she agree with her newest disciples. "Do you know, in London, one of the hardest, most dangerous jobs is to be the laundress?" she asked.

Each child shook their head slowly. Michael even gulped.

"It's true," Amelia said. "Clothes are an easy thing to steal, and you can get a lot of money for some nice pieces. I know some laundresses that carry knives with them when they're hanging the clothes so they can defend themselves against thieves."

"Really?" Kitty asked breathily. Eli could almost see the huge knife the girl was envisioning in her head.

Amelia nodded gravely. "You two are lucky. I wouldn't hassle with a laundress or her things all the way out here in Essex. Who knows what might happen?"

Was she threatening his children? Eli wondered. The idea of their laundress, sixty-five-year-old Sarah, having a knife hidden under her skirts was preposterous. Though the children didn't seem to think that …

"Did …" Michael gulped again. "Did *you* ever steal from a laundress?"

Amelia's brows went up to her hairline. "Do I look crazy to you? Never!" She bent her fingers back and studied her nails, adding off-hand, "I did a short stint as a skinner, though."

"What's that?" Cecily asked, practically stretching her torso across the table.

Eli didn't want to know and had to restrain himself from covering his ears with his palms. He had to remind himself that this was all his idea—and his fault. He'd forced the woman to come to his house; he'd asked for these incorrigible stories. *Forgive me, Father,* Eli prayed silently. *I know not what I do.*

Amelia flashed her teeth, as if she'd been waiting for the question. "That's when we lure little rich children like you into a dark street with candy and toys. Once we get you there, we steal all your clothes and force you to walk back to your home in only your underthings." She shrugged. "Sometimes bare feet, if we like your shoes enough. Your parents like to dress you lords and ladies up in expensive fabrics."

"Were you ever caught?" Kitty said, close to tipping in Amelia's lap.

"By the authorities? Never." Amelia sighed. "I was caught by a laundress one time. She'd been watching the little lord because his nurse was out sick."

"What did she do to you?" Kitty asked.

"You don't want to know," Amelia said sternly. "It's like I told you. Clothes are a dangerous thing. By the way, does food always take this long to come out?"

CHAPTER TWELVE

BELLY FULL AND pride satisfied, Amelia was just about to close the door to her bedroom when a boot slammed its way across the threshold.

Eli's incensed face met her on the other side. "Was that truly necessary?" he asked.

Ignoring the question, Amelia slammed the door on the boot, but he wouldn't yield. Damn the man! He didn't give her so much as a yelp.

"I have no idea what you're talking about," she returned calmly as if repeatedly trying to maim a man's foot was her pre-sleep ritual. After the third attempt, Eli had had enough, and he pushed out his arm, stretching the door wide open.

"You know exactly what I'm talking about," he said. "Terrifying my son and daughters half to death with sordid tales of stripping children of their clothes in the streets wasn't what I had in mind when I brought you here."

Amelia gave him an odd look. They hadn't seemed terrified; on the contrary, they'd appeared quite entertained.

But she'd clearly touched a nerve. Eli's color was high, and his dark hair was sprouting out of his scalp like a wild fern. She wondered if he'd been pulling at it while he debated giving her a dressing-down after dinner. However, *Angry Eli* had to be her favorite Eli. There was something so animated and visceral about him, something so much more alive and textured than *Haughty Eli*.

It was why Amelia didn't retreat into her room, forcing space between them. She appreciated his energy, the way his tempter simmered off him like a low-burning fire, the embers so hot they turned blue. There was a beautiful alchemy to it all.

She dismissed his complaint with a glib smile. "I thought that's why you hired me ... to scare them onto the straight path. That story wasn't even that bad. They ate it up like Sunday pudding."

"And now they'll have nightmares."

Oh. She hadn't thought of that. Amelia had experienced so much of the world that her nightmares were tame in comparison. "Do your children have nightmares often?"

Eli's features hardened as if the temperature had instantly dropped to freezing. His jaw clenched a few times before he replied with a barely contained sneer, "No, and I'd like to keep it that way. I assume you'll be able to come up with some cautionary tales that aren't so explicit and horrifying."

Amelia picked through her brain. Nothing was coming to mind. "It's not my fault your children are so sheltered," she countered. "You're doing them a disservice by hiding them in the country, away from life."

"Don't you dare tell me how to raise my children," he replied. "I'm keeping them safe."

"From who?"

"People like you!"

Amelia threw her hands up around her, bewildered. "Well, you're doing a terrible job!" she snapped.

Eli surprised her. The lines at the corners of his eyes deepened, and he released a puff of air that she realized was a laugh. Amelia might have joined him if she wasn't so incensed by the ridiculous conversation. Did she have to remind him that he'd forced her here? Why bring a snake into your midst if you were petrified of being bitten?

They stood there in limbo for a long minute. Amelia considered shutting the door again, but there was something about Eli's expression that stopped her. He was staring at her hands with such ferocity that she almost hid them behind her back.

"Is that how you got the scars?" he asked quietly, finally meeting her eyes.

"What?"

He nodded at her knuckles, at the white nicks growing whiter as she squeezed her fingers tighter. "On your hands," he continued. "Was it a laundress who did it to you?"

Amelia frowned, her mind playing catch-up to realize he was addressing her story from earlier. Finally, she laughed. "Ah, no. I might have embellished that a tiny bit." And by a tiny bit, she meant all of it. "Laundresses have been known to be tough, although I've never actually seen one carry a knife. Once, when I was younger, a giant of a woman grabbed me by the hair when I tried to steal a pretty blouse." She rubbed the crown of her head as if she could still feel the blinding pain. "She almost pulled a chunk out of my scalp, but she was taken care of right enough."

"But who?" Eli asked, one corner of his lips quirking up.

She hadn't thought of this story in forever. "Jimmy Donovan—one of Harry's Boys. When the woman was yanking on me, he ran by and snatched a pair of trousers from her basket to take the heat off me. He hadn't any idea how fast she was, though—none of us did. She caught up with him by the next block and sent him back to Harry black and blue and trouserless."

Amelia chuckled at the memory, though it faded fast when she noticed Eli's assessing stare. "Is Jimmy your man, then?" he asked with a quiet edge.

She huffed. "I was six when that happened."

"Is he your man?" He pulled his shoulders back. "Women like you tend to swoon at heroic actions like that."

That wasn't the first time he'd used that expression. "*Women like me*? You mean, *attractive*?"

"Foolish."

Ah.

"No, Jimmy isn't my man. Never was, even though he certainly asked enough. Despite what you think, his heroics didn't turn my foolish head."

"But others have."

Was that a question? Amelia decided to go with it. "Wouldn't you like to know?"

Eli didn't back away. He didn't budge at all, but Amelia still had the sensation that they were being drawn closer like two magnets. His pulse jumped in his throat, giving Amelia the only indication that he felt anything at all.

His voice, bored and flat, wasn't helpful. "Funny enough, I think I would like to know. Your stories are rather entertaining, even if they are barbaric."

Amelia's voice rumbled out of her throat. "I'm so happy I can amuse you."

"Are you?"

"I wouldn't say it if I didn't mean it."

He cocked his head, peering at her curiously. "You seem to say a lot of things you don't mean."

"Rest assured, when I called you an ass, I meant that," she said sweetly.

Behind his glasses, Eli's eyes fell to half-mast as he stared at her lips. "You also kissed me. Did you mean that? Or do you kiss all the men who chain themselves to you at night?"

Amelia could have been blown over by a feather. How had they gotten here? And why did he need to keep insinuating she was some experienced courtesan? Just because she worked the streets, that didn't mean she used her body to do it. Amelia understood how lucky she'd been by avoiding that kind of existence. For women, there was a thin line. Too many nights with too many empty bellies could make or break the decision to go down that path.

She tilted her nose in the air, pretending to count. "Let me think—you're going to have to give me time to remember them all."

Eli rewarded her with a lazy smile. It completely transformed his face, making him seem younger, more carefree, human. "Are there that many?"

"Why do you need to know?" Were they flirting? Amelia had very little experience with flirting. She'd scared men off for so long that they rarely flirted with her anymore. The ones that did used feats of strength and over-the-top theatrics as their preferred methods. Peacocks, blinding her with their showy feathers.

There was nothing showy about Eli, and yet he always managed to keep her attention. "I'm realizing it's best to be prepared where you're concerned. I want to be ready when your knight in shining armor comes to steal you away."

"That makes you the villain."

"In *your* story it does."

Was it her imagination, or did he almost look wistful when he said that? They were definitely *not* flirting, Amelia finally concluded, but she couldn't put her finger on what they were doing. Talking seemed too simple; arguing too aggressive; getting to know one another too innocent. They were more like two opponents circling each other, searching for the other's weaknesses without the slightest idea of what they would do once they found them.

"Alas, dear villain, you have nothing to worry about," she joked, attempting to lighten the situation. "There will be no knight riding up on his glorious steed. Unfortunately, if I am going to break out of your chains, I'll have to do it on my own."

Eli tilted his head and looked over her shoulder, his eyebrows raised. "If these are chains, I'd hate to find out what the hulks look like on the inside."

Amelia swung around, appraising the bedroom. He was right. There was nothing prisonlike about the way Mrs. Hutchinson had set up her stay. The room was gorgeously appointed in yellows and blues, large but still comfortable, with an idyllic view of the gardens at the back of the house. Furniture was sparse, though carefully planned out around an ancient bed that could easily sleep ten people. In all honesty, it was the nicest room Amelia had ever laid eyes on.

"Charles II slept in that bed," she heard Eli say. Amelia's nod must not have been deferential enough, because his voice became more clipped when he added, "You do know who Charles II is, don't you?"

Annoyance flared. Amelia twirled to face him. "Of course I do. He's that man who did that thing that one time. It was wonderful."

With sick satisfaction, she watched the pendulum of emotions swinging on his face. Apparently, Eli didn't know if he wanted to laugh or shake his head in disgust. Probably both. She capitalized on his loss of speech. "I may not have had your level of education, but I did get one, you know. It just didn't take place in a classroom."

Eli studied her with the fierceness of the tutors she never had before finally relenting. "I know that," he said, throwing her off balance. "I apologize. I didn't mean to demean you."

"Didn't you?"

Color swept over his cheeks. "I apologize," he repeated.

"Why did you give me this room if it's so important?" Amelia asked.

"I didn't. Mrs. Hutchinson did."

She frowned. "You could have changed it."

Eli lowered his head ruefully. "Mrs. Hutchinson runs this house; I merely live here. If she placed you in the king's room, then she must have had good reason for it. Besides, even with your prodigious talents, it might be difficult for you to try to steal the bed in the middle of the night. Your pockets aren't that deep."

Amelia giggled. Not at the funny picture he'd planted in her head, but at his continual disbelief in her abilities. If she wanted that bed, she'd find a way to get it out of there. Best not to tell him that, though.

"I promise not to steal the bed," she said, noticing the faint lines across his forehead relent with her admission. Did she really make him that nervous? How sheltered *was* this family? Even she had been surprised by the way the children flocked to her so easily. Amelia wasn't used to children or acceptance. She'd figured that she would have to show a few more magic tricks to gain their trust. But she was no stranger to hunger—both the physical and mental kind. And she'd recognized it in Eli's kids. Their bellies were full, but they were starved for something more in their lives, something he clearly wasn't giving them, or simply didn't know how.

Eli blinked and eventually straightened from his lean, as if concluding that they'd conversed enough for one night. Or perhaps he was remembering that he'd told her that they wouldn't be seeing each other anymore? It had only been a few hours since those fateful words, and she'd already ambushed their dinner and now he was outside her room again, just as he'd been the night before.

They faced each other awkwardly, each waiting for the other to say goodnight. Amelia wanted to dismiss him first. She loved slamming her door in men's faces, but she couldn't bring herself to do it. Because it was then she noticed the father had the same appearance of his children. That hunger. It didn't scare her like it did when it came from other men. This hollow deprivation was different somehow. The yearning. The tension wasn't born of carnality but rather emptiness. For all of Lord Eli's hair and scruff and height and dress, there was something missing, something Amelia couldn't put her finger on.

He slid his hand over the frame of the door, back and forth, knocking it with his fist a few times before eventually retreating into the hallway. He arched a brow one last time. "You will behave? This is my home," he stated.

Amelia wasn't sure what she needed to say to reassure him enough to leave. She also wasn't sure if she wanted to find those words. "I will do my job and then I will go. You'll barely notice that I was here at all." *And, hopefully, you won't notice everything that I've taken with me.*

Eli tried for a smile, though it looked incredibly pained. He nodded and walked down the hall, though Amelia could hear him say, "I doubt that very much."

CHAPTER THIRTEEN

KITTY AND CECILY sat next to each other on the settee in the drawing room, their hands clasped in their laps, the tips of their toes balancing on the floor.

No wonder Amelia had never considered being a governess. Four eyes set upon her, waiting for—nay, expecting—brilliance to rain down from her lips.

But she couldn't think of where to start. Amelia usually had a story for everything. Her life was one big, colorful cast of characters and London was the backdrop—and yet here she stood with two little girls at full attention and she couldn't think of anything to say.

The grandfather clock chimed in the corner, causing Amelia's heart to smack into her ribcage. Fifteen minutes had gone by! Kitty's pink-slippered feet began to wave back and forth under the furniture, her cupid's-bow mouth puckering in irritation. If Amelia didn't say something soon, they'd mutiny. And then where would she be? Attentive children were bad enough; she hadn't the slightest idea what to do with inattentive ones.

Amelia took a deep breath. The twins leaned forward as if to catch whatever came out of her mouth as soon as it landed.

"So … there was this whore," she began, a rush of relief blowing through her.

The twins slammed back against their seats. And just like

that, the relief vanished. Had Amelia said the wrong thing?

"Ugh … I mean … Let me start over," she stammered, beginning to pace back and forth in front of the settee. She scratched at her head. "See … she wasn't a whore—I mean, a fallen woman—yet. She was just like me. Well, not like me. Because she got caught—" Amelia squinted down at the twins. "Do you understand what I'm saying?"

They shared a look, their blue eyes as large as the ocean. Kitty nodded. "Definitely."

Amelia nodded in turn, confidence faintly restored. "Good. All right, then. So, Stronghand Sally they called her because … Well, you don't have to know why. Anyway, she was out one night on a job. She knew a girl working as a maid in some lord's residence and had been told he would be out for a week. The maid had left the back door open for her, and Sally came in one night, hoping to lift a few things—nothing to be noticed, just a little something to get her through the next couple of months."

"What kinds of things?" Kitty asked with enough interest to make Amelia uncomfortable.

"Oh, you know, a candlestick here, a vase there. Nothing too big, nothing you can't hide in your clothes when you make your escape." She swiped a hand in the air. "Anyway, so it turns out the maid got it wrong. The lord's *family* was going to be out of town, not the lord, and suffice it to say, when Sally ventured into the master chamber, she found more than a few candlesticks."

Cecily sat on the edge of her seat, gnawing on her bottom lip. "What did she do?"

Amelia shrugged. "What could she do? She ran, and almost made it too, but the lord got a hold of her by the time she made it to the back door."

"Did he turn her in to the authorities? Was she shipped off to a penal colony?" Cecily asked. "Or … or did they hang her?"

"What? No, of course not!" Amelia grimaced. "He asked her to be his whore. I don't know why—no one knows why—but he took a liking to poor Sally, and she was already long in the tooth and not exactly known for turning heads. He put her up in a posh home in town, gave her servants and anything else her heart desired."

"Oh," Kitty replied, slightly dejected, her gaze down as she mulled over the story. "So … she was a kept woman for the remainder of her life, scorned by all those around her?"

Amelia scanned the ceiling as if her body might float there any second. "Not exactly," she answered slowly. "Now that I think of it, the lord's wife died a few years after that and he married Sally. Made her a baroness, I think? I can't remember now; I get confused with all of you and your titles."

"Is Sally still alive?" Kitty asked. "Or is she dead now from some disease due to her unfortunate life decisions?"

Amelia scratched her head again. "Oh no. Sally's alive and as healthy as a horse. Eating three meals a day in her fancy town-house."

The twins continued their disconcerting stares, stretching a silence out. "So …" Cecily began. "It's a love story?"

"What? No!" Amelia exclaimed. "It's a lesson that even the best get caught and you never know what might happen. Once you start down a questionable path, it's difficult to control the outcome. One minute you're working at the top of your game, and the next, you're a kept woman." *Was* that the lesson? Amelia wasn't really sure anymore, and the twins definitely weren't convinced.

"It sounds like a love story to me," Cecily said. "Sally got her happy ending."

Amelia supposed she did, though "happy" was definitely up for debate. Sally got caught, pure and simple. In the gang, she would wear that shame forever, just as Amelia was now doing. There was no escaping it, though Amelia wondered if Sally even cared while she was having love lavished upon her by her husband. And he did love her. Amelia had gone to the wedding. The lord had been disgustingly open about it.

"All right," she announced, racking her brain. "Let me try this again. I have another story; just wait a minute—"

"I don't want to wait," Kitty said, hopping off the chair. "And I'm tired of sitting. The governesses always made us sit."

"I'm not a governess," Amelia said.

Kitty grinned, her blue eyes deepening. "Exactly."

Ten minutes later, the trio was lost in the grounds in the back of the estate. The late summer sun rained down from a cloudless sky, lighting everything in Amelia's path, making it sparkle like a jewelry box waiting to be pinched.

She could have kissed Kitty for suggesting the walk. Barrington's gardens were magnificent in their wild splendor. It was part quintessential English garden, with its clean lines and straight hedgerows, and part wildness, with its smattering of raucous wildflowers, and Amelia was certain she could spend the rest of her life navigating this slice of heaven and never get tired.

Which was saying something, since her companions were intent on driving her crazy with their questions.

"How old were you when you stole something for the first time?"

"Was it just like *Oliver Twist*?"

"Have you ever been shot at?"

"Girls, girls slow down," Amelia said, stopping to caress the silky petal of a salmon-colored rose along the path. Rubbing her fingers on her pounding temple, she could smell the flower's sweet, powdery fragrance. "Let me see ... I was five when Molly let me out to work; life on the streets is nothing like *Oliver Twist*; and I've only been shot at once, but it wasn't because I stole something. A man at a pub had had too much to drink and shot at his friend because he thought he was trying to steal his wife. The bullet just grazed me. I was in the wrong place at the wrong time."

Kitty's mouth dropped open. "Amazing," she breathed, staring at Amelia as if she were the queen herself.

Oh, no. Amelia wasn't *exactly* sure what Eli wanted from her, but that look *definitely* wasn't it.

"No, no, no," she said, shaking her head. "It is *not* amazing. Life on the streets is difficult. Dickens makes it seem exciting, even fun at times, but it's not all daring escapes, spine-tingling capers, and long-lost relatives."

"It isn't?" Cecily asked, quite put out.

My God, Amelia thought. *I am doing a terrible job.*

"Of course not," she stated. "Even with the protection of a gang, you are in complete charge of your life, which means you only have yourself to depend on. You're alone for long periods of time and you can do whatever you want. There's no real structure or purpose other than filling up days with money and food. Sometimes, if you're lucky, you can sneak in to see a show or exhibit. The days can be so long because even though you have nothing to do, there's so much to do. Staying alive takes a lot of energy. It's … exhausting."

Amelia didn't know how true that was until she said it. Every day she had to wake up and think about how she was going to keep going. What was the new trick? What was the new angle? She could never just *be.* Maybe Sally had been right to leave it all behind—the thrill, the girls, the independence.

"I don't understand," Kitty said, kicking the dirt while she walked. "That sounds divine. I would love to have that life."

Amelia laughed bitterly. "Trust me, you wouldn't." She lifted her hands toward the house, which sat like a centurion above them, the bricks of its foundation the source of so much security and assurance. What Amelia would give for a little of it. Thanks to Molly, she'd always had a home, but they were always getting kicked out or forced to move when situations became too hot. She always wondered what it would feel like to live in a place longer than six months at a time.

Amelia had almost gotten there. She'd lasted a whole month living above her tiny flower shop before it went under. Those were the happiest days of her life.

"Even I had enough," she said softly. Coming upon a tiny pond, she stopped at its edge, admiring the lily pads that covered the surface like speckled spots on orchids. "I tried opening my own business. Going straight."

"You did?" Cecily asked. She picked up a smooth pebble and skipped it expertly across the water. "What kind?"

"A flower shop," Amelia answered, a tinge of embarrassment gripping her stomach. She was speaking to children and yet she was still abashed to mention her dream; perhaps because it had failed so miserably.

"What happened?" Kitty asked, finding another pebble for her sister, though not throwing one of her own.

"No one came," Amelia said, her voice hollow as she watched Cecily's ripples grow bigger and bigger in the water until they disappeared. Just like her shop. "I couldn't pay my rent and had to close it."

Kitty tilted her head, squinting against the sun. "Why didn't people come? Everyone loves flowers."

"I thought so." Amelia bobbed her shoulders. "I had this idea that I could design arrangements, bouquets, for people to buy instead of doing it themselves. Perhaps I wasn't any good at it."

"That can't be it," Kitty argued. "You're good at everything."

Amelia's chest warmed. "Thank you. But I assure you, I am not."

"So, you went back to pickpocketing?" Cecily asked gently, sensing the delicate turn of the conversation that her sister did not.

"I had to," Amelia said, backing away from the water to the path. The girls followed her, though kept a distance. "I owed money," she went on. "Molly had helped me start the shop and asked Harry's Boys for a loan. I was so sure of myself—so sure I would pay it back in no time. But no one came! No one. Maybe for a week, I got some customers, but after that, it was like I was a ghost. No one would come near me. I still don't understand, to be honest."

Amelia could feel fat tears hanging to her lower lids, just waiting to fall. She hadn't cried, not once since it happened, and now, she thought she could weep for days, like a fountain with an endless supply of water. "I still owe them, and that's the worst feeling in the world—to owe someone. Harry's Boys won't stop until they have their money back."

Kitty stepped lightly to her side. "What will they do?"

Amelia couldn't bear to look at her. "You don't want to know," she intoned, before swiping a hand over her face, stopping any tears before they got started. "This is why you need to listen to your father, girls. Do what he says. Live nice, simple lives with nice, simple husbands. You have golden years ahead of you. Don't ruin them like I did."

Cecily came up on her elbow. "You didn't ruin anything," she said. "All you did was try."

"I suppose." Amelia sighed. She sounded pathetic, but at least it was working. There was no doubt in her mind she'd scared the girls properly straight. Eli would kiss her with happiness.

No, she remembered. He wouldn't.

"We have flowers," Cecily said, so off-hand that Amelia almost missed it.

"Yes, you do," she agreed, sucking the air into her lungs, drinking in the mixture of nectars. *When in doubt, smell roses.* That was what Molly always said. They had a way of making any situation a little brighter.

"No, not these flowers," Kitty said, breaking Amelia's little meditation. "We have others. So many others, we don't even know what to do with them."

Amelia cracked one eye open. "What do you mean? Where?"

Kitty nodded across the grounds, to where Amelia could just make out a structure hidden behind two large weeping willow trees. "The greenhouse. It's where Father does his work, but half of it is filled with Mother's flowers. No one takes care of them anymore," she added. "Father isn't much for flowers. He only cares about his strawberries."

Cecily skipped out in front of them toward the greenhouse. When she turned back, her expression was particularly ecstatic, and her blue eyes had a shine that immediately put Amelia on edge. "We could sell them!" she said, clapping. "You could teach us what to do, and then we could go to the village, and the neighboring ones, too. Then you can pay back Harry's Boys."

They were sweet. Did Eli have any idea how sweet his girls were?

Sweet and smart.

Could it work? Amelia would need a lot of flowers and, more importantly, a lot of customers …

She shook her head *and* the idea away. She didn't need their mother's flowers. Her plan to ransack the house would bring her enough money to pay back her loan. "I don't think so, girls. I appreciate you thinking of me, though."

Kitty scoffed. "This isn't only about you. We're bored, Miss Amelia. Bored! If you don't let us help you, then who knows what we'll do until the next governess comes?"

Cecily bobbed her head eagerly. "I can feel myself itching to cause trouble. Help us, Miss Amelia. Help us!"

Were they threatening her? Amelia usually knew a threat when she heard one, but these girls were masters at sandwiching their words between saccharine smiles and musical voices. Amelia couldn't risk it. If the girls acted up while she was here, she knew Eli would blame her. There was no telling where she'd end up after that.

Each girl grabbed one of Amelia's hands, tugging her along with their pleas. "Plus…" Kitty said, "if you let us do this then Father will be so overcome with gratitude over our docile behavior that he'll let you leave. It's a winning solution for all of us."

"Only if we sell enough flowers," Amelia returned uneasily.

"We will." Cecily giggled. "I'm sure of it."

Oh, to be a child and filled with such naïve confidence. Had Amelia ever been that young? No, she hadn't, which was why she was pragmatic to the core.

"Lead the way," she said, letting the girls drag her toward the looming structure, "but I'm not promising anything." She would indulge them for now; there was no harm in taking a look while she told them more stories. She would let them down gently later. Amelia hated to tell them no, but to be honest, after their thinly veiled threat, she was almost scared to do it.

Harry's Boys were one thing, but the ladies of Barrington were quite another.

CHAPTER FOURTEEN

S OMETHING WASN'T RIGHT.

Eli had sat through an entire dinner without barking at his children once. He didn't even catch that delightful fact until they were on dessert, when his shoulders began sliding down his back, his blades flattening around the curve of his ribcage. He couldn't quite place the feeling. Was it … peace? No, he was too worldly to believe that. Eli had three children—two of them girls—and he wouldn't have peace until they were good and married. And yet … something odd stirred within him as he took a bite of rice pudding.

Dear mother in heaven, could he actually be *enjoying* himself? In the sixty minutes they'd been sitting at the table there'd been no hair pulling, no kicking, no incessant teasing, no outlandish storytelling, and no crying from Michael. Eli couldn't believe it. Could it all be because of Amelia? He'd hate to give her too much credit so early, but she was the only change from the past week to this. Could she already be making headway with his girls? Not for the first time, he wondered what kind of woman he was dealing with.

"Have I told you how handsome you are, Father?" Cecily asked, startling the spoon out of Eli's hand. It clanked heavily on his bowl.

He cleared his throat. "Um, no you haven't, Cecily," he said gruffly.

Cecily's pink lips spread wide over her teeth. "Well, you are. Looking very handsome."

"Thank you."

"You're welcome, Father."

She stared at him for a beat too long, opening her mouth as if to say more before going back to her pudding.

Thinking Cecily wished him to say more, Eli searched for an easy question to keep up the convivial conversation. "And how was your day with Miss Amelia? Did you learn anything interesting?"

Cecily's forehead creased in thought, her spoon stalled in midair. "Yes, Father. We did," she answered in a serious tone. "Never get caught." She pointed her spoon at him. "Unless you're a whore, and in that case, you might marry a baron."

Eli's spoon hit the bowl again. "Cecily! Where did you hear that word?" What a stupid question. He glowered, though his daughter only returned a guileless look. "Ladies don't speak like that."

"Oh, yes," she said, before taking a bite of pudding in consternation. "Miss Amelia used another term. What was it?"

"Fallen woman," Kitty added helpfully.

"Yes!" Cecily said. "Fallen woman. Is that better, Father?"

So much for the pleasant dinner. A headache began to pound at the top of his head. Eli rubbed his eyes behind his glasses, downing the remainder of his red wine in one gulp.

"Is that … is that all you learned?" he asked, his insides turning to jelly. He'd never been so afraid of an answer in his life.

"Oh no, we learned boatloads of things," Kitty announced joyfully, taking over for her sister. "Like one must always have an inside man working if you want to steal from a house, and never, *ever* borrow money from Harry's Boys."

When his spoon fell that time, Eli didn't bother picking it back up. "How the hell—?" He breathed deep, trying for a modicum of patience. "I apologize," he said, softening his voice.

Again, it didn't matter. Kitty was just as impervious to his outburst as her sister had been. She was more interested in scooping up the last bits of pudding in her bowl. "Who, may I ask, are Harry's Boys?"

Kitty's head popped up. "A truly vicious gang in London. They steal and fight and cheat for a living. They are utterly ruthless."

"And Miss Amelia told you that good girls have nothing to do with men like that, correct?"

Kitty's lip curled up in disappointment, as if she'd been speaking to a person for an hour and only just realized he hadn't understood a word she'd said. "No. She made us swear we would never borrow money from them."

"Why on earth would you borrow money from Harry's Boys?" Eli demanded, crumpling his napkin into a ball and throwing it on the table.

"We just told you we never will," Cecily explained patiently. "We promised Miss Amelia."

The headache was going full speed at this point, closing in on Eli's brain as if it was in the mouth of a nutcracker. His hands were shaking when he placed them on the table—in anger or fear, he did not know. "Michael?" he asked through gritted teeth. "How was your tutoring session today?"

"Fine," the boy answered glumly, eyes downcast. "Not as interesting as the girls' day," he muttered.

Eli dismissed his sulky tone. "How is your Greek coming?"

"Fine."

"Why can't I learn Greek?" Kitty asked.

"Because," Eli replied dryly, "you like to burn your governess's clothes."

"But you wouldn't let the governess teach us Greek even before we burned her clothes!"

Irritated, Eli placed his napkin back in his lap. He could feel it coming. The atmosphere was shifting into more familiar territory. "Young ladies don't need to learn Greek."

Kitty leaned her elbows on the table. Eli stared at the offending limbs so long and hard that he thought his eyes might fall out of their sockets. "What if my husband wants me to know Greek?"

"Then he can teach you Greek," he answered easily.

Kitty slammed back in her seat, crossing her arms. "Why does Michael get to learn everything fun?"

Michael gulped. "Greek is not fun," he said meekly.

Kitty opened her mouth to, no doubt, whip back a hot retort, but she caught Cecily's eye. Instead of shouting at her brother, Kitty closed her mouth, pressing a rictus smile onto her face before returning to her pudding.

Eli watched the whole encounter, lost on what had happened. One minute he was readying for another volcano to erupt over the dining room, and the next thing ... nothing. Silence. Peace, again.

Until Kitty claimed the silence with a last, unnerving statement. "You really do look handsome today, Father."

ELI ESCAPED FROM the dining room as soon as the meal was finished. He couldn't sit there any longer listening to his girls wax on about his "finer features." What the hell had come over them? They were trying to get on his good side. But why?

After enjoying a drink in his study, he meandered through the house, listening to the sounds of his children dissipate into the night as they grumbled up to their rooms. He'd contemplated receding to his greenhouse, checking on any new developments with his strawberries, but lacked the energy to drag himself outside. Eli accepted he was in one of *those* moods. The greenhouse was his escape, his salvation, but it also haunted him when he was contemplative and out of sorts. He was definitely that tonight.

Marianne had ordered the greenhouse built as a wedding

present. She'd told Eli it could be a place they shared together. The only thing that had stunned him more about the generous structure had been the fact that she actually wanted to spend time with him while he worked. She'd ordered dozens upon dozens of flowers brought in for her side of the glass enclosure, though didn't realize until later that one had to have a passion for gardening. And Marianne did not. Nor, she sadly came to realize, did she have a passion for her new, studious husband.

Marianne soon grew bored with the bucolic idea and moved on, finding other amusements that suited her personality more than a serious husband.

It hadn't taken her long to find them. At the time, Eli had thought children might strengthen the bond between them, but the pregnancies only seemed to make her resent him more. His freedom. His work at the estate. The babies didn't keep her interest. Marianne was perfectly content handing them over to wet nurses and nannies as she went on with her life in London. Eli had had no qualms letting her enjoy the city without him, desperate as he was to keep her happy.

The whispers came fast and furious after that.

He had heard the gossip. He knew there were some who thought Michael wasn't his child, since he took after Marianne so fully, but Eli was positive the affairs hadn't started until after the boy was born. Marianne could be selfish and cruel, but she was not a monster. She would never do that to him.

In the end, they married too quickly. They did what their elders had told them to do, and Eli had been so swept up in Marianne's beauty and vivaciousness that he hadn't recognized the signs. They weren't a good fit; it was as simple as that. Their arguments were relentless, her misery ever-present. When Marianne had told him she was leaving, he didn't put up a fight. What would have been the point? Why force a woman to stay? Marianne was content to leave the children with him, and they were all he wanted.

All Eli asked was that she stay on the Continent, away from

the constantly wagging tongues of London. He should have known the English Channel wouldn't be wide enough for Marianne.

Stories of her antics reached his tucked-away enclave. The more Eli heard of her gambling and lovers, like her infamous scandal with Lord Charles, Earl of Somerset, the more he retreated into Barrington with the children. When she died a year after leaving him, Eli had genuinely mourned her—not for what they had, but for their youthful innocence, what they once believed they *could* have had.

They had never fit. Eli saw that now. He was the square peg, and she was the round hole.

Eli had no business getting married at twenty. But he'd been all alone. His parents had died when he was young, leaving him with his taciturn grandfather. After the old man passed, Eli believed he was finally a man who could make his own decisions. No one was there to inform him that, though he was a viscount, he was not yet a man. Marianne had been the family he'd always wanted. It had crippled Eli to realize that he wasn't the same for her.

And now it was like history repeating itself.

The outside world was cruel. Whenever he went to town, Eli still got looks, still heard the snickers. Soon, his children would too. And soon he would have to give them the truth about Marianne: that she hadn't died in childbirth as he'd initially told them—she'd left them. Left all of them. The *ton* was merciless with scandals, even toward children. That was why he hid them away at Barrington. That was why he pushed them to be better, smarter, so well behaved that no one could point at them and compare them to their mother.

Was it a losing battle? Eli had pushed Marianne to love him, and she did not. He was now pushing his children for perfection and was facing the same pushback. With horror, Eli was learning his children were growing older, and all signs were pointing to the fact that they were not going to be content to sit obediently on the outskirts, as he was.

More. The children wanted more from him. And damned if Eli knew if he could give it to them—

"Holy fuck! What the hell are you doing in here?" he shouted, practically jumping out of his skin.

In the middle of the drawing room, a guilty-looking Amelia gawked back at him, a pristine Grecian vase held tenuously between her scarred hands.

A spark had only recently been started in the fireplace, and the low-level light danced across her spooked features, highlighting her furtive fear of being discovered.

"I-I'm so sorry," she stammered, placing the vase back on its table. "I thought you were still with the children."

His heart reclaiming a normal rhythm, Eli ventured to the table, nudging the vase a few inches to the right, back to its correct spot. He was a stickler for that sort of thing, and he was buying himself time. Eli hadn't seen the woman since yesterday, which was exactly how he'd planned it. Amelia Driver was like too much sugar—no good for him. She made his blood rush and his tongue loose. All day, he'd recounted the disastrous conversation they shared outside her bedroom the previous night. What the hell had compelled him to go there? He should have stayed away! But gone he had, and he'd made an ass of himself. Worse … he'd gotten to know more about her, and that had only made him crave knowing more. People didn't want to believe, but Eli knew the truth. Sugar was a drug as dangerous as opium.

"I thought you said we weren't going to be seeing each other anymore," she pointed out cheekily.

"I wasn't actively looking for you," he argued. "I was merely walking around my house. This is my house, you remember? Why aren't you in your room?"

"I couldn't sleep."

Eli tried not to picture her prone on that giant bed, her legs lashing back and forth fitfully as she tried to doze. Instead, he ran a finger over the lip of the vase. "This is smaller than the bed, but

I still would find it hard to believe you could get this in your pockets without anyone noticing."

Amelia drew in a sharp breath, and Eli took pleasure in the way her chest rose fitfully against another of his sister's proper and restraining dresses. Yet again, the ensemble was too long for her, but the deep blue silk played against her black hair in a way that made the word "sultry" come to his mind. He would have preferred another.

"You are obsessed with my perfidy," she said in an irked fashion, casually sauntering away from the vase. Amelia hooked her fingers behind her back, as if she had to physically restrain them from nicking something of their own accord. Muscle memory. "You have a beautiful home, my lord. I was merely admiring its splendor."

Eli didn't believe her for a minute. Pity the man that ever believed a word that ever came forth from her supple little mouth. Sadly, that didn't mean he wanted her to stop. He was quite certain he could sit and listen to her read *Johnson's Dictionary* with no complaint. Beyond a doubt, he believed that she could even make that dull tome entertaining.

A game of cat-and-mouse commenced. As if to further make her point, Amelia circled the room touching and moving everything she could get her hands on. Eli followed, righting everything to its natural place. The game became ridiculous quickly enough. Did the woman really need to punch a pillow at its top and redistribute it to the middle of the sofa? And did Eli have to give a put-upon sigh and replace it back at the side? Yes. Of course he did. Whoever heard of putting a pillow in the middle of a sofa? Only barbarians considered such things acceptable.

"I think you have a problem," Amelia mused as she watched him adjust the ormolu clock to the exact center of the mantel.

Eli fiddled with the piece, not stopping until the cherubs' wings were facing directly forward. Dropping his hands to his sides, he replied, "If by problem, you mean you, then yes, I have a problem."

Amelia chuckled, and he was pretty sure it was directed at him. "You seem to have an unhealthy preoccupation with *things*," she announced, saying the word as if it was dripping in oil. "Though I should have known that when you chased me for the pocket watch."

"I don't have an unhealthy preoccupation with anything," he griped, noting to himself that he was definitely not preoccupied with *her*. "And I chased after you for my watch because it was *my watch*."

Amelia shrugged a dainty shoulder, moving on to pull books just slightly from the shelves without having the courtesy to push them all the way back in. No matter—Eli would do it tomorrow. "I know it's a Breguet, but it's just a watch," she said. "You could have bought another."

Tomorrow wasn't soon enough. Eli shouldered past her, shoving the books flush into their rows. "It had nothing to do with it being a Breguet. It was my father's watch. It's one of the only things I have that was his."

Amelia's finger halted on the spine of another book. "How old were you when he died?"

"Nine. My mother died shortly after." She hadn't asked for that piece of information, but he gave it anyway. And it seemed he wasn't done giving. For a man who liked to keep his own counsel, Eli was unusually loquacious that night. He'd only had one drink after dinner, so he couldn't blame the alcohol. Blaming Amelia didn't seem fair, though that didn't stop him from doing it. There was something about the woman that made him want to open up. Most likely the fact that their relationship was limited. The end date was a blessing for his conscience. "My grandfather raised me, mostly. One of his favorite lessons was to tell me that we are only passing through. Some faster than others," he added ruefully, thinking of his father. "The viscounts of Barrington are stewards of this land, of this great house. My role is to protect all that I have so that Michael will have something to inherit. It is the job of the nobility."

Amelia's brow furrowed, making Eli second-guess what he'd just said. There was nothing to frown about. Was there?

"I suppose that's a noble role," she remarked, her uncertainty evident. Walking behind the sofa, she skated her hand over its edge. "But in the end, these are just things. If they broke or got lost, no one would remember them after a few days." She gave him a look. "Or maybe a few weeks, in your case."

Eli huffed. What did a street urchin know about family history? He tried not to let her ignorant words injure his pride.

He failed.

"They are hardly just things." He jutted his chin toward the mantel. "Those candelabra were given to my family by Henry VIII."

"I'm glad the fat king treated your family better than his wives," Amelia cut in dryly.

"And for Christ's sakes, you're standing in front of a Caravaggio!"

She swirled to take in the painting, not giving it nearly enough appreciation time before she turned away. "I've seen paintings just as well done on the streets for a few shillings. I'll show you."

Eli could feel the rush of blood to his head. "I don't need you to show me!"

She shrugged. "Your loss." She paused for a beat, seeming to think over her words. Eli readied himself for the worst. "Is that why you're so hard on him?"

"Who?"

"Michael."

"I'm not hard on Michael. What are you talking about?"

She flopped on the sofa, the little hairs around her face flying up from the unladylike exertion. "You keep him inside with tutors all day. It doesn't seem fair, especially since the girls and I are having so much fun."

He narrowed his eyes at the woman as she curled her feet up

underneath her. Feet on his sofa! He, literally, did not have the words! "Might I remind you that your job is not about having fun—"

She waved an insolent hand between them. "I know. I know. I'm working on that. We did have some interesting conversations. But mostly we walked the grounds, getting to know one another. You have very intelligent little girls, Eli. You should be proud."

He shifted his stance. "The other governesses told me they cannot be taught and are too rambunctious for their own good."

Amelia rolled her eyes, a lightning bolt of anger striking her features. "People always say that about active girls. They are no different from little boys who need to express their energy and ideas. Why should girls be held to such ridiculous standards and kept inside all day?"

Eli had never thought of it that way before. Amelia was right, though. His daughters were strong creatures who could climb trees and skip rocks better than most boys. Even always looking down at his plants, it had been hard for Eli not to notice that. Exercise was considered beneficial for boys—critical, even. Why should it be any different for his daughters?

Like Kitty wanting to learn Greek. Why had he been so against it? Just because he had heard he should be?

"Yes, I've heard about some of these conversations," he said. "Whores? Fallen women? I hoped you'd be a bit more scrupulous with your choice of words. These are gently reared girls, after all."

Eli expected a rebuke, but he got nothing. Well, not nothing. Amelia flushed, her cheeks pink with … embarrassment?

"I'm sorry," she said, amazing him. "It just came out. I'll be more circumspect in the future. Sometimes I forget all little girls weren't raised like me."

"And how were you raised?"

The side of her mouth tilted up, though the effort seemed to cost her. "I wasn't raised at all. Sometimes I think I came into this world fully formed, like Athena born from Zeus's brain."

Eli shook his head. The things she said. "How does a pick-pocket know about Greek mythology?"

Amelia's smile grew. "I didn't only steal pocket watches. Books are easier to pinch than you think."

Eli laughed, despite the criminal confession. "And Greek mythology was your favorite?"

She grabbed the pillow next to her, hugging it to her chest. He didn't have the heart to tell her that it was purely decoration and not to be used in that way. Besides, it looked right in her arms. Amelia had a knack for making whatever she did seem natural. A chameleon, she could fit anywhere, do anything, even have a conversation with him.

"Hardly," she replied with a youthful chuckle. "I preferred manuals the most. Anything that could teach me how to do something new."

"More weapons for your arsenal?" He regretted the words the moment they were out of his mouth. A shadow of hurt passed over her eyes, and Amelia squeezed the pillow even more, probably pretending it was his rude neck.

"Not everything about me is tied up in my profession, much as I'm sure not everything in you is tied up in this house."

Eli threaded his fingers together behind his back. She was right, of course, but he couldn't afford to see her in that light. Amelia Driver was safest to him as a pickpocket. On the outside, that fact made no sense, but he understood it perfectly.

Luckily, she changed the subject, though it wasn't any better for him. "Why did you take Michael to the tournament? It was obvious you didn't want to be there."

Had it been? Eli thought he'd done a decent job hiding his disdain for the ridiculous theatrics—the ones he didn't even allow the boy to see in the end. "Ah … we made a deal. I told him that I would let him go if he refocused on his education. He's been … distracted of late."

"He's been a child, you mean."

Eli's indignation rose. "He's nine. The same age as I when … when …" He ran a hand through his hair. "He needs to be prepared, that's all. He has a duty—"

"Surely there's enough time in the day to be a child *and* prepare for his future role?"

Her eyes were sparkling. Was she laughing at him? Eli hadn't said anything remotely funny.

"One must be ready for any eventuality. He will thank me when he's older," he said.

Amelia lifted herself from the sofa, throwing the pillow haphazardly behind her. "I think he would thank you more if you played with him," she said softly, her skirts rustling against the carpet as she retreated to the door. "Take it from someone who grew up too fast—a little play never hurt anyone, especially a child."

CHAPTER FIFTEEN

Amelia tried to take her own advice. Over the following week, she kept the girls outside as much as possible, running them like the stallions that they were. Molly had always told Amelia that she'd been an odd child, never causing trouble other than the kind they made for other people. Amelia had never had the heart to tell Molly that it wasn't because she was some angelic youth; she was always too tired for any mischief—especially in the beginning of their relationship. Molly had kept her busy learning the trade inside and out. There was simply not enough time in the day to get up to no good. And no one to care if she did.

So, Amelia kept the girls moving, only letting them inside the house for eating and sleeping. True to form, they didn't let up on their demands to sell the flowers, and there was one particularly rainy day when they were forced to stay inside that Amelia almost relented. Her hope to pilfer items from the house seemed more and more far-fetched as the days wore on. Eli had proven that he would recognize something the moment it was stolen. And he wouldn't rest until he found every last piece—and her. For all his gentlemanly behavior, he was a stubborn man and, as if Amelia was just another of his things, relished putting her in her place.

Which left her with quite the dilemma. For the time being,

she was safe. Harry's Boys would be coming for their money soon, but they'd never think to look for her in Essex. But she couldn't hide forever, nor would Eli let her. When she returned to London, she would need to do it with her pockets full. Thanks to Eli's obsessive compulsion with the items in his household, her options on how to obtain that money were rapidly dwindling.

Late in the afternoon, the shadows on the ground stretched long and dark. Amelia had towed the girls down the sloping lawn to the giant fountain where a statue of Prometheus stood prominently in its center. Not one for art, she had surprised herself by loving the gory marble sculpture, which featured the kind Titan attempting to gain his feet with fire cupped in his hand, all while an eagle pecked at his side.

"I'm bored," Kitty said, tossing her makeshift sword on the ground and kicking it for extra measure.

Amelia had sensed a mutiny was coming—she was becoming so much better at reading the signs, but she'd still insisted on one more round of "pirates" before retiring for dinner. Exhausted twins were less likely to pick on their brother during the meal.

"I'm tired of this game. Let's go steal some of Mrs. Hutchinson's biscuits!"

Cecily clapped her hands as if it was the most brilliant idea she'd ever heard. "Oh yes!" She tossed a beseeching look at Amelia. "Mrs. Hutchinson is the worst. We can never get anything by her. Show us some of your pickpocket tricks!"

Amelia stared at the girl incredulously. "Have you gone mad? Your father will throw me on the first boat to Australia if I teach you anything of the sort. Besides, I already tried to pinch some biscuits from Mrs. Hutchinson. It's next to impossible. The woman has eyes at the back of her head."

She relaxed from her fighting stance, untying the cloth she'd wrapped around her one eye for roguish effect. "How about we build a fort? I saw large sticks in the forest we could drag here. Shouldn't be too difficult."

In answer, Kitty plopped on the ground, crossing her skinny

arms. "I want to learn about flowers. I want to learn about owning a business."

Amelia raked her wooden sword into the ground. She hated to tell Kitty that the girl would have better luck learning the trade from someone whose business had succeeded. "Ladies don't own businesses."

"You did."

"Case in point. I'm not a lady."

"Would you want to be? Like your friend, the whore—the fallen woman," Cecily said.

Amelia stopped herself from laughing out loud. The idea was preposterous, and one she'd never wasted any thought on. Her? A lady? It was so far beyond the realm of possibilities. They might have asked her if she'd ever considered being queen. "I suppose I would," she answered truthfully. "Who wouldn't want a life like this? Cozy and surrounded by such beautiful things."

Kitty huffed. "Beautiful things," she muttered. "Father won't let us touch half those *beautiful things* in the house."

"I don't just mean what's inside the house," Amelia said. She lifted her arms, highlighting the outdoors like a canny salesman. "Look at all you are surrounded with. I used to think London was the only place that held beauty and magic. I was wrong."

Kitty tore at more of the *magical* grass. "And *you* won't let us touch the flowers," she griped.

Amelia dropped her arms to her sides, deflated. "What makes you think your father will even let you sell them?" she asked. "Have you even asked him about the flowers?"

"Of course we have," Cecily answered, picking up Kitty's sword and handing it back to her. "We've been buttering him up all week."

Amelia pinned the girl with a stare. "And he actually said yes?"

Cecily nodded, but the fact that she didn't say the words gave Amelia pause—though not as much as she'd had before. The facts were the facts. The girls hadn't been lying. The greenhouse was overgrown and bursting with plants that would wither and die any day now. Selling them made the most sense. And a decent profit could be made. Would it be enough for Harry's Boys? Definitely not. But it might be enough to buy her time to make more. And that was all Amelia needed at this point—more time.

She groaned. "Ah … I'll think about it," she said, eliciting whines from the girls. And claps. Because they knew they had her. So did Amelia, for that fact. Her pride was the only thing keeping her from telling them. Tomorrow would be soon enough. The sun was setting as it was, and they would be going in to get ready for dinner soon.

Michael's tutor must have left for the day, because Amelia spied his little face watching them through a back window of the house. Her heart broke for the boy. His tutors let him out for exercise, but it was all so preordained and manly. Lots of bats and balls … and rules. Which was fine. But the way his face turned ashen whenever he saw his sisters pick up one of their swords was enough to make Amelia want to steal him away from the house, along with the family's ancient china.

"If all you girls are going to do is sit and pout then I'm going to look for a better companion to play with." Amelia cupped her hands around her mouth and caught Michael's eye through the glass. "Michael, come out here. I need help!"

He hesitated for a second, but then Michael's face left the pane of glass and, soon enough, he stoically exited the house. He cast the twins furtive glances as if wondering if he was walking into a trap. Amelia snatched Kitty's sword away from her, eliciting a "Hey," and handed it to Michael, who grasped the handle readily. "I know you had to leave the medieval tournament early on my account," she began, "but I have a feeling you know how to spar. Would you care to try with me?"

Michael bit his lower lip, trying to hide a smile, but it was no use. His cheeks were as red as the inside of a beet. "I'm not very good," he said shyly.

"Oh, wonderful," Amelia replied, backing away to lift her

own sword in the starting position. "That means I'll win. And I love to win."

"You're not very good either," Cecily chimed in.

Kitty would not be outdone. "Yes, you're actually quite terrible."

"Be quiet, you two," Amelia said from the side of her mouth. "Michael and I are knights, and you are the damsels in distress."

"I don't want to be a damsel," Kitty complained, tearing at more blades of grass.

"Good." Michael laughed. "Because I don't want to save you."

Amelia lowered her weapon. "Do you know? I don't want to save them either!"

Michael's smile was so wide it almost hurt Amelia's heart. "So, what are we fighting for? Honor?"

She cocked her head. "No. I don't think I've got enough honor to warrant fighting over."

"Gold, then?"

Amelia grinned. "Gold! Yes, I'll always fight over gold."

Michael giggled and settled himself in position. Right away Amelia recognized that the child knew even less about fencing than she did. And the little knowledge she'd accumulated was obtained by rifling through a stolen copy of Sir William Hope's *The Scots Fencing Master*, written in the late 1600s. Amelia had to assume it was a touch outdated.

She decided to go easy on the child—but not that easy. As she'd said, she liked to win.

Amelia struck first. Her style of fighting was a solid mishmash of fencing and Viking-like brute force. With all of her interest in Sir William Hope, she'd never once memorized anything having to do with footwork.

Catching on that their fight wasn't respectable in the least, Michael quickly lost his noble inhibitions and parried and struck with the demented efficiency of a cornered cat. It took no time at all for their faces to be crimson and their breaths to be pathetically heavy as they chased each other around the lawn, using the twins as shields and any available stick or rock as worthy projectiles.

If Amelia had known another person had come to watch, she might have tried for a semblance of decorum … or at least not have scooped up a handful of water from the fountain and thrown it in the little boy's face (it was rather unsportsmanlike), but she was too intent on her opponent, too focused on finding a weakness.

She climbed onto the edge of the fountain, hoping the higher ground would grant her an advantage. Michael didn't necessarily have skills, but he was a child, which meant inexhaustible energy. He would never stop.

No, only his father could make him do that.

"Michael! What on earth do you think you're doing?"

The child's body immediately went rigid. He snapped away from Amelia's feet. He'd been diligently trying to trip her into the foundation.

All laughter evaporated, the only sounds coming from their ragged chests and the water Amelia stood in front of.

"I'm sorry, Father," Michael replied, eyes dutifully downcast.

Eli came forward, his features hardened in disapproval as he stood over his son. A swarm of anger enfolded Amelia, and it took everything within her to hold her tongue. Would it kill him to bend? What did it serve to be such a taskmaster all the time?

"You didn't answer my question," Eli said, waiting for Michael to lift his head. The poor child couldn't.

It was too much for Amelia. "It was my fault, my lord. I forced Michael to come out and play with me. Your daughters were too busy whining."

"We were not!" Kitty countered.

"Yes, we were," Cecily added with a casual shrug.

Eli eyed his daughters before returning to his son. "Where's Mr. Samuels?" he asked, referring to the tutor.

"He's gone for the day," Michael whispered.

Eli hooked his hands behind his back. "Then you should be studying so you can be ready for tomorrow."

Michael's meek reply almost ripped Amelia in two. She hadn't understood her feelings for the boy until now. He reminded her of herself when she was that age. Molly, for all her generosity, had been an unyielding taskmaster as well. Nothing Amelia did had ever been good enough—especially at the beginning. The woman worked her day and night until Amelia could go off and work on her own, earn her keep. She'd told Amelia it had been for her own benefit. She'd been making something of the girl. One day, Molly had told her, Amelia would be grateful.

She glanced down at her knuckles, rubbing the dappled white scars with the tips of her nimble fingers. She was grateful. But she was also conflicted.

One night long ago, over an empty pint glass, an old barman had once told Amelia that recollections were an elusive thing. He couldn't remember what his mother had looked like, but he could always remember the way she'd made him feel.

Amelia couldn't remember Molly slapping her knuckles with her leather strap anymore. She'd blocked those memories as easily as she'd blocked Michael's parries. Nor could she remember many kind words or warm clothes.

She remembered fear, though. She remembered it all too well.

"He was only having fun," Amelia argued, leaning down from her perch. "What is the crime in that?"

Eli fixed a stare on her, the corner of his mouth inching up. "Odd choice of words," he replied. "Coming from you."

She rolled her eyes. "Yes, yes, I'm a pickpocket. I'm a drain on society, a worm under your feet. I know what you think of me," she replied bitterly. "But I'm also a person with two eyes. And your son was happy. Can't you stop being a stick in the mud for a few minutes and just let us enjoy each other? Can you just look the other way or polish your beloved silver that some long-dead emperor gave you until we're done?"

"King James," Cecily piped up.

"Sorry?" Amelia asked.

The little girl's eyebrows rose to her hairline at the sudden attention from the group. "King James gave our family the silver as a gift."

Amelia released a long exhale. "Of course he did."

She returned her ire to Eli, who stood there watching her curiously, as if she were an animal who'd just begun to talk in perfect English.

"I have nothing against fun," he said softly.

Amelia *humphed*. "You could have fooled me."

Eli reached for his son's sword and cradled it easily in his hand, admiring the dull wooden blade. His next words were spoken to the weapon, not to her. "If I have a problem, it's that there is a proper way to do things and an improper way. There's a right time and a wrong time."

"Let me guess," Amelia said. "Now is not the right time?"

He raised one eyebrow, suddenly smiling at his son. Michael returned the smile uneasily at first, until some conversation seemed to flow between them that Amelia couldn't decipher. She only had the distinct impression it didn't bode well for her.

"Do you want to learn how to fence?" Eli asked the boy.

Michael nodded eagerly.

"Do you want me to teach you?"

The boy nodded so hard that Amelia thought his head might fly off.

Eli's expression relaxed. "Then let me give you the first lesson. Never, ever let your opponent gain the higher ground. You're as good as done when that happens."

Amelia *tsked*, leaning on her sword as if it were a cane. "Everyone already knows that."

Eli reacted in a flash, moving so quickly that Amelia never saw it coming. Whipping out his sword, he knocked hers out of her hand, throwing her off balance. Grappling for purchase,

Amelia swung her arms around and pitched back into the fountain. Water covered her on all sides as her behind hit the shallow bottom. Not missing a beat, the fountain spray continued to pour over her incredulous head.

The children's gasps were drowned out by their laughter.

Amelia simmered, heating the water like lava under a hot spring. "Any other brilliant lessons for the day?" she seethed.

Pointing his sword at the statue, Eli said, "Yes. Prometheus was also a thief who got caught. And look where he ended up." To his daughters, he added, "Make sure she empties her pockets before she gets out. I don't want her to steal any of my fish while she's in there."

CHAPTER SIXTEEN

As HE SAT down at the evening meal, Eli's stiff muscles ached. He wasn't complaining, quite the opposite. It was a delicious pain. The kind that reminded someone that he had used his body in the way it was meant to be used. The kind that reminded a person that he was alive.

Fencing agreed with him, as did teaching his son. For the past week, Eli and Michael had practiced together, Eli relinquishing everything his fencing tutor had imbued in him so long ago, and Michael gobbling the information up like it was candy.

Eli hadn't expected himself to enjoy it so much. Like most things he did, he considered the joint venture to act as a means to an end. Just with the tournament, he figured the lessons would be an incentive for Michael to focus on his schoolwork and attract more of an interest in the estate. If that was happening, Eli wasn't aware of it. In fact, he hadn't even asked. Their fencing bouts were ... fencing bouts. No more, no less. If anything, Michael seemed even more dreamy about knighthood, even referring to himself as the Knight of the Flowers. Eli didn't even ask why the boy had chosen that moniker, thinking it just some fanciful notion for the nine-year-old.

Dinner turned out to be another subdued affair, with the girls on their best behavior yet again. Cecily only broke character once to screech at her brother (almost blistering Eli's eardrums) when

Michael voluntarily tattled that she'd snuck into his room and tied his shoelaces together while pretending to look for a missing toy on the floor. When the clueless boy had stood up from his desk, blissfully ecstatic that his studies were over for the day, he'd promptly landed straight on his face. The knot had been so tight, it had taken him thirty minutes to extricate himself.

Clearly, after two weeks in his household, Amelia's job was not done.

That realization didn't bother Eli like he thought he might. He told himself it was because he valued a job done to completion, though he wasn't positive that was the *only* reason.

After wishing the children a good night, Eli decided air was what he needed. He ventured out to the lawn toward the fountain where Michael and he conducted their lessons. His back spasmed at the sight, and he twisted it to free up the muscles tightening from the repeated strain of the week. He would need to hire Michael a fencing teacher before long. Eli was self-aware enough to admit he wasn't the best fencer, had always been mediocre at best, and would soon be of no use to his son.

Growing up at Barrington and being sent away to boarding school at the first chance, he'd had a first-class education just like every other gentleman; however, even though he was well versed in the noble pursuits of fencing and shooting, his heart had never settled there. He loved the outdoors but much preferred using his body to build the land rather than to take from it. It was why he never shied from joining his tenants whenever a house needed to be constructed or a fence needed to be mended. Plus, that gave him a chance to speak to the farmers, and ascertain what crops were failing or thriving so he could go back to his greenhouse and puzzle out solutions. His grandfather would have never approved of such easy relations between master and tenant, but although the old man had espoused the importance of a good relationship between lord and farmer, he'd never stipulated exactly how Eli should do that. Eli liked his way. It worked for him and his estate, which was thriving from his active attention. He was determined to continue that success for Michael as well.

Eli filled his lungs with the crisp late summer breeze. A pervasive chill caused him to shudder, and he wrapped his arms around his chest, warding off the signs of autumn. The moon was big and round, casting the grounds with a pearly, luminescent light that reminded him of a dusting of snow. He could never understand why people dreaded the winter. When he pictured withered plants and brown grass he never thought of death, only rebirth. As a horticulturist, he appreciated the natural order of things. One couldn't appreciate a bud if one didn't understand all that little miracle had gone through to survive on this planet. It was breathtaking in its daunting simplicity.

Eli had even tried that tack with his parents and Marianne as a way of coming to terms with their deaths, though the premature nature of those events always made it so much more difficult. Which was why he'd decided long ago that it was best not to think about them at all. Taking care of his house, his children, his family's relics was the safest way to preserve their memory without actually having to bear the heartache of reflecting on them.

However, if that was the case, why on earth had he allowed a thief in his midst? Like opening the door to a henhouse and inviting a fox right in, Eli's decision had made no sense. And yet if he had to do it all over again, he would have done the same thing. That either made him stupid or crazy. Or enamored.

He would settle on stupid *and* crazy.

Eli shivered again and had turned to go back inside when a noise stopped him. Searching past the fountain, he only saw gradations of shadows eventually leading to pure darkness. The hairs on the back of his neck stood to attention. It was probably nothing more than an animal—an owl or badger looking for food—but when he saw a flicker of light move away from the house toward the path, he knew he'd made the right decision to wait.

And he also knew he was right not to consider himself enamored. He wasn't in the slightest. But he wasn't stupid or crazy either. If Amelia was determined to steal from his home, he was just as determined to stop her.

Eli didn't go back into the house to find his overcoat. He followed Amelia's footsteps right away, leaving just enough room to evade detection as she traveled toward the village. He wasn't cold anymore anyway. He was bloody on fire.

ELI DIDN'T WASTE time with convoluted schemes. It was obvious what Amelia was doing as she took a seat in the pub and ordered a drink. A lady didn't drink ale alone late at night. Neither did a pickpocket. She was waiting for someone.

She just didn't know that person was him.

Ignoring the surprised looks thrown his way as he strolled the length of the pub, Eli slid into the seat opposite Amelia, thrilled at the way her eyes grew large over her glass as she sputtered her first sip.

Eli paused until she put the glass down. But she wouldn't do it. Amelia kept drinking, her throat the only thing moving as she swallowed one large gulp after the other. He was just about to grab the drink away from her when she clunked it on the table, heaving deep breaths and wiping her mouth with the back of her hand.

"Thirsty, were you?" he asked lazily.

Instead of answering him, Amelia called out to the barmaid, raising her nearly empty glass when she got the woman's attention. Eli lifted his hand, insinuating he would have one as well. Although he frequented the pub from time to time, he wasn't certain when it closed. He gathered the hour must be soon, since the patrons looked knackered, with those that could still use their legs retreating to the exit.

Her co-conspirator must be running late, he mused as he

watched her try to gain her bearings on the other side of the sticky table. Amelia was wearing yet another dress of his sister's, this one a demure light green and pink plaid that somehow didn't seem so grand and ostentatiously out of place in this rough establishment, as it should have. Perhaps because Amelia felt so casual and comfortable, something that continued to amaze him about her. She'd left her bonnet at home and wore her hair half up, with the rest trailing down her back as if she'd been undressing before she got the notion to leave the house, which made no sense to him if she'd planned to meet someone. Still, Eli's confusion didn't hinder him from appreciating the way her long, silky hair lay over her shoulders, like a waterfall sliding over rocks that had been smoothed from years of motion.

"You followed me," she asked—no, stated—cutting to the quick before Eli had a chance to, which bothered him more than he cared to admit. "Why?"

He settled in his seat, adopting his best arrogant stare. "Why don't you just tell me whom you're meeting so we can get this over with and I can go home and get some sleep? Better yet, why don't you empty your pockets now so I can take everything home before he even gets here."

"He?"

Her innocent blink almost made him laugh. "Your accomplice. The man you are obviously passing my things off to so he can take them to London and sell."

"Ah," Amelia said, nodding thanks to the barmaid, who'd returned with their fresh pints. She took a sip before answering. "Would it kill you to know I just came here for a drink and a think?"

Eli wasn't positive, but he confessed to himself that it just might. "Do you take me for an idiot?" he returned, before swallowing some ale to keep his temper in check.

Amelia scrutinized him for an uncomfortable moment, ripening a vulnerable feeling in him. "To be honest, I don't know how to take you."

Eli didn't like what the words did to him. It was bad enough how his body continued to react to the defiant woman. The way his heart clenched and his stomach dropped whenever he caught her citrus smell. Or the way his collar felt too tight when he watched her fingers circle each other. Because he wanted to touch those fingers, feel the upraised lines of skin where her scars stood out like heat lightning in the humid summer night.

"Can you be honest with me for once?" he said, searching within for the anger and indignation that was his only shield against her. "You can think and drink at my home."

"But it's too quiet there."

He scoffed. "That makes no sense at all. The house is insufferably noisy."

"Maybe to you," she pointed out patiently, using the tip of her finger to swipe a drop of ale off the corner of her mouth. Eli held the untenable desire to lick it off her finger. "But I grew up in town. It's difficult for me to go to sleep without the hum of a fistfight in the background. Your house is too tame for me to gather my thoughts properly."

Eli should have known better than to ask the woman for an honest conversation. His house too tame? His children? "What could possibly be on your mind that you need to come all the way out here at this hour? It's not safe, by the way."

She snorted in her glass. "I can take care of myself."

A chuckle breached his lips. "Of that, I have no doubt."

Amelia took another sip of ale. A tiny rivulet went unnoticed and inched down her chin, highlighting the smooth skin down her neck. *He* noticed. Eli yearned to reach across their divide and wipe the lonely trail with his palm. But she wouldn't want that ... would she? Sometimes, when she was glaring at him just right, her dark eyes eating him alive, he thought maybe ... just maybe ... she did?

"What does anyone ever think about?" Amelia asked.

Without hesitation, they both answered her question at the same time.

"Work."

She giggled, clinking her glass with his, almost upsetting his ale as he watched on, stultified. A woman had never done that before. It was ghastly. He liked it anyway.

"I would think your work is going well enough," he said, allowing the conversation and her company to lull him into an easy rhythm. "I almost can't believe how well you're doing with the girls. In all honesty, I didn't expect them to take to you so quickly. And what you've done for Michael—" Eli's words caught. A sharp sense of caution took hold. One that he ultimately avoided. "You saw things that I didn't. I should thank you for that."

Amelia inched to the edge of her chair, resting her recalcitrant elbows on the table. "You're welcome. But I also see why the girls have behaved so abominably. They're bored, Eli. They need a change. It wouldn't hurt for you to take them to London, let them enjoy Town."

"London is dangerous," Eli replied quickly, searching for the barmaid for another ale. How had he finished it so quickly? As a rule, he never imbibed overly much. Loose lips were never a good thing. Amelia's cup was still mostly full. When she stayed quiet, Eli felt compelled to continue. "I don't want them to get hurt."

She scrutinized him over the top of her glass. "Why would they get hurt? I lived in London all my life, and I have barely a scratch."

Immediately, Eli zeroed in on her scarred hands. "Forgive me for not believing you."

Amelia rolled her eyes, letting the conversation drop. They drank in silence, with Eli's agitation spreading like a weed. The only thing more agitating about the woman's willingness to speak out of turn was that there was some truth to what she said. He didn't fight it, since in his darkest hours he even acknowledged it to himself—when no one else could hear and he could easily pretend he hadn't entertained those thoughts.

"You think you know everything," he muttered in every direction except for hers.

"No," she said, her smile leaden with pity. "But I think I know what it's like having your future ripped away from you … and the solace that hiding provides for a time—"

"Who says I'm hiding?" Eli asked petulantly.

Amelia ignored him. "The only difference between you and me is that I don't have a past that I can retreat into. Moving forward is my only choice."

"What future was ripped away from you?" His voice turned deep, the malice surprisingly gone.

Her smile flickered brighter, like a firefly calling out to another. "Oh, I don't think there's enough ale here to get me to tell that story right now."

"Another day?" Eli asked hopefully.

She issued a soundless laugh. "Another day."

CHAPTER SEVENTEEN

*A*NOTHER DAY TURNED out to be the very next one. And then the one after that. Eli and Amelia never technically agreed on it, but when she picked up the lantern that second night and walked on the path, she'd known that Eli would follow. Her silence had been her invitation.

Their conversations never matched the depth of that first night. It was as if they'd both realized an invisible line had been smudged but were too hesitant to test if it had been erased entirely.

Eli changed into a completely different person away from Barrington House. It seemed that the further he ventured from the estate, the fewer burdens he carried. Amelia acknowledged that the stress of the home, the children, his previous marriage maintained a hold she didn't truly understand. But she remained open to learning.

With the table between them and a few ales in them, the unlikely couple talked about everything. The grafting that Eli experimented with in the greenhouse … the proper education for young ladies, if or when Michael would begin boarding at Eton.

The topics were seemingly endless; they felt safe in the realization that once Amelia left Barrington, everything divulged would float away as if it had never been spoken at all. The relinquishing of their thoughts and opinions to someone who inhabited such a different sphere of life was a momentary respite from their everyday burdens.

Despite all that, Amelia still couldn't tell him about the flower shop. It was still too raw, an open wound that refused to scab over. Her pride also kept her lips shut over the simple fact that she was embarrassed. She'd tried and she'd failed, and she desperately didn't want Eli to know that side of her. She preferred that he think of her as the brilliant pickpocket instead. He still didn't approve of her humble profession, yet it was making an impression on him.

"How about him?" he asked, jutting his chin toward a man sitting at the bar, gray hair peeking out underneath his workman's cap and his shoulders hunched over the shiny surface like a naked bough overburdened with wet snow.

Eyes shining, Amelia pursed her lips, feigning consideration. Eli was hopeless; he would make such a terrible thief. He had no knack for choosing an appropriate mark. She shook her head.

"Why not?" he asked, adorably flustered. Amelia couldn't pinpoint when Eli had turned the corner in their evenings and become adorable—after her first drink or his? The healing waters of the ale loosened them up around each other, leaving their inhibitions and suppositions at the door. Though, truth be told, Amelia didn't think it had so much to do with the alcohol anymore. She had to stop herself from thinking him adorable the moment they took their seats.

She returned her flagging attention to the workman. "First of all, he's all alone. It's much harder to con a man when he has nothing to divert his focus. Also, look at his forearms, his figure." She paused, allowing Eli to do as she said, taking in the white, curly hairs on the man's rolled-up sleeves, the way his forearms flexed and rolled as he shifted in his seat. "He's fit. I might be able to outrun him in the long run, but I can't be certain about the short. I'm not saying I couldn't do the job, but you should only pick a sure thing. Like the young man to his side. Look at his feet. Look at his legs. They're as long as a giraffe's, and he trips each time he gets up from his seat. He's the better choice, even if he is decades younger."

Eli's smile danced behind his glass despite the lecture. "And what about me?" At her questioning glance, he went on, "At the tournament. Why did you pick me?"

"Oh." Amelia could feel her cheeks brighten. "I didn't. My partner did."

"But you went along with it."

"Yes," she agreed.

"Don't I look fit?"

She gulped, avoiding the whiskers on his chin, the sweet way his hair was mussed in all directions from his forehead. "Yes."

"Don't I look quick?"

"Yes."

He folded his arms over the table, leaning into her, the light from the lanterns glinting off his glasses. "Then why me?"

"Y-you were a sure thing."

A lazy grin crawled on his face. "How so?"

Amelia took a drink. How was it so hot in here all of a sudden? "Michael … children always slow a person down."

He cocked his head. "They didn't slow me down."

"You didn't chase after me."

"I did … in my own way. And you never looked over your shoulder."

"I thought I was in the clear."

"You were overconfident. Hardly the behavior of a professional."

Amelia's pride hurt. "No, it wasn't," she agreed through gritted teeth.

"You know what I think?" Eli asked, twirling his pint around in his hand. "I think you wanted me to catch you."

A great guffaw flew from her throat. Not her most ladylike moment. "You're insane."

"Perhaps." He shrugged before finishing off his ale, his Adam's apple pumping underneath his cravat. "But that doesn't mean I'm wrong."

"Well, you are," Amelia replied, her tone hardening. Now she remembered why they never talked about important things … it had the potential of leading to a fight. "Why would I want you to catch me? Do you think I want to end up hanging in the town square or, worse yet, in the colonies?" She fell against her seatback, irritation pricking all over her skin like she'd been caught lying on an anthill. "Your hubris knows no bounds, you know that? You are such a pompous ass."

Eli laughed in her face, not apologetic in the least. "You just don't like to hear the truth."

"You have no idea what the truth is!"

"Of course I do," he said, signaling for another drink. "You were desperate for a way out of that life and, when you saw me, instantly knew that I was the only man strong enough to pull you out of it." He frowned as if something suddenly came to him. "That reminds me. I offered to teach Michael how to shoot, but he said he didn't want to. He said you told him that guns were for cowards. Why?"

How dare he change the subject so easily, like he hadn't just been denouncing her talent? What did he think they were? Friends?

Amelia finished her drink and began to gather her things.

"Where are you going?" he asked. "I'm not done."

That didn't deter her. She scooted out from the table and was halfway out of the pub before she rounded back to a still-seated Eli. "You want to know why I told Michael that, *my lord*?" Amelia bent so that their noses were almost touching. She watched his eyes dilate and his tongue flick out to lick his full lower lip. She resisted the urge to bite it, and smiled. "Because guns are for cowards. Michael wants to be a knight, and only true knights know that if you're going to take something from anyone, especially something as special as a life, then you must be prepared to get close enough and look them in the eyes when you're doing it."

⇥⇥⇥⇥⇤⇤⇤⇤

AMELIA HADN'T DRUNK too much. She never did. But she still made a point to lose her footing when passing the gray-haired workman as she escaped the pub. He hardly noticed. They never did.

Her fledging freedom took her just outside the building before a hand yanked her from the path.

"Let go of me—" Amelia yelled as Eli wrangled her into the alley at the side of the pub, the narrow space equally deserted of bodies and light.

Even when she stopped struggling, he gripped her by the shoulders, pinning her up against the wooden slats, the flash of his limpid blue eyes showing her just how precipitously she'd nudged him toward his edge.

"Give it back," Eli stated.

Amelia blew a disgruntled exhale in his face, flattening her shoulder blades against the wall. "I didn't take anything."

"You are such a bad liar."

She laughed. "I am an excellent liar."

He returned an arrested stare. "That man works hard every day for all that he has."

"So do I."

"Just give it back, Amelia. You made your point."

With a disgruntled sigh, she reached into her pocket and pulled out the workman's wallet, slamming it into Eli's waiting palm. She wasn't *really* going to take it; she'd had every intention of slipping it back into the man's jacket the next time she saw him … probably. The need to prove to Eli that she could do it had been too great. The incorrigible man always thought he had her number, that she was easy to read.

Without inching away from her, Eli slid the wallet into his coat, and his arm skated across her chest as he made the solemn movement. His chin rose the tiniest amount, just enough to spark her fury anew.

"You were definitely trying to get caught that time," he said. The tenor of Eli's voice, guttural and disapproving, made Amelia's heart beat so hard against her ribcage that she was certain something would crack. Most likely, her sanity.

Her words came out low, even more so when she realized he was staring at her lips while they moved. "That's the last thing I wanted."

Eli's mouth curved, a genuine smile that belied his roguish, whisker-covered face. "See what I mean?" he said to her lips. "Such a bad liar."

This time when he kissed her, Amelia was ready for him. There was no room for shyness or innocent pecks in that lonely alleyway. A torrent of emotion opened between them, unleashing itself, consequences long dismissed. Eli's pelvis lay against hers as his hands cupped her face, angling her mouth for his onslaught. His tongue swept inside her mouth, cutting off any chance of Amelia's rebukes or proper thought. She didn't mind. Not at all. The last thing she wanted to do was talk about what they were doing or contemplate why they shouldn't be doing it.

Despite what it looked like from the outside, Amelia's life was made up of careful calculations, ascertaining the odds of a decision before she made any leap. She didn't want to do that with Eli. Besides, somewhere deep down, she was already well aware of the answer. The chance that whatever boiled between them would end badly was close to one hundred percent. A smart girl would have buttoned up her dress (yes, because he was unbuttoning it now) and run for the hills, keeping any sense of self-preservation she could. Molly would have been so disappointed in her … but Molly wasn't here.

Eli's rough fingertips flicked her dress open and lay flat against her neck. His kisses had lightened, and their mouths rested against each other as their spicy, ale-tinted breathing mixed. He tapped his middle finger in the hollow of her throat, much slower than the pulse she could feel running riot within.

"I thought you said we weren't going to see each other much," Amelia said, breaking her need for silence. She couldn't help herself. He was making her so nervous; her body was humming with so much anticipation, each hair on her skin stood up and screamed for him to act.

He chuckled, raising his eyes to her. "Every day I wage a war with myself," he said, sliding his finger lower until it stopped over the lip of her corset. "I tell myself that I will not talk to you, will not leave my office to see where you are, will not hide behind a door while you tell the children another of your inappropriate stories." Slowly, he peeled her corset lower, releasing one breast from its confines. The cool night air instantly made the nipple pucker and reach toward Eli as he circled it delicately with the pad of his thumb.

Amelia clawed at her bottom lip with her teeth, suffering through his ministrations, worried about letting out any sound. It had nothing to do with where they were; the shadows worked as a perfect cover. Her reluctance came from her inexperience. She'd never truly done this before—whatever this was—and was afraid to make a mistake. A born perfectionist, Amelia hated doing anything wrong, even when it was her first time.

So struck was she by the sensations he was giving her breasts, Amelia didn't notice his other hand travel down her skirts, casually lifting them as if she was prone on a bed and not up against a pub wall. Her skin sizzled, like water flung on a hot fire, when his palm found her naked thigh, following the heated path higher and higher up her body.

"You even haunt me at night," he said, licking the side of her neck, biting the tender patch so hard she gasped. "Do you know what it means when I say I pump myself?"

Fighting through the fog of her mind, Amelia nodded. She couldn't give him specifics, but she had an idea.

He leaned in to kiss the swell of her breast, and she felt him smile. "Each night. I can't go to sleep without doing it. I hold my cock, dreaming I am inside you, dreaming you are the one finding release and not me."

Now, she had no idea what he was talking about. Not that it mattered. The only thing that did matter was the roving hand that had a mind of its own as it caressed between her thighs, massaging and tickling along the way. When Eli reached the spot he was searching for, Amelia was too curious to be shy. In fact, her legs fell open even more as he played with her hair, stroking the lips of her core until one finger moved inside her.

Amelia's spine jerked straight against the wall. Eli might have said something, might have warned her, but at the same time he lowered his head to capture the nipple he'd been tormenting, waving his tongue with the same rhythmic insistence as his hand underneath her skirts.

It was too much. It was not enough. Amelia wrapped her arms around his head, keeping him closer, but also keeping herself from falling. He waged a war against her, dismantling her defenses one by one. She was absolutely helpless against the sensations he released on her.

Amelia's shock wore off quickly as her body reminded her that her mind was no longer needed; it could take it from there. She echoed Eli's movements, at some point even grabbing the lead, grinding her hips against his hand, pushing her nipple against his magical teeth. Overcome by the alchemy of his actions, she gave herself up to them like a sacrifice at an altar, knowing her supplication was for the greater good.

She egged him on—begged him, more likely—as she contorted her body to take more of his finger. His breathing became ragged as he inserted another, and the pain was worth the pleasure because a conflagration arose so mightily inside her that Amelia thought she would singe anyone who looked at her.

Her head banged back on the wall, and she saw stars, bright bursts of light that opened up the night sky, threatening to drag her up. She might even have encouraged it.

It was all over too quickly. Amelia's skirt was flicked down, her dress buttoned up, her conscience reclaimed before she was ready for it.

To his credit, Eli stayed with her. With an edgy expression, he arranged his trousers and fell against the wall, his shoulder butted alongside hers. The only evidence of their clandestine experience was the shallowness of their breaths, the swaths of sweat Amelia spied on the top of his forehead, similar to her own. That was where the similarities ended. She felt entirely boneless, to the point where she worried how she would make it back to the house. He, on the other hand, was strung as tight as a corset string, his stilted movements giving off the impression that he would, once again, enjoy the company of his hand that night. Amelia would have laughed if she'd had the energy.

When she felt the muscles on his side tense as if to move, Amelia knew she had to speak. She couldn't let his possible regret ruin one of the most informative moments of her life.

"Please don't say you were out of your mind."

Eli turned to her, his expression difficult to read. When he opened his mouth, Amelia almost put her hand over it, so afraid was she of what he might say. In the end, she didn't have to.

The pub door swung open, diverting their attention.

Two men, their feet unsteady, fell out into the moonlight at the end of the alleyway. "Someone must have taken it! I didn't just drop it. I'm not some simple-minded bastard."

The workman! He must have just realized his wallet had been stolen. Amelia pinned herself to the wall even more, sliding down the alley away from the voices.

"Oh, nowsh, Jack. I never shaid you were," the workman's friend replied, his words all slurring together in a drunken babble. "I just meant maybe you'll have better luck finding it at home. I'm too tired to look around now."

"Oh, what do you know, you drunken idiot!" the workman said, peering into the alley.

Eli straightened away from the wall. Amelia tugged him back to her. "What are you doing?" she whispered. "Stay here. He can't see us."

He gave her an incredulous look. "I'm going to return the man's wallet."

"Not now! It's not the best time."

"It's the perfect time."

Amelia's eyebrows shot to her hairline. "Eli—"

But he was already gone. Eli left her behind and walked toward the drunk men as casually as if he were attending a Sunday picnic. Still, Amelia did not budge. This wasn't going to be pretty. Happy or sad, drunk men never were.

"Gentlemen," Eli said, cutting off the men from their argument. From her vantage point, Amelia could see them eye Eli suspiciously, squaring their shoulders at the man whose accent and clothes were so different from theirs. If they remembered him from their shared time in the pub, they didn't let on. "I think I have something you are looking for," he said to the workman.

The man snatched the wallet out of Eli's hands the moment it was presented. No thanks, not even a grunt of appreciation. "How was it that you had it, in your pocket, no less?" the older man sneered.

To his credit, Eli didn't seem to be put off by the rude behavior. "I spotted it on the ground on my way out. I was just on my way back to the pub to ask if it belonged to anyone."

"Is that right?" the workman asked, not believing Eli's story for a minute.

His friend nudged him with his elbow. "That'sh the viscount," he whispered. "Good evening, my lord," the friend offered to Eli while trying for a bow that almost toppled him.

Eli stretched his hands out and righted the man before any harm was done.

The workman didn't appear half so impressed. Just as they were rarely pretty, drunk men were rarely impressed. "The viscount, eh?" He chuckled. "Barrington, is that right?"

"It is," Eli replied, his voice flinty. Amelia's whole body tightened. The stupid man. She'd told him not to confront them. Nothing good ever came from confronting someone who was angry, let alone as wet as the ocean.

The workman tipped toward his friend. They both seemed to be using the other to keep standing. "You'd think a man with all that money wouldn't go around stealing an honest lad's wallet."

"As I said," Eli murmured. "I was keeping it safe until—"

"Keeping it!" The man guffawed. "From what I heard, you couldn't even keep your wife. And now you think you can keep my wallet?"

"Come on now, Jack," his friend said, casting an apologetic glance at Eli. He threw his arm around the workman's shoulders, steering him away. "Off to bed with you."

The workman, wallet safe, let himself be towed. But his laughter kept cutting into the air like picks to an ice block, his words "Couldn't even keep his wife ..." trailing into the maudlin night.

Amelia watched Eli for an interminable minute. Watched as he didn't move, not even a flinch as the men departed. When she couldn't take the silence anymore, she crept toward him. Reaching out a hand, she'd almost touched his shoulder when he spun around to her.

"We should go," he said. Flat. Emotionless. Final.

Amelia only nodded. Enough had been said in that alleyway.

CHAPTER EIGHTEEN

THE WALK BACK to Barrington was quiet. Amelia had so many questions, but she didn't know how to broach their silence, or if she even should.

Eli walked next to her, not shying away when the back of his hand brushed against hers. It stunned Amelia how much she wanted him to reach out and take her hand, and they could just hold on like a pair of innocent sweethearts. But they weren't sweethearts, and after their time in the alley, they weren't innocent either.

Then it struck her. When had Amelia ever lived within the realm of propriety? Eli wouldn't hold her hand; that was fine. He still needed someone to hold his. And she would do that for him.

Quickly, before she talked herself out of it, she wrapped her hand around Eli's, squeezing for extra measure. When he returned her squeeze, she let out a silent sigh of relief. And couldn't find another breath. They were holding hands! And she liked it so very, very much. It made the entirety of her skin tingle and pop like fireworks.

"My wife is dead."

There went the fireworks.

Amelia searched Eli's face, but found nothing more than a serious, matter-of-fact expression. "I know that," she replied softly.

"No," he said. "You don't know how she died … when … how …"

"Not in childbirth, then?"

Eli sucked in a deep breath. Amelia used her thumb to caress the side of his hand, encouraging him to open to her. In this charged moment, he reminded her of a dormant spring flower that had been tricked into blooming in the winter. With enough warmth and attention, she could make anything open.

"We married when we were twenty, young enough to believe that we were marrying because we loved one another and that it had nothing to do with our families. Marianne was so beautiful. I was just so damned grateful that someone like her would ever look in my direction."

Amelia's chest hurt. Guilt. She didn't want to hate the beautiful Marianne, but she did. Desperately.

Eli went on. "But it didn't last. Marianne was bored in the country. So I took her to town. It was then I realized that she was just bored of me. She liked the parties and the gossip, being in the middle of the *ton*'s vicious games …" His words stuck, lost in the web of memories. "I tried to give her what she wanted. I was so desperate to please her, but she didn't want me. She never did. She wanted men like Lord Charles."

Amelia stopped short. That name was familiar. She didn't know much of the aristocracy, but one would have to live under a boulder not to know about Lord Charles. He was one of the most popular knights in the Eglinton tournament, and the newspapers barely went a day without mentioning him. "The earl of Somerset?"

Eli nodded, his lips in a thin line. "He was rumored to be one of her affairs, among others. Stupidly, I thought the children would bind her to me, but with each pregnancy, she only hated me more, what it did to her body, the demands it made on her. Motherhood didn't suit her. When she asked to leave, I didn't have the heart to fight for her. I just asked that she live on the Continent, to save the family from the gossip." He gave her a wan smile. "I should have known it wouldn't work."

Amelia's heart was breaking for the poor man. She tried to imagine a young Eli, so fresh with love, so intent on creating a family that he'd never known. To have it all crash down so disastrously in his face. No wonder he hid away; no wonder he acted so bitter.

"Did you hear from her?" she asked.

"Not at first," he said. "Marianne stayed true to her word, but then I'd hear about the gambling debts, the wild parties, the paramours. It all happened so fast. Then, out of nowhere, I received a letter. I thought Marianne was just asking for more money. I threw the letter on my desk, never opening it. A month later, her lawyer wrote to tell me she was dead. When I finally opened her letter, I realized she'd been asking to come home. She'd realized she was sick and wanted to live out her last days with her children. She'd begged for my forgiveness. I was angry at her for so long, and now I don't think I'll ever be able to forgive myself for how I treated her. She didn't deserve it."

Amelia squeezed his hand again. "Maybe you need to forgive both of you. You were so young, Eli."

A rough sound came from his throat. "Does that matter?"

She leaned into his side. "You know it does."

Eli didn't say anything to that, though Amelia thought she saw a sad smile flit across his face. The hand holding hers became firmer; his shoulders seemed to straighten as if a mysterious load had been lifted.

They walked a few more beats before Eli broke their lull. "Thank you," he said. "And I was out of my mind." When he saw Amelia's brow furrow, he added, "Back at the pub, with you. I *was* out of my mind." He brought her hand up to his lips and kissed it. "But in the best way possible."

The butterflies in Amelia's stomach fluttered double time after that.

She feared the silence of the night would make the journey uncomfortable, forcing them to make conversation or excuses for their behavior, but it was just the opposite. The obsidian backdrop of the path, devoid of texture or perspective, acted as a bubble, hiding their feelings from the outside world. For those twenty minutes, they were just Eli and Amelia, man and woman. Not lord and pickpocket. They could breathe and just be. Perhaps that was why they ambled so slowly.

"Do you see that?" he asked, breaking Amelia from her giddy trance.

She blinked awake, following his gaze toward the darkness ahead. It took a few seconds, but eventually, her vision focused on a lump in the road ahead of them.

"Must be an animal," she said, grateful that they had something concrete they could speak of, something that pulled their minds off one another.

Eli's steps took up speed; he dropped her hand as they came within a few feet of the object. Amelia told herself she didn't care, though she couldn't help but notice how cold her palm became without his around it.

"Amelia, stay back."

"Why?" she asked, recognizing the alarm in his voice. Before she could make out the form, he pushed her behind him, obscuring her sight.

Not to be waylaid, she nudged his shoulders out of the way, her feet instantly halting as she finally saw what was on the ground.

It wasn't an animal at all. It was a body. And even though it was bloated and bloody, even though it was covered in dirt and mud, Amelia would have recognized it anywhere.

Jenny.

She covered her mouth, masking a wail that threatened to splinter her apart.

Eli's voice rang out harsher. "Goddammit, Amelia, I told you to stay back."

But she wouldn't listen. Couldn't. Her friend's body lay crumpled on the ground, limbs tucked into each other neatly as if she'd decided that a patch of dirt was as good a place as any to lie down for a nap. For a ridiculous moment, Amelia almost hoped her friend *was* sleeping there, but the ragged cut across Jenny's neck quickly dispelled that notion.

"Fuck," she heard Eli murmur as he crouched next to the body. He moved Jenny onto her back, making it easier for Amelia to see her friend's once-crystal-blue eyes open and sharklike, dead and cloudy, no light shining from within. Quickly, she scanned Eli's face to check if he remembered the girl but found it was unnecessary. Jenny wasn't wearing her blonde wig. Bright red hair lay like limp tentacles across her face and shoulders, tangling over the blade mark.

The slash at her neck was clean and straight, making it evident to Amelia that this wasn't just an ordinary murder.

"What did you say?" Eli asked, startling her. Had she said something? Amelia didn't think so.

He straightened to stand next to her, peering at her curiously. "You said there was no blood."

Had she? Amelia shook her head; this was all so surreal. She couldn't believe this was Jenny. How had this happened? No, not how ... *why* had this happened?

"Um ..." Amelia extended her arm to point at Jenny's neck, shaking it a few times to get it to stop trembling. "Her neck. There's no blood there. Only on the clothes. Someone must have killed her a few days ago and dumped the body here."

Amelia didn't like the way Eli was looking at her. Like she knew more than she was saying ... which she supposed she did. "Why would someone do that?" he asked.

"To distance themselves from the murder."

"Why?"

She met his gaze. "How should I know?"

Frozen in thought, they continued to stare at the body, only relenting when Eli asked, "Do you know her?"

Amelia took too long to answer. Molly would be shaking her head at her bad show, but Eli wasn't like Molly. He trusted people. "No," Amelia whispered.

That word, so small and so untrue, was enough for Eli. With a ragged exhale, he ran a hand over his face as if willing himself to take action.

"I'm sorry," he said, wrapping his arms around her, moving her further away from her friend … the corpse. "I don't know why I asked you that. Let's get back to the house so I can make plans on what to do. What a waste of life."

Amelia let him guide her down the road, allowing him to hold most of her weight. Her head didn't stop spinning until sleep pulled her into its depths much later. Her last thoughts were the same ones that had run on a loop ever since she recognized her friend.

This wasn't a waste. It was a sign.

CHAPTER NINETEEN

A MELIA COULDN'T GET out of bed.

The following morning, after trying, and failing, to extricate herself from her sheets, she claimed defeat and informed Mrs. Hutchinson that she was too ill to work with the children. There was no way she would be able to put on clothes and a smile for the twins. She was strong, but not that strong.

And she needed to think.

Harry's Boys. It had to be.

There were the only ones with a score to settle with her, and they knew she and Jenny had worked together. Even though their line of work made this sort of ending plausible for someone like Jenny, Amelia couldn't shake the supposition that this had been a warning for *her*. Harry's Boys had found her—most likely they'd wrangled the information from Jenny—and they were done waiting for their money.

Even Jenny's expensive emerald ring hadn't been enough to bargain for her life. Before Eli had whisked her away from the body, Amelia had spied Jenny's finger, noticing a mark from where the ring had been taken. Jenny had told her that she would keep the ring for herself and not give it to Molly. It seemed that she'd kept it as long as she could.

Amelia wrenched herself from the tall seat near the window where she watched Eli and Michael conduct another fencing lesson. Kitty and Cecily cheered while sitting near the fountain, always on Michael's side despite the constant heckling of their brother.

Amelia slumped to the basin and ewer that a blessed servant had noiselessly refilled this morning, and splashed water over her face. What was she going to do? She couldn't stay here while her presence put the family in danger. However, she couldn't go back to London with nothing to show for it. Stealing from Eli's home was out of the question; she'd known it for days but hadn't found the courage to acknowledge it.

She ventured back to the window, leaning against the sill as the family broke out in hysterics. Eli was hiding behind Cecily as Michael charged at him, causing the girl to beam from the attention. For all his faults, Eli's decision to keep his family in the country had been the right one. The love, though not evident at first, was obvious between the father and his children. He only ever sought to protect them from the relentless hurt and disappointment the world was so good at providing. Their mother had made a mistake, and their world would never let them stop paying for it.

Melancholy swarmed Amelia like an insidious fog. The girls resented their father's overprotection, but they had no clue what he was shielding them from. Did they realize how much he loved them? Could they appreciate anything that had been given so freely?

Would Amelia's life have been different if she'd had a father like Eli? Would she have been a baker's wife? Or a shopkeeper's?

A lord's ...

Ridding her head of that nonsense, Amelia dashed away from the window, her gaze falling on a bunch of bright pink peonies crowded in the vase by her bed. Mrs. Hutchinson had the flowers changed daily, no doubt because the greenhouse held so many.

Too many.

The girls had been right when they showed her the neglected plants. The majority of them would die within the next few weeks. It would be a waste.

Perhaps this was one waste Amelia could do something about.

THIS WAS GETTING ridiculous, Eli thought later that night as he retreated into his greenhouse. He'd barely given his strawberries any attention that week. His focus had been on other things … and other people.

With heavy feet, he walked to his worktable, measuring how well his plants were accepting his latest grafting experiment. *So far, so good.* With any luck, this latest combination would prove successful, and he'd be able to plant the offspring in his fields next spring.

Eli never knew what to say when his colleagues and other landowners asked him why he held such a fascination with strawberries. They weren't exactly a necessary staple of the English diet, more a luxury for those who could afford the sweet fruit. A jolt of anguish locked him too tight when he remembered that strawberries and a dash of cream over poundcake were his mother's favorite dessert. Certainly, that couldn't be the source of his obsession. He could hardly find another reason for the allure. Apples, pears, cucumbers, squash … those would make a more respectable, reasonable crop to pile his energies into.

But Eli was coming to terms with the fact that he wasn't as reasonable as he thought. And the rope that was tethering his reason was only getting laxer. He had one person to blame for that.

Which was another reason he was in the greenhouse. From his stool, he had a perfect view of the back of his home and would be able to see if Amelia ventured to the pub. And, most likely, he would follow her, strawberries be damned. Because now that he had tasted Amelia again, he didn't think he would ever be able to stop wanting to.

Eli's life would be so much easier if she didn't leave her room that night. It did his ego no favor knowing that he was helpless against Amelia—the temptation to be with her was too strong. It served as an uncomfortable reminder of his youth, when he'd behaved the same way around Marianne, trailing after her like a puppy, performing for scraps of her attention.

But Amelia was different. She'd seemed willing enough last night when he finally kissed her—more than willing. And during their talks at the pub, she appeared to value his company, even enjoying the combative conversations. Still, Eli applied caution. He couldn't lose himself in his wishful thinking. He'd done that before with another beautiful, ardent woman. And that one had deemed him not enough. Not passionate enough; not loving enough; not man enough for her.

Wouldn't Amelia, a woman who'd been molded by the hectic vibrancy of London, eventually do the same? She would never be able to convince him that there weren't men waiting for her in the city. Men who could shoot and fence with finesse, swashbuckling, dangerous types with no pasts or responsibilities holding them hostage.

"I am a fool."

But even saying the words out loud did little to hasten the punch of rightness Eli received when he saw Amelia step out of the house and into the moonlight. Her mere presence did that to him.

He picked himself up from his stool, ready to follow her down the path to the village, but Amelia surprised him by changing direction to the greenhouse. Did she know he was there? Probably not.

She entered quietly, gravitating toward a great palm frond before striking a match and lighting a lantern at the far end of the structure. She looked so peaceful, meandering through the plants, lightly caressing the petals that reached out to her as if she was the sun. It amused Eli to think he had something in common with a flower.

He needed to make his presence known, lest she think he was some creepy voyeur—which he was in danger of becoming. But he'd lost control of his voice, and it boomed like a cannon, making her jump. "You shouldn't be here," he called out from his end of the greenhouse.

Amelia dashed a waxy leaf out of her face, squinting toward him. "You scared me to death!" she wheezed.

"My apologies," Eli replied, lowering his voice. *Get a hold of yourself, man!* "But it isn't safe for you to be out here."

"I'm sure you will restrain yourself," she called back, her voice clouded with insolent amusement.

"I didn't mean me," he muttered. There was a killer on the loose, for fuck's sake. Though, now that Amelia mentioned it, she wasn't particularly safe from him either. His control was like water in his palms, leaking from every crack.

Eli threw his pencil on the table and fixed his glasses over his nose. *Contain yourself,* he admonished himself as he walked the length of the structure away from his carefully manicured experiments into the wild growth of vegetation he'd never had the heart to clear away. It was like entering another world, one of exotic color and untold mystery. As usual, when he found Amelia, she looked perfectly at ease within the chaos.

"This is *my* space," he said, keeping his distance. Coward that he was, Eli was hoping for a signal, something to clue him on how Amelia felt. After their lustful foray, he thought there might be a second, and (hopefully) a third, but then they'd found the body in the road and life had bled into his dreams. Not particularly spiritual or religious, Eli wasn't one for signs. He wondered if she was.

Amelia didn't seem the type, but Eli didn't even know if she had a type. A chameleon of vast degrees, the woman was a mixed bag, a little bit of everything, an amalgamation of fearlessness and adventure. An exquisite one.

But that didn't mean she was oblivious. The children had

informed Eli that she'd decided to stay in her room that day. Clearly, the body had unnerved her, which was saying something, since she'd grown up with London as her playground. Amelia must have still been out of sorts, because she'd come outside in her nightgown. Blessedly, the diaphanous white dress was covered with a robe, thin though it was, and she held a stack of papers in her hand along with her own pencil. Eli should have averted his eyes, but he hadn't the willpower. This was *his* greenhouse! So, he soaked in her curves, his temperature rising as he noticed she wasn't wearing a corset and her body was as unrestrained as his desire.

Amelia's owl eyes blinked at him before turning toward the overgrown flowers that were so abundant and out of control that they looked to be growing out of the ceiling like in some silly fairytale. "I thought you would take better care of your workspace."

Eli's jaw tightened. He opened his mouth to explain that the area she was in was not technically his workspace, but thought better of it.

"What are you doing here?" he said instead. Gruffly. To make a damn point.

She placed the papers on the table. "Taking inventory," she replied, the lilt in her voice betraying excitement. "I spoke to the twins before they went to bed. We are determined to get started as soon as we can."

Get started?

"Thank you again for letting us use the flowers," she went on, not recognizing his confusion. "I know they were your wife's; I promise we won't take them all." Amelia dashed a waxy palm out of her face. "Besides, plants should be pruned. It helps them grow better in the future. I'd thought you would know that."

Eli held some much-needed questions on the tip of his tongue. He had absolutely no idea what the woman was chattering on about, but his ego pushed itself to the front of the line. "I *do* know about that!" he said, stomping in her direction only to be smacked in the face by a monstera deliciosa. In his embarrassed rage, he almost ripped the damn thing from the root. "I know more about plants than—"

Amelia skirted around him, her earthy fragrance hitting him like a punch in the gut. "So these are the infamous experiments?" she asked, her genuine curiosity doing the most to assuage his temper. "I've never seen so many plump strawberries in all my life!"

Eli's indignation ebbed like a low tide as he watched Amelia meander to his side of the building and scan his tables. He didn't have that many strawberries. He preferred to work with only a handful of plants at a time, knowing the constant care and attention they needed. However, she was right about one thing, he concluded with pride. They were plump. Wonderfully so.

"Don't touch that!" he barked suddenly.

Amelia's finger stalled in the air. Her eyes did their magic, taking up the whole of her face. And then she smiled. Patronizingly. "Why not? Aren't strawberries meant to be eaten?"

Eli ran a disgruntled hand through his hair. "Not these. Not yet, anyway." He hadn't meant to sound like such a hungry bear, but dammit, he wasn't used to having people in his greenhouse … touching things. It made him feel entirely too exposed, like he was naked in front of all his peers. But Amelia wasn't his peer. And he would much rather she be naked with him.

He desperately needed to stop thinking like that.

She needed to leave. Now. Or else he wasn't sure what might happen. Damned if the fantasies weren't already swirling in his head though.

Eli tried for a polite smile; he was fairly sure he just looked constipated. "Isn't it time for you to be going to bed? I'm glad you took the day off, but I'm sure the girls will run you ragged tomorrow. By the way, your job is far from done. They are still hellions. Cecily fed her pony ale again. The damn thing couldn't walk straight for an hour."

Amelia sniggered, backing away from the strawberries.

"It's not funny!" he railed. "You're supposed to be helping me."

He began to crowd her. It wasn't lascivious in nature, even though Eli could feel the hair on his arms start to tingle the closer he came to her. Amelia was like a damned magnet attracting his very essence. Raising his arms, he attempted to herd her away from the table, back to her side of the greenhouse.

But she wouldn't budge, intent on leaning over his strawberries again. "I've told you. It's simple. They're bored. Women need purpose, just like men," she said absent-mindedly as her nose dipped much too close to the red fruit. Her brows shot up. In appreciation? Was she impressed by the size? She should be. Most women would be.

Goddammit, now *he* was growing in size. What the hell was wrong with him? Eli had stood next to many women. No, that wasn't true. Definitely not lately. And no one like her.

"I'm amazed how you got them so big," Amelia said, much too innocently. "Grow them any bigger and a lady won't be able to get them in her mouth."

Eli suppressed the loudest groan of his life. For a woman on the streets, there was still a lot for her to learn. Or was she playing with him? A few days ago, he might have answered yes, but now he wasn't so sure. Despite all her worldliness, there was an incorruptibility to Amelia, which continued to perplex and enthrall him.

Surreptitiously, he shifted his cock in his pants. It didn't help. "They're not that big," he replied modestly.

"They're extraordinary," she breathed, bending further over the table. "Is this your best crop so far?"

"Um, yes," he admitted, speaking to her like … well, like a colleague. "I'm keeping an eye on it, but so far, it's incredibly resistant to diseases. The rootstock is hardy, and I grafted it with a scion from one of my most proficient fruiting strands."

Amelia stood up to face him. "What will you do then?"

"I'll have to write a paper of my findings, and lecture at the

Horticultural Society. If this varietal is as strong as I think it is, many landowners will want to grow it."

She smiled, and it was like she was wrapping two strong arms around his heart. "And then everyone will be eating strawberries and cream."

Eli nodded, slightly abashed. "As you say."

Amelia swiped a few strings of black hair off her face, tucking them behind her ear, upsetting her pencil from its precarious perch. At the same time, they reached for it on the ground, just narrowly missing bumping heads.

Eli came out the victor, snatching the pencil and handing it to her, not obsessing over her hand as it grazed his, the way her skin felt as downy as Jerusalem sage.

He was too close now. He'd warned himself and, dolt that he was, didn't listen. Eli could see the golden striations in her eyes, the lines in her lips, the wisps of baby hairs that clung along her forehead that she was never quite able to pull back in her bun.

He cleared his throat. And then had to do it again. "Um ... you mentioned purpose? Women need it? I ... uh ... thought marriage was their purpose."

Amelia sniffed, though she didn't move away. Did she want him to touch her again? Like he had last night? He could still smell her on his fingers; still feel the insides of her core pulsing restlessly against him. Needing him.

"It might surprise you to know that marriage isn't the only thing on a woman's mind. We grow up with other dreams too."

"And what was your dream?" Eli asked.

Slowly. Excruciatingly slowly, Amelia licked her bottom lip. "Why do you ask?"

"I'm just trying to get to know you."

"I thought that's what we were doing at the pub?"

He shook his head. "No. You were holding back from me there."

"So were you."

That was true. "Why do you think that is?" he asked.

Amelia's smile was wistful. "Because we're afraid the other might not like what they hear. Although ... maybe we would surprise each other."

Eli could see the wanting in her eyes. How could a woman like her ever want someone like him? Boring. Set in his ways. A widower. Not a knight.

Before he could stop himself, Eli reached out and skimmed his fingers over the little hairs on her forehead. They were so soft, as soft as baby's breath. "The only thing you do is surprise me."

He felt her hands at his waist, pulling him toward her. That was the signal he was hoping for. She wanted him just as much as he wanted her. Thank the Lord.

When Eli finally lowered his head, Amelia reached toward him—

—and then jerked away.

Evil. So evil. "I'll only kiss you again if you let me eat one of your strawberries," she said, her eyes in full sparkle mode.

This was why a man's brain and his cock would never truly be friends. Because everything inside Eli screamed at him to drop Amelia like the bad habit she was becoming and then pick her up and carry her back to her room, dumping her gracelessly outside her door.

However, his brain wasn't in charge. It never was when she was around. So, he did what any man would do when a beautiful, annoying, willful woman said there was a chance he could kiss her again. He plucked a damned strawberry. Hell, he plucked ten just to be sure.

Eli wanted to kiss her until she was too tired to stand. And then he wanted to kiss her as he laid her on the ground.

He could always grow more strawberries. Just as she'd declared—he was good at what he did.

Amelia watched, curious, her mouth slightly open, her breathing harsher, as he lifted one luscious strawberry to her lips, offering her the pointy tip. When she went to bite it, Eli played with her, moving it just out of her reach. He did that a few more times before she caught up with him, snagging the fruit, and the luscious juices spilled out in a heavenly burst. She made a humming noise that Eli was certain would haunt him forever.

Transfixed by the way her lips pressed together as she swallowed, he rubbed the remainder of the strawberry over them, painting them red, teasing them until they were as crimson and decadent as the fruit he based his life around.

I could base my life around her, Eli thought sinfully, not having the strength to chastise himself. He had all day to do that tomorrow. For now … for now, he would feast.

He popped the rest of the strawberry in his mouth and kissed her with a sense of hunger he'd never experienced before. Her mouth was sweet and warm, welcoming and full of his tongue. He plundered, allowing his need to release the fantasies that had wrecked him since the day they met.

Eli wanted her. Unabashedly. Completely.

Just as Amelia wanted him. Her hands were everywhere. Tugging his shirt up at his waist, throwing his jacket off his shoulders, upsetting the glasses on his nose. She painted her body to his, pressing into his chest, hooking a foot behind his calf. It astounded him. Eli had never had a woman express herself so freely with him. He'd never experienced a woman want him so much. It was a heady feeling, like drinking a bottle of champagne in one gulp. It made him feel like a real man—the only man for her.

Which could only explain his uncharacteristic actions. In a fluid motion, Eli picked her up off the floor and sat her on the table, swiping—though not hurting—his plants to the side to make room. His lips never leaving hers, he unbuttoned her dress from her neck all the way down to her solar plexus, opening the fabric wide so he could relish the swell of her breasts as they strained above her corset. He palmed one with the delicacy and respect he used in his work, coaxing the luscious mound from the undergarment so that the nipple—rosy and peaked—strained expectantly toward him.

Amelia broke away from their kiss, her breath heaving, her dark eyes full of the animation and disbelief that he shared. How had they gotten here? Had it been inevitable?

She was waiting for his move. She braced her hands against the table, her shoulders wide. Gently, Eli focused on her other breast so that both nipples trembled back at him. He wanted to lick them until she screamed, but his strawberries caught his attention.

He brought one more to her lips, allowing her to take another bite. Then he stroked the strawberry over her nipple, gently rounding it over the pale expanse, over the peaks and valleys of her skin, soon following with his tongue. She'd been correct—the strawberry was delicious, but it was nothing compared to the taste of her. The earthy, salty, tangy, overwhelming flavor of her body.

Eli had heard people say that you ate with your eyes first. He'd never agreed, though now he was reconsidering. His hands clung to Amelia's sides as he lavished her with tongue, sucking and drinking her until he'd committed her memory. On his deathbed, this was what he would remember. This moment was what he would relive. Tonguing the tiny mole just above her right breast. Biting her nipple just hard enough to hear her yelp with the perfect mixture of pain and excitement. Being thoroughly intoxicated.

But like any other drunkard, Eli wasn't satisfied. He craved more.

In one fell swoop, he lifted her off the table and turned her around, bending her until her cheek pressed against the wood.

"What ... what are you doing?" she asked, her limbs tensing under his guidance.

"Something you'll enjoy," Eli said, raising her skirts, one tantalizing inch at a time. He forced himself to be patient, for his benefit as much as for hers. He didn't know when he'd have this opportunity again. He didn't want to rush it.

Over her shoulder, he saw Amelia's hands make fists against

the table before flattening out. When he tried to spread her legs further apart, she rebelled slightly, requiring more gentle coaxing until she did his bidding. "Shh," he whispered in her ear, tugging the lobe into his mouth. "Let me do this. I'm desperate to know what you taste like."

"T-taste?" she said, her voice low and husky.

Eli nodded against her head, trailing wet kisses along her neck and shoulders, down her back until he was kneeling on the floor behind her. He skimmed her undergarments down her legs until her bottom half was completely naked in front of him.

He heard her gasp when he looped his hands underneath her pelvis and pulled her bottom out even more toward him so he could admire everything. Eli had read once about a flower in America that only bloomed once a year. People would come from all over to wait in the dead of night for this shy cactus to open its petals and reveal its beauty. Even as the dedicated horticulturist that he was, Eli couldn't imagine wasting his time for that one moment.

But now, as he kneeled at the altar between Amelia's thighs, he realized that 365 days was nothing. The wait was nothing compared to the vision he now saw unfurling before him. He smoothed his hand over Amelia's creamy backside, marveling at the succulent globes, enamored by her body—by the fact that she was even allowing him to touch her.

Eli couldn't wait any longer. He lowered his head into the pink folds of her sex, offering a delicate lick. Amelia lurched into the table, and he chuckled against her, making her squirm even more.

"Sorry," he said, pulling back. "I should have warned you."

She laughed nervously. "I don't think anything you could have done would have warned me of that."

"Do you want more?" he teased.

"Yes, please."

Without pause, Eli returned to his work, giving the woman what she wanted. Or hoping to. Because ... he'd actually never performed this act before. The only thing that calmed his nerves was that it seemed like Amelia was a novice as well. He hadn't expected that. To be honest, he always felt like a bumbling fool around her when it came to things of a sexual nature. Eli wasn't naïve; Amelia's childhood and lifestyle most likely made her more experienced than him. Marianne had been the first woman he'd made love to, and their lovemaking hadn't been the experimental kind.

Eli's head housed in between Amelia's thighs was pure imagination come to life. He didn't want to condemn it with self-doubt, though he desperately didn't want to appear like he didn't know what he was doing, either.

He was a technical man, one who liked order and books, rules to follow, arrows that pointed the way. He had none of that here; he had to feel his way along. And listen for clues.

It took Amelia some time, but luckily for Eli, she began to offer them.

Sinking deeper into her sex, he found the little pearl beneath her hood and sucked it with the vigor of a penitent. Amelia mewed on the table, her body seemingly at odds with the sensations, pulling away and pushing into his mouth. When her breathing increased and her body found a rhythm against his tongue, Eli realized he was on the right path.

He increased his speed, playing with her, broadening his strokes, tasting her fruit, coming to the conclusion that nothing tasted better than pure woman. When his tongue couldn't move fast enough, Amelia worked against him, using him to reach fulfillment. It was all so carnal and eye-opening, finding what made this woman come, what made her cry out and grip the table like she was splitting in two. He could only watch in abject wonder as she came apart, tensing and then releasing, her folds opening further in deep relaxation and satiation.

Eli wiped his mouth against his sleeve, sitting back on his heel as Amelia slumped against the table. This couldn't be gentleman-ly behavior, but he wondered if she would let him sit like this all night. When she shuddered, he shook his head at his nonsensical, love-struck thoughts, pulling her undergarments up and flicking her skirts down so she was covered and warm against the cool night air.

Amelia straightened her arms against the table, picking herself up to stand, though she still didn't turn to face Eli. Immediately, worry plagued him. Had he done something wrong? Gone too far? Could the most erotic sexual act of his life have been one-sided and selfish?

Eli's cock pulsed angrily in his trousers, ready and waiting for him to relieve himself. He hadn't even considered it. All he'd wanted was to bring her satisfaction.

He cleared his throat as he watched Amelia pass her hand over her head, combing the hair off her face. Eli wanted to say something, anything, but he didn't trust his voice. He was also afraid he might apologize, and doing that might absolutely crush him. He'd thought she enjoyed it. Had he been wrong?

Finally, Amelia turned. Her face was damp and flushed, her eyes bright and shining and hooded with … embarrassment? Eli had the urge to do it all over again. Kiss her until their embarrassment melted along with their inhibitions. He wasn't sure what to do. He'd never had to deal with this before. But, then again, he'd never eaten a woman while standing in his greenhouse. Most—all right, all—of his sexual encounters had been accomplished in his bed with the lights off. That was the way his wife had wanted it, and he'd been too young and excited at the prospect of touching a woman to debate her on it.

Eli shouldn't have worried so much. He should have known Amelia would take the lead. She hooked her fingers together in front of her. "I'm not sure what to say—"

"Me neither," Eli breathed in relief. My God, he was a thirty-year-old man, not a boy. Why was he so damned nervous? And grateful? So very, very grateful.

She smiled, her unease abating slightly. "I've never done that before."

"Me neither," he repeated, making laughter burst from her chest.

Eli could feel his cheeks flaming. For all his accomplishments, he was certainly not a man-of-the-world lothario.

"Did … you enjoy … it?" he asked.

Her smile turned polite. "Yes … thank you."

Eli shoved his hands in his pockets, balancing back on his heels. "You're very welcome."

"Um …" Amelia's gaze found the exit. "I should probably go. I have a busy day with the girls tomorrow."

"Of course, of course," he said, nodding. "I expect you do."

"I do."

"Yes. No doubt."

"Good," she said.

"Good," he concurred.

Amelia raised her brows. "Very well, then."

"Very well."

She turned to leave. Stopped herself. Opened her mouth and then shut it. Nodded one time and then fled.

As soon as her skirts disappeared from view, Eli leaned against the table, wiping a hand over his face.

Well, that went downhill fast.

Tomorrow, he would avoid her. Unequivocally. Eli would not show his face. He needed space to forget his embarrassment.

Space.

He fell to sleep dreaming about his head clamped between Amelia's strong thighs.

CHAPTER TWENTY

ELI CLEARED HIS throat. Again. Louder. And *definitely* more irritated.

Even from his end of the greenhouse, the guttural noise still interrupted Amelia's mini-lecture.

Kitty and Cecily gave her a look as if to say, *What is wrong with him?*

Amelia shook her head, directing them back to the flowers in her hand. They had too much to accomplish today and would have to ignore Eli's grumbling. He'd been doing it ever since they entered the greenhouse first thing after breakfast, and, even though midday was past, his temper showed no signs of letting up. Amelia almost sent for some chamomile tea for him. He was certain to lose his voice with all the incessant growling.

They'd ended their night on a perfectly civil, perfectly amiable note. Amelia had no idea what was troubling the man so. She hadn't asked him to do what he did to her, though she'd remembered to thank him. They'd simply gotten carried away. Had she done it all wrong? *He* was the experienced one. *He* was supposed to lead the way. Amelia had merely followed his charge. Eli had been polite. A little wooden, but courteous. A gentleman. It had all been so … so … awkward. Not the first part! The first part had been mind-blowingly, life-alteringly wonderful. The second part … not so much.

"You see, girls, it's all in the language," she continued, holding out her pages for them to follow along. She had made sketches of the most popular flowers they would be selling. "If someone asks you for flowers that signify love, you have a few options, so you have to ask more questions. Do they want roses for love and appreciation? Or larkspur for the strong bonds of love? Or maybe even narcissus."

"Narcissus?" Kitty asked.

"Yes," Amelia said, towing the girls over to the corner where a group of orangish-yellow daffodils were standing at attention. "For self-love."

"What's self-love?" Cecily chimed in.

Eli coughed loudly, hacking like he'd swallowed a bouquet of narcissus and couldn't get it down.

Amelia took a pause. "Self-love is …"

He whooped louder.

Beyond annoyed, she twirled to his section. "Do you mind? You are quite distracting."

Sitting at his table, Eli glanced up from his notebook with an infuriatingly incredulous expression. Amelia appreciated the anger that filled her; it prohibited her from admiring the way his pants fit snugly against his long legs and the way his hair branched out along his ears in a wayward, dashing fashion.

"*You're* the ones being distracting," he snapped, going back to his book, penciling in a note as if to show how important his time was and how she was burning through it. "I'm working. You're—"

"So are we!" Amelia cut in.

Eli *humphed*, refusing to meet her gaze. What had she done? Why couldn't he look at her? Besides his animalistic noises, he'd avoided her like the plague all day.

Determined not to let him make her feel silly or cheap, Amelia dug deep for some resolve. "You said we could be here," she muttered.

Eli slammed his pencil down on the desk, and it rolled dutifully to the floor. "When? When did I say that?"

"Last night!" she roared back.

Kitty shared a dubious look with her sister. "When did you speak last night?"

"Last night—" Eli stopped himself, abruptly fishing for his pencil under his seat as if remembering he didn't want to think about that moment. Amelia's heart sank. She hadn't known what to think after she went up to her room after their interlude; she hadn't known what it all meant. Clearly, though, it hadn't been as positive as she'd wanted to believe. Why did she keep falling for him like that? She'd passed through twenty years on this planet with hardly even looking at a man. What was so disarming about this one? He wasn't *that* handsome. And it certainly wasn't his prickly personality.

Did Eli have to be so curt and dismissive? Didn't he know how thorny a situation like that could be for a woman? No one had ever touched Amelia like that before; she'd never allowed anyone to. With him, she'd thrown caution and self-preservation to the wind for a fleeting take at what could be. It made her feel alone and stripped down, as transparent and fragile as the greenhouse glass.

Eli bristled in his seat, dismissing her for his work. "Last night I specifically remember telling you about Cecily's love for getting her horse sotted—"

"Buttercup was thirsty!" Cecily cut in.

He shot Amelia a harsh stare. "You're supposed to be telling them your stories—about the dangers of lying through life—not wasting their time with this flower nonsense."

Flower nonsense! If the bastard would take his stick out of his behind, he might realize that this "flower nonsense" was made for men like him who couldn't actually express themselves. Maybe if Eli had the courage to say what he felt, he would stop being so horrid toward her and move on. They didn't have to touch each other again; that was fine. But Amelia would be damned if she had to suffer through his barbed tongue for the entirety of her stay just because of *another* momentary lapse in judgment.

Eli sulked back into his work, and Amelia returned to the girls, who'd been watching the whole exchange with curious expressions. She avoided their questioning gazes and went back to the flowers, supervising as they cut the stems and placed them in the baskets they would cart into town.

But confusion and anger continued to rumble in the pit of Amelia's stomach.

Lies. Eli wanted her to warn the girls off lying. Didn't he know all lies weren't created equal? Sometimes people needed to lie to themselves to get through the day, as she did now when she told herself she wasn't hurt by his caustic behavior.

Amelia swiped a hand over her eyes, proud that there were no tears. "All right, I have a story for you," she began, the tale ripening in her memory. "Barman Bert ran the local pub that me and the girls would go to at the end of a long night. Bert was always nice to us, never tried to cheat us, which was always a welcome surprise. The place had belonged to his pa, and Bert had inherited it after he died. Well, one night, Bert goes up to Jim, his best friend, and wraps his arms around his neck and lays a kiss right on his lips."

"His best friend?" Cecily asks.

Amelia nodded, slicing off a stem. "The very one. See … it turns out Bert was actually Bertha. She'd always been a woman, and her father had had no other children to give the business to. Scared that it might go to a lousy, good-for-nothing cousin, her father raised her as a boy from a young age, encouraging her to keep up the act so she could run the pub without anyone harassing her. Bertha expected to go on like that forever … until she met Jim. She told me she tried not to let her love run away with her, but she couldn't help herself. Every second Jim was in the room, all she ever wanted to do was kiss him … until one day she did."

"What happened next?" Kitty asked, completely forgetting about the flowers.

"Everyone left the pub," Amelia answered. "Bertha lost a lot of money that night. A *lot* of money."

Kitty glowered. "Who cares about the money! What did Jim do?"

Amelia shrugged. "He did what he wanted to do. He married her."

Kitty sucked in a breath. "Wasn't he upset she lied?"

"I supposed he was at first—especially since she kissed him in a roomful of very shocked people. But he got over it quick enough. Eventually, all the customers came back. Bertha and Jim work the pub together now and have eight—no, ten children."

Cecily's pink lips pinched as she twirled a rose in her hand. "So ... it's a love story?"

"What?" Amelia startled. "No, it's about losing money because of a lie ..." She trailed off. *Dammit; it is another love story.* For being such a bleak place, London sure did have its fair share of happy endings.

"That's a wonderful story," Kitty breathed dreamily.

"Yes, so lovely," Cecily concurred.

On the other side of the greenhouse, a pencil slammed to the table again. "Those are not the stories I had in mind," Eli called out.

Amelia frowned. "You told me to tell them about one of my friends who'd been caught in a lie!" she yelled in return. "It's not my fault no one died at the end of it!"

He sighed, cradling his head in his hands on his desk. "Tell them something real, something gritty, something that won't have them dreaming up ways to dress as a man and own a bar one day." A distinct edge of warning glinted off his last words. "We had a deal."

Amelia held his gaze—and her breath—as she thought it over. Yes, they had a deal, but it seemed like it had been broken somehow, or muddied it in some way, like they'd drawn lines in the sand that had been swept away by all the crossing they made back and forth over it.

Now, here Eli was, insisting she remember how their relationship started, completely overlooking how (or why) it had evolved into something completely different.

"Fine," Amelia seethed. "Something gritty. Something real." She gave the girls a sympathetic smile as if to apologize in advance. "This one is about lies as well. It even starts out as a love story." She cocked her head in Eli's direction, though he was pretending to be interested in his work. *Now who's the liar?* "Don't worry; it doesn't stay that way."

Returning to her flowers, Amelia started telling them about Walter Bowery—the leader of the Bowery Gang and Molly's noxious beau, who came and went out of their lives like a traveling salesman. Walter had never liked Amelia much. Supremely hated her, more like. The feeling had been mutual. She couldn't remember a day in her youth when Walter didn't say Molly would have been better off dumping her in an orphanage or—better yet—at the bottom of the Thames. But Molly, being Molly, always put her foot down, saying she could train the little girl, and make her the best thief Walter had ever seen.

Walter, being Walter, would usually get drunk and forget most of the arguments. He tended to do that a lot in those days. In the end, it didn't matter so long as Molly kept making money and splitting it with him. And that was exactly what she did. Without fail.

Even when Walter left for months at a time, Molly would take him back the second he knocked on the door, shoving Amelia as far away from his disdain—and his pipe—as she could. Amelia could still smell that pipe—the hideous burned aroma emanating from it. Whenever Walter accused her of misbehaving, he got a sick thrill out of threatening her with that pipe, saying he would stick her finger in the lit bowl until her skin singed off. Luckily, he never took it that far, but children know; and from a young age Amelia understood spending the days on the streets was safer than spending them alone with Walter in the home.

"It didn't matter how much money he needed, or how badly he beat her," she said, staring off at a mound of yellow leaves on the ground. "Molly always took him back. He would lie and say it was the last time, that he would treat her better, that he'd even marry her, and she'd let him come crawling home, knowing full well he didn't mean any of it. Walter was like a drug to her. Molly is the strongest woman I've ever known. Half of London is scared to death of her, and the other half would be if they knew who she was. And yet this man could reduce her to nothing time and time again. And even though I pleaded with her never to listen to him, she would always believe him over me."

"Is she … is she still with him?" Cecily asked slowly.

Amelia broke out of her trance, giving the girl a sad smile. "No, not for a long while. A couple of years back I walked in on him. Walter was going in on Molly pretty good because she'd told him she didn't have enough money to buy him out of some scrape he'd gotten into. Her face was so swollen she couldn't open either of her eyes. That's what saved her, actually. She didn't see me when I snuck up behind him, so he wasn't alerted when I picked up a bat and smashed in the back of the head."

"Did you kill him?" Kitty gulped.

"Nah," Amelia replied wistfully. "But I did manage to knock a few teeth out. I haven't seen him since then; I heard he was sent off to the hulks soon after—"

"I think that's enough for the day," Eli said, cutting in. He wasn't sitting at his desk anymore. Amelia hadn't noticed that he'd walked over to stand behind the twins. "Why don't you take a break?" he said. "Girls, why don't you go inside and ask Mrs. Hutchinson to bring out some tea and cakes?"

They nodded. "Good idea, Father," Cecily said. She tugged Kitty's hand, and they both broke off toward the house.

Amelia shook her head, trying to get the visions out of her mind's eye. After all these years, they were still so foul. She could still smell Molly's blood in the air, see the splatter of the red as it sprayed off her face onto the walls. She could still feel the ringing in her tiny forearms as she brought down the bat. Again and again until her muscles screamed as loud as Molly.

"Come on." Eli put his arm around Amelia's waist and guided her outside, where the air was crisp and clean, the metallic scent of blood nowhere to be found. She shivered, tightening her arms around herself, over his hands, which refused to leave her.

He directed her toward an ancient-looking weeping willow that stood sentry alongside the pond where the girls liked to skip rocks. Its limbs hung heavily, skating against the ground. Amelia wondered if it felt as old as she did.

"I'm sorry I made you tell that story," Eli said, stunning Amelia out of her stupor.

She rubbed more heat into her arms. "It wasn't your fault. You were right; we had a deal. I'm here for a reason."

He relinquished his hold and moved to stand in front of her, his blue eyes capturing hers so vividly. "Maybe so; nevertheless, I didn't intend to hurt you. I had no idea—"

Amelia puffed a harsh breath. "You had no idea about what? That my life before you knew it might have been difficult? That the reality you want me to tell the girls might be more unsavory than you bargained for? You know, Eli, just because I choose to smile and laugh and smell flowers whenever I walk past them, it doesn't mean I haven't experienced pain and sorrow. It just means I choose to embrace life as much as I can because I know how fleeting it is. That might be difficult for you to understand locked away in your ivory tower—"

Eli kissed her, planting his lips on Amelia's, leaching the pain from her body.

When he backed away, Amelia forgot what she was saying; her thoughts vaporized into mist.

He rubbed a thumb over her bottom lip. "I'm sorry. I know your life hasn't been easy, and I will never know the extent of that. I suppose I forgot because you make everything seem too effortless. If you don't want to tell the girls any more stories, you don't have to. I don't know how you're doing it, but they haven't been this well behaved since before they could crawl. You're weaving some sort of magic here."

"It's not magic, Eli. I'm just letting them be themselves. I'm not forcing them to fit in some mold of someone else's choosing."

"And what does that have to do with flowers? How do you know so much about them, by the way?"

"I told you—I didn't always steal jewelry and pocket watches. Sometimes I snagged books. Molly called it my rebellious stage when I'd read everything I could get my hands on instead of practicing diving with the other girls.

"And … flowers?" he asked.

"They spoke to me, I guess," Amelia replied, feeling more exposed now than she had last night. "Life can be so gray and unrelenting. Sometimes I would stand on the street and watch men buy flowers for their ladies. The women's faces would light up like a bonfire blaze, so enchanted by something that would die in a matter of days. Then I realized it wasn't the flowers so much as what they were trying to convey. The petals would wither, but the message and the feeling of receiving it would live on. There was something so beautiful in that."

"With your knowledge, I'm surprised you didn't try to make a profession of it."

"You think I would have made a good flower girl?"

"I think you would make an expert salesman." Eli laughed. "No one would ever get anything past you, and the service would be fast."

Amelia's expression clouded. "Well, there you are wrong. I'm sorry to disappoint you, but that's what got me into this whole mess to begin with. I had a store. I saved and scrimped and borrowed to open it, tried to do things proper for the first time in my life."

"What happened?"

She snorted dismissively. "Didn't work out."

"What does that mean?"

"It means, it didn't work out."

"Can you be more specific?"

Amelia blew out an irritated hiss. "You said I didn't have to tell any more sad stories."

Eli nodded. Light as air, she felt him brush the tips of her fingers, taking her hand in his. "Please, Amelia. Tell me what happened."

She didn't think she'd ever heard the viscount say please before. She told herself that was why she relented, when in actuality she *needed* to tell her story. For too long it had been a cancer inside her, eating away at everything that was healthy, left over from her disappointment. "It's simple, really, not much to the story. I opened a shop and no one came."

"What do you mean no one?"

Amelia lifted her shoulders in exasperation. "Not no one, I suppose. The first week was right enough—more than right. I was doing good business, was even thinking I could open another shop the following year if it kept up, but then …"

"Then?"

Amelia snapped her fingers. "Like a well, it all dried up. The first few days had been a fluke. Everyone stopped coming, preferring to go three blocks over to a different seller. He was good, I'm not saying he wasn't, but there was nothing special about his flowers, no imagination to what he created." She bit on the inside of her cheek, warding off tears. "No use dwelling on it. I tried and I failed. Some people don't even get that far."

"Why did you quit?"

"I didn't just give up, if that's what you mean," Amelia answered hotly. "I wanted to keep going. I tried getting more loans, but I couldn't pay back the ones I already had. Rent was due and I was in the lurch. I had to close so I could go back to pickpocketing. It was either that or end up six feet under, if you understand my meaning."

Eli nodded. "Who gave you the loans?"

"You don't want to know."

He tugged on her hand, forcing her to stop. He waited until

she tilted her head up to look at him before speaking again. "Harry's Boys?"

He muttered a curse when Amelia nodded.

"I know!" she said, flapping her arms out hopelessly. "You don't have to tell me. I was a fool."

"You weren't a fool—"

"Yes, I was. I thought I could change my fate, change who I was. But I have learned my lesson. I am Amelia Driver, the best damn pickpocket in London. And that is who I will stay." She paused to consider her words. "That is, if I can pay Harry's Boys back in time. If not, well then, Eli … it was lovely getting to know you."

"Wait a second," he said, snatching her back. "That's why you were in Eglinton … to make enough to pay off your loans?"

"Obviously."

"And I stopped you and now I'm keeping you here."

Amelia pointed her finger. "Right-o!"

"So, essentially, I'm holding you back from paying off your loan?"

"Wrong," she said with feigned cheer. "You *were* holding me back from paying my loan. But the girls and I have figured it all out—or they figured it all out. I took some convincing."

She thought she saw Eli shudder. "What do my girls have to do with this?" he asked.

She returned a disbelieving look. "What are you talking about? We discussed this last night."

"We did not discuss this last night," he said, expanding his lungs.

"We most definitely did. The girls told me they explained it all over dinner and got your blessing. That's why I came to the greenhouse. Why do you keep shaking your head? It's all been taken care of." Amelia's stomach sank. "Please tell me the girls asked you if we could sell the flowers."

Eli's eyes froze into ice chips. "They did nothing of the sort."

"I don't understand," she said, hands on her hips. "What did you think we were doing in the greenhouse today, cutting all the plants?"

"I hadn't the faintest idea. I thought you were teaching them about the language of flowers, showing the girls how to arrange them like other ladies."

"Why would I know anything about how ladies do things?"

"I have no idea!"

"I'm not a bloody governess!"

"Christ, don't remind me!"

They paused, each catching their breath, the anger and confusion whirling around them like moths to a flame. Amelia gathered her courage. It wasn't so difficult, since she had no other choice.

"Well, all our cards are on the table, then," she began, plastering an optimistic smile on her face. "Can we sell the flowers? What's worse to you—the girls behaving badly or going into business?"

Eli gave her his back, allowing her worry to fester like an open wound.

"Well?" she asked.

"I'm thinking."

"Oh, come now. What's the harm in it?"

"The harm is that you've turned my daughters into peddlers."

"No, I'm encouraging them to be industrious, to have purpose. And it's working. Despite Cecily's penchant for drunken horses, they are getting better. If you're determined to keep them at Barrington, this is what they need, Eli. Don't take it away just because someone told you ladies should behave differently. After all, someone probably once told you that thieves were horrible people, and look at me. You like me."

Turning back to her, Eli cocked his head. "Do I?"

"I think so," Amelia said, her voice wobbly. "Do ... do you usually go around kissing people you don't like?"

Pink splotches brightened his cheeks. "About that ..." He ran a hand through his hair. "I bungled it, didn't I? I never know what to say to you … to excuse my behavior."

The vague anxiety that had been following Amelia all day immediately disappeared. "You don't have to excuse anything. But is that the reason you've acted like such a bull today?"

He ducked his head sheepishly.

Amelia's smile split her face. "Do you see? This is another point for the flowers. They help men like you who have a difficult time expressing yourself. Your daughters and I would be providing a service. The women of this village would thank us."

Eli studied her for a short pause. "Give me your expertise now, then. What should I have sent you to save myself all this embarrassment today?"

"That depends," she said slowly. She'd meant her comment about the flowers to be humorous, to relax the tension around them, but it only seemed to have built. "What did you wish to say?"

His Adam's apple bobbed over the top of his cravat before his words flooded out, tripping after themselves. "That every time I touch you, I want to peel off your clothes and lick every inch of your skin."

In an instant, Amelia lost her breath. The air congealed, too thick to breathe, his words hanging there like forbidden fruit. Eli watched her expectantly, his face a mixture of bashfulness and hope. But not shame.

Fighting all the careful levels of self-preservation she'd created for herself over the years, Amelia raised her hand, hovering her fingers near his face. Slowly, she traced the sharp indentation of a cheekbone, all the way down to his jaw, and the prickly hairs of his unrelenting beard tickled her soft skin.

"Oh," she said. "I'm not sure there's a flower that says all that."

"Pity," Eli replied.

CHAPTER TWENTY-ONE

LATER THAT NIGHT, Eli lay in his bed, restless. Lack of sleep—that had to be it. But how could he sleep when Amelia was occupying the same house? How could he close his eyes when he could still feel the way her smooth hand glided over his chin as if she owned it? Owned him?

He wanted her, though the logistics of that wanting continued to confound him. He could make her stay—force her, even. Eli was a viscount, she a pickpocket; the power was his.

No, he was fooling himself with that ridiculous assertion. Her mere touch reduced him to a puddle. Eli had never felt so weak and uncertain—the power was all Amelia's.

The following morning proved just as frustrating because he woke with an erection that wouldn't let him out of bed until he relieved himself. Waking up in such a fashion wasn't necessarily new to him, although the insistence of the need to be assuaged definitely was. The problem was that he couldn't get Amelia out of his mind. The harder he tried, the more elusive it was. She was just a woman—yes, an unusual one, but just a woman. Considered an eligible bachelor, Eli had had women thrown at him his entire life. He'd made it an art dodging each and every one. Yet this one got under his skin like no other, like fresh dirt under too-short fingernails.

Eli loved fresh dirt under his fingernails.

Which was a terrible metaphor! No one would ever liken a beautiful woman to dirt, nor understand its appeal to him. No one except her. Eli was certain Amelia would comprehend what he meant.

Desire tempered, for the time being, he ventured down to breakfast, thinking time listening to his children squabble was just the thing to take his mind off his thief. But when he arrived in the dining room, he found it empty, though traces had been left behind. The sideboard along the wall had been picked over and crumbs were scattered near the opposite end of the table.

It seemed that Eli hadn't been the only one who couldn't sleep this morning.

He strove to enjoy his meal. It wasn't every day he could spend it in peace, but he found himself rushing through the act, stuffing food in and swallowing without tasting it. Tea scalded the roof of his mouth because—impatient twit that he was—he hadn't tested the temperature first. Composure was nowhere to be found, and decorum was absolutely lost.

There was no use denying it. The only thing he wanted to taste was what was between Amelia's legs. Anything else was just a placeholder.

With nothing to delay him further, Eli shuffled off to the greenhouse. His work had never failed to divert him before, but that was before he'd decided it would be a good idea to bring a pickpocket into his home. Amelia had told him time and time again that she was the best at what she did. Eli had to concur. She'd stolen his focus—and his sanity.

An hour he spent on his strawberries, categorizing and ana-lyzing the subtle changes that had happened overnight, writing down his observations on the different soils used, the plants that appeared to be grafting harmoniously.

But his heart wasn't in it. His head kept swiveling to the other side of the greenhouse, which looked like it had been ransacked. Once full—much too full—of various colors and overgrown bulbs the size of snowballs, the area now appeared manicured and sparse. As if she'd taken a machete to it, Amelia had thinned out the flowers, cutting everything that had fully bloomed, leaving very little else.

Mrs. Hutchinson had informed Eli that Amelia and the girls had loaded the carriage this morning with all of their stems and gone to the village, which seemed horribly optimistic of them. He hoped the girls wouldn't be too disappointed when they came back with most of the lot. The village wasn't particularly large. Full of good, hardworking people, it didn't boast a flower shop for good reason. The people in these parts were sensible; they didn't waste their money on frivolous things like curated blooms, not when they could go to the nearest meadow and pull some adequate wildflowers.

Eli would ask Mrs. Hutchinson to plan a special dessert tonight. That would salve the twins' moods, and, hopefully, Amelia's as well.

The next few hours were some of the most laborious Eli had ever spent in the greenhouse. Every sound he heard—every squeak of wheels—brought his head up to check if the girls had returned. When the afternoon came and went, he figured he must have missed them. There was no way they were still out. Perhaps they'd returned to Barrington while Eli had gone inside for his tea. Though that seemed unlikely, since his ears had been just as on alert inside as they'd been outside.

He was finally put out of his misery when the vehicle approached just as the sun was starting to lower over the horizon. At the sound of the horse, he bounded out of the greenhouse to see his stable boy, Jimmy, bringing the cart up the lane, and three young ladies sitting in the back of the wagon with three equally thrilled smiles. There wasn't a single stem sharing the wagon with them. They'd cleaned house.

Eli met the wagon at the stables, issuing an impressed whistle as Cecily and Kitty hopped off the back, their hair windblown and the fronts of their dresses smudged with dirt. He should have been furious, or at the very least disappointed in their hoyden appearance.

He wasn't. They were simply too ecstatic for him to be anything other than the same.

"Don't tell me," Eli said, putting his hands up to stop the chatter poised to explode out of them. "You were robbed. Someone stole all your flowers and that's why the wagon is empty!"

"Father, really!" Kitty said, going back to the wagon to grab a pouch next to Amelia. She remained seated, and Eli could feel her watching him as he interacted with his thrilled daughters. Her joy was more tempered, but he could still see the same rosiness in her cheeks, the same energy radiating from her lithe form.

"We sold everything. Every last flower," Kitty said, thrusting the pouch into his chest. Eli heard the jingle of coins and felt the bottom of the sack, noting how heavy it was. "Amelia let us take turns holding the money on the way home."

He shot Amelia a wry look. "That sounds too trusting to be true."

"And she said we can take it upstairs to our room to count it now," Cecily said, ignoring his comment. She snatched the pouch from her sister, and they made a break for the house, barely acknowledging Eli as he told them not to be late for supper.

After the girls were out of sight, Amelia edged off her seat. Remembering himself, Eli caught her waist in the nick of time, securing her torso as she slid to the ground. He let his hands stay on her longer than needed, riding them up her sides, remembering too vividly the way her skin felt as he peeled her undergarments down her legs.

Tilting her head up, Amelia smiled with half her mouth. "Too trusting?" she said, though from the flash in her eyes, Eli knew she was teasing. "I can be trusting."

In the vague recesses of his mind, he understood they were not alone. There had to be no less than ten servants milling around while Eli made calf eyes at this woman, and yet that didn't seem to faze him. The temptation to touch her, to be near her, was too great.

"I will just have to take your word on that," he said, making her eyes narrow into two almond slivers. "I was led to believe that trust wasn't a major characteristic of a thief."

"On the contrary," Amelia replied, placing her hands over his, which were still resting on the delicious dip of her hips. He tensed, thinking she was going to push him away, but they remained there, as if she, too, was desperate to feel a swath of his skin.

Eli tightened his grip in appreciation.

She continued, "Trust is at the very heart of our gang. We couldn't be successful without it. Without a shadow of a doubt, we need to be sure that we are looking out for one another, that we won't leave anyone behind."

"Like the girl at the inn?" Eli asked before thinking. Instantly, he found it was the wrong thing to say. Their sweet moment of levity evaporated, and Amelia's expression became grim.

"She was right to escape."

"Even if meant leaving you behind with me?"

Light as a feather, Amelia's fingers caressed the tops of his hands. The soft flutters created a frenzy in his blood. "She knew I could handle you."

"Is that what you're doing ... handing me?"

Amelia regarded him, the serious moue still apparent. "I don't think you mind it so much. For now, anyway."

For now, anyway. Always there was a sense of an ending between them. A warning that it would all be over soon.

And their spell was broken. Amelia pushed away from his arms. "I should wash up. It's later than I thought."

Shadows draped long and forbidding against the grounds, but Eli didn't want to end this conversation. He yearned to keep this going a little while longer.

"How did you manage it?" he said, nodding to the empty wagon where broken stems and dead petals littered the vehicle's floor.

Amelia followed his gaze and grinned as if suddenly remembering all that had happened. "I know it will trouble you greatly to hear this, but your daughters are born saleswomen. They are quite ferocious when it comes to customers."

Eli managed a polite chuckle, yet all he wanted to do was throw his head in his hands and wallow in self-pity. Had it really been such a good idea to pair Amelia up with his daughters? True, he didn't want them to continue to be arsonists; however, salesmen weren't much better. Some in their social circles probably considered it worse. To aristocrats, ladies who enjoyed a good fire every now and again could be excused as quirky. Sales, on the other hand, defied explanation.

It was impolite to discuss money, but anything was better than his business-savvy daughters. "How much did you make?" he asked, steering the conversation into calmer waters. "Do you have a chance of paying back the loan?"

Eli realized he was holding his breath as he waited for Amelia to answer. It was then he realized what a bastard he was—because he wanted her to say no. If she said no, then she could stay longer. It wasn't forever, but longer was still better than nothing.

"Not yet," she replied, and he had to repress a grin. "But we're getting there. I can't believe it. The people were positively ravenous for what we had to offer."

Eli felt in perfect accord with the villagers. Ravenous was a prime word for it.

"I told the girls we could go travel to another village in a few days." She frowned. "If that is all right with you, I mean."

Ha! The annoyance was plain as day on her face; it killed her to have to ask for permission. The woman was positively feral. She'd been allowed to live with entirely too much independence.

Eli sighed, digging his hands into his pockets. He wasn't sure if he was going to regret this—he probably would. But the notion of making Amelia smile again was too enticing for him.

"If you're going to another village then you're going to need more flowers."

"Oh, we should be fine," she said quickly. "There is plenty left in the greenhouse for us to harvest—"

"Be that as it may," Eli interrupted, "I gather the girls didn't show you the other greenhouse yet."

"Other. Greenhouse?"

"My grandfather was quite the amateur horticulturist as well." That was putting it mildly. The old man wasted much of his time in those damn buildings, ignoring every living person around him. "It's just on the other end of the property. I'll have the girls show you in the morning."

Eli adored seeing her so shocked and so grateful to him. "Is it ..." She gulped. "Is it just as overrun at this one?"

He shrugged. "Probably."

Eli watched as a battle waged within her. Brow furrowed and lips puckered, Amelia desperately wanted to take him up on the offer, but something was holding her back. She shook her head. "I shouldn't take all those flowers. They're yours. Just because you don't appreciate it now doesn't mean the girls won't help you do so in the future."

"You're not going to pull out the roots, are you?" Eli asked, leaning so far down that his nose skimmed hers. A sweet blush rose on Amelia's cheeks.

"Of course not!"

"Well, then you'll be doing me a favor. Wasn't it you who told me that plants need to be cut and pruned to become healthier? You could be my gardener, since, apparently, the one I pay isn't doing an adequate job."

"You shouldn't say that," she replied. "Edgar is a saint. Look at all you have. It's a lot for him."

Who the fuck was Edgar? And how did Amelia know him, while Eli didn't?

Her face sharpened like a knife, cutting to the very heart of him. Eli had to resist pulling her into his arms and kissing her senselessly. Then she would go soft again. He could make her that way. "You'll be doing me a favor," he said, resisting the urge to stare at her lips and remember how when he sucked and pulled on them, they turned a lovely cherry shade. "You earned them anyway. So far, my daughters haven't made anyone cry today."

"Oh, they did!" Amelia exclaimed, before adding hastily, "One of the boys in the village hid behind Kitty and yanked her hair when she wasn't looking. When she turned around, he tried to kiss her, and she punched him in the jaw instead." She lowered her gaze bashfully, avoiding his eyes. "See? Not all my stories have happy endings, my lord."

Eli surprised them both with a booming laugh. Then, whether people were looking at them or not, he brought Amelia to his chest, placing a loud kiss on her shocked lips. When she pulled back, her face was open with astonishment.

"I thought you'd be angry," she sputtered.

"Are you joking?" he asked. "That was the happiest ending of them all."

CHAPTER TWENTY-TWO

AMELIA SPENT THE next two days in almost constant work with the twins. As Eli had said, the second greenhouse was just as dilapidated and overgrown as the first, and the flowers were in desperate need of culling. She used their time together to teach the girls about the plants and their different languages. In particular, she demonstrated the difference between deadheading and pruning and what the various flowers preferred.

Kitty particularly enjoyed deadheading and had to be reined in from "Henry the VIII-ing" all the flower bulbs that showed any hint of dying. The girls had a natural inquisitiveness that made the work truly enjoyable. Amelia loved teaching, especially a profession that didn't have the potential result of her ending up in shackles. The days flew by quickly because of the pure joy she felt working in the soil, and the fear of the looming debt washed away as easily as the dirt from her hands.

For his part, Eli steered clear, giving them room to plan without distraction. Although disappointed, Amelia was equally grateful. From the very beginning, she knew her time at Barrington would be a temporary situation, a means to an end. But as the clock ticked against them, her regret was too palpable to be ignored. For the first time in her life, Amelia wanted to share an intimacy with someone. Instead of wishing to take something from Barrington, she hoped to leave a piece of herself behind.

Unfortunately, she wasn't sure how to proceed. She only knew she hurt. And not like she used to hurt when Molly and she would practice diving. The older woman would smack Amelia's knuckles with her leather strap each time she made too much noise rummaging in a pocket. That had smarted like the devil—and she still had the scars to prove it. However, this needy, achy feeling in her chest throbbed more. Amelia wondered whether if she looked inside her body, she'd see tiny nicks and white marks like the faded ones on her hands.

On the day of their trip to the next village, Amelia woke early and met the girls near the stables, where Jimmy was already packing their flowers. They'd spent the previous afternoon sorting the flowers by variety and had also made a few bouquets designed for the special customer in mind. Amelia settled on a "new love" cluster featuring deep red roses, hot-pink peonies, and soft white carnations, as well as an "I'm sorry" cluster including lily of the valley, daffodils, and sturdy purple hyacinths. Not wanting to be left out, Kitty designed her own bouquet for people with an ax to grind. Including yellow carnations, petunias, and buttercups, she explained that her pre-made item was for those running away from love, not toward it. Though reluctant at first, Amelia acquiesced in the end, concluding that the idea was brilliant. The world was a complicated place, and a good businesswoman was ready for every eventuality.

She was just about to order the girls into the wagon when she heard a scuffle of footsteps behind her. Cecily let out a squeal. Amelia turned to see Eli walk up to Jimmy, and—after a series of nods and low speak—the stable boy retreated back to the house.

"What's happening?" Amelia asked. "Where is Jimmy going? It's time to leave."

Instead of answering, the frustrating man perched on the front seat of the wagon, flicking the reins until he had the two horses in his command. He glanced down at the three females impatiently. "Well, are you coming or not?"

With another squeal, Cecily was the first to jump into the wagon bed, Kitty not far behind. From a thick fog, Amelia heard them batter their father with questions and exclamations, beyond thrilled that he was accompanying them for the day instead of Jimmy. She vaguely heard his answers, though could tell they were distracted as well. Amelia could feel his eyes on her as he waited for her to climb onto the cart. A stickler for plans, she hated a last-minute change. It threw her off balance.

Coming to terms with the new driver, Amelia picked up her skirts, rounding to the back to join the girls when his words stopped her. "Come up here with me," he ordered her, leaving no room for argument.

"I'll be perfectly comfortable back here with the girls," she said lightly, nose in the air. That was a lie. Thanks to the abundant blooms, there was barely enough room for three in the back, and the planks under her behind would make her bottom go numb in less than ten minutes.

Eli turned in his seat, flashing her a lopsided grin. Amelia wasn't fooled. The morning sun glinted against those white teeth, and she only saw a predator used to getting what it wanted. If the lion wanted to converse with the lamb before he ate it, then that was the way it was going to be.

Concluding Eli wouldn't get the wagon moving until she acquiesced, Amelia huffed—loudly—and went around to the front, taking his hand as he lifted her in the spot next to him.

The bench was tight and narrow, and Amelia's thighs were pressed up against his so much that she might as well have been sitting in his lap. The thought didn't only make her blush, it made her armpits break out in a sweat.

Eli stared straight ahead, whipping the animals to get them started, but out of the corner of her eye, Amelia could see his smug smile, as if he'd just won some magnificent ten-round boxing match.

When he spoke next, his words were dangerously casual. It was the kind of voice that could lull one into a false calm if one allowed it. "Now, isn't this better?" he asked. "Cozy."

"A little too cozy," Amelia muttered, placing her hands primly in her lap. Too much of her was plastered against him; stubbornly, she would not hold on to him if she didn't need to.

Unfortunately, Eli made sure she needed to.

Fifteen minutes later, Amelia was glued to his side.

"Whoops, sorry there," he said, swerving the cart in order to miss another hole in their path. "This road had definitely seen better days."

Laughter floated from the back, where Kitty and Cecily were thoroughly enjoying their father's reckless driving. Amelia sucked in a breath, peeling herself off him yet again. She hadn't seen that hole in the road, just as she hadn't seen any of the others. Either her eyesight was going, or Eli was more of a fiend than she thought. She placed her money on the latter.

"Will you stop that?" she seethed, straightening her skirts.

"What?" he asked as innocent *and* unconvincing as a little boy with two stolen biscuits behind his back. The rascally smile said it all. For some reason, he still wore it, and it worried Amelia more than his driving. "Why had you so edgy?"

"You weren't a part of the plan; Jimmy is supposed to be driving."

"Don't be angry with me." He chuckled. "You can hardly blame me. I wanted to see what all the fuss was about."

Amelia raised her chin away from his, gazing at the countryside, letting the pastoral atmosphere settle her temper. She had never seen so much space in her life. Born and bred in the city, she always thought it completely natural that people lived on top of one another. Here, surrounded by so much land, she realized that wasn't the case. This was nature. This was natural. Meadows as far as the eye could see; trees so high it made the Jack and the Beanstalk tale seem possible. Amelia was certain she could walk along the tall grass for hours and not see another person. The idea was both inviting and frightening.

Eli must have sensed her contentedness, or else grew tired of his childish game, because he let her be for a long stretch of time, allowing the ocean of the countryside to swallow her under its rich waves of golds and reds, the turning of the seasons as rich and vibrant as any magical lost city under the waves.

"Pretty, isn't it?" he asked softly.

Amelia stared at a long oak tree in the distance, its roots erupting through the ground in scraggy tentacles. It was a fine place to sit and read a book, she thought—if one *liked* sitting and reading under a tree in the middle of the day in the middle of nowhere. Which she didn't. At least, she didn't think she did.

She shook her head, returning to the path in front of them. The road that led to the village, to civilization, to people. "Yes, quite."

"Makes London pale in comparison."

"Oh, I don't know about that," Amelia returned lightly as if they were two friends enjoying a pleasant conversation on a pleasant drive. Or two people courting. Which they definitely weren't. "London has its share of beauty."

Eli chuckled. "Is it the rancid scent or the inexplicable trash on the ground that you find so dazzling?"

She scrunched up her nose just thinking about the unappetizing smells. He was right, of course. The city's unfortunate aroma did leave much to be desired. But it was her city. The only city she had ever known and, with things the way they were going in her life, the only city she would probably ever know. She could not let him disparage it. "London is more than the sum of its parts," Amelia defended the city—gallantly, she might add. "From the architecture to the parks, to the palaces and the museums, there's so much to see. One can never grow tired in London."

"It's full of people," Eli returned as if he'd just tasted something he couldn't wait to spit out.

Amelia gawked at his response, fending off the tightness in her chest as she drank him in. He was all haughty and straight-spined, and his fine clothes and expert tailoring were as incongruous to the ratty wagon as Amelia was to a fine carriage. And yet he wasn't completely out of place. The way his hands expertly guided the reins, the long tendons moving as rhythmically as piano keys; the way the muscles in his thighs were outlined through his trousers; the way the wind hit his hair, pulling it up away from his high forehead, tanning his skin.

He wasn't so out of place. Sitting there next to her.

Eli caught her staring at him. Her neck tightened as she turned away, her cheeks flushing. "People aren't the worst thing to be surrounded by," she said, cringing at the wavering in her voice.

"Depends on the people."

"Yes," she agreed. "It depends on the people. And London has the very best." Amelia closed her eyes, thinking of anything but him. She conjured Piccadilly Circus and the hordes searching for entertainment. And Hyde Park milling with fine carriages just waiting to see others and be seen in return. She let the current of expectation and anticipation flow through her, the belief that not only something could happen, but that something would happen at any moment. London was the place dreams were made and the place dreams happened. The people felt it. That was what made it special.

Eli *humphed*. "I've never thought of it like that before."

Amelia's hands flew to her lips. Had she just said all that out loud? She was always so good at keeping her thoughts to herself.

"It must be difficult for you to be away," he went on, his voice taking on a flintiness at their differing viewpoints. "You probably can't wait to get back."

She twisted in her seat, smiling at the girls, who were busy making flower crowns for each other. "It hasn't been too bad, all this considered."

"Because you've been handling me." His tone was back to being lighthearted, and yet Amelia couldn't judge whether he'd asked a question or made a statement. What was unmistakable was that he was alluding to their time together.

"Perhaps you aren't as easy to handle as I'd thought," she

replied diplomatically.

He chuckled. "Between me and the girls, I assumed I would be the easier option."

Amelia laughed in kind, although an uneasiness settled over her. She was unsure of what they were truly talking about. "The girls weren't so hard. Like I said, they just needed a purpose, something to work toward."

"Am I so different?"

"I don't know," she said honestly. "What are you working toward?"

Eli threw her a suggestive smile. "Not what, but whom."

CHAPTER TWENTY-THREE

"So, IT LOOKS like Father will be the shill, then," Kitty stated.

Eli's hands stalled from unloading another carton of flowers. He whipped around to find Kitty, hands on her hips, sizing him up as if he was a racehorse before a big race.

He was so taken aback by her statement, his words weren't so much angry as aghast. "What did you call me?"

Cecily strolled up next to her sister, a matching thoughtful expression on her face. She shrugged. "I suppose there's no one else. Amelia? What should we do?"

Eli stood his ground, though he could feel his knees falter under his daughters' bewildering inquisition. What in the world was a shill? And did he want to be one?

Amelia left the makeshift table stand she'd set up on the perimeter of the village square and joined the girls. The fact that she'd heard the girls' discussion was evidenced by the devious glint in her eyes. Stopping in front of Eli, she gave him a slow— dare he think it lascivious?—inspection from the tips of his toes to the top of his head. "Yes, I think we have our shill."

Eli tongued the groove in his molar before replying, "I think not."

"You have no choice," Amelia answered, bobbed her shoulders helplessly. "You sent Jimmy home, which means you're our new Jimmy."

Eli wasn't sure what he hated more, being the new shill or the new Jimmy. The girls were watching them expectantly. A film of disappointed resignation settled on Kitty's face, as if she'd known from the beginning that her father would ruin their fun. That look gutted him, and he made an effort to unclench his fists. "And what, pray tell, is a shill?" he replied, eyes closed, gathering his courage.

Amelia skirted around him to grab another box from the wagon, but Eli hopped her out of the way, unloading the box instead. He carried it to the table, absorbing the twins' chatter.

"It basically means you're the first customer," Kitty said, skipping next to him. "You have to come up to the table and act interested in what we're doing. That way the people in the town can learn what we can offer them."

Eli placed the box of flowers on the ground and frowned at the girl. "But why would I be a customer when I came here with you? That doesn't make any sense."

Cecily approached him cautiously. "That's why you have to leave for a while. Give us a half-hour and then come back and act like you've never met us before."

"But that would be lying."

"It's not lying!" Cecily said, her brows puckering together before she shot Kitty a questioning look. "Is it?"

"Of course not!" Kitty answered, though it was obvious she wasn't sure herself, because she turned to Amelia. "Is it?"

Amelia kept her focus on arranging the flowers on her table, but Eli could sense her consternation as she fiddled overly long on getting the daffodils to stand without drooping too heavily. He wondered how she was going to talk her way out of this one.

"Well …?" he prodded. "Is it a lie? Because it definitely sounds like one to me."

Shaking her head like she was arguing with herself, Amelia blew out such a frustrated breath that the daffodils hung their heads, refusing to stand at attention. "It isn't a lie, per se," she began. "It's merely a simple, innocent way to entice the buyers.

There's no harm in it. It's best not to overthink it."

But that was what Eli did. He overthought everything because everything deserved thought. If people didn't weigh decisions, then they were nothing better than animals or lawless thieves.

This was a gray area. And Eli didn't like gray areas. Actions were either positive or negative; beneficial or detrimental. Either the plants grafted successfully, or they died. There was no room for this land of in-between—a land that Amelia frolicked in.

Cecily broke his mental exercise. "Please, Father. You have to help us. It's so difficult getting people interested at first. Jimmy did it," she continued pitifully, as if Jimmy doing it would invite Eli's competitive spirit to come out and play.

"Jimmy did it wonderfully," Kitty added.

Amelia laughed. "Jimmy was the best shill I've ever had. That boy needs to move to London and begin a life on the stage!"

All right, so maybe it *was* working. Eli's competitive spirit was raising its pathetic little head. There was no harm in helping them in their venture, and if he was creative, he could do it without lying to show the girls that businessmen—businesswomen—could be successful and maintain their ethics in the process.

Eli's resolve melted. He noticed it had a habit of doing that around Amelia. "But won't people remember that I came with you? I can see some looking at us right now!"

The girls craned their necks to witness these mysterious people. Save a few children milling around chasing one another, it was still too early for a crowd.

Amelia's expression was dubious. "I think we're pretty safe," she said, a hint of teasing in her voice. "Why don't you go to the pub for a drink and come back when you're done? We'll be ready for you then."

Eli pressed his lips together, powerless to continue the debate, and left the women to do their work. It seemed that he was the new Jimmy, and Jimmy did what he was told.

Why the hell had he sent the poor boy home? What had spurred Eli to jump in the cart? It wasn't like he didn't have things to do today. Amelia and the girls hardly needed him. In fact, thanks to Jimmy's acting prowess, they didn't need him at all.

Eli had been curious. But, if he was being honest with himself, it was something more, and this took longer to come to terms with. He wanted to be included. Not only in Amelia's excitement, but in the girls' as well. He'd never seen them as alive as when they'd come back from their first outing. Being a part of their success lit him up. He'd spent so many years disciplining them, chastising them. It was time Kitty and Cecily witnessed his being proud of them.

Despite his orders, Eli did not lose himself at the pub. It wasn't even midday! Jimmy might imbibe like a drunken sailor, but Eli would not. Instead, he spent his time, wandering the area, reacclimating himself with the village he hadn't visited in years.

Eli had shut himself and his children up for so long under the unfailing determination that Barrington was safe. After Marianne died, he'd closed the doors of his London home and that way of life forever. He had assumed that Barrington would make him whole again, but, if anything, the chasm within him had become deepened the longer he stayed there, surrounded by the unchallenged familiarity. It was cowardly. He understood that now. And weak. Death had a way of breaking down the living, like a hog, piece by piece until there was nothing left.

People could run from that pain or withstand it. They weren't so different than the plants Eli grafted. They could choose to accept the cut and become something different—maybe even stronger—or wither from the trauma.

Eli wasn't sure what he'd become in the last nine years. Plainly altered, but he wasn't so sure if he was stronger.

It was with that heaviness that he trudged back to the village square, his steps less sure and steady as when he'd left only thirty minutes before. Amelia and the girls had asked him to come back as a different person, someone they could pretend not to recognize, be their shill. Eli didn't think it would be that difficult now.

With the morning in full bloom, the square was picking up traffic, with more people walking about, dodging around the few riders and carts bullying up the path. Amelia and the twins had transformed their little table into a perfunctory flower shop, showcasing as much of their petals and varieties as they could on the tiny surface. The twins worked the road, enticing people to come closer and see what they had to offer, stringing words together that would make Eli's grandfather roll over in his grave. "How about some sweet stems for your sweetheart?" Kitty yelled. Not to be outdone, Cecily called out, "We have just the thing to put a smile on your missus tonight!"

They were two steps away from being street urchins in a Dickens tale.

But Eli's daughters were exultant. Their smiles traversed from ear to ear. Their voices—though much too loud to be ladylike—were sure and proud. Kitty and Cecily commanded their space. It was wrong, utterly, unmistakably wrong for two young ladies to be behaving this way—in public, no less! And yet Eli was charmed by their effervescence. Pleased with their confidence. They would grow up to be women who would never be strong-armed by others. They would not falter in who they were.

They liked themselves. And what greater lesson could you give two young women?

And that was when the realization hit him. Like having a stinging nettle rubbed in his face, Eli felt like his skin was on fire. Amelia was finished. She'd done it. In no time at all, damn her. She'd taught his daughters a lesson, and she'd done it her own way. She hadn't taught them to be fearful of what they could turn out to be; she'd taught them to embrace who they were. And that small distinction had made all the difference.

Eli's goal to keep his daughters safe from gossip and the blunt truths of their mother had always been a losing battle. But in his pain and rejection, he'd spurned that idea, grasping at some form of control over his life. He shouldn't have bothered. Instead of focusing on perfection for his children, he should have concentrated on strength. Their inner resolve, their backbones and boldness, was what they would need to navigate life. And his daughters and son had those characteristics in spades.

As Eli ventured closer, Cecily's pale eyes locked on his, and her features were so intent and full of joy that he almost dropped to his knees. "Hello, good sir," she crowed merrily so everyone within a twenty-foot radius could hear. "You look like you're in the market for some flowers, am I right?"

Eli nodded grimly, not knowing what to say, mortifyingly uncomfortable with everyone watching him. Despite taking the time to think, he hadn't actually considered what he would say once he got up to the table.

Amelia was the only one not showering him with attention, too busy attempting to lure an older man with a walrus mustache to purchase one of the readymade bouquets. The man was a window shopper if ever Eli saw one. He stood on the side of the table, making contemplative facial expressions followed by lengthy sighs as if he was being coerced into buying his own coffin.

Amelia's gaze flickered to Eli's, though it didn't stay long, which bothered him more than he cared to admit. "Uh, yes," he began self-consciously. Why did he sound like a third-rate actor spouting Shakespeare in the park? "I would like flowers."

"As you can see," Cecily said through her rictus grin, "we have plenty to choose from. What did you have in mind?"

Eli shrugged. "It doesn't matter. Any will do."

Cecily's shoulders slumped, her smile vanishing. Eli suspected she was wishing for Jimmy right about now.

Amelia saved the awkward interaction, dismissing her decision-impaired customer to sidle next to his daughter. "That won't do at all," she said with an air-clearing laugh. "Might I ask ... are you buying for a lady? A *special* lady?"

Eli hadn't the faintest idea why she put the emphasis on the word like that. Was he buying for a lady? A *special* lady? But, wanting Cecily to stop shooting daggers into him with her eyes, he played along.

"Yes," he replied gruffly.

Amelia nodded patiently, as if patting a dog on the head for finally understanding the "sit" command. "Well then ..." she drawled, more to the crowd than to him, "it does matter. It matters greatly because every lady deserves her own special bouquet of flowers—one that speaks to her directly. Tell me, sir, what do you wish your flowers to say?"

Eli's tongue stuck as if he'd swallowed tar. Amelia had asked him that question before; however, he had a feeling his previous response wouldn't be appropriate at their current venue. "I ... ah ..." He could sense people crowding behind him, waiting for his answer. "That I want to give her flowers."

Amelia's tone was as dry as his mouth. "Yes, we gathered that." Her eyes narrowed. "What else?"

Eli's feet shifted in the gravel. Why was this so hard? Why was *she* making this so hard? He was doing what they'd asked of him. He was buying flowers. Did it have to be such a production? When words continued to elude him, she went on. "Why don't you tell us about the lady. What does she look like?"

"Look like?" Eli's straightened his glasses over his nose. Maybe Mrs. Hutchinson would appreciate some nice flowers? No. She might accept them but then look at him like he was insane while she was doing it. There was only one person he could think to give flowers to, and she was the annoying woman putting him on display for all to watch. Well ... two could play that game.

Eli straightened his spine. "Black hair," he said, projecting for the crowd. "Maybe even purple in a certain light. The kind of black that absorbs everything around it, so every time she comes near, all you can ever see is her. And dark brown eyes that take up so much of her face that one wonders how she can ever hide what she's thinking."

The growing throng tittered at his remarks, a few women even sighing. Amelia's face softened, though, ever the professional, she didn't break from character. When she spoke next, her voice was demonstrably weaker. "She sounds lovely."

"Indeed."

"And … what is this lovely woman like?"

Eli smiled. "That is a little harder to explain."

"Her behavior doesn't live up to her beauty?"

"On the contrary," he responded, his voice carrying across the square. "Her behavior is what makes her so beautiful." A splash of wind hit him, and he turned to see an older woman using a newspaper to fan herself. Taking that as a good sign, he went on. "That was why I was so reluctant to come here. I'm afraid there is no flower I could give her that would be good enough. This is the kind of woman that deserves gold and jewels, precious gifts that will last forever."

Amelia shook her head. "Such cold things that dull in time."

"At least they don't die."

"Flowers die; you're right," she said. "But I assure you, the memory of this gift will live on forever in your lady's mind. She will cherish the time and effort you took picking out each stem. That romantic consideration will not be lost because no one will ever be able to *steal* it away from her."

Amelia had emphasized *steal*, leaving no doubt she'd intended to use the volatile word. Eli nodded, conceding her point. And it was a good point. He still knew she was wrong. A woman would always want jewels over flowers—most women, anyway. However, for the benefit of the crowd, he let her win.

Eli lifted his hands at his sides. "You have me, then, miss. What do you suggest for this paradigm of wonder and virtue I've laid at your feet? How can I tell her how much I love her?"

"Love?" Amelia asked, her pitch high and untenable.

Shit. Eli hadn't meant to say love. Had he? Maybe he was taking this whole thing too far. Jimmy wouldn't have.

He had to go with it now. Eli thought the words would be

harder to say the second time around … but they weren't. "Yes. Love."

Amelia blinked a few times. If Eli were closer to her—as he always wanted to be—he would be able to feel them tickle his face, and then he'd kiss them and calm them to a stop. As many kisses as it took.

Kitty held a red rose up to Amelia, and the stiff petals scratched under her chin. She stared down at the luscious bloom—and frowned. "Roses?" she said, seemingly to herself. "Roses." Along with the onlookers, Eli watched as Amelia's mind seemed to turn the idea around and around in her head, working through a difficult equation like a stumped mathematician. "I think we can do better than roses."

"Better than roses?" a voice shot out from the crowd. "Nothing is more romantic than roses."

"That's true—most of the time," Amelia allowed, her eyes sweeping over her flowers. "But I have a feeling that roses wouldn't work for this particular woman. She reads to me as being a little different. Is that right?"

Eli chuckled. "Oh, she's different. *Very* different."

"I'm sure she's not *that* different," she muttered.

"Very different," he repeated.

Amelia stuck her chin out. "Well, being 'very different' is hardly a bad thing—"

"I didn't say it was bad," he replied firmly. "She's perfectly wondrous in every way."

Shit. Those were more words he hadn't meant to say. Compliments were dripping out of him like water from a leaky faucet. Which wasn't to say he *didn't* think Amelia was wondrous. In fact, saying the word only made it feel more correct.

"So, what would you give her, then?" the voice from the crowd challenged.

Amelia appeared to clam up, her eyes locked with Eli's. She seemed to be searching him, ascertaining how much of this was an act and how much was true. He couldn't have answered her if he'd tried. Not because he didn't know the answer, but because he wasn't sure he wanted her to know yet.

But how could Amelia not know how he felt? Here he was, standing like a dolt in front of all these people, practically spelling it out for her. And still she stared. With those ruthless eyes that betrayed nothing.

"I ... I ..." Amelia started, swallowing the remainder of the sentence.

"What about chrysanthemums?" Kitty asked. "Or sunflowers?"

Breaking the tether of their gaze, Amelia leaned down to Kitty, who was presenting both of her suggestions. Amelia regarded them for a while, touching the petals tenderly as if saying goodbye to an old friend. Finally, when the crowd began to murmur and its curiosity could no longer be allayed, Amelia returned to Eli, offering a sad half-smile. She reached behind the table into one of her boxes and pulled out a bunch of tiny blue flowers, all charmingly identical with their tough five petals and yellow center like a bullseye to the heart.

With great care, she arranged them in a bouquet, tying the dark green stems with a simple white ribbon. Shyly, as if she was gifting the flowers to him, Amelia presented him with the offering.

"Forget-me-nots," Kitty said dubiously, moderating the interaction. "Why those?"

Attention fixed on Eli, Amelia answered, "It's a promise. That no matter what happens to them, wherever their lives lead, he will always keep her in his thoughts."

Kitty was still not convinced. "It's a little simple, no?"

Amelia shook her head, a lovely pink climbing onto her cheeks, as promising and hopeful as the flowers she sold. "Life can be complicated. Sometimes simple is best. I think for this woman, these are the best choice."

Eli accepted the flowers, not registering the people swarming around him, fighting to be next in line. Shoulders and hips bumped him, but he didn't move. Even as Amelia gave him one last little smile and turned to her customers—attentively listening as they describe who they wanted to give flowers to—Eli stood his ground, lost and adrift in his feelings.

Eli's fist tightened around the stems, his knuckles turning white.

Flowers were a language, Amelia had told him.

Flowers said what people were too afraid to say themselves. Amelia was saying something unmistakable to him. And Eli didn't like it. He didn't like it one little bit.

CHAPTER TWENTY-FOUR

ELI DIDN'T ORDER Amelia to sit in the front of the carriage with him on the way home. He didn't ask her to either. In fact, even before Amelia approached the wagon, he asked the twins if they wanted to ride beside him, bribing them with the chance to take turns holding the reins and directing the horses.

Amelia sat in the back the entire journey, alone with her feet dangling over the edge of the cart, the discarded broken leaves and stems scattered alongside her, the bag of coins heavy in her lap.

The only solace she took—though why she needed solace, she wasn't sure—was that Eli hadn't thrown the forget-me-nots on the side of the road like she'd assumed he would. Nor had he given them to the girls. The tiny blooms remained clenched in his hand throughout the whole ride. He never placed them down or dropped a single petal, not even when he had to grab the reins from Kitty and haul the animals under control after she'd incited them to a roaring gallop.

That had to mean something, didn't it?

Nothing felt right. The twins and she had made another killing, selling flowers hand over fist. At this rate, Amelia might even be able to pay back Harry's Boys and be in London by next week. And yet that realization did little to curb the unsettled feeling in the bottom of her stomach. There was a gnawing ache there that had nothing to do with Kitty's poor driving and the bumps in the road. And Amelia didn't know how to salve it.

Michael was waiting for the family, hopping and waving near the stables as if they'd just come back from conquering Jerusalem. The girls wasted little time filling him in on the day and the part their father played in its success. As the children flittered around Eli, he stooped low to pick up Michael and give her a smacking kiss on his cheeks, making the little boy giggle with pure surprised ecstasy. Michael was shocked for a whole two seconds before he stopped dwelling on the "why" of his father's actions and just accepted them gleefully. Eli placed Michael back on his feet, listening to the girls piping into the stories whenever they went off on tangents.

To Amelia, it was a lovely familial scene. However, the moment she caught sight of her position regarding it—on the outside as usual—an overwhelming loneliness soaked deep into her bones, making it difficult for her to stand.

Amelia didn't trust herself to leave, lest she fall flat on her face, so she leaned on the wagon as Eli unloaded the empty carts, placing them back in the stables. Without a word to her, he traveled back and forth, not giving her any inkling of what he was thinking. Amelia always thought she had the power to read anyone, and yet this man continued to be such an enigmatic puzzle. Hot and cold; dismissive and then bursting with questions. She'd never met someone so intent on holding all his cards so close to the chest. And she'd grown up around the best card sharps in London!

Eli passed her a few more times, holding her flowers in one hand, hiding his emotions in the other. When Amelia couldn't take his aloof demeanor a second longer, she wished the children a good night and went to her room. Counting her money after a long day had always massaged her ego and her conscience before, but halfway up the stairs, the weight of the money bag in her hand, she came to the conclusion that counting wouldn't do her any good tonight. Her ego and her conscience were fine; it was her heart that felt brittle and stiff. People assumed that money made you happy, but Amelia had learned long ago that that wasn't the case. Money could buy food and lodgings, clothes and even friends, husbands and titles, but happiness was beyond its power. It could never bring back her real mother, or make Molly see her as something more than a golden goose. It could never earn trust or loyalty or respect or love. And those were the traits needed for relationships to flourish—real relationships.

Like families.

Deep down, Amelia understood that Molly loved her in her own way, but the gang in London wasn't her family any more than the twins were. They were her partners. Good partners. Loyal partners. But partners are all the same. Partners that ran when you found yourself in a jam rather than sticking around to help you find a way out.

Which was why Amelia had wanted to move on. She'd wanted out of the gang because she didn't want to spend the rest of her life looking over her shoulder; that was true. But she'd also dreamed of creating a family that was completely hers, one that didn't revolve around a set of draconian rules. Amelia had dreamed up the flower shop because she wanted a place where her daughters could learn the benefits of hard work, where friends would know where to find her, where her husband could watch her thrive. Where a collection of people could experience a shared life built around trust and love.

Amelia trudged into her room, disrobing herself in record time then crawling onto the lush confines of her bed. She just wanted to sleep. And sleep and sleep and sleep. And maybe in all that sleeping, she might find a new dream, one that didn't involve going back to London and working with Molly again. One that had a happy ending. She didn't believe in those sorts of things. They were dangerous.

But, for tonight, she let herself be.

THE WALLS WERE vibrating. No, more than that. They were damn near shaking! Amelia's head popped up from the bed, hair tangled all over her groggy face. The room was dark, and it took her a solid minute to remember where she was or how she got there. She'd fallen asleep over her blankets, just her thin chemise covering her chilled body.

The walls pounded again, the sound increasing in volume and temper.

"Amelia. I know you're in there," a booming voice called.

Amelia held her head in her hands. Eli. What had she done now? And why the hell couldn't he wait to yell at her until the morning?

Without thinking, Amelia lugged herself out of the bed, her limbs feeling like they were made of pudding, and marched to the door. When she swung it open, she didn't know who was more surprised.

Eli's glasses always made his eyes look unnaturally large, but they almost fell off his face as he gaped at her state. His gaze ran over her barely clad body, and words stalled on his lips.

Amelia looked down and yelped, dashing into the room to grab the robe draped on the back of her chair. Fiddling with the tie, she knotted it securely before returning to the door.

"I was sleeping," she said, half grudgingly and half apologetically. "Why are you here beating my door to death?"

"First of all, it's my door," Eli said, getting over his stupor, anger refilling. "Second of all, I have something I have to discuss with you."

Without waiting for her to respond, he sailed past her into the room, striding along its perimeter. *Probably wants to make sure I haven't stolen anything yet*, Amelia thought bitterly.

"I was sleeping," she said again with much more indignation. Eli didn't seem to mind. His face settled into its usual stoic demeanor.

"It's not that late," he replied dismissively, sighting her bag in the corner. He walked over to it and, with one finger, lifted up the flap so he could peek inside. The nerve!

Amelia stalked toward him, ripping the bag away from his prying. "It doesn't matter how late it is," she seethed. His eyebrows leapt up, as if it were *her* behavior that was shocking. "What matters is that I said I was sleeping, and you haven't even apologized—"

"You can't go."

Amelia flinched back as if he'd just tried to dive into her pockets "What?"

Eli's expression lost some of its arrogance. He ducked his head, chagrined. "You can't go ... yet."

"Yet?" she repeated, trying—and failing—to understand what he was saying. Of course she couldn't leave yet. She still didn't have the money she needed. And the girls were ... What were the girls?

"The girls are still holy terrors!" he announced, folding his arms across his chest. Now that he'd spit out the statement, his confidence appeared to be restored, his superiority back in its rightful place. "You haven't helped them as we'd agreed."

Amelia couldn't seem to form an idea and hold on to it. On the surface, she understood the situation she was in. Eli was in her room, at night, and he was yelling at her about his daughters. But her mind still couldn't process why.

One thing she did understand was that he was angry. Very angry. Even with the scant moonlight streaking through the windows, Amelia could see that his color was high, his neck muscles straining from under his collar. Well, too damn bad. She'd been sleeping!

"First of all," Amelia said, echoing his infuriating tone, "our agreement only involved my coming to your home and speaking to your daughters. How they continue to behave has nothing to do with me. That is your problem." She poked him right in the center of his chest, upsetting his glasses. "You are their father."

He fixed his glasses over his nose. "How dare—"

"And you"—she poked him again—"need to be more specific. What do you mean they're still terrors? Your daughters have never been terrors. They are sweet, hardworking, intelligent girls—"

"I know that—"

"So what did they do?"

"What?"

Amelia stood back, her finger hurting from poking him in the chest so much. "What did they do that got you so upset?"

"I'm not upset," Eli declared icily. "Women get upset. Men do not get upset."

Oh, for the Lord's sake. She sighed. "Fine. What has you so … disappointed. Angry. Perturbed. Disgruntled."

"Dinner," he said, the muscle in his jaw flexing. Had she gone too far with the teasing? Did she ever care?

"What about dinner?"

"They kicked Michael's chair."

Amelia paused, breath held, waiting for more of the story to unfold. After a few seconds, when nothing came, she sucked in a loud exhale, her lungs billowing wide. "And?"

Eli arched an eyebrow. "And I've told them repeatedly not to."

"So … keep telling them."

"I have!"

What wasn't she getting? Eli was scowling at her as if he was speaking Greek and expected her to understand everything. But she didn't. Not at all. Amelia tossed her hands up. "Why am I getting blamed for this? They are your daughters. And, by the way, kicking a chair is a far cry from lighting a governess's clothes on fire."

"That's precisely my point!"

"What is?"

"Your work isn't done. You can't leave yet!"

The words came out like a roar, pushing Amelia's hair off her face. She roared right back. He. Woke. Her. Up! "Who said I was leaving? I know I'm not done yet. Why are you yelling at me?"

"Why are you yelling at me?" he yelled back.

"I asked you first!"

"Because … dammit, you gave me those damn flowers." Eli faltered, his voice losing half its volume.

"Flowers? What are you talking about?"

"The blue flowers," he said. "You were telling me something with them, giving me a message with your silly coded language."

Incredulously, Amelia replayed the day's events in her mind. "The forget-me-nots? You're upset that I asked you not to forget me?"

Eli's head shot up, eyes smoldering with intensity. "Yes, forget you," he said, stepping closer, eating up the space between them. He wasn't poking her in the chest, but Amelia still felt the force he directed at her. "You are asking me not to forget you, which means that you are planning on leaving soon."

Was *that* what he'd gotten out of the whole thing? That was where his mind had swirled? "It … it was meant to be a nice gesture," Amelia stammered. *Maybe even a romantic one.*

He loomed above her. "It was meant to be *final.*"

"But …" She licked her lips. They were so dry, as if all the fire in Eli had sucked up all the moisture in the room. "You *want* a final. There has to be a final."

"Who says?" He crowded her. Amelia backtracked until she hit the wall. But he didn't stop. He kept going until he clung to her like a blanket she'd always yearned for but never hoped to receive.

"Everyone says." Amelia shrugged and immediately regretted it. Her breasts rubbed against his chest and her nipples strained through her chemise. His slow smile told her that he'd felt them too. "Life says," she whispered.

He shook his head. "Not yours. And certainly not mine."

CHAPTER TWENTY-FIVE

"W HAT ARE YOU saying, Eli?"

Eli glanced over his shoulder at the bed and then back at Amelia. "I'm saying that I am not leaving this room tonight."

She stared at the large, historical bed. The ornately decorated room. His. All his. Amelia was a thief. She knew the laws better than most barristers. Possession was everything. And right now, here in this moment, Eli had her. The only question she had to ask herself was: did she want him to?

Yes.

The answer came to her freely, without effort. Tonight, Amelia wanted to belong to someone. She wanted to be a part of something real and true, something not taken but freely given.

Eli lifted his fingertips, caressing her shoulder. Had she been shaking? "Don't be afraid—"

"I'm not afraid," Amelia replied quickly. "I just ... I ..."

The words cemented in her mouth. How could she explain that there was a gulflike divide between fear and trepidation? Amelia Driver was no coward, but she also made it a habit never to jump into the unknown. And making love to Eli would force her to jump into a pool of water where she couldn't see the bottom.

What would it feel like to break the glasslike surface, float with the current while the waves crashed around her? To be so unmoored?

Would it feel like his hand as it lowered down her shoulder, over her forearm? The rough, callused fingers made the goose-bumps prickle over her skin, the hairs on her arms stretch from the riotous static.

Eli ventured down until he found her hand. Intertwining their fingers, he gave her a reassuring squeeze. "I want more from you than flowers," he said, pulling her off the wall, towing her to the bed. Sitting down, he held her in front of him, widening his legs so she could stand in between them.

If Amelia was being honest with herself, she would have acknowledged that this moment had seemed inevitable since the moment Eli kissed her in the inn in Scotland. And yet she still felt unsteady, unsure of what to do next. Her arms seemed out of place at her sides, as useless and ornamental as her old pregnancy costume. She gnawed on her bottom lip. "What if flowers are all that I can give?"

A deep chuckle sounded from his chest, and Amelia felt a frisson of excitement, knowing that soon she would be able to witness the source of that sound, feel his bare skin beneath her palm.

Eli's eyes caught hers, the blue orbs warming her insides like a sun-drenched sky. "I'm not asking for much ... only your body ... and your mind ... and your soul ..."

Amelia laughed. "Only that? Those things might be difficult to give."

Eli worked on the knot of her robe, slipping off the gauzy article before he answered. "Oh, but you forget," he drawled, a lazy smile playing on his mouth. His hands dropped lower, finding the hem of her chemise. "I've been living with a thief for the last few weeks. I've learned a thing or two about stealing."

Amelia gasped as he lifted the fabric, one tantalizing inch at a time, the cotton skating on her skin eliciting dizzying pleasures and sensations. "And what is that?"

Behind his frames, Eli's eyes dazzled with awareness. "That sometimes the best way to steal something is when you're in plain sight. All you need is a little distraction."

With the chemise lifted to Amelia's chest, he stopped moving. The drafty air hit her, causing her skin to tighten and her nipples to pucker to attention inches away from Eli's rapt face. He stared at her body like a scholar, studying it, reading it, desperate for all the knowledge it could bestow. Power engulfed her like it never had before. She knew Eli desired her, but to see it so desperately … She was the one with barely any clothes on, and yet he seemed more naked than her.

He dipped his head and caught a nipple in his mouth, swirling his tongue around it, sucking gently, letting the heat of his mouth warm every corner of Amelia's body. Her arms remained limp at her sides as he delved into her, kissing her mounds and the hollow space between them. Eli left no patch of skin un-kissed, no line unread.

Amelia's head lolled back, and she stared at the cream-colored ceiling, luxuriating in the rasp of Eli's tongue, the sharpness in his teeth, the way his hands now shook while he held her chemise. Finally, he dropped the flimsy fabric so he could grab hold of her behind. He clutched her with a searing intensity that made Amelia yelp. The explosive sound was soon eaten up as his mouth found hers.

It was a demanding kiss, one of pure need. Their tongues mingled together as their heads canted, leaving no space between them. Her body snapping to attention, Amelia held Eli's head in her hands, slanting him to just the right degree, having never known how important it was before. But it was. She needed him at just the right angle to have all of him, leaving nothing behind, savoring all he had to give. Eli tasted of wine and sugar. Amelia thought if she kissed him long and deeply enough, she'd be able to decipher where the grapes were planted, the herbs that shared the soil.

He burrowed into the cave between her breasts, taking deep

breaths as if to settle himself. She cradled him against her, loving the way his hands never stopped moving. Even when they found something they liked—a turgid nipple, the wetness between her legs—they roamed freely like there was so much more to discover. So much more to her.

Amelia let herself get lost in the splendor. When he sucked her nipple again, she cried out. Her screams were a prayer. To him as well. Because he increased the pressure on the delicate points until her scream grew louder, not stopping until her voice became hoarse.

Her body moved of its own accord now, undulating under his, dancing in its own rhythm. Eli's breath warmed her; his body cloaked her; his fingers in her sex excited her. And when she came, his moan honored her.

"Goddammit," Eli said roughly, hiding his head into the notch under her neck. "I fucking love when you make that sound."

Amelia laughed, twining her fingers in his hair. "Not as much as I love making it, I assure you."

He lifted his head. "How about we make it together this time?"

His enthusiasm was infectious, soaking through her reluctance. Not wanting to seem like a complete novice, she unlatched his trousers and reached for his manhood, closing on him like a steel trap. Eli's head fell like a lead ball straight to her chest.

"Not … so hard, darling," he choked out.

"Oh!" She recoiled as if an adder had bitten her. "So sorry!" Humiliation consumed her. One didn't grow up on the street without seeing some unsavory activity in dark alleyways, and Amelia was no different. However, she would never describe what she'd been privy to as loving. The motions were always hectic, perfunctory and battering, two people in a hurry to find pleasure and/or an ending as quickly as they could. No one had ever intimated that the act should be different.

"It's fine, it's fine," Eli reassured her through heavy pants. He took her hand and re-placed it on his rod. "I liked it. Very much. I just need to work up to that. Took me by surprise, was all."

He wasn't the only one. With a job like diving, Amelia thought she'd felt everything. People wouldn't believe what one could find in a man's pocket. But this ... this was something else altogether. Eli was smooth and long, delicate as a rose petal, and she treated him with the same care. His hand over hers, he taught her how to manipulate the skin, not to snag or yank it while she pumped up and down, slow and first, and then increasing in speed. She followed his breath, his hips. His growls. And then she went faster. Harder.

"Stop now, baby, you have to stop," Eli said, though he wasn't stopping, nor did it really seem like he wanted her to. Amelia pumped even harder. "I want to be inside you," he rasped, his eyes open, watching her work him. It *was* a mesmerizing sight—his manhood, so powerful and hard, straining in her capable hands.

With an ungraceful, panicked swoop, Eli flung her hand off his rod and lifted her up. He sat Amelia on his lap, arranging her legs on each side of his while he tore her chemise over her head. The frenzied motions made her giggle, but that soon fell away as she felt him at her entrance, the blunt tip of his shaft poised to enter her.

Amelia's thighs burned as she held herself up over him, her gaze boring into his.

Eli kissed her lips, lightly, reverently, one hand cradled behind her neck. "Mark my words, Amelia my love. I will steal your soul and your mind and your body, but I won't steal your trust. Tell me to stop now and I will wait."

Now he asked her if she wanted to stop? When she could feel the lips of her core molding over his straining shaft?

Amelia could barely form a sentence in her passion-befuddled mind, and he was asking her to speak? She decided to stay with the tried and true. "You are such an ass," she whispered into his lips.

Eli didn't smile. Like her, Amelia figured he didn't have the extra energy. His skin was flushed and sweaty and his glasses held a foggy sheen. "I take it that means I should continue?"

She nodded. "You'd better," she said.

In one fluid movement, Eli impaled her. Amelia screamed out, clutching his head between her breasts, reveling in his serrated breaths as they stimulated her sensitive nipples. They stayed like that for a long moment, twined together like a ball of yarn, no end and no beginning. To Amelia, the pain between her legs was secondary; their entire unit appeared to throb, from the top of her head to the bottom of his toes. They were one. And when Eli began to lift her, their bodies moved as one.

Amelia had planned to lie. She'd witnessed enough back-alley situations to know that they were mostly for the men's benefit. In those cases, those women were merely props, vehicles for male satisfaction. But the noises Amelia heard from herself seemed utterly foreign. They came freely from her body, in tandem with the sensations Eli provoked in her. As he lowered her onto his shaft, they slid and rubbed and created a friction that was beyond the mortal plane. And Amelia could feel it build.

She canted her pelvis against his, angling it more, taking him deeper, needing his shaft to hit a certain spot higher. And when he did—when he did!—it was like her entire body took flight.

"Oh, God, yes," Amelia mewed, before Eli's mouth took hers again.

He felt bigger inside her now, thicker, more determined. He ground her bottom down, so hard and so full she thought she could feel him touch her womb. And what would that be like? If he filled it tonight with something beautiful …

"Fuck yes. Talk more. Say more," he said.

Say more? Amelia had no idea she'd been talking. "What do you want me to say?"

Eli licked around her nipple, not giving her what she wanted. "Say anything. Everything. Tell me you want me."

"I want you."

"Tell me you love me inside you."

That cataclysmic burst was almost there. Amelia's voice hitched as she arched for it, stretched out for it. Just a few more strokes. Sweat dripped down her forehead; it was like being drenched in a baptismal font. "I love you inside me."

Then Eli stopped. Holding her captive on her shaft, their insides vibrating frantically, he planted his forehead against hers. "Tell me you won't ever leave me."

Held prisoner in Eli's arms, held captive by her torrent of emotions, Amelia gave him the words they both wanted. "I won't leave you," she promised.

He thrust again. And Amelia broke. Mind and spirit and soul.

And Eli picked up all those pieces and stole them in plain sight.

CHAPTER TWENTY-SIX

ELI STRETCHED HIS long arms over his head. "You know … *this* is a very comfortable bed," he murmured. "No wonder the king loved it so much."

"Ugh," Amelia groaned into her pillow. "Please stop talking; it's too early for words and sentences."

He smiled to himself. Again with the aching muscles. He hadn't felt this utterly transcendent in … he didn't know when. Never.

He could hear the house come to life underneath them, the servants hurrying through the hallways to begin their daily chores. The children would be awake soon. Eli should have risen hours ago, not only because it was his habit, but because it would be unseemly to be caught in Amelia's bed.

That only made his smile wider.

He glanced down at his bed partner. Amelia might have uttered words a few seconds ago, but she was right back to sleep on her side, hands tucked underneath her pillow, legs hitched into her chest as if she was trying to squeeze herself into the smallest form possible. The mammoth-sized bed was wasted on her. Luckily, Eli was here to appreciate it.

And he would continue to do so.

With a light finger, Eli brushed a curtain of black hair off her face, tucking it over her shoulder. She trembled under his touch, and her thick eyelashes batted against the pastel-colored skin under her eyes. A sliver of empathy rankled Eli, though it didn't last long. He hadn't allowed Amelia much sleep last night. Just as much as she'd allowed him. He should give it to her now … But the more Eli perused her, the hungrier he became. Even with the crust in her inner eyes. The tiny rivulet of drool staining her pillow. The breath that didn't have a snowball's chance in hell of being minty fresh. All of it. He wanted all of it. All its loveliness. The exoticism of the ordinary. Everything that he'd been missing in his life until he found this extraordinary woman.

A faint beam of pale light shone through the windows, landing on her pale face. With a foul mutter, Amelia twisted in the sheets away from Eli to her other side, snuggling until her bottom was pushed up against him.

A man could only take so much.

He draped over her, wrapping his arms around her compact torso, taking her hands in his. Over her shoulder, he studied them, the faded pink welts that crossed over the tops like thick brush strokes on an oil painting. He'd hoped she would let him in on her history, tell him about the woman who'd hurt her under the guise of love and tutoring. The twins had been the ones to inform Eli, but he would never let on that he knew. He wanted to gain her trust. Until that time, he would wait patiently.

But he wouldn't be idle. Eli nuzzled into the curve of her neck, this time eliciting a less offended grumble from Amelia's sleep state. He kissed her downy skin, rubbing his nose along the ridge of her scapula, appreciating the sheer strength hidden just under the surface.

Eli had never made love in the morning before. In all his thirty years, he'd never had a woman when the sun was rising. With no shadows to shelter behind, he thought it would hinder his ardor, and yet the opposite was true. There was something freeing about daylight. No hiding. His passion, his need, was firmly on display. Eli liked that. He wanted Amelia to not only feel it all but to see it as well.

"I thought you said your wife called you passionless," Amelia said, wiggling her behind against his growing manhood even more. "There's nothing passionless about this."

Eli chuckled into her hair, filling his lungs with the lavender and orange-peel scent. He kept his head there until all thoughts of his wife evaporated from his mind. He didn't want to think about her, didn't want her memory to mar anything he was developing with Amelia. Marianne *had* called him passionless. For a long time, Eli assumed he was. It wasn't until he met Amelia that he realized that passion and lust were two different things. The twenty-year-old Eli had experienced lust for his new wife, though little passion. Just as he'd loved Marianne but had never been in love with her. Those phrases—so similar—had miles between them. And those miles were where marriages died.

When Eli found his voice, he whispered in Amelia's ear, "I have too much passion for you. Will you let me show you, Amelia? Will you let me show you one more time?"

He knew he was asking a lot, but tried not to be too embarrassed over it. The last thing he should be doing was entering Amelia's tender body again, but she answered by rocking against him. He captured one breast, weighing it in his hand like it was gold. Eli tweaked the rose-colored nipple with his fingers before tracing a path down between her legs, which were still damp and sticky with the seed he'd left. He entered her with his finger smoothly, hushing Amelia with soothing tones while he circled his thumb over her clitoris, rocking into her from behind with his pelvis.

"Can you do it for me, Amelia?" Eli asked, tracing her ear with his tongue, sucking the lines and grooves as she shivered. "Just one more time?"

"What do I get in return?" she asked cheekily. Eli decided then and there he would never again guess what Amelia was going to say. He was destined to always be wrong.

Nipping at her neck, he licked the jump in her pulse. "How about an orgasm that will shake the house from its foundation?"

She shook against his hand, her breath quickening. "Surely you shouldn't promise something that enormous. Hasn't anyone ever told you that pride comes before the fall?"

"Don't tell me you stole the Bible too?"

Amelia laughed, a husky, erotic noise that made his balls tighten. Eli couldn't wait any longer. He arranged himself behind her, planting his shaft at her entrance, lifting her right leg up and over his own to spread her wider for him.

Inching inside her tight space, Eli felt harmony overtake him. Amelia was completely his. He would always have the answer to her every need.

When he could go no deeper, he hugged Amelia with a fierceness that stole his own breath. This. Was. Perfect. He'd never known that heaven was on earth, but here he was. Hadn't he once referred to Amelia as one of Lucifer's fallen angels?

Once he began thrusting, it didn't last long. Eli was too thoughtful that morning, too overwhelmed with whimsical ideas. The second he felt Amelia's inner muscles begin to spasm, he unleashed himself, filling her with his seed and his future. There was no separating them anymore. It was all he wanted with Amelia. It was all he would accept.

When her breathing had evened out, she twisted in his arms and placed a sweet kiss on the scar on the top of his lip. Soft and undemanding, the action was so different than the rampage of fervor that had just exhausted itself between them. Eli was shocked by how much it affected him. It felt like love. Simple love.

Her eyes sparkled when she tilted her head up to his. "The house is still standing. I was worried for a minute."

"You have nothing to worry about, my love. This house was built to last."

As are we.

A small patter sounded at the door. "Miss Amelia?" Mrs. Hutchinson said. "Apologies for bothering you this early, but ... you have a visitor."

Amelia pushed her hair out of her face, popping up from Eli's chest. "Who is it?" she called out.

On the opposite side of the door, the chatelaine hesitated. "Um … an older lady. Says she's your mother?"

The color in Amelia's face fled, and her mouth dropped open.

"Your mother?" Eli asked. "Or your mother-like figure?"

Pulling the sheets to cover her chest, Amelia slid to the side of the bed. "Tell her I'll be down at once," she called out.

Mrs. Hutchinson's forthright footsteps could be heard retreating down the hallway.

"I have to get ready," Amelia said, her back to Eli. How quickly the levity of the morning had vanished. How quickly the light had brought in the day.

Eli hated to be confrontational, not when so much had been achieved between them, but he had so many questions that his tone was more abrasive than he would have liked. "Who is that woman to you?"

Amelia's shoulders pulled back. She stared ahead at the wall. "She raised me. That's all you need to know."

"She raised you to be a thief."

"She raised me."

Eli edged up behind Amelia, circling her with his arms, though she didn't fall into him as she would have before. "Don't leave."

From the corner of his eye, he saw her blink as if awakening from a dream. "Why would I leave? You already told me my job isn't done yet."

The attempt at a joke fell flat; neither of them had the heart to pretend.

"Let me come down with you—"

"No, please," Amelia snapped, too quickly for his tastes. He must have looked put out, because she took his face in her hands. "She won't be here long. Let me speak to her alone. And then she'll go." She caressed the sides of his face with her short nails. "Just promise me one thing, Eli. Don't let the twins near her.

Keep them away."

"What? Why?"

"Please? Just trust me. I'll explain everything later. You asked for my trust last night, and I gave it. Now I'm asking for yours."

Eli scowled. He hated relinquishing control of any kind, but she had a point. Amelia had given her trust. Now, it was his turn to do the same. He didn't have to like it, though.

"Don't be long," he grumbled, before giving her a hard kiss.

Amelia kept her lips on his longer than necessary, as if unwilling to be parted from him. That little action scared him more than anything she wasn't telling him.

CHAPTER TWENTY-SEVEN

AMELIA HURRIED TO the drawing room, checking herself before she entered. She waited just outside the door, patting down her dress, taking a settling breath. In her rush, Amelia hadn't come up with a decent reason for Molly to be there. Whatever it was, it couldn't be good. Molly never left London. Country life was as useless to her as a fingerless pickpocket—or a retired one.

"I know you're there; you might as well come in," Molly called out from the drawing room.

Amelia's neck wilted. That was why she was Molly Diamond. Always two steps ahead of her, Molly was.

Amelia sailed in the room, feigning confidence. "I came as soon as I could," she said, walking toward her mentor, stopping before they were close enough to hug or kiss. There was no need for it. Molly had never been one for displays of affection. The closest she ever came was a hearty pounding on the back whenever Amelia brought something unexpected home after a day on the streets.

Molly pursed her lips, scrutinizing her protégée, seeming completely out of place in Eli's home. Even decked out in her finest day dress with matching bonnet, the older woman was incongruous. Her crimson silk was a shade too deep, the feathers in her bonnet a hair too long. Everything about her screamed *outsider*. Perhaps Amelia was just being touchy. But even Molly's lemon-yellow hair offended her. The older woman dyed the grays away because she never wanted people to consider her old. Older people were victims, easily manipulated, and Molly would never be that.

She arched a thin, light brow. "Since when do you have to pause on the other side of a room before coming to see me? It was the soap," she said, noticing Amelia's eyes widen in wonder. "I can always recognize that smell. Bergamot. Smells like oranges. You've used it since you were a little girl. Ever since I bought a block for you. Expensive tastes."

"I wonder who I got that from." Amelia laughed, attempting to lighten the room. The atmosphere had a charge to it; one spark and everything might blow.

A shrewd smile lifted Molly's narrow face. She retreated, wandering around the room, picking up various knickknacks and placing them back down, no doubt estimating their worth with the speed of a banker. "Why haven't you written? After your first letter, I assumed another would be coming soon. We've all been waiting."

"Were you worried about me at all?"

Molly placed a crystal candleholder back on a side table. "Of course! But you told me you were fine. Don't forget who trained you. I knew you would be able to handle this little predicament."

"Then why did you come?"

For the first time, Amelia sensed alarm in the older woman's expression. It was gone before she could study it further, though it tugged at her memory, transplanting her to a regrettable time and place.

"We're running out of time. Something's happened," Molly said.

"Jenny." Even though Amelia would never consider the girl a bosom friend, it still hurt to say her name. Visions of her crumpled body came to the forefront of her mind, making Amelia's stomach roll. No one deserved to die like that.

"Yes, Jenny." Molly sighed, continuing her perusal of the room. "Harry's Boys sent a letter informing me of what they'd done. I never saw the body. They said they were sending it to you."

"I … got the message."

"Good," Molly said coldly, meeting Amelia's gaze. "Then you know you are out of time. You need to get me that money so I can pay them back."

"I don't have it yet—"

"What are you talking about?" Molly said, raising her arms at her sides. "You're surrounded by it. Just name the day and I will have the girls come and clean house. You're sitting on a gold mine! That's a Caravaggio behind me."

Amelia shook her head. Why was everyone so impressed by that Caravaggio?

"We can't steal from here. It's too risky. Eli—"

"Eli?"

Amelia swallowed. "Viscount Barrington will never let us get away with it. He's too … attached to everything in this house."

Molly scoffed, rearranging the ormolu clock to get a closer look at the cherubs. Amelia would have to remember to put it back exactly as it had been before Eli came in the room. "Then we'll only take small things; things he won't possibly care out."

The words rushed out of Amelia. "He'll remember everything. I'm telling you … it's too risky. Besides, I have a better idea. I've been making some money already. It's not a lot, but it can be soon. I'm selling more flowers than I ever did—"

"Flowers?" Molly spat the word out like it was a mouthful of mugwort, her countenance slipping into rank disappointment. "Honestly, Amelia. Haven't you learned your lesson yet? I thought you'd finally come back to your senses."

One by one, the words pierced Amelia's skin as if they were a swarm of bees stinging her for her stupidity.

Molly walked over to her, taking hold of her upper arms. Her expression softened, the wrinkles she tried to cover up with makeup sinking deeper into her powdered skin. "My little dear. I'm sorry it is I that must keep telling you this. Truly, I am. But you failed. The flower shop was a disaster, and it isn't just you that is paying for it. I'm the one who initiated the loan from Harry. I have to pay him back. Now, I don't know what's going on here. I don't know why you won't steal from these people who obviously have enough to give, but you need to get your head on straight. We are in trouble; make no mistake. Your little flowers got you into this mess, but they won't be able to get you out." Molly pounded a fist into her chest. "*Me.* What I've taught you. That is your salvation, just as it always was. Now, do you understand?"

Amelia shook her head, stunned. It was all she could think to do. Molly would never understand. She'd only let Amelia start the flower shop after she had begged for months. Now, looking into her mentor's concerned hazel eyes, Amelia knew the truth. Molly Diamond might be a world-class criminal, but Amelia had grown up and learned everything from the woman. She knew when she was lying. Molly had wanted her to fail. From the very beginning. If only to teach her another lesson.

Molly dropped her arms with a relieved smile. "There now," she said, pulling up the gloves on her skinny arms. "I'll be expecting a letter in the next week. I'll tell Harry's Boys they'll have their money soon after. And then you can come back, and we'll move on. Pretend all of this never happened."

But it had happened. Brushing it under the rug wouldn't work this time. The flower shop. The twins. Barrington. Eli. They all happened, and Amelia would never be the same.

Impotence crushed her. She'd never felt so out of control. Amelia Driver could get out of any scrap. There were no handcuffs she couldn't unlock. So why couldn't she fix this? Molly's mere presence seemed to paralyze her, turn her back into the helpless child she'd been all those years ago.

"What if I went to Harry?" she asked, stopping Molly from turning toward the door. "I've always had a good relationship with him. He'll listen to me. Like I told you, I have some money. I'll give him that for now and buy some time. It will work. I know it will."

Molly put up a hand, each finger shining with a bauble that Amelia's teary eyes were too cloudy to appreciate. "Don't you think I've already tried that?" she asked. "I've pleaded. I really have. They are done waiting. Times are hard for all of us. Money is short in the game. The new police force is cracking down on the gangs. I'm afraid this is it, my dear. We need to band together if we're going to succeed. You can't talk your way out of this one. Finish this so you can come home."

Home. A word Amelia had revered her entire life. Only now that Molly had said it, it seemed to have lost all its shine, like a sterling silver spoon tarnished over decades in a cupboard.

"I don't know if I can," Amelia whispered shamefully, lowering her head to miss the anger she knew was coming. In all their years together, Amelia had never betrayed Molly nor questioned her. She'd seen others do it and rue the consequences.

But a swift slap across the face did not come, nor did a fit of rage. It was something much worse. Disappointment. "You don't think you can?" Molly asked, creeping so close that Amelia could smell the tobacco on her breath, see the stains on her yellow teeth. "Let me tell you something else Harry said. Poor Jenny was just the beginning. Don't think for one second that I don't know what's going on here with … *Eli.* And Harry knows as well. He'll come for him and the children."

Amelia's head sprang up.

"Oh yes," Molly said. "He knows about them too. Twins. How delightful. What Harry would do with twins …" She let Amelia's imagination go wild with all the ways a person like Harry or Molly would take advantage. "Girls get lost in London all the time. Stolen. I'd hate for that to happen to this poor family. It's seen enough scandal already. Wouldn't you hate to be the cause of more?"

Amelia's throat wobbled. She refused to break Molly's stare, but it took everything to keep from falling in a heap on the floor. The twins! She should have known Molly would find out. If Harry brought his retribution to Barrington, there was nothing Amelia could do to stop him.

Molly cupped her cheek, caressing her with her thumb, making Amelia only want to retch more. "You've run out of time, my love. But don't you know I will always take care of you? Didn't I promise your mother that on her deathbed? I've raised you since you were two years old, and I've never let you come to harm, and I don't intend to start now. You are my masterpiece. You are my heir. Everything I do, I do it for you. Don't you see that?"

With monumental reserve, Amelia nodded.

"I wish it could be different," Molly said. "You have no idea, but I need you, Amelia."

Again, Amelia registered something in the older woman that she hadn't recognized in a long time. Fear. Molly was scared for her. For them all.

Amelia had no choice but to make it right.

CHAPTER TWENTY-EIGHT

ELI WAITED TO go to Amelia. Even after the garish older woman departed, he kept his distance, hoping Amelia might come to him. But she didn't.

He had done what she'd asked, hiding the children while her guest was in the house. He'd taken them to the greenhouse and spent the time listening to the twins chatter on about all they'd learned about commerce and the art of starting a business of their own. Eli should have been mortified. In all honesty, he was a little bit, but his pride beat that away. Amelia was right—Cecily and Kitty were brilliant little creatures, with vivid imaginations and quick minds. Whatever they decided to do in life, he was certain they would do it well. They would never be model debutantes, never the belles of any balls. They would make their own way, and Eli would be there to clear the path for them to the best of his abilities. That was his role as their father.

His fear for their futures was swiftly disintegrating, because what he was equally sure of was that they would never be their mother. Yes, they had her spirit and rambunctious nature, and yes, they shared her uncommon beauty, but Eli could now see Marianne for the tragic figure that she was. The world, their society—even Eli—had put her in a box and expected her to stay there regardless of her wants or passions. And she'd rebelled soundly. Drastically. Fatally.

Eli would learn his lesson with his daughters. If they wanted a purpose outside of marriage and children, then they would have it. If they decided they wanted marriage and children too, then they could have that as well.

The world was moving so quickly. With its innovations and modernizations, the nineteenth century was barreling toward his children with the speed of a locomotive. Eli had no doubt they would be ready for it. The whispers, the gossip, the innuendoes … they would meet them head-on. Eli would make sure of it—with Amelia at his side. He couldn't do it without her. He didn't want to do *anything* without her.

Which was why after his two hours of waiting, Eli's patience had reached its limit and he searched the house. After checking the garden paths, the weeping willow tree, and the second greenhouse, he finally located Amelia in her room, sitting silently, motionlessly, on her bed, staring off into space.

The door was open, but Eli knocked anyway before stepping softly across the threshold. "Amelia?"

Her eyes barely flickered.

"My love, what happened? What did that woman say to you?"

She blinked. "That woman is my mother," she whispered.

He ventured toward her, taking his time as if she were a cornered animal. "I thought she was a *mother-like* figure."

"She is my mother," Amelia repeated, her tone stronger, almost like she was trying to convince herself.

Eli knelt at her feet. He tried to catch her gaze, but she wouldn't let him. "Mothers have their children's best interest at heart; does yours?" He cradled Amelia's hands in her lap, clasping them as if they were made of glass. "I don't know what she said to you or is asking you to do, but maybe it's time you started to see her for who she really is."

"She raised me," Amelia replied flatly.

"To be a thief."

She went on as if she hadn't heard him. "She fed me and

clothed me, made sure I always had a warm place to sleep. She didn't have to do that. She could have left me in an orphanage. She deserves credit."

"I won't deny that," Eli began, "but she also taught you to lie and cheat and steal to line her pockets."

Finally, Amelia met his gaze, and Eli felt it like a bolt to the chest, the emptiness in those dark pools of light. "It's not just me. Molly saves girls society throws away. She helps them stand on their own feet. You wouldn't understand."

She tried to yank her hands away, but Eli wouldn't let her. He turned her hands up so he could kiss the jagged scars on her skin, each and every one. "I understand what she did to you. And what she's going to keep doing to you if you go back. That isn't your life anymore. And the longer you stay, the more scars you will get"—he placed his hand over her chest—"in here."

"How do you know about my scars?"

"I made the twins tell me," Eli answered, hoping she wouldn't blame the girls. "They told me that woman would whip your hands every time she felt you steal from her. Hardly the action of a loving mother."

Brushing him back, Amelia stood up, hurrying over to her bag. "After that, did you explain to your daughters about Marianne? How she left them? Don't be a hypocrite, Eli. Don't ask me to see the fault in my own mother while you continue to shield your children from theirs. You want me to be ashamed of my mother; I won't be. She did what she had to do. Women don't have many opportunities in this world. We do what we can to get by.

"If you don't want your children to be ashamed of their mother, then you have to stop being ashamed of her. I'm sorry she didn't love you. I'm sorry she ran away. But not everyone is a villain. People are layered. Tell them the good things you remember. Stop hiding. The longer you wait, the harder it will be for them."

"You know why I wait," Eli said, pushing to his feet. "I'm

saving them from the pain."

Amelia's skirts fanned out as she rounded toward him. "There's no such thing as being saved from pain. It's all just an illusion! You can hide them here all you want, but the outside world will always find them. I have to go. Please, don't make this harder than it already is. The longer I stay here, the worse it will be for everyone."

Panic gripped his heart, followed swiftly by anger. "That's not true! You can't leave. I already told you—you haven't finished your end of the bargain."

"I'm sorry," Amelia said over her shoulder as she began stuffing all the clothes she'd accumulated during her stay into her bag. "It's out of my control. I have a debt to repay. I'm done here."

Eli watched her, the old feeling of being left behind racing back to him. What was it about him that was so easy to leave? First his parents, then his wife. Well, he couldn't save his parents, and he couldn't make Marianne love him. But Amelia did. Of that, he was certain. He would never be mistaken for a knight, but he would fight for her until his final breath left his body.

"Done here or down with me?" he asked.

Amelia froze. Like a sunflower deprived of light, her head hung even lower. With a bitter chuckle, she answered him with the same words she'd used the first time they met. "Does it matter?"

Eli spun her around to face him. "Yes. It. Does," he said, shaking her with every word. "It matters. You matter. To us. Just as we do to you. Don't deny it."

Tears flowing down her face, Amelia struggled to break free, but Eli's hold was too strong. Too determined. "I can't deny it," she said, sobbing. "But that's why I have to leave. If I don't go back, then Harry will come here. You don't know these people like I do. He will hurt you. Hurt your children. I can't let that happen."

"No one will hurt my children. Or you."

Bitter laughter collided with Amelia's tears. "You can't stop

Harry. *I can't stop Harry, which is why I have to leave. Please, Eli … we always knew this was going to end."

She shook him loose as the truth of her words bled into his conscience. Faith. She might have trusted him last night, but that was as far as she was willing to go. She had no faith in him. No faith that he could be the man she needed. To protect her. Save her.

"Let me pay him," Eli said. "I can sell—"

"No!" Amelia cried. "You can't do that. I got myself into this mess, and I can get myself out of it. Besides, if you paid for me, then I would be nothing better than your whore."

"Whore!" Eli raked a hand through his hair, upsetting the glasses on his face. "What aren't you hearing, woman? I want you to stay. I want you to be my wife. The mother of my children. Not my bloody whore!"

Amelia's tears gained speed, and her face crumpled with his admission. "Me? Your wife? You're out of your mind, Eli—"

"In the best way."

"No." She shook her head, hiccupping through a sob. "I won't bring any more scandal to your doorstep. I love your children too much to do that."

Eli was out of ideas. Amelia's decision was firm. He was throwing everything at her, and she was lobbing it right back. He released a long breath, glancing around the room that had once held a sleeping king. However, in the future, whenever Eli thought of this room, he would only think of Amelia.

"You can come back," he said, annoyed by the childish hopefulness in his tone. All he heard was weakness. Failure.

She began to pack again. "You won't want me back after I do what I have to do."

"I love you."

There. He'd said the words. And still Amelia clawed at her things, her hands covered in tears.

"Thank you."

"Thank you?" he echoed bitterly. "Is that all you can say to me? After everything?"

Like a beaten man trying to rise to his feet, the corners of Amelia's lip attempted to lift. "I assure you, you will thank me when I'm gone. Maybe not tomorrow or the day after. But in time, you will."

Eli backed away from Amelia, afraid that in his despair he might tie her to the bed as he once had. It hadn't worked before, and it surely wouldn't work now. Though that gave him an idea … "At least … at least"—he racked his brain, trying to find a way to keep her there a little while longer, until he could discover a viable solution—"leave in the morning. You can take the carriage. Give the children one more night with you."

Amelia sighed, her actions losing their speed. "What would that accomplish? What would we do? The day is half over already."

It came to Eli. Something he should have invited her to do a long time ago. "You will have dinner with us," he said. "One last time. As a family."

CHAPTER TWENTY-NINE

DINNER WAS A subdued affair. Even though Eli had opted not to tell the children that Amelia was leaving, they still sensed something was awry. That wasn't to say the meal wasn't enjoyable. There were plenty of laughs and the conversation never stopped flowing—however, there was an undercurrent of effort, as if everyone was putting on an act to keep things light and airy.

To her credit, Amelia was the best performer, regaling the kids with more stories of her days on the streets. Not once did Eli cover his ears with his hands, despite some of the tales being more sordid than usual. He wanted to hear them all. He wanted the constant reminder that what he was about to do was necessary and excusable. That what he was saving Amelia from was worth the underhandedness.

As the dessert plates were being taken away by the servants, Michael whined for one more story. Eli was ready for the request, already shaking his head. "Sorry, son. Time to wash up for bed."

Kitty piped up. "Please, Amelia. Just one more."

Amelia shared a look with Eli, and he relaxed back in his chair. "If the lady is up to it," he said.

She smirked at his use of the word "lady" and swept a hand over her forehead dramatically. "Another story, another story," she said, squinting up at the ceiling. "You've put me on the spot. I can't think of anything."

Placing her elbows on the table, Kitty shimmied her chair closer to Amelia's. "Of course you can. You always have more to teach us."

It was such a tiny movement—Eli was certain he was the only one who noticed Amelia flinch at the remark.

"I think I might have something," she said, almost wistfully, as she relaxed back in her seat. The whole room seemed to brace itself.

Amelia smiled softly at the twins. "Once there were two girls. They were the best of friends. Molly and Emily. Each of their parents died when they were young, and they met on the streets, practically raising each other. There was no one they trusted more. London can be a hellish place for two young girls, but Molly and Emily were special. Smart and fearless, they became something to be reckoned with, and other girls flocked to them, wanting to be a part of their gang. By the time they were twenty, they were making a name for themselves in London's underbelly, gaining respect. Molly thought she had everything she'd ever wanted, until one day Emily came to her and said she was leaving. She'd fallen in love and was going to have a baby. They wished each other well and didn't speak again.

"Two years later, Molly got a letter from Emily inviting her to her home on the other end of the city. When Molly arrived, she did her best to hide her disgust at the rancid way her friend had been living. Such poverty. It was everything they'd worked so hard to rise out of. Emily told Molly that she was dying of consumption. Her husband had vanished, leaving her alone to take care of the baby girl. She had been too embarrassed and ashamed to go back to Molly before, but now that she was dying, she had no one else. Emily made Molly promise to take care of the child, see that she didn't end up like the mother— brokenhearted and ruined. Taken advantage of.

"Now, Molly wasn't used to self-reflection, but even she had to acknowledge that she wasn't mother material—though she did what her friend asked. She took the little girl back to her gang and raised her the only way that she knew how. Molly taught the little girl to look at something from all angles. They solved riddles and puzzles. They played hide-and-go-seek even after the little girl realized it wasn't just a game. There wasn't much laughter, but there weren't many tears either. When the tears did come, they mostly came from Molly when she used her strap on the little girl's hands if she felt something was stolen from her pocket. 'You must be as quiet as a ghost,' Molly would tell her in between slaps from the thin leather, her tears mingling with the girl's blood. 'Being a ghost is your only hope; hiding in plain sight will be your power. It will save you from all the danger that comes for a woman whether she looks for it or not.'

"So the little girl grew up resourceful. She grew up proud ..." Amelia's dreamy expression hardened as she fought to finish her sentence. She shrugged. "She grew up strong."

Silence settled in the room.

Michael leaned toward his father. "Is that it?" he whispered.

Amelia chuckled. "Sorry, not much of a story."

"It's not that," Kitty replied, her expression pensive. "I just don't know what you want us to learn from it."

Amelia shrugged again, her forehead creased. "Nothing, I guess. It was just a story."

"A love story," Cecily added hopefully.

"Yes." Amelia offered with a thin-lipped smile. "Yes, I suppose it is."

LATER THAT NIGHT, Amelia and Eli walked the stairs to the third floor hand in hand. When he followed her into her room, she offered him a questioning look.

"If you think I'm sleeping by myself tonight, you're gravely mistaken," he said, tugging at his cravat. "If this is my last night with you, then I'm going to make the most of it."

Amelia's cheeks flushed prettily, the only source of color in a face that had grown dourer as the night wore on. Even though he still had no intention of letting her escape, it salved his pride to know that she took no pleasure in her departure. She didn't want to leave him. That was all he needed to know.

Eli tossed his cravat on the side chair and slowly unbuttoned his shirt, riding the scene out as Amelia pretended not to watch. But she was. Even if he hadn't been staring at her, he would know. His skin pricked whenever her gaze fell on him, like the sun drying water off his skin.

His jacket and shirt discarded, Eli made short work of his shoes and trousers, ridding himself of the stuffy items until he stood before Amelia, naked and free, untethered to everything except his need for her.

"Come here," he said.

Hanging back near the hearth, Amelia hugged herself, warding off a shiver. "No."

"Amelia," he said. "Come here."

"Why must you do this to me?" she whispered, the fire reflecting off her eyes.

Eli held his arms at his side, determined to stand his ground. "I am only doing what you want."

"What I want?" she repeated, her voice ragged with unfettered emotion. "I want you to leave me alone. I want you to stop trying to make me stay here when you know I can't. I want to go and forget that I ever met you."

Eli shook his head. "I cannot do that. I love you—"

"Stop saying that. You don't—"

"I do," he continued. "I will continue to do so for the rest of my life. Which will be easy, since you'll be at my side while I do it."

Amelia sucked in a breath, battling for control. "You are not listening to me—"

"You're right," he cut in. "I'm done listening to you tonight.

I've already said everything that needed to be said. I want you. Now. Here. Forever. I want to argue with you, make love with you, infuriate you and delight you. I want to debate until I'm blue in the face and lose happily every time. I want to make a home with you, make a family. I want everything. No more. No less. Now, come here."

Eli was determined, but he was also hungry. He didn't know how much longer he could wait until she was out of her dress and under him. Luckily, Amelia took pity.

Glacially, haltingly, she moved her feet by inches. Less than inches. It didn't matter to Eli. Let her keep her pride; she was coming toward him. Not running away. It was a win by any measure.

He met Amelia halfway, scooping her up and carrying her to the bed. Eli took greater care with her clothes than with his, putting time and effort into removing the layers one by one, until she lay resplendent on top of the covers. He sat back on his haunches, admiring the fluid beauty of her form, the way something so small and compact could reduce him into such a raw, primal being.

Never in Eli's wildest dreams had he imagined someone so breathtaking, so strong and confident and capable, would want a man like him. For years he's suffered under the pain of being left behind, not worthy, not good enough. Yet this remarkably fearless woman gave herself to him without shame, without asking for anything in return.

"Give me your hand," Eli demanded.

With a shy smile, Amelia placed her hand on his knee, languidly moving up the curve of his thigh, with a clear destination in sight. Eli caught her before she could waylay his plans. "We'll get to that." He chuckled, taking her hand in his. He began massaging her palm, pressing into her skin, kneading the tiny muscles at the base of her thumb. Amelia's head dropped back on the pillow, where she let out an orgasmic groan that went straight to Eli's cock.

He switched his focus to the other hand, performing the same soothing rubs, making sure to give each finger its own attention. He caressed each digit, stroking the lengths, balancing pressure with ticklish sensations.

"Your hands were one of the first things I noticed about you," he said lightly, kissing her knuckles.

Amelia let out a husky laugh, bending her knee to dig her heel into the bed. Eli's mouth watered at the creamy limb. "You told me to get my hands off you."

He smiled ruefully, leaning down to kiss the mock offense off her face. She tangled her arms around his neck, attempting to keep him on her, but he broke away. Eli had more to say. "Not at the tournament. At the inn when I saw your real hands for the first time. I knew right away they weren't a gentle-born lady's hands."

Amelia pulled, but Eli wouldn't let her out of his grasp. "The scars—"

"It had nothing to do with the scars," he said, kneading. "The knuckles were red, the veins an ocean of color. There was so much strength in those little hands ..."

"Not enough to escape you that night," she whispered.

"Not enough to escape me ever."

Amelia yanked again, just managing to pull her hand out of his. She sat up on the bed, kneeling next to him, placing a palm over his cheek. It was still warm from his caresses, the blood just underneath the surface. Her dark eyes caught his, dragging them into their abyss. "You must know ... I'm not Marianne. I'm not leaving because I don't love you," she said quietly. "I'm leaving because I do."

Eli kissed the inside of her palm, filling his lungs with her earthy scent. "That makes no sense."

Her lips trembled. "It makes more sense than a viscount and a pickpocket."

"*Ex*-pickpocket."

"There's no such thing as an ex-pickpocket," she lamented,

dropping her hand. "I'm just another of your possessions, Eli, one of the treasures in this house. You'll miss me for a time, but you'll soon get over it. Everyone thinks the pain of losing something lasts, but trust me, it doesn't. You'll move on. Everyone will move on."

Eli couldn't take it anymore. He hated listening to Amelia lie to make herself feel better. If she truly thought she was going to leave him, fine, but he wouldn't listen to her talk her way out of the pain any longer. Pushing his weight into her, Eli placed her prone on the bed, blanketing her body with his own. The friction of the slide, skin on skin, was blissful beyond compare.

He held himself up on his forearms, looming over Amelia. "You once asked me why I would bother chasing after a pocket watch when I was rich enough to buy another," he said, his throat tightening, his passion pumping him into a frenzy. His cock was hard and ready and poised along the soft mound of her belly, jumping with his every word. Amelia's breasts pointed up at him insistently, begging him to suck them, but everything had to wait. "What did I tell you? What was my answer?" he asked.

She stared at him curiously, as if trying to recount the conversation in her mind. Eli knew the moment she found it. Her dark eyelashes batted nervously against her cheekbones as she shook her head in disbelief. "You …" She licked her lips. Then Eli licked them for her. She shook her head again as she gathered her thoughts. "You told me that you chased after it because it was yours."

He nodded. "That's right. Just as you are mine. You aren't my possession, Amelia. You are mine, though. Now and forever."

Lowering down on his elbows, Eli reached between them and positioned his shaft at Amelia's entrance, easing in slowly, letting her succulent body do the talking. Gritting his teeth at the exquisite torture, Eli could feel her tiny muscles clamp him, swallow him, invite him to grant their mistress pleasure.

"Your body knows. Can you hear it?" he asked, flexing his hips, pulsing into Amelia's center. "It knows you belong to me.

Listen to it call for me—listen to it beg."

Her mouth dropped open, her eyes burning. "I'm not begging, you ass. And I don't belong to you. I don't belong to anyone. There's no knight in shining armor to come rescue me, remember?"

Good, Eli thought. He was the villain in her story anyway. With one harsh thrust, he cushioned himself inside, utterly enveloped in his woman's embrace. They lay there together, feeling—just allowing—the acceptance of their persons, the conflagration of their souls.

"Fuck," Eli groaned, resting his forehead on her shoulder, licking the salty sheen of her skin. "I've wanted you all day."

"I've wanted you too," Amelia admitted.

He smiled at the timidity in her voice. "Even when you were telling me you were leaving me?"

"Especially then."

He stayed inside her, waiting for Amelia to take her pleasure first, his shaft throbbing from the restraint. And then it happened. Like the hesitant flutter of a baby bird's wings, Amelia shifted her hips, backing off Eli's shaft before encapsulating him.

The pleasure was too intense; he couldn't move. He didn't have to. Amelia did it for him. Lazily, she worked herself on him as he held himself over her. Gently at first, and then hard and gritty, running her body up his pole, milking him with a greedy insistence.

Eli did what he could. He couldn't keep his lips off her. He captured her mouth in long, drawn-out kisses that left them starved for air. He sucked on her nipples, licked the curves of her breasts, nipped at the ridges of her clavicle. His hand was caressing and squeezing, gripping Amelia's plump ass to make her buck harder. And harder.

There was nothing romantic about this lovemaking. Carnal and gluttonous, a point was being made, a message made clear. A brand was being burned into their flesh. *You are mine,* it said. Bold for all to see. For them each to feel, the pain of the seared skin forever singeing their nerves.

When Amelia came on his cock, Eli shouted from the beauty, her slick cave squeezing him into his own little death.

He collapsed on her body, not ashamed of his weight, nor the fact that this competent woman could handle it. His woman could handle anything, especially his wiry, broken self. Nor did it rankle him that she hadn't agreed that she belonged to him. Eli was man enough not to need the words. They would come. He had the rest of his life to fight for them.

As Eli and Amelia fell asleep that night, they each stretched to their sides of the giant bed, unconsciously eating up the space with their exhausted bodies. Only their hands reached across the divide, fingers tangled as effortlessly as the links on an ancient gold chain, its value, its significance, immeasurable.

CHAPTER THIRTY

AMELIA BLINKED DROWSILY, the familiar noisy chirrs of the sparrow nudging her awake. Roaring an indecorous yawn, she stretched out her legs, reveling in the ache of her tender muscles as the night's escapades flew back to her in a delicious jolt.

For a brief suspension in time, Amelia let herself believe she wasn't leaving Barrington, that she could wake up in this lovemaking grandeur for the rest of her life. Presumably, her partner would be there with her—unlike now.

Amelia's back was cool without the blanketed warmth of Eli's chest, which informed her that he'd snuck out hours ago. She tried turning to see if he left a clue as to where he'd ventured off to, but a biting cinch in her wrists trapped her stubbornly in place.

"What in the bloody hell …?" She gasped, fighting against the shackles pinning her arms around the right bedpost corner. "That slimy bastard! How dare he!"

Her first intention was to scream. However, after opening her mouth wide, she immediately slapped it shut. Screaming would only bring unwanted spectators to her indecent situation.

Eli had thought ahead and made sure Amelia was naked while he cuffed her to the bed. She was hardly a prude, but she wasn't in the mood to have half the household gawk at her while they broke her out of her constraints. She was on her own.

And she had no one to blame but herself. The stupid man had told her he didn't have a dungeon—but he did have handcuffs. Amelia twisted her neck, getting a better view of the offending steel.

Seventeenth century, indeed. Eli clearly didn't know his handcuffs. These were Hiatt Darbys, and definitely of this century. This decade, more like.

What had he been thinking? He knew she could escape from anything. What was he playing at? What was his point in locking her away for a few extra minutes?

Curling her legs up, Amelia reached one foot out to the bedside table. Using her toes, she opened the drawer and reached inside, hoping that the everyday item she was searching for could be found. Sweet relief coursed through her when her toes closed around the skinny, smooth metal. Carefully, ever so carefully, she carried it up to her mouth.

This shouldn't take her too long. By her calculation, she would have her hands free to choke Eli's neck in less than an hour. Then she would leave for London. She was in a hurry, but she had time for that.

⸎⸎⸎

THIRTY MINUTES LATER, Amelia was stomping down the stairs, freshly dressed, her bag packed and over her shoulder. She'd need to find Jimmy and ask him to drive her to London in the carriage. Growing up in the city, she'd never had the time or inclination to learn how to ride. As it was a two-hour journey, she'd be sure to pay the stable boy handsomely for his trouble.

The house was quiet, unsettlingly so, as Amelia wandered the ground floor, pacing through the rooms. "Eli's probably hiding from me," she muttered to herself as she peeked inside the vacant library. "Won't face me after his childish attempt to make me stay."

Hadn't he known it wouldn't work? Nothing could work. Amelia was doomed to her life. Clearly, as evidenced by this morning, she was only good for one thing—thieving. Why pretend being something different? Eli might have a past he was proud of—a lineage worth saving for posterity—but Amelia didn't. Her past would always come back to haunt her, wearing her down until there was nothing left.

Turning a corner, she finally heard the telltale sound of the twins, their giggles giving away their location outside, near the fountain. She marched down the lawn to greet them, interrupting the pair as they sat on the lip of the fountain, a game of knuckle-bones between them.

"Good morning," Kitty sang out absent-mindedly, tossing a stone up in the air while she swiped three bones in her palm then catching the ball before it hit the ground. Ever her sister's supporter, Cecily clapped her hands at the dexterous move.

"Good morning," Amelia replied. "Have you seen your fa-ther?"

"He left," Cecily said.

Amelia's stomach dropped. "Left? Left where?"

Cecily shrugged, rearranging the bones in front of her. "He had business in London. He said he'd be back as soon as he could."

The duplicitous snake! "What kind of business?" Amelia asked. When Cecily tossed the stone into the air, Amelia snatched it away. "What kind of business, Cecily?"

The young girl huffed, lolling her head to the side. "He said he had to talk to a man about a debt. That's all. Why?"

Amelia frowned. She couldn't possibly be referring to Harry, could she? Eli couldn't be that idiotic. What in the world did a horticulturist think he could do to Harry Holmes, one of the vilest thieves London had ever produced? Amelia rubbed at her temples; a headache was swiftly brewing. The stupid man. What had he gotten himself into? For her?

"When did he leave?"

"A few hours ago," Kitty answered. "Maybe. I don't know. I was barely awake. Does this have something to do with that woman?"

Amelia felt like someone had tripped her into the fountain all over again. "What woman?"

"You know." Kitty rolled her eyes. "The woman that Father hid us from yesterday. The one with the ring." Amelia opened her mouth to speak, but Kitty went on without taking a breath. "We know we weren't supposed to let her see us, and we didn't, we swear! It's just … we had to see what she looked like. It was your mother, right? The lady you told us about?"

Amelia nodded, her tongue too thick to move.

Kitty frowned. "She was different than I expected. Smaller. Not as scary. Though I did like the way she dressed, and her jewelry was lovely. Did you see her rings?"

"Yes," Amelia answered flatly, feeling the ground tip underneath her feet. She hadn't wanted the girls to witness that part of her world, wanted them to keep believing it was a place found only in her ridiculous stories. That was the only way she could keep them safe. "She's always loved pretty rings."

"They weren't just pretty," Kitty continued, her enthusiasm gaining speed. "She wore a green one that was the biggest I'd ever seen. I doubt the queen even has something like that."

Green ring? "I didn't notice it," Amelia said, suddenly feeling clammy, as if a ghost had walked through her.

Kitty bobbed her shoulders. "She wore it around her neck. We only saw it when she bent over to pick up her skirts to get into her carriage. It fell out from under her dress."

Amelia dropped to the ground, scattering the girls' game into the fountain in her haste. She grabbed Kitty's knees, her grasp making the child wince. "How big was it? The size of a walnut? The color of fresh moss?"

The girls nodded in unison, with matching stares of confusion.

"Holy hell," Amelia said to herself, falling back on her behind.

There was no way ... It couldn't be ... Molly never would have ... Unless ... She was scared. Amelia *had* recognized that.

She sprang to her feet, making for the stables where she hoped Jimmy was waiting. "You two stay here. I have to go."

"What should we do?" Kitty called after her.

"Behave." Amelia stopped in her tracks and turned around. "On second thought, I have a job for you."

The twins leapt from their seats, at the ready.

"Girls, I need a gun. Do you know where your father keeps his—"

Amelia didn't get a chance to finish her sentence. Cecily and Kitty were already halfway through the back door. That was one of the benefits of capable young women. There was no squeamishness, no questions. Just action.

Amelia was on the road fifteen minutes later, a Smith of London percussion pistol hidden in her skirts.

◆──────❖──────◆

CHAPTER THIRTY-ONE

LOCATING HARRY HOLMES hadn't been as difficult as Eli thought it would be. He'd intended to spend all day in London's less-hospitable corners, interviewing duplicitous-looking creatures about the infamous gang leader's whereabouts.

However, standing on the outskirts of a busy thoroughfare, surrounded by young urchins in desperate need of a bath, Eli had been reminded of his inquisitive, wise-beyond-their-years girls and gotten an idea. All it took was the promise of a pound and a hot dinner and, minutes later, Eli was on his way.

The boy couldn't have been older than Michael, but he directed Eli to The Lucky Fish with all the assurance of a seasoned cutpurse. Eli had assumed they were on their way to the Rookery or another downtrodden patch of the city. When the boy's swift feet brought them to St. James—home of some of the most upstanding establishments on offer to the upper crust—Eli thought he'd been duped.

Now, confronted with The Lucky Fish's imperious butler, Eli decided it was time to reevaluate his opinions of Harry Holmes.

"What's your business with Mr. Homes?" asked the older gentleman, acting as the gatekeeper for the gaming hell.

"I'm here to pay a debt," Eli replied quietly. Standing in the foyer, he caught sight of patrons in the adjoining rooms. He didn't recognize anyone, but that didn't mean they wouldn't

259

recognize him. He wasn't necessarily hiding his presence in the gaming hell, though he surely didn't desire to flaunt it either.

"What was that?" the butler asked, shifting his right ear toward Eli.

He bristled. So much for discretion. "I'm here to pay a debt."

The old man straightened. "Oh, well, why didn't you say that? I'll take you to Mr. Holmes right away. Ordinarily, he orders me to tell everyone he's busy—especially before the night crowd comes in—but seeing as how you're paying a debt … He always has time for that."

"I'm sure," Eli replied tersely, following the butler up the gleaming marble staircase all the way to the fourth floor. A series of doors, all closed, filled the corridor. The old man led Eli all the way to the end, knocking lightly at the last room. When a grunt answered from the other side, the butler ushered Eli into the room with a wave of his elegant hand.

"The Viscount Barrington is here to see you, Mr. Holmes," he announced grandly, as if Eli was taking an audience with the queen. Actually, it was grander. The queen's man wasn't half so polished.

Harry Holmes kept his gaze down on his desk, where a mess of ledgers lay in front of him. Holding a cigar in one hand and a glass of brandy in the other, the businessman appeared to be reading every one at the same time.

"I don't know a Viscount Barrington," Holmes answered casually, smoky plumes puffing around him like the chimney on a steam train.

Eli stepped around the butler. "That's because we've never met," he said impatiently. "I'm here to pay off the debt of a friend."

That got his attention. Holmes leaned back in his chair, biting his teeth around the cigar as he considered his guest.

Another mistake of Eli's—he'd thought the infamous gang leader would be older. Though there was a sizeable amount of gray around the man's ears, Holmes still had a full head of thick hair and nary a line on his face. His body was thick and broad, but not necessarily tall. Holmes reminded Eli of a ram that would bash and thrash until he'd demolished everything around him, coming away without a scratch.

"Friend?" Holmes asked, stringing out the word. Eli was about to explain when Holmes placed his crystal glass on the table with a thud. "Wait. I have heard of a Barrington. Some scandal …" He rubbed his thick paw over his face a few times as if to wake his memory. When he dropped his hand, his eyes shone a brilliant green—a devious green—and he snapped his fingers. "That's right. It wasn't you. It was your wife. Used to come in here a bit before she was shipped off to the Continent. Good decision on your part. Bad for my pockets, but I would have done the same in your shoes. She was a terrible gambler. Wasn't she carrying on with the Earl of Somerset? Was that the straw that broke the camel's back?" he asked gleefully, his straight white teeth reminding Eli of a wolf.

Eli cleared his throat, not scrounging up a lie. What was the point? Amelia was right. Marianne had left him; she'd been the source of so much of his pain. But he'd been a source of hurt for her as well. If forgiveness was ever going to start—if the family was ever going to move on—it would have to start now. "My wife left me for a different life," he said plainly, his chest oddly light. "I commend her courage."

Holmes's brow shot up. "Courage, huh? Is that what you're calling it?"

Eli squared his shoulders. "I only say the truth."

"The truth," Holmes echoed. "It's too early in the day for that." He waved his cigar in the air. "Forget I mentioned anything—besides, even a bastard like me knows it's not right to speak of the dead. Now, what friend are you paying off? I got to say, this is a surprise. Not many people have generous friends like you. Most of your ilk can't even get their fathers in here to settle their accounts."

Eli nodded, quite content to steer the conversation back on

track. "Amelia Diver. She took out a loan a few months ago. I'm here to pay it off with the condition that you stay away from her from here on out. Don't contact her. Never again will you have anything to do with her."

Holmes paused, his mouth widening into a chilling smile around his cigar. "Isn't that sweet? But I'm afraid I can't let you do that, *my lord.*"

Eli stalked closer, flattening his palms on the desk. Holmes, to his credit, didn't flinch. Eli ran through the odds. If need be, there would be a brawl. Holmes might have more power, but Eli had the length *and* the determination. It wouldn't be an equally matched fight, though the outcome wasn't set in stone either. "Why the hell not?" he asked, his muscles tingling in anticipation.

Holmes hooked one leg over the other in a devil-may-care motion. "Because, my friend"—he laughed—"I've never loaned Amelia Driver money in my life."

Eli's fingers curled into the ledgers. Holmes was playing games with him. "Fine, then. Molly Diamond. You loaned the money to her, and she gave it to Amelia to use for the flower shop."

"Oh, the flower shop—now I know what this is all about." Holmes uncrossed his legs, slid his papers out from under Eli, and stacked them in a tidy pile. "I always thought it strange that Molly borrowed all that money only to later ask me to make sure the flower shop failed. Seemed like a whole lot of wasted effort to me."

Eli jerked away like he was evading a punch. Holmes's confounding words landed harshly all the same. "What do you mean, 'make sure the flower shop failed'?"

"I blame Amelia," Holmes went on. "I always liked her; she's a smart girl, one of the best divers I've ever seen. She should have known Molly wouldn't let her out of the business that easy. The girl brought in too much loot, *and* she was the heir apparent— Molly's legacy."

Eli put up his hands. "Wait, just wait a second. Are you trying to tell me that *Molly* is the reason the flower shop failed? She hired you to … what? Kill the business?

"What can I say?" Holmes replied with a self-satisfied grin. "My boys are good at scaring people. Easiest money we ever made."

Eli's arms slumped to his side. How was he going to explain that to Amelia? She loved Molly as much as any daughter loved her mother, maybe even more, because blood wasn't the natural bond between them. But what Molly had done was deplorable. Wicked. Selfish to the core.

However, it didn't change anything. Not for Eli. Not now. He still had a debt to pay. So, he would deal with one degenerate at a time. Eli would pay Holmes first and deal with Molly's perfidy second.

"Please," he said, fighting a sudden onslaught of weariness. "Just tell me how much Molly owes so I can let you get back to your work."

Holmes chuckled. To Eli's frazzled nerves, the sound was as off-putting as nails scratched across a chalkboard.

The gambling hell owner shook his head. "Sorry, friend. I'm afraid I can't do that for you either."

"Now why?" Eli shouted.

Holmes leaned his elbows on the desk. "Because Molly already paid me back months ago."

CHAPTER THIRTY-TWO

MELIA'S SUSPICIONS WERE confirmed the instant she stepped through the front door of the townhouse. She wondered why she hadn't noticed it before she left for Eglinton's tournament. Surely there had been clues. Had Molly been better at hiding it then, or had Amelia been too heartbroken over the flower shop to acknowledge anything other than her own sorrows?

The vestiges of tobacco clung to the home. The aroma pervaded Amelia's lungs, making her stomach clench and her heart pump rapidly like she was six years old all over again. That fear, that uncertainty, tripped her feet over themselves as she took the stairs to the first floor, knowing that Molly could always be found at this time of the day enjoying the midafternoon sun from the comforts of her drawing room. It hadn't always been so. From an early age, restlessness clung to Molly like a millstone around her neck; she kept Amelia moving, always changing addresses, hoarding money for that ever-threatening rainy day. It wasn't until recently that the gang leader had allowed herself to settle on a permanent location. Covent Garden was the logical choice. A bustling, seedy part of London, it was home to all kinds of people, and rarely judged them for how they made ends meet. And thanks to its celebrated market, it was a prime place for a den of thieves.

For a moment, Amelia wondered if Molly might be waiting for her in the room, watching the door with the same intensity as a hawk scouting a chicken coop. But as she entered the stark space, she found Molly head down with a fresh newspaper in her lap, the glasses she wore when no one was looking resting on the tip of her nose.

The older woman appeared demure sitting there on her modest furniture—not too expensive, not too cheap. An extension of that sparse lifestyle, the room was similarly outfitted with a few adornments, yet nothing so special and dazzling that anyone would speak about it later in awed tones. Molly hated wasting her money on furnishings. Never saw the point. Her clothes and jewelry … now that was different.

She wore a brilliant azure day dress, modest in design to the untrained eye. Amelia was not fooled. The devil was in the details, and she had no doubt that Molly had spent a fortune on the carefully crafted gown that fit her slender form like a second skin. It was all about balance. The dress didn't need to shout; that was what the jewelry was for.

Amelia counted five rings on the older woman's fingers, though Jenny's green treasure was missing.

"Are you going to stand there all day or are you going to say something?" Molly asked, still intent on her paper. "I was expecting a letter from you. You shouldn't be here."

Amelia's words hardened like concrete in her throat. She'd spent the whole journey from Essex planning what she would say when she finally confronted Molly. Now, in this place that she'd once considered home, her courage faltered. Closing her eyes, she conjured Jenny's body, the contorted, broken limbs of a young woman whose only fault had been associating with Amelia.

One lonely tear ran down Amelia's cheek. Quickly, she swiped it away, praying that this once she could contain the rest long enough to unload what she needed to say. "Please …" she began, her voice coming out choked and strangled. "Just tell me you didn't do it. Tell me you didn't kill Jenny for the ring."

The newspaper floated down from Molly's fingers, and she looked up. This was the one time in Amelia's life she wished she didn't have her talent for reading people. Because what she saw on her adoptive mother's face ripped her to shreds.

"Amelia," Molly said, stretching out the word like spun sugar. "Don't get any ideas."

"What ideas should I get, Molly?" Amelia said, storming into the room, not stopping until she stood over the woman. "That Harry Holmes killed Jenny? Guess who I ran into on the way here? Jimmy Donovan. I asked him about the debt, and he said it was all paid up. So, who do we owe, Molly? Who have you been siphoning all of the gang's money to? Who would you kill one of your girls for?"

Amelia knew the answer; she just wanted to hear the gang leader say it.

Molly's eyes sank into her face, and her skin was plump and swollen in its agitation. She rubbed her temple with shaking fingers. There was no mistaking the anxiety Amelia had spotted at Barrington, nor the purple bruise near her ear that Molly tried to hide with her yellow hair. Amelia understood what the bruise meant. But she couldn't allow herself to feel pity for Molly. Her pity was only for Jenny.

"I loved that girl," Molly said. "I sold the ring right after I saw you. Maybe I wore it to keep her close, I don't know. But I would never kill one of my girls. You know me better than that. I have only ever cared about their safety."

"So, it was Walter. He killed Jenny and … what? Dumped the body to scare me?" Amelia watched as Molly picked at her nail beds. When she stayed silent, Amelia sighed. "How long has he been back?"

Molly ducked her head even lower, as if she was crawling into her body to hide. "He was released from the hulks a few months ago. Right before you opened the flower shop."

"You didn't tell me."

"I didn't want to hear what you would say. I didn't want you to look at me like you are now."

"Because you knew I would speak the truth," Amelia said, fighting the way her heart always melted when Molly looked like this, so dejected, so small. "That he's bad for you. You're the strongest person I know, but whenever he comes into the picture, you become a shell of yourself. Why do you let him have this hold over you?"

"He doesn't have a hold."

"He does." Amelia sat next to Molly on the settee as the puzzle pieces snapped together. "What did he tell you? That he'll kill every one of us unless you give him what he wants?"

Molly shuddered, her shoulders slumping under the invisible weight of the truth. "He got into some gambling debt." She slid her tongue over her top teeth, making a sucking sound. "He owes the Elephants ten thousand."

"Ten thousand!" Amelia was lucky she was sitting, or else she would have keeled over. There was no way Molly could come up with that money to pay back the Elephants. It would take them years. "Tell him no!"

"I can't."

"Yes, you can!"

"Why couldn't you have just stayed in the country?" Molly asked. She crumpled up the newspaper in her lap and threw it on the floor. "That score would have solved everything."

"Not for me, Molly. It would have ruined my life."

The woman laughed bitterly. "Don't you understand? I'm trying to make sure you *keep* your life!"

From the side, Amelia noticed two missing teeth from the corner of Molly's mouth. It was why she never smiled wide, hating what it did to her appearance, hating how it betrayed her humble beginnings. So much about Molly was artifice, Amelia realized, bright colors and fanciful trinkets to distract, to convince her gang that she was in control when she was anything but. It wasn't just the gang. Amelia had thought that too. Molly had always stood on such a high pedestal to her. It crushed her to find out her hero, her mentor, her adoptive mother, was woefully human.

"Is that what you told yourself when you ruined the flower shop?" she asked, her voice oddly restrained, the anger not at the ready as it had been hours before. "That you were saving me?"

Molly scowled pitifully. "How did you—"

"Jenny," Amelia answered. "She said something at the tournament, something I didn't consider until I found out you had the ring. She said, 'Sometimes I wish she hadn't ordered us to stay away.' That was you, wasn't it? You scared people away from my shop so I'd fail and come back to you with my tail between my legs. Help you keep up Walter's payments."

Molly rubbed at her eyes. The rims were red and moist. "I didn't want to, love. Please know that. I thought I could let you go, but then Walter came back, and I needed your help. No one dives like you. You bring in more money in one day than the other girls make in a week. I was desperate. You have to understand that."

Amelia did. That was the horrible part. She did understand Molly's reasoning, which made hating her and resenting her futile—and returning to Eli impossible.

Eli!

Amelia threw her head in her hands and groaned. "Dammit!"

"What is it?" Molly asked.

"Eli—"

"You mean Viscount Barrington?"

Amelia gave her a pointed look. "Eli came to London this morning. I think he's going to confront Harry. He thought ... And then I thought ..." She shot off the seat. "I've got to get to The Lucky Fish, stop him before he does anything he'll regret."

Molly followed Amelia to standing, wearing an odd expression. "Seems like you didn't leave Eglington empty-handed after all. Came back with a knight of your own."

Amelia snorted. "A knight that doesn't like to shoot, can barely fence, and hates being around people."

Molly gave a halfhearted chuckle. "They can't all be Lancelot."

Amelia started to leave. "I'll be back soon. Then we'll talk. I have no intention of giving Walter one shilling, but I'm sure I can think of a way out of this."

Molly's voice was as soft as a child's. The emptiness, the helplessness that Amelia heard sent a chill up her spine. "I can't kill him. I … I don't know why. I just can't. He saved me when I was young. He helped me … kept us safe in his own way."

Amelia couldn't dwell on what "in his own way" meant.

"You won't have to kill him," she said. "I will. I'm not a little girl anymore. I'm not scared of Walter. You shouldn't be either."

A *tsking* sound met Amelia in the corridor, forcing her to back-pedal into the room. "That's the problem with women," Walter said, standing in the entrance, leaning lazily on its frame. "You'd figure they'd know by now that thinking never does them any good."

It had been years, but Amelia's body still shut down, paralyzed at the sight of him, even if Walter was half the man he used to be. In her memories, he'd taken on a mythic size, resembling an ogre or giant. His current dismal state confused her. He was pallid and rail-thin, his cheekbones cut sharp across his face, and his fashionable clothes hung like they were on a washing line. His shrewd eyes crowded a nose that had been broken numerous times. Age had made the terrifying man even more gruesome. But the way Walter looked at her—with so much unmitigated venom—hadn't changed at all.

And yet all that was secondary, background noise, because what really grabbed Amelia's attention was the shiny pistol he pointed straight at her.

Though the fear in Molly's voice alarmed Amelia the most. "Walter, put the gun down!" she whispered so thinly that Amelia barely heard her.

"Shut it," Walter sneered, entering the room, making Amelia step back until she and Molly were sitting side by side again on the settee. "I'm tired of waiting for you to get my money. You're lucky I don't sell you again, but you're too damned old and ugly. You, on the other hand …" Walter's watery gaze centered on

Amelia as he licked his chapped, bloodstained lips. "You have some potential. Might be beneficial for you too. Fuck the bitch out of you."

Another time, Amelia might have been terrified by the disgusting remark; however, she was too caught up in the revelation of his words. "You worked for him?" she asked Molly. "With my mother?"

"Oh, she never told you that story?" Walter asked, before chuckling to himself and bending over in a fit of phlegmy coughs. He wiped his mouth with the back of his dirty hand. "Well, I could see how that might tarnish the glorious legacy of the notorious Molly Diamond. At one time, long ago, little Molly was just another whore. *My* whore. And not a very good one, I might add. Frigid. Like you, probably," he said, bobbing the gun at Amelia.

She heard a sob but couldn't look at the older woman. If Amelia saw Molly's tears—saw her break—she didn't know what she'd do. Her composure needed to stay intact so she could determine a course of action. View the situation from another angle.

But thinking was difficult, especially since the buffoon was in the mood to talk. Walter's skeletal legs wobbled as he continued, and Amelia noticed his pistol was having a difficult time staying straight. The drunk was drunk. No surprise there. Good. She could work with that.

"I had myself a good little operation going," he went on, lost in the glories of his youth. "Molly and her little friend, that nasty mother of yours who ran off. If I hadn't been sentenced to the hulks that first time, I would have set up my own gaming hell teeming with young girls, better than that bastard Holmes's." He scratched the whiskers at his jaw before his gaze alighted on Molly. His lips curled as he ran a black-nailed finger over her trembling cheek. "By the time I got out, Molly had made a name for herself. Clever girl, she was. I should have known she'd be better at stealin' than whorin'. Natural-born liar. We made a decent pair before you ruined it."

Amelia gripped Molly's hand. "Why can't you just leave her alone?"

"Because she's mine," Walter snapped, slapping Molly hard across the face. She fell back against the seat, holding her cheek. "She'll always be mine. I may leave or get sent away, but I always come back. And don't let the bitch fool you; she wants me too. If it weren't for me, she would have died on the streets like all the other whores. She needs me now as she needed me then. And, unfortunately, we need *you*."

He leaned over Amelia. She suffered through his rank tobacco breath and the dangerous glint in his dead eyes. How many times had this man made her real mother cower? How many times had he slapped her across the face?

White flecks of spittle collected at the corners of Walter's mouth. "Do you know how long I've dreamed of killing you? Ever since you bashed my skull in with that bat. I'd planned to strangle you that night, but when I went out to drink off the pain, I got nicked by police for some old theft they'd pinned on me. So, I bided my time, living like an animal on the hulks until I could get back here."

"Molly said you've been out for months," Amelia replied, her blood pounding in her temples. She felt like she was caught underwater, listening to everything through murky depths. "Why did you wait?"

"Maybe I've softened." He coughed out another disgusting laugh. "Though, truthfully, it's probably all the money Molly was shoveling me to leave you alone. But that ran out quickly while you were playing the whore in the country. It was my brilliant idea to use Jenny to get you back to work. And look! Here you are!" His spittle landed on Amelia's nose. "Time for you to start diving again, little girl. My benevolence and your special hands are the only reason you're alive. You should thank me."

Behind Walter, a blur of a shape took focus at the edge of Amelia's vision. In a familiar, clipped accent, it said, "And I'm the only reason you're still alive. Why don't you turn around and thank me?"

Chapter Thirty-Three

THE DAMN WOMAN didn't have to look so surprised, Eli thought as Amelia fixed her gaze on him. Maybe it would help if his hands stopped shaking. He couldn't help it; he was furious and operating on pure adrenaline. After Holmes had told him where Molly lived, Eli had gotten to the townhouse as fast as he could. He certainly hadn't expected to find a picturesque familial scene; however, stumbling upon Amelia being held at gunpoint rocked him to his core.

Eli flexed his forearm. He straightened his cane sword out in front of him and hoped he was exuding pure, masculine confidence. Scanning Amelia, he breathed deeply, seeing she didn't appear to be hurt. Only angry.

"Who the hell are you?" Walter grumbled, less alarmed and more put out by the interruption. Pointing his gun at the women, he twisted half his body to Eli. The man was so skinny he almost disappeared when he turned sideways. If Eli could knock the gun out of his hand, he was certain the rest would be easy. But he had to get across the room without being shot at first.

His mind swelled with ways to answer Walter's simple question. For some reason, he thought of Michael and his knights and dug deep for the bravado that courageous men loved to showcase. "I'm the man that's going to kill you," Eli said, squelching a grimace. Like a coat three sizes too small, the words felt ill-fitting.

He took two steps into the room. "Release the women and I'll let you live."

Walter shot a comically inquiring glance at Molly. "What the hell does he think he's going to do with that stick?" To Eli, he continued, "You do know how guns work, right? That skinny thing can't do anything from all the way over there." He paused to consider. "Unless you throw it. Can you throw it?"

"Of course I can," Eli answered. It wasn't convincing even to his own ears.

Walter shook his head, puffing out a laugh. "No, you can't."

"So that's your Lancelot?" Molly asked Amelia.

"Yes," Amelia replied firmly.

Even in this horrendous situation, Eli's body tingled with the idea that Amelia had talked about him. It also warmed him to realize that she hadn't taken her eyes off him once.

"He's sweet," Molly said. "I like his pretty blue eyes, not to mention the fact that he came all the way here to save you."

Amelia nodded, a small smile curving her face.

"I do wonder," Molly drawled, "why he doesn't trust you enough to get out of this scrape yourself."

Amelia lolled her head to the side, clicking her tongue in irritation. "He does trust me. He's trying to help, that's all."

Molly didn't look convinced. "Is that why he brought a stick when he should have brought a gun?"

"It's not a stick!"

"It's a stick," Walter added.

"It's perfectly serviceable!" Eli declared. He yearned to point out that the weapon was a gift to Eli's grandfather from Earl Cornwallis in the eighteenth century but thought it best to hold on to that interesting information for another day. He also wanted to explain that he was using the stick because of the comment Amelia had made to his son about cowards and guns. Clearly, she wasn't getting the significance; he would be sure to fill her in later. "It will run you through just fine," he concluded grandly, wondering if anyone else thought he sounded like he was starring in a very bad play.

Walter sighed. Pitifully. His head hung from his twiggy neck. "Look, son. I don't know what you're thinking, but you're in over your head here. Don't waste your life on these two. They're stinkin' thieves." He stared right at Molly and Amelia while he said it, grinning at the hateful looks they returned. He chuckled before facing Eli. "They're liars, plain and simple. Evil women. Stupid woman. They'll smile in your face while reaching into your pocket. They've got you hypnotized. That's what they do. Now, take that nice, fancy stick and run along with your kind before you get hurt."

Eli and Walter heard the eerie *click* sound at the same time. With a one-shot pistol aimed at the back of Walter's head, Amelia said calmly, "Poor Walter. Maybe you should have taken your own advice."

The Adam's apple on Walter's throat jumped, though his wan features remained impassive. During his soliloquy, the fool had dropped his arm; his own weapon was now pointed uselessly at the floor.

"Don't do anything stupid now, girl," he said, his gaze still holding Eli's.

Amelia laughed. "But I thought that's what I was ... just a stupid girl."

Molly nodded at Amelia's pistol, which looked mighty familiar to Eli. "You had that the whole time? Why did you wait so long to bring it out?"

Amelia rolled her eyes. "I was waiting for the right moment, wasn't I? Don't give me that look. At least I came prepared."

At that, Molly reached into the pocket of her voluminous blue skirts, presenting a pistol of her own. It was newer than Amelia's, and her barrel wasn't as thick, but it was still a single-shot. Eli had no doubt she could use it well.

Molly cocked the hammer and lined her weapon up next to Amelia's. "Did you really think you were the only one?"

Amelia's eyes went wide. "I thought you said you couldn't

kill him?"

Molly's lips pinched. "I still don't know if I can, but I do know I'm tired of getting hit in the face," she said. "Luckily for me, your little knight came with his pointy stick."

Eli's ego was truly taking a beating. But he didn't care. Finally, he could breathe again. Walter was covered on all sides. Amelia was safe. Thanks to him … Molly even confirmed it.

Eli was pulled back into the mother/daughter bickering.

"Don't call him that," Amelia snapped.

"Why not?" Molly asked. "He looks like a knight with his little sword."

"Stop calling his sword 'little.' You're teasing him, and he doesn't deserve that. You have no idea how much trouble you've caused for all of us. But, then again, you never do."

"I told you I was sorry about the flower shop," Molly exclaimed. "I'll help you start another one, all right? Let's just deal with this bastard first, and then we can talk about it."

"I don't want to talk about it with you," Amelia grumbled. "I'm done. I'm out. I don't care if you need me to run the gang. You're going to have to learn to do it without me."

Molly glared at her daughter. "Now why are you saying mean things like that? You're just mad at me right now. You'll get over it and things will get back to normal. You'll see."

Amelia's head fell back as if she was asking the Lord for patience. "That's just it, Molly. I don't want things to get back to normal. I want a new normal."

Eli cleared his throat. "Excuse me, ladies," he said, trying to break through the argument. The women didn't hear him. Or probably just ignored him.

Molly stuck a hand on her hip. "So what are you going to do? Live out in the country with this one? Leave me like your mother did? What happens when he's through with you? I didn't raise you to be a mistress."

"I wouldn't be a mistress!" Amelia seethed. "He asked me to marry him."

"Marry?" Molly spat. "Why would you ever do anything like that? Something so permanently awful?"

Eli stopped trying to end the conversation. Suddenly, he really wanted to hear the rest of it. Amelia's eyes shifted to him while her cheeks grew red. "I love him," she said softly.

"What was that?" Molly asked. "You're going to have to speak louder."

"I said I love him," Amelia yelled.

Eli's heart surged in his chest. He already knew Amelia loved him, but hearing her scream it (in anger) almost melted him to the floor.

"Ugh." Molly grimaced, leaning around Walter to sneer in Eli's direction. "I know I called him sweet, but he's a bit odd, isn't he?"

Eli threw up his hands. "I am standing right here, you know."

"Is he one of those lords who sits around all day in his castle petting sheep, teaching exotic birds to speak?"

Amelia's jaw tightened. "He's a scientist. He experiments on strawberries."

"*Strawberries?*" Molly said.

Not for the first time, Eli wished he worked with a more masculine fruit.

Molly was still not over it. She dropped her arm holding the gun, rounding on her daughter. "He plays with strawberries all day?"

Eli squeezed his eyes shut, forgetting that Walter was watching him like a hawk. That split second was just what the older man needed to make his move. Springing with surprising speed, he spun around, slapping Molly again with the back of his hand. Before Amelia could react, he snatched her wrist, bringing it down as he raised his knee, slamming the tender limb with enough force to force her to drop her pistol.

It felt like he was wading through sand, but Eli was on the man in seconds. Without thinking, without pondering the implications of taking a life, Eli flung his sword arm back, ready to make the final strike—

Bang!

A single shot rang out, filling Eli's eyes with smoke and his ears with an interminable ringing. He stopped dead in his tracks; Walter was staring at him again, a contemplative expression on his face as his arms slackened away from Amelia down to his sides. In a daze, he stumbled before glancing down at his stomach, where a small hole showed in his jacket. Eli wondered if the man needed to see the blood flow to realize he'd been shot by Molly. He knew *he* did.

Walter stuck his finger in the hole, and a gurgling laugh came from deep within his throat. He raised his finger to Molly, revealing blood so fresh and crimson it appeared black. "You'd be nothing without me," he said, collapsing to his knees.

With a shove of her boot, Molly kicked Walter to the floor, where, after a few foul convulsions, he stopped breathing altogether. "Remind me to thank you later," Molly replied softly.

Eli had no idea how long they stood, transfixed by the body. It felt like an eternity to him, both a dream and a nightmare.

Amelia broke through the fog first. "You did it," she whispered. "You finally did it."

Molly's head remained bowed. A tear held on for dear life at the end of her nose before finally dropping. She sniffed. "I should have done it a long time ago. I'm so sorry it took me this long."

Slowly, Amelia reached and took the pistol from Molly's shaking hands before tossing it onto the settee behind them. Then, inch by awkward inch, she folded Molly into her arms for a hug. The older woman's entire body stiffened as if she'd never been touched before. Like a boa constrictor, Amelia held on, adding more pressure until her prey relented. When Molly finally hugged Amelia back, they both broke out into joyous sobs.

No words were used; Eli realized that no words were necessary. The two women, linked by soul if not by blood, only needed to hold one another.

When he was quite certain they'd forgotten he was there, he

shifted his weight on his feet. "I should go," he said. "Someone should alert the constable."

Amelia's head lifted from Molly's shoulder, her eyes shiny with tears and mirth. "You aren't going to turn me in?"

"That depends," he answered. "Do you plan on staying by my side?" His skin was on fire. All he wanted to do was touch her.

Amelia seemed to sense that need, because she came to him then, wrapping her arms around him like the salvation she was. Their bodies instantly recognized the peace and grace that they gave and received.

She smiled. "Always and forever."

A tinny voice swam along the periphery of their love-drunk haze. "What about me?"

Incredulous, Amelia turned in Eli's arms toward Molly. His hands held firm. That was as far as he'd let her go for the moment. "What about you?" she asked.

Eli had to hand it to the older woman—she had no shame. With a chuckle, he remembered thinking the same thing about Amelia at one time.

Molly lifted her palms up like a beggar. "I need help. Just for a little while," she added hurriedly when Amelia opened her mouth. "I've given this bastard everything. He's cleaned me out." Molly kicked the body again, putting an exclamation mark on her words. Eli noticed he was the only one who flinched at the indecorous action. Walter was a bastard, but the man was dead, after all.

Molly's thin eyebrows rose. "I promise. Just a little while. Then you can ride off with your strawberry knight and I will never bother you again."

Amelia sucked in a tight breath. "You're still teasing him! You can't even ask for my help without trying to make him look like a fool."

Molly put her hands up in defense, her expression comically innocent. "I'm not teasing him. You're the one who told me he plays with strawberries—"

"I *experiment* with strawberries," Eli cut in, but they were back at it with their squabbling.

Hands on her hips, Amelia wrangled her way out of Eli's clutches. "He's a scientist!" It was her turn to kick the body. "You are the last person to lecture me on my taste in men."

"There's nothing wrong with your taste in men!" Eli interjected.

She burned him with a brilliant smile. "I know that, my love." But he recognized that look in her eye. She was ready to fight. Before she could round back on Molly, Eli slid in between the women and reached into his pocket.

Molly's reaction was just what Eli was hoping for when he pulled out his father's pocket watch. "A Breguet," she said matter-of-factly, trying and failing to hide her interest.

Amelia clawed at his back. "No, Eli, no!" she said. "I won't let you do that. Just go home. I'll follow in a month. Let me just do this, and then I'll be rid of this *dastardly woman* once and for all."

Molly snorted at the abrasive description. "You've always been so ungrateful. The sacrifices I made for this girl," she said, jabbing a thumb at Amelia. "Spoiled is what you are."

"Spoiled!" Amelia screamed, taking out her aggression on Eli's coat.

He managed to hold her back with a stiff arm and shoved the pocket watch in Molly's hands. "Just take it," he said. "Sell it, keep it, I don't care. But from this moment on, we're even. Amelia is out of the family business."

Molly bobbed her hand up and down, weighing the precious piece. She eyed her daughter a long time. Eli would never have considered himself a romantic—and would never have been confused for one—but he saw something in that exchange, something that a million of those pocket watches could never amount to.

"Do we have a deal?" he asked.

"Eli!" Amelia screeched. "It was your father's. It's your past."

"And you're my future," he said without missing a beat.

"Nothing else matters." He continued to hold Molly's gaze. "So?"

As an answer, Molly placed the watch in her pocket. "I suppose you'll be leaving, then," she said.

Certain that Amelia wasn't going to inflict harm, Eli released her to stand at his side. "Yes, I'm leaving," she said instantly.

"You know where to find me."

"Always," she replied.

It was Amelia who nudged Eli toward the exit. They had almost made it out of the drawing room before Molly's words stopped them.

"You're going to miss this. You don't think so now, but you will."

Giving his hand a squeeze, Amelia turned back. "No, I won't miss this," she said. "I'll miss you."

Eli waited until they were out on the street before speaking. All the adrenaline seemed to evaporate from his body at once, and he felt discombobulated and hollow, like an empty ship adrift at sea. As always, Amelia was his anchor.

She tilted her face to the sky, letting the waning sun baptize her with what little fire it had left. It occurred to him that she felt as unfettered as he did at this moment, and was handling it much better.

Her lashes flickered under the light before she opened her eyes to him. He wondered if he would ever get used to those eyes, ever not feel so starved for them. "Where to now?" she said. "Home?"

Home. That one word used by her was enough to feed his soul for a lifetime. Not only did she want him, but she also wanted a home with him.

Before he could answer, Amelia went on, "You don't have to worry about a constable. That's the last thing Molly needs. She'll call some people and get it all sorted."

The way she casually spoke about dealing with a dead body on a carpet should have appalled him, but it didn't. Eli was more shocked her hand was in his, and showing no signs of letting go.

"How did you know how to find me, by the way?" she asked.

"Harry," he replied, finding that speaking was harder than he'd thought. What was wrong with him? It was done. All was right in the world. He had the girl. They were going home.

Amelia didn't seem to notice his issues. She chattered along easily enough as they put space between them and the townhouse. "I can't believe you went to him. I should be furious. I *am* furious! I also can't believe you shackled me to the bed. Why did you do that? I told you I could handle everything!"

"You told me you were leaving me and never coming back!"

She lowered her head sheepishly. "I know I said that. I think I even believed it. But the second I got back to London, I realized I couldn't stay here. Not without you."

Eli tugged Amelia to stop, turning her to face him in the middle of Covent Garden. "Say it again."

"Say what again?"

No longer able to contain himself, he leaned in, placing his lips over hers in a kiss that washed everything else away. He retreated just far enough that he could speak. "Tell me that you'll stay by my side. Forever."

"I thought you trusted me."

"I do. I just want you to say it again. And then again and again."

"I will stay by your side forever," Amelia said, punctuating the declaration with a fleeting kiss. "Now can we go home?"

"Yes," Eli said, keeping one arm around her waist. "Now we can go home." He gave her a funny look when she started to giggle. "What?"

"I was just thinking," she answered slyly. "Not many men would be brave enough to spend the rest of their lives next to a pickpocket."

"Yes," he drawled. "But you're not a pickpocket anymore. You're done with that life, right?"

"I have one more job, but you needn't worry about it."

He frowned. "What could you possibly have left to steal?

You've already stolen my heart."

She took his hand. Together they walked, their fingers intertwined like the roots of a tree, strong and determined. Amelia lifted his hand to stare at his fingernails. She did that often. Soon, Eli would have to remember to ask her what was going through her mind when she did it. "I didn't steal anything, my love," she said thoughtfully. Lowering his hand, she gifted him a lovely smile. "You gave it to me."

EPILOGUE

One Month Later
London, England

I T WAS SHAPING up to be a good day. Molly Diamond was back on top, or at least she would be there soon. After the vestiges of Walter had been wiped clean and his debts were cleared from Molly, she'd been able to spend the month searching for girls that were hungry to make their names. Finding unwanted, down-on-their-luck girls in London was simple. What made Molly so successful was that she could always spot a tiger, a girl who had the brains as well as the courage.

No one could take Amelia's place; that went without saying. But once news got out that Molly had killed Walter in retribution for Jenny, she'd been received by her fellow thieves with a more accepting eye. She wasn't just the leader of a female gang. Molly Diamond was the leader of a *gang*. One that was well trained and organized. One that wouldn't be intimidated. And one that every enterprising girl in the city wanted to be a part of. Yes, things were looking up for Molly Diamond.

"Excuse me, miss, would you like to buy some flowers?"

Molly glanced down at the little urchin barring her way down the street. The grimy little blonde girl must be new. No one stopped Molly Diamond in Piccadilly. Every hustler was aware that she was too busy hustling herself.

With a flick of her hand, Molly brushed the girl out of her way, though she couldn't help but notice how attractive she was. Even disheveled, there was no mistaking her golden curls and pale blue eyes. Too young, though. Molly had considered accepting a young protégée, but never took the last step. She doubted she would ever do it again. Children tended to get too attached … make things overly emotional.

"Annie, there you are!" Another little girl ran up to the blonde one with the flowers, blocking Molly's escape yet again. "I told you, we have to go!"

Fixing her bonnet, Molly glared at the tiny interlopers. She was skirting around them when it struck her. The new little girl's hair wasn't as long; it only reached her shoulders, but that was where the differences ended. Same color hair, same height, same porcelain skin and button nose. Only someone as discerning as Molly would notice the slight contrast in their blue eyes.

Twins.

Twins!

Molly fought to disguise her eagerness as she confronted the pair. Leaning down to their level, she threw an indignant hand at the basket. "I'm sorry to say, little ones, but you're never going to make any real money selling those lowly flowers."

The girl called Annie looked down dismally at the pathetic, half-dead roses in her basket. "Beth says we have to. Says we can't come home until we sell every one."

"Who's Beth? Is that your mother?" Molly asked.

"Oh, no," the second girl answered. "Our mother is dead. Beth took us in. She's …" She gnawed at her bottom lip. "She's not very nice."

"I'm sorry to hear that," Molly said. "I've found that not many people are nice to little girls."

"Are you?" the girl asked hopefully. Molly returned to standing, her spine cracking in a few places. In all her years, she'd never had twins. What she could do with twins!

"I can be nice," she said truthfully. "And I can teach you how to make more money than you've ever dreamed of."

"How much?" Annie asked.

Molly loved greed. It was a beautiful thing. Where would she be without it? But she loved ambition more. "More than you can count."

"She can't count," the sister said, nudging Annie with her shoulder.

Annie shoved her back. "I can too!"

"No, you can't!" the sister yelled, smacking Annie in the chest.

Annie balled up her fist. "You don't know anything," she roared, smacking her sister just as hard.

Before Molly knew it, a brawl started in front of her, a petty maelstrom of wild fingernails and aggressive hair pulling.

Guarding her investments, she flung herself in the middle of the fracas, pinning the sisters on separate sides with an iron grip. "None of that, none of that," she shouted as the termagants continued to go at each other, bumping and bruising her with their fiery little tempers. Molly had encountered some of London's absolute worst, and these girls still stunned her with their unrelenting venom. "Stop it *now!*"

Immediately, the twins stopped, glued into place.

"There now, that's better," Molly said, straightening her skirts. Maybe she didn't want these nasty little cats. They would take a strong hand. But if there was one thing she knew to trust about herself, it was her hands.

She leveled them with her harshest stare. "You two don't know who I am, so let me tell you. I'm Molly Diamond, and I run the best gang in London. If you come and work for me, I'll make you queens of this city. But we can't have any more of that. You will need to listen to everything I say. Do you think you can do that?"

They nodded in unison. It positively tickled Molly to see it. She could almost feel all the loot they would steal already lining her pockets.

She placed her arms around their shoulders, directing them to walk in front of her. "All right, then. Why don't we set you up at my place? Then we can get to work."

Annie's feet were cemented to the sidewalk. Then she twirled around, her angelic expression apologetic. "We have to get our things."

Molly pushed them. "No, you don't. I have things for you."

"No," Annie replied stubbornly, pulling nervously at her curls. "I have a keepsake from my father. I won't leave without it." Her eyes watered, making the irises appear almost white. "Please, don't make me leave it behind. We won't take long. We just live around the corner."

"All right, all right. Don't start bawling." Molly sighed, glancing around. "I can't take another scene. I'll wait here for ten minutes. If you two aren't back in time, then I'm leaving along with my offer. I promise you girls, no one will give you a better one in your life. You work with me, and you'll never have to rely on anyone ever again."

They nodded again before taking off. Molly watched their lithe figures disappear among the crowd as her excitement built. Twins! What a day.

Before she could catch herself, the thought came to her that she couldn't wait to tell Amelia. But she hadn't seen her in a month, not since she ran off to marry that strawberry lord. What an odd girl she turned out to be, even if she was the best damn diver Molly had ever seen.

Perhaps Molly would pay her a visit. She'd heard the family was splitting their time between the country and London, something about wanting to be close to the son while he attended school. *Humph!* Well, at least she wasn't stuck in the country. What an inane existence that would be. Molly wouldn't wish that on her worst enemy.

Tapping her fingers against her belly, she meandered toward the shop windows, gazing absent-mindedly at the wares. She couldn't wait to sic the twins on those shops. They'd be like ghosts; the proprietors would never see them coming. *If* Molly could stop them from killing each other.

Her fingers continued to tap. How long had she been waiting? Five minutes? Eight? If the girls wanted to impress her, they would have been back by now. Molly tucked her hand into her pocket, searching for her watch. She probably should have sold it, but the money she'd received hawking Jenny's ring had been more than enough to keep the gang happy and the business running. Besides, Amelia didn't really think Molly was going to sell a Breguet, did she? Only historically devoid idiots sold a watch like that.

Coming up empty, Molly searched another pocket. Nothing. *Where the hell is it?* She never left the expensive piece at home; she always kept it near her person in case one of her girls decided to do something incredibly dumb.

A cold feeling crept up the back of her neck. Ten minutes had definitely come and gone. She would give the twins a few more. One had to make allowances for windfalls.

But as the minutes ticked on, Molly's composure began to fade. What was it about those girls that seemed so familiar? She'd certainly never seen them before. She would have remembered. Not to mention their nasty behavior. The way they showed no regard for bumping and rocking into her—

Molly probed her pockets again.

No.

Couldn't be.

There was no way.

Those eyes. Those blue eyes. So familiar.

And then, in the middle of Piccadilly Circus, Molly Diamond laughed.

She laughed until she cried.

About the Author

Margaux Thorne is a lifelong reader of romance novels. Some of her earliest memories are sneaking into her mom's room at night and stealing any books she could find.

After moving around quite a bit, she's finally put down roots in New England with her two sons and husband. She's always been a writer, starting out in newspapers, but it wasn't until her sons began going to school full-time that she began working towards her dream of becoming a romance author.

She enjoys crocheting toys for her kids, hiking with her Saint Bernard, watching all the Real Housewives franchises on the couch with her very old and very fat pugs, and the rush of feeling she gets *after* she finishes a long run (though not a second before).

www.ingramcontent.com/pod-product-compliance
Lightning Source LLC
Chambersburg PA
CBHW072027220726
48293CB00016B/495